ACTS OF SEDUCTION

Miranda and Shreve lay side by side for a long minute, only their little fingers touching. Gradually their heartbeats slowed.

"I got a marriage license," Shreve said quietly.

Her eyes flew open. "When?"

He was not looking at her. "The day you ran away to Wyoming."

She searched his face incredulously. "After all these years. But you never said a word about—"

He nodded as he finally met her gaze. "I didn't have any thought of marrying you. I never thought about the future. It seemed we'd go on and on together. I never thought you'd even want to leave me. When I realized I didn't have any claim on you, I'd waited too late. You were gone."

She looked away. "A marriage isn't supposed to be a prison."

She expected him to argue, but instead he nodded shortly. Then the dark lashes slipped down over his eyes as he pulled her close, his knowing hands searching out her secrets. "I waited too late."

She tried to pull away, but he had caught her unawares. She had been seduced as only he could seduce her, as he had always been able to seduce her from the first night they had come together . . .

DISCOVER DEANA JAMES!

DEANA JAMES

ACTS OF LOVE

ZEBRA BOOKS
KENSINGTON PUBLISHING CORP.

For Great Performances

Errol Flynn as Robin Hood

Douglas Fairbanks as Sinbad

Stewart Granger as Scaramouche

Tyrone Power as Zorro

and

Lawrence Olivier as Hamlet

Never!

Never was swash buckled so romantically!

THE PLAYERS
Act III, Scene 3

In the Wyoming Territory, 1883

The Actor	Shreve Catherwood
The Actress	Miranda Drummond
The Makeup Artist	Ada Cocks
The Business Manager	George Windom
The Colonel	Theodore Armistead
The Sergeant	Will Trask
The Widow	Ruth Drummond Westfall
Her Daughter	Rachel Drummond Westfall
The Trader	Adolf Lindhauer
His Wife	Blue Sun on Snow Lindhauer
His Son	Victor Wolf, born White Wolf's Brother
The Senator from New York	Hugh Smith Butler
The Private Investigator	Frank de la Barca

Act IV

In New Orleans and Mexico City, 1883

The Pimp	Poteet
The Mexican Minister of Foreign Relations	Ignacio Vallarta
The Madam of *La Yegua Blanca*	Celestina
The Captain of the *Pride of Narragansett*	John Ward
The Ship's Doctor	Thaddeus Clinton

Act V

In London and Washington, D.C., 1884

The Producer	Billy Beresford
The Old Actor	Freddy Franklin
The English Nobility	
Maurice Francis John,	
Lord Edgemont-Canfield	Shreve Catherwood
Amelia Mary Elizabeth,	
Lady Edgemont-Canfield	Miranda Catherwood
The Senator from Virginia	Chester Waldron
His Wife	Cassie Waldron
The Assassin	Billy Steubens

Epilogue

In Chicago, 1884

The Owner of the new Imperial	
Theater	Nehemiah Horowitz
The Heir Apparent	Drummond Catherwood

Act III
Scene 3
Wyoming Territory, 1883

One

*Well there's one yonder arrested and carried
to prison was worth five thousand of you all.*

"I'm just an actor!"

Shreve Catherwood breathed in carefully trying not
to disturb his bruised and exquisitely painful ribs.
"Some man paid me to wear a costume, ride in on a
horse, carry — "

A fist hooked upward into his face and landed
squarely on his mouth mashing his lips against his
teeth. His head thudded back against the wall of the
guardhouse. "Try again, purty boy."

Groaning and sobbing, Shreve let his head roll on his
shoulders and loll down onto his chest. He could taste
his own blood in his mouth. It oozed into the stubble
on his chin. "Don't. For God's sake, don't! I didn't
know what he was going to do. I didn't have any idea.
Listen, I wouldn't have been within a mile of him if I'd
known. I was out of work and he offered a couple of
dollars." He let his voice trail off into a pathetic whimper. Head hunched between his shoulders to protect
his face, he poked his tongue against his front teeth.
Damn! One — no — two were definitely loose.

"Push his head back, Sergeant Trask."

A rough palm bumped into his forehead, lifting his
face, pushing him back against the wall. With a con-

11

vincing moan, Shreve relaxed completely, allowing his body to slide to the floor.

"You've hit him too hard."

"Naw! He's playin' 'possum."

"Catch him."

"Sure thing." The sergeant tangled his fingers in Shreve's hair and yanked the prisoner upright.

Shreve grunted, his face contorted in pain, and his limbs stiffened to bear his weight. Obviously, the moan hadn't been convincing enough. It usually convinced audiences, but they probably didn't have this bastard's expertise at torture. He scraped his legs back under the bench to relieve the pain in his scalp.

Trask chuckled. "See. He's awake."

Col. Theodore Armistead nodded. "I do see." He leaned forward to inspect the bruised, bleeding face. His breath was rank. "You'd save yourself a lot of misery, fella, if you'd cooperate."

He waited a moment, then straightened with a show of regret. "Better make it easy on yourself. You're going to tell us what we want to know one way or the other."

Shreve squinted through the blood and sweat and tried to think above and beyond the pain. He needed to remember everything. It would give a new dimension to future heroic performances. He let his head sag lower.

A hard fist punched his shoulder. "Hie up there! Don't play 'possum on the colonel, purty boy. It don't work."

Shreve swayed with the blow. *God! The bastard was enjoying himself.* His lines, however, were too melodramatic to be believable.

Armistead leaned forward again until their faces were only inches apart. "Listen, Phillips—"

"Phillips," Shreve groaned. Important to stick to the script. "Phillips. Mark Phillips."

Armistead's lip curled. "Whatever you want to call yourself is all right with me. The point is we can make

12

a deal. We've got a dozen troopers who'd step forward at a minute's notice to say that you were completely without fault in that shooting out at Fort Gallatin. You can be free in twenty-four hours. Twelve even. Just give us the name of the man who pulled the trigger."

Shreve hesitated, dreading what would follow. At length, he drew a deep breath. "Never saw him before."

With a shrug Armistead stepped back. "Sergeant Trask."

The blow caught Shreve on the temple and knocked him into the wall. The rough bark scraped off a patch of hair and skin. Hot blood oozed down the back of his neck. The sergeant waited for his victim to fall forward, then hauled him back up by the hair. Rotten teeth bared in a grin, he wallowed Shreve's head from side to side. "He sure ain't gonna have much left of that purty face at this rate."

Barely clinging to consciousness, Shreve tried to locate the source of the voice. He blinked rapidly, but he could not clear his vision. Instead he was aware of blackness slashed through and through with red and yellow streaks of lightning.

Armistead's voice borne on a gust of foul breath came from right in his face. "Listen, to me, you idiot. The same troopers can also say you pulled the trigger. Within forty-eight hours, we're going to find the man who killed that old man. We've got our orders direct from Washington. They take a dim view of somebody riding into the middle of a Fourth of July celebration and gunning down a brigadier-General. Especially if that general's some senator's pet appointee. Hell, whoever did it shot the director of Indian Affairs for the Mountain District."

"I didn't know what he was going to do," Shreve insisted wearily. "God, why don't you believe me? I didn't —"

Armistead interrupted him. He stared intently into the prisoner's bruised face. "Look, fella, *when* I get the credit for solving this, I'll get a commendation, maybe even a promotion. I could be transferred to Washington. My wife and all her family'd be pleased to death. Understand what I'm saying to you? I mean to get the name of the man who hired you. Sergeant Trask isn't going to stop until I get it. Do I make myself perfectly clear?"

Shreve opened his mouth. More blood oozed out of the corner of it. Tears trickled from his eyes. His vision began to clear, though the ugly faces of Armistead and Trask were distorted like reflections in a bad mirror. He tried to swallow. "I've told you everything I know." His voice rasped out of his dry throat. "But—swear to God—I don't know anything that's worth anything to anybody. That fellow hired me and another man to ride down with him. He said it was part of the celebration."

Armistead drew back. "Sergeant."

"No." Shreve hunched his shoulder, small protection with his hands manacled together behind his back. "Don't. Don't hit me again. Don't!"

Shreve's squawk of pain when the sergeant struck him was entirely real. His head slammed back against the wall again, but this time the sound was mushy as his scalp split. Blood flowed, soaking his collar, trickling hotly down his back, mixing with sweat. *The costume was going to be a total loss—*

The same fist thudded into his belly below his diaphragm. It drove the breath up out of his lungs in a powerful whoosh of agony. He started to slide again; this time no torment the sergeant inflicted brought him back upright.

"Where is Miranda?" Ruth Westfall pressed her fist tight against her mouth to hold back another storm of hysterical weeping. "Surely she would have found some way to send us word. Are you sure she hasn't been caught?"

Blue Sun on Snow Lindhauer put her arm around

Ruth's shoulders and hugged her tightly. The woman's entire body vibrated in her efforts to contain her grief. The Cheyenne lifted sloe-black eyes to her husband's pink, grizzled face.

Adolf Lindhauer met his wife's stare and shrugged helplessly. A German by birth, he had a stoical man's intolerance of a woman's tears, one of the reasons he loved and respected his Indian wife's self-control. Still, he bowed his head before Ruth's grief. Her husband of thirteen years was dead, shot down in a duel with her daughter. The division of loyalties was tearing the woman apart before his eyes.

He reached out his hand, then drew it back. "Miz Drummond," he began gruffly. *"Ach, Gott,* Ruth. Please don't take on that way. Miranda got clean away. They didn't even guess that she wasn't a trooper. They're out beatin' the bushes for a man."

"But they caught her friend." Ruth's voice rasped out of a sore and swollen throat. "They caught her friend — Mr. Catherwood."

Adolf heaved a sigh. "Chances are they'll just ask him a few questions."

"But what will he say? He rode in with her. He was part of it. It's been three days now. If they just wanted to ask him a few questions, he'd have been free by now." Ruth shook her head agitatedly. "They don't believe him. I know it. After all, what excuse could he give? What could he say?"

"My guess is he's saying that he was just hired to be part of the celebration. You know, like the speech-making and marching and singing. He'll tell 'em that he doesn't know anything. They'll stand around and cuss and discuss it. And then they'll have to let him go."

"But — "

"Ruth, listen," Adolf hurried on. "He dived off his horse the minute the shooting started. Hundreds of people saw him. Nobody's going to think he was anything but what he is — an actor."

15

At the mention of the shooting, tears welled in Ruth's eyes. She bowed her head. Blue Sun on Snow put her other arm around the woman and turned Ruth's face into her strong shoulder.

Adolf spread his hands helplessly. "Now what did I say?"

His wife waved him to silence, and with a shrug, Adolf took himself away, glad to escape from such a display of emotion.

The owl screeched from among the inch-long thorns of the black locust. Then it spread its wings and sailed noiselessly away. The weary horse flicked an ear in that direction but otherwise did not react. Its equally weary rider dismounted and plodded toward the steps.

"You made my mother cry again."

Rachel's voice had an eerie quality that made the hair rise on the back of Miranda's head. Slowly, she peered into the deep shadows of the Lindhauer's porch.

"She's cried and cried. For my father. Because of what you did."

Miranda's heart beat like a drum against her breastbone. "I'm sorry," she whispered. "I —"

"What did you expect? You shot her husband."

"He killed her husband." Desperately, Miranda repeated the timeworn statement.

"That's a lie."

"If you say so." Miranda put her booted foot on the first step.

"Don't come in here," Rachel warned, stepping out to bar her sister's way. The bright moonlight tinged her skin blue at the same time it sank her eyes in shadows. "You're not wanted here. My mother's had enough of you forever. After everything else you've been, now you're a murderess."

"I—I meant to make him confess his crime," Miranda protested. "I just wanted him to confess."

16

"Liar. You wanted to kill my father."

Miranda pressed her palm hard between her breasts. "He wasn't your father."

"He was the only father I ever had."

"Only because he killed your real one."

Rachel shuddered. "I hate you."

Miranda climbed another step.

"Your actor friend's been arrested," Rachel announced triumphantly.

Miranda groaned. "Shreve? Why?"

"Because they caught him. At least he didn't get away. They're going to see that someone pays for what you did."

"But he didn't do anything."

"He was part of it. They've caught him. And they'll catch you, too. You won't be getting out of this. They'll make him talk and then they'll catch you."

No longer willing to listen to her sister, Miranda mounted the porch to face her sister on the same level.

As she retreated, Rachel's voice rose hysterically. "You'd better run for your life. Don't waste time coming in here. You've done what you set out to do. Now leave my mother and me alone."

"I have to see her."

"No, you don't. If you take one step more, I'll make you sorry you were ever born."

"You're too late." Miranda stepped around her sister's slender frame.

"Stop! I swear I will."

"You're too late," Miranda repeated. Her hand twisted the doorknob viciously. "I've been sorry more than half my life."

"How'd y' like y'r day in th' hole?"

Shreve Catherwood's face was scarcely recognizable. Hideously bruised and swollen from the beatings, it was also blistered fiery red. Located behind the guardhouse was the hole, a dry well that had been

17

brought into service for holding dangerous prisoners. A well cover placed over it and bolted down turned the place into an oven in the July heat.

"How'd a little water taste 'bout now?" the sergeant went on.

Shreve could not even lick his lips. Shielding his eyes with his manacled hands, he squinted up at the black silhouette against the sun.

The sergeant set a bucket on the edge of the well and dipped water up from it. "Sure does taste good. Water from around here tastes real good. Mountain water." He tipped the ladle. A silver stream fell into the hole, spattering on the prisoner's hands. "Just say the word and we'll pull y' up."

Shreve dropped his arms. His chin fell forward onto his chest. He tried to speak, cleared his throat, summoned up enough saliva to wet the parched tissues inside his mouth. "Mistake," he rasped.

"What? Can't hear y'."

"Mistake! You're making a mistake."

"Wrong! Wrong answer, purty boy. Y' sure are dumb." The sergeant stepped back from the opening. "He ain't done yet!" he yelled over his shoulder. The cover slid back into place, and the bar rammed home across it.

Shreve staggered back a couple of steps where his back collided with the wall of the hole. Slowly, he slid down it. His manacled wrists draped over his knees as his head sank back on his shoulders. He took a deep breath of the hot, stale air. At noon he had told himself that the heat wasn't much worse than the footlights at the State Street Theater in Chicago. By three o'clock he knew himself to be a liar.

He coughed and wallowed a pebble back and forth behind his clenched teeth. It did little good. *He ain't done yet*. Shreve touched his fingertips to his forehead. The skin felt dry; no perspiration slicked it. He

18

grimaced. Baking time would be only a matter of hours.

He had never thought to end his life in a hole. He pushed at the pebble with his swollen tongue. Maybe a different size would help. Through slitted eyes, he looked around him in the dimness. Dust motes swirled through the shafts of burning light that sliced between the boards on the well cover. Thank God, he wasn't claustrophobic. He allowed one corner of his mouth to twitch upward in a smirk.

The movement reminded him painfully of the bruises on his face. These army brutes had a real enthusiasm for their work. Still and all, he credited his performance with averting some of the worst damage. Even when the pain was making him sick enough to puke, he had managed to keep his head down and to roll with the punches.

He felt his nose gingerly. Still unbroken. The terrible wounds in his eyebrows and at the corners of his eyes could be covered with makeup. His mangled lips would heal. But his nose. That was another thing entirely. A nose once broken, particularly by a blow from the very physical Sergeant Trask, would never heal straight. Shreve patted it gently, congratulating himself on his success in guarding his profile.

Concentrating on protecting his face, judging where the next blow was coming from by the sway of his torturer's body and the shuffling of his manure-encrusted boots had taken Shreve's mind away from the pain. Over and over like a litany, he had repeated the same lines, told the same story, until he believed it himself. That was the secret of great acting. *Believe it yourself.*

And he had.

Each hour of his imprisonment allowed him to relax a bit more. Miranda had gotten away without a problem. No one suspected that a woman had been the rider from the mountain, dressed in Francis Drummond's clothes, riding Drummond's horse Wellington. Miranda's trail was cold.

19

All he had to do was wait this out. He did not doubt that somewhere friends were working to get him released. Eventually, they would prevail or he would convince the army that he knew nothing or both.

Reassuring himself with those thoughts, he concentrated on Miranda. When he got out of here, he would make sure that she never left the theater again except to buy a dress. How could she have been such a fool?

Even her long dead father, the mythically heroic Capt. Francis Drummond, would never have pursued the same vengeful course with such tenacity. Shreve gave a short grunt, all he could manage of a cynical laugh. No, Francis Drummond, army officer and career soldier, would have shrugged, cut his losses, and moved on.

Men made boasts of eternal vengeance. The dramas of Shakespeare, Jonson, Marlowe, and Kyd were cemented together by their vows. But in real life practicality wooed them away. Only Miranda—

He smiled again, then groaned softly at the pain in his face. His lover, his partner, his creation, his almost wife, only she would carry out her vow. Because she knew nothing but drama. Nothing but theater. She was what he had made her—an actress. She knew nothing of reality.

Thank God she was safely away. Ada and George would take care of her until he could get this misunderstanding cleared up and get back to her.

He heaved a sigh. The hot air seared his nostrils as he breathed in the air he had expelled. He stared around him at the rough walls, at the hand and foot holds in the sides of the well, scraped out, no doubt, by desperate men. He had studied those niches and memorized them just like an important piece of theatrical blocking. Then in the dead of night, he had climbed them. But the cover of the well was immovable. He was truly baking in an oven.

Miranda. He intended to have it out with her about this. She would have to fan him with a pair of Japanese fans and bring him iced drinks and run her cool hands over his body. He smiled ruefully. Even in hell Miranda was the center of his thoughts.

"Fool, there was never man so notoriously abus'd." Malvolio's mournful words fell from his lips. Instantly, he regretted the waste of moisture. "Just fool," he murmured. And closed his aching eyes on a smile.

"Civil jurisdiction doesn't extend to an army base," Armistead said stubbornly. "You know that, Lindhauer. I'm surprised that you'd even come here with a lawyer."

"Everyone is entitled to representation," the black-coated attorney declared stoutly.

"Besides, Mrs. Westfall is real interested in what you're doing to find her husband's killer," Adolf lied. "She saw what happened, don't forget. This fella that you're holding didn't do anything."

Armistead flushed angrily. "We're doing everything that can possibly be done. You just trot back to her and tell her that we're getting close to getting the information from this fella. He'll make a full confession before long and then we'll know who hired him."

The old trader ducked his head and scratched his chin reflectively. He had a good idea what was being done to Shreve Catherwood to get a full confession. How long the actor could hold out was a question. "You're sure you're not barking up the wrong tree, Colonel? Who is this fella anyway?"

"Well, now, he says his name's Phillips. 'Course that's probably made up. He claims he was just hired to ride in and be part of the celebration. Says he didn't have any idea what was goin' to happen. Says someone just dressed him up in a fake uniform and handed him a made-up flag to carry."

Adolf nodded his head sagely. "I'd 'spect that's pretty much what happened. He probably doesn't know any more than you do."

21

"He knows," Armistead insisted doggedly. "And he'll spill his guts before long."

"Or he'll be dead and the killer'll be all the way to the Canadian border and you won't be any closer to an answer that'll satisfy Washington." Adolf's white eyebrows drew together in a ferocious scowl.

Armistead thrust out his jaw pugnaciously. His hands balled into fists on the desk in front of him. "Why don't you just turn your tail around and let me see it waggin' goodbye?"

"Mrs. Westfall has a lot of friends in Washington that'll be mighty unhappy if you mess this up," Lindhauer prophesied. "Seems like you ought to be covering the territory trying to find the man who pulled the trigger instead of beatin' up on some innocent bystander."

"I'll handle this business my way. You get the hell out and stay out. Corporal!" he barked. "Escort these men off the post."

Once outside the gates, George Windom, business manager and sometime actor, removed his stovepipe hat and used his handkerchief to wipe sweat and greasepaint from the inside band. "Lord above, it's hot! Is there any chance at all that we might break him out?"

Lindhauer tapped the reins across the horse's back and the buggy gathered speed. " 'Fraid they've got him in the guardhouse with an around-the-clock guard. Unless they've got him in the hole, which is worse."

Windom squinted upward into the brutal sunlight and shook his head morosely. "I can imagine."

"Looks like it's up to Ruth."

"Don't suppose they'd believe us if I told them he had an infectious disease and we had to get him off the post?"

Lindhauer looked sideways at the old actor, who was carefully stripping off his thick gray eyebrows and sideburns. "Not much chance of that. You'd have to go through the army surgeon. They've heard every excuse and looked at every symptom in the book. They'd never buy it."

"It worked in Chicago," George mourned.

"Maybe Ruth's telegram to Washington will get some results."

Sen. Hugh Smith Butler stared at the telegram from Ruth Drummond Westfall. His face paled, then reddened. He laid it down and flexed his fingers as if his arm hurt. Noting the man's distress, his secretary came around to the side of the desk to pour water from a carafe.

Butler extracted a small metal box from his pocket and popped a tiny pill into his mouth. He accepted the glass. The water sloshed as his hand shook.

When his color began to return to normal, he picked up the telegram again, read it, laid it down, and pushed his spectacles up on his forehead. Benjamin was dead. Butler rubbed at his eyes. He should have sent a younger man, but his former son-in-law had been ideal. A man obsessed and utterly ruthless, no sentimentality would have clouded his judgment. He would have treated the Indian problem with ruthless dispatch.

Butler thought of the hundreds of thousands of dollars from investors now in danger of slipping through his fingers and the fingers of his partners.

He looked again at the telegram. "Killed in a duel with a person unknown." *A duel!* Butler snorted. Benjamin Westfall was not the dueling sort.

The senator had made it his business *not* to know the true nature of the man's disgrace. Likewise, rumors of violent deaths, accidents, unsolved crimes occurring coincidentally in the vicinity of the general. He had not even looked deeply into his own daughter's death. Benjamin Westfall had been a perfect career soldier, a self-serving man. Such men could be depended upon.

23

No. Westfall's death could not have been anything so simple as a duel perhaps fought to settle a dispute. In all probability rival political forces were at work here. With Benjamin's death, Butler had no one in mind as a successor. The next person in line for the job might not be trustworthy, might not be easily manipulated.

He slapped the telegram down on the desk and reached for his handkerchief to wipe his forehead.

"Is there anything else I can do, sir?" His secretary still hovered beside the desk.

Butler nodded. "Send a messenger for Frank de la Barca. And another to ask Senator Waldron to have lunch with me."

The secretary noted each name. He hesitated. Butler looked up irritably. "And to Mrs. Westfall?"

Butler wadded the piece of paper and tossed it contemptuously into the wastebasket. "Nothing."

"He's passed out down in the hole," Sergeant Trask reported to Colonel Armistead.

"Real? or is he faking again?"

Trask scratched his head briskly, then regarded the white flakes in the black soil under his fingernails. "Reckon it's real. He ain't had nary a drop for twenty-four hours."

Armistead frowned. "Haul him out and douse him in the horse trough. If he doesn't sing real loud, drop him back in for another day."

"A courier, George. What about a special courier, carrying orders from Washington for his release?"

The old actor looked hopeful, but Adolf Lindhauer shook his head. "It'd never work, Miss Miranda. They'd never buy it. There's a documents pouch that comes once a week. It's sealed."

"But we've got to do something." Miranda Drummond turned to her mother. "Mother, we've got to do something."

"I've sent a telegram to Senator Butler, telling him that Benjamin was killed during the celebration. I've told him that the army is mistaken in the man they're holding." Ruth shook her head. "We'll just have to wait."

Miranda put her trembling hands to her mouth. Her voice had lost its trained timbre. It was high and thin with fear. "We can't wait. They'll kill him. He's just an actor, for heaven's sake. He didn't do anything. He's the sweetest, dearest man in the world. He didn't know I was going to shoot Westfall. I swear on my life, I didn't know I was going to shoot him until he pointed his gun at me."

"Miranda—" Her mother put her arms around her.

"Shreve is forty-one years old, Mother. Once someone threw a knife at him on a riverboat in Saint Louis. He was a young man. He pulled the knife out, and then he fainted in his own blood. He fainted. He's not rough and tough. He's a gentleman. He talks and reasons and persuades. He acts the sword-wielding hero, but it's all pretend. No one has ever laid a finger on him. He's the most talented man I've ever known at pretending to take a blow, but never in his whole life has anyone actually hit him. We've got to get him out of there."

"Miranda, I think Senator Butler will respond immediately to my telegram. He liked Benjamin and respected him. I think he'll be happy to do whatever I ask him to do. He'll trust my judgment." Her voice faltered. "That is—"

"You're not sure?!"

"Well, no. I didn't want to come here. I'm afraid I made a scene. He might decide that he didn't want to be bothered with me."

Miranda looked around her at the solemn faces of her mother, Adolf Lindhauer, and her dear friends,

Ada Cocks and George Windom. "Then I'll give my-self up."

"No."

"Oh, Miranda, no. You can't."

"No, ma'am. Good Lord, what those troopers would do to you if you were locked up in that jail house wouldn't be fit for God himself to know about."

"But Shreve's in there!" She groaned. Her fingers trembled until she clenched them into fists. "Shreve's being hurt."

"He's a man, Miss Miranda," Adolf continued. "They aren't going to hurt him the way they'd hurt you. And even if you turned yourself in, they wouldn't let him go. The only difference would be that there'd be two of you instead of one to try to figure how to get out."

"Then we've got to do something. A special messenger has got to arrive."

Adolf looked at her doubtfully.

"The disguises were good before. This time they'll have to be perfect. We'll need costumes."

Lindhauer shrugged. "You can have whatever I've got in my store."

"And props. What does this documents pouch look like?"

"Maybe I've got an old one. But it's real old. They might be using a different kind."

Ruth smiled cynically. "Those things never change. If the leather's worn and cracked. It'll just look more authentic."

Miranda drew in a deep shuddering breath as she turned to the wardrobe mistress. She took her friend's strong clever hands. "Ada, this is going to be your greatest challenge. My makeup has to be perfect."

Colonel Armistead stared at the special courier from Washington. The slight lieutenant with the face full of dark whiskers wore a uniform so dusty that it looked more gray than blue. Likewise, his face was so begrimed that he looked as if he had ridden through a dust storm. The leather pouch that he passed across the desk was so old that the government seal was worn slick and shiny.

Nevertheless, Armistead's key turned in the lock. He withdrew the contents — a single letter — and stared at the senatorial seal with real trepidation.

So far his prisoner had not talked. He had finally been forced to take him out of the hole. Two days and the man was so dehydrated that the post surgeon declared he would not last a third. Chained in a cell in the guardhouse with all the water he could drink, he continued to deny that he knew the man who had hired him.

Trask had suggested a good whipping, but the visit by Lindhauer and the lawyer had made Armistead cautious. Lindhauer had mentioned the late general's widow had sent a telegram to Washington. Now evidently her telegram had borne fruit.

The letter was a direct order to transfer the prisoner to Fort Leavenworth, Kansas, where he would be questioned by a Federal marshal. The whole thing was being taken out of Armistead's hands.

He heaved a sigh. So much for finding the killer and having his success entered into his record. If he could just have another twenty-four hours at the man, he was sure he could break him. He pretended to scan the orders again.

The lieutenant shifted impatiently.

The colonel looked up, his eyebrows beetling. "I'll need to study these documents more carefully, Lieutenant. The junior officers' quarters — "

"With all due respect, sir, Senator Butler wants this matter investigated with all dispatch. I need to get to Cheyenne in time to take my prisoner on the train back east."

Armistead could not remember what day the train came through. "You've got plenty of time," he lied.

27

"The junior officers' quarters will accommodate you very comfortably."

"I must return immediately," the lieutenant insisted.

With an angry scowl Armistead stuffed the orders back into the envelope and rose. "You're a very obstinate fellow, Lieutenant."

"I have my orders, sir."

"Then I'll provide an escort to the railroad."

"That won't be necessary, sir."

"I'll be the judge of that." Armistead overruled him. "This man's a dangerous criminal. He's an accomplice to murder. He'll be transported under guard."

"Very well, sir."

He studied the young man's face critically. Despite the chin whiskers it was very youthful, just the sort of fresh, upstart aide-de-camp he'd expect to find on the staff of a senator who didn't know a damn thing about what went on in a western fort. "You'll thank me for this when you get to sleep nights on the road."

The lieutenant merely shrugged. "If you say so, sir."

Two

Receive what cheer you may:
The night is long that never finds the day.

The Palace Hotel in Cheyenne, Wyoming, was no
palace. Consequently, the rooms were cheap. The
lieutenant arranged for four, one for the two
guards, one for the prisoner, with each of the
guards taking turns with him, one for himself, and
one for Sergeant Trask.

The Union Pacific to Julesberg, Colorado, and
points east did not come through for forty-eight
hours. At that point, Sergeant Trask and his men
would return to Fort Laramie and Lieutenant Shaw
would continue with his prisoner.

"You're wastin' the gov'ment's money," the sergeant observed. "We could've put him in the town
jail and bunked in together."

Shaw looked at him coldly. "I snore."

"Hell. So do I. But when I'm asleep, I cain't hear
it thunder."

"I'm a light sleeper."

The sergeant wallowed the cud of chewing to-
bacco to the other side of his mouth. "Suit yourself.
Jes' tryin' to be accommodatin'."

The lieutenant turned to the other two. "You men
are dismissed to eat your supper. Eat it here in the

hotel, the army pays. Drink it at the saloon down the block, you pay for your own."

The two troopers looked at each other. One grinned. "Reckon we could do both."

"You stand first watch, Perkins," Sergeant Trask informed him.

The pudgy young man hung his head. "Yes, sir."

Lieutenant Shaw intervened. "I'll stand first watch, Sergeant. I've a few questions I'm supposed to ask the prisoner. Senator Butler wants answers sooner than later."

Trask thumbed his suspenders and rocked back on his heels. "I'm jes' the man to get 'em fer y'."

"I didn't notice that you had succeeded in getting any before."

The suspenders snapped back into place. The sergeant growled around a partially unintelligible remark about sissy-butted shavetails.

The lieutenant folded his arms. His piercing blue eyes stared the man down. "He's my prisoner. I'll be sure that he's locked up tight for the night. Perkins."

"Yes, sir."

"Have a plate of food sent up from the kitchen."

"I'll bring it myself, sir."

Shaw hesitated only for an instant. "Very good."

"Shreve, Shreve. Can you hear me?"

He could barely see. His eyes were so swollen. Blackness like slats in a jalousie slid across his vision. His head still buzzed from the many blows. But through the buzzing came Miranda's urgent whispers at his ear. He must be dreaming.

Cool water bathed his face and caressed the ugly contusions and abrasions with infinite gentleness.

He struggled to open his eyes. "Miranda?"

"Yes, darling. Oh, yes."

The water dribbled into his swollen mouth. He

swallowed. His voice gathered strength. "Miranda."

Instantly, her hand covered his mouth. "Ssssh, darling. You mustn't say my name."

"What're you doing here?" He could barely get the words out through his mashed swollen lips. Dimly, he tried to open his mouth wider. His jaw might be broken. He tried to raise his hand to touch it. His chain clanked ominously.

"I've come to get you away."

Get him away! He must still be in prison. He had been groggy with pain and exhaustion when guards had fastened irons to his ankles and connected his manacles to them by a chain. Then they had put their hands under his armpits and dragged him out of the cell into the blinding glare of the noon sun. Then lifting him by the irons, they had slung him into a closed wagon. As it jolted away, he had been too weak to raise himself to the tiny barred window even if he had cared where they were taking him.

Now somehow Miranda was here with him. She must not be. "Get away," he whispered. "Don't stay."

"Yes, darling." Her lips were next to his ear.

Hair tickled him. He managed to open his eyes. His vision cleared for an instant. Then he saw that she was heavily disguised. The sight of the grease-paint and crêpe hair chilled him to the bone. "No. Get away," he repeated, more strongly. He tried to lift his arms. "They'll catch you. Don't want you—"

She smiled encouragingly. "We'll be going together in just a few hours."

"No. You mustn't wait." Suddenly, he felt so damned heroic he wanted to cry. He had hurt so much for so long. He didn't want her to leave. He wanted her to take him in her arms and hold him against the pain that was wracking him. But he couldn't because the woman he loved was going to be hurt if she helped him.

31

Heroism stank.

Even as he forced the bruised muscles of his face to sketch a travesty of a smile, he wanted her to keep him safe from Trask's beatings. Even as he tried to think of the words to send her away, he didn't want to be slung back into the well. He could feel the tears starting in his eyes.

"Shreve," she whispered. "Oh, Shreve." She put her arms carefully around his face and pressed her lips to his forehead.

"Miranda." His lips formed the word, but no sound came. His fear for himself was magnified to terror for her. He closed his eyes to try to gather strength.

"No one will beat you again. I swear."

He made a tiny shake of negation within the circle of her arms. "You can't stop them. Get away."

"We will. Together." She kissed him again.

The tears were stopping. The trembling in his belly subsided to a persistent ache. At length he released a shaky breath. "Where are we?"

She lifted her head. "In a hotel in Cheyenne, waiting for the train."

He could hear the soft splash of water. A wet cloth bathed his forehead, his temples, his bruised cheeks, wiping away the hot tears beneath his closed eyes. It dipped again, then resumed laving his neck, bestowing blessed coolness to his body that felt burnt and blistered.

"How?" His voice was stronger than he had meant it to be, but his control seemed to have lapsed.

Again she put her finger over his swollen lips. "Don't talk, darling. Don't. We're in danger."

He tried to open his eyes, blinked them twice, three times. Through a haze, he looked up into her face, the face of a bewhiskered stranger. "You look like a man."

32

She smiled. "Thank God. Ada's makeup is a miracle."

"You're in danger," he whispered.

"Yes, but only a little. We're both waiting for the train. Under guard. Sergeant Trask—"

At the mention of the man's name, Shreve felt hatred course through him in waves. He cursed long and vividly. His body began to shake uncontrollably.

Miranda put her hand on his shoulder. "Shreve, don't get so—"

A knock sounded at the door.

He stiffened, his curses silenced.

She dropped the rag into the pan and slid them under the bed. "Remember, darling. You don't know me."

He set his teeth. "Yes. All right."

Squeezing his hand, she rose. Through the ringing and buzzing in his ears, he could hear her boots tapping across the floor. Even in boots he recognized the rhythm of her walk. The door opened.

"Here's the tray, Lieutenant."

"Thanks, soldier."

"I'll stay with him while he eats and you can go on down."

"You go ahead, Private Perkins. I'll see that he eats and then get him settled for the night. I've got the key to his chains. I want to be sure he's anchored down good and tight."

"Right, sir."

"Come back at eight, soldier."

"Yes, sir."

He heard her footsteps returning. Her weight came down on the bed beside him. She bent over him. Her lips touched his forehead, the wounds in his eyebrows. "Oh, Shreve."

"Pretty bad, huh?"

"Pretty bad," she agreed.

33

"But they didn't break my nose," he croaked. He tried to raise his hand, but again the manacles connected by a short chain to his ankle irons restrained him. "Feel it."

Her cool fingertip slid down his nose. "You're right. It's not broken."

"I ducked," he said with quiet pride.

She kissed his nose. "Clever darling." And the nasty abrasion on his cheek. "Oh, Shreve, what have I done to you? I never thought they'd arrest you for just riding up on a horse."

He shrugged one shoulder. "You can't depend on the army to have any sense. I told you so. Life isn't like the theater. Real people don't see logic the way playwrights do. Or they do, but it's their own kind of logic, based on keeping their jobs and getting promotions." He stirred trying to find some way to ease his aching body.

She shook her head. "I've made a mess of things. I never really thought beyond confronting Westfall and making him admit that he sent my father out to die. Have I ruined everything for us?"

He heaved a sigh and tried to open his eyes to see her clearly. "Miranda. So long as they don't know who you are, they'll eventually have to let me go. After all, I didn't do anything."

"But they're hurting you." Her voice was strained.

"They've about given up on that," he lied, shuddering as he thought of Trask somewhere nearby. He had to convince her to give up this scheme to set him free. It was probably as harebrained as the one that had gotten him caught in the first place. "Look, sweetheart, I love you for coming here. I don't know how you did it. But you've got to go. They'll catch you. And what they did to me will be minor compared to what they'll do to you."

She kissed him one more time and straightened

up. "Now don't waste your breath. I've got some food. You must be starving."

He shook his head, then regretted the movement as the pain lanced behind his eyes. "You've got to get out of here."

"*We've* got to get out of here, but we can't go until the train comes."

"They'll find you out."

"How can they, when you didn't even recognize me?"

"I can't see very well. But they'll see right through that costume."

"Shreve. I'm a better actress than that."

He tried to rise, managed to push up on one elbow, chains clanking. Fighting pain in his jaws, in his ribs, in his temples, he stared her up and down. "You look like the lead in a girls' school drama production."

"Only to a trained actor. You know what to look for." She sawed off a tiny piece of the tough steak. "Can you chew?"

He slumped back, muttering curses behind his swollen lips. "I doubt it."

"You've got to try." She held the piece to his mouth.

He shook his head once again, fractionally. "Teeth loose."

She closed her eyes, struggling to keep from crying. She could not shed tears and spoil her makeup. She had not counted on forty-eight hours until the train. The crêpe hair would last, though it would itch like the very devil, but she had not Ada's skill with the paint. "Shreve," she whispered. "You must eat. You have to keep up your strength. At least until I can get you on the train."

"I'll make it," he murmured and turned his face away on the pillow.

"Shreve!"

He had lost consciousness.

For several minutes she sought to get herself under control. First, she performed all the deep-breathing exercises he had taught her. As she breathed, she went over her lines and her moves analyzing her performance. So far it had been perfect. Nothing less would have served. She had to remember everything and maintain a consistent characterization for forty-eight hours.

It was the role of a lifetime. Women played men in farce, but never in drama. It would be the performance of her life.

When her hands had stopped trembling and the hard lump in her throat had dissolved, she unbuttoned Shreve's shirt with the idea of making him more comfortable. The sight of his chest made her gasp. He was a mass of purple contusions from armpit to waistband. Surely some of his ribs must be broken. What if one had punctured his lung? She closed her eyes for a moment against the tears that threatened again.

Imagine that it's makeup, she counseled herself. *Some of Ada's best. Just like mine. I can't cry. I have to go on any minute. And I can't make any mistakes.*

Opening her eyes, she wrung out the washcloth and began to bathe his body. He moaned at her gentlest touch. His skin jumped and flinched even though he seemed to be unconscious. At last she buttoned the shirt, refolded the washcloth, and laid it across his forehead. He sighed and opened his eyes.

"When did you come to?"

He managed a travesty of a smile. "You didn't know, did you?"

"It doesn't take much talent to play an unconscious body." She gave him her stern look of command as she forked up a bite of beans. "No more

36

passing out now, Shreve. Eat this food and get your strength up for the performance. You can't miss your cue."

One corner of his pitiful mouth quirked upward. He allowed her to push the food between his swollen lips. With concentrated effort he chewed, grimacing as he did so. When he had swallowed, he managed to raise one abused eyebrow. "You just be sure you give me the correct line. I'll make the cue."

Downstairs, Miranda helped herself to a plate of food off the cold meal on the bar. Thankfully, the place was almost empty. Nevertheless, she sat down in the darkest corner of the room. Private Perkins was taking first watch with Shreve. The other trooper was nowhere in sight. She had taken up her tin fork when Sergeant Trask appeared in the doorway.

He did not appear to have put his free time to good use in such things as bathing, shaving, or even beating the dust from his clothes. His narrow face still bore dark stubble. His campaign hat was pushed back on his head. Lank, greasy hair flopped in his eyes. Despite the obstruction he searched the room until he found her. Extracting a toothpick from between his teeth, he spat in the direction of the spittoon and swaggered toward her.

"Mind if I set down." He twirled the chair opposite her around on one leg and straddled it crossing his arms over the back. The stench from his armpits made her eyes water.

"How's the purty boy?"

If his body odor had not completely done away with her appetite, his question would have. The biscuit crumbled in her hand as she clenched it. Still she must eat. Not bothering to answer Trask, who should not have presumed to sit down with an officer, she let the crumbs fall to the edge of the plate and took up her fork and knife. Ignoring the rank exhalation of breath from across the table, she cut herself a bite of meat.

Not offended by her behavior, Trask chuckled. "I reckon he don't look so purty no more, but when he was brought in, whoo-ee-ee. He looked just like a girl."

Miranda chewed slowly, remembering her part, conscious that she was a lieutenant in the U.S. Army. The meat was dry. She reached for the draught of beer.

Trask tilted his head to one side. "He was damn near as purty as you."

Her hand stilled. Her eyes flashed to the sergeant who was grinning, wind-blistered lips peeled back from rotten teeth.

"Sergeant, you're out of line."

Trask chuckled again. "Now don't go gettin' the wrong idee, Lieutenant. I ain't sayin' a thing, if'n y' don't take my meanin'."

She stared at him. *What was the man saying?*

Trask grinned even wider. "Now, I see y' don't, and that's to your credit. I do hate them young fellers that jes' don't have no pride."

Miranda frowned. The man was saying something to her that she was too naive to catch. For a moment she thought he might have guessed she was a woman. But that couldn't be. He wouldn't be sitting here across the table talking to her about pride—

Shades of Freddy! Frederic Franklin! The sergeant, unless she was very much mistaken, was making her a proposition. She wanted to laugh. The whole thing was so ludicrous.

"Good night, Sergeant."

"Just thought y' might be inter'sted. Things're purty quiet 'round here. Don't get many chances." His scabby eyebrows waggled, his mouth quirked up

38

at one corner. He pushed his hips forward as he rose still straddling the chair. His dirty hands hooked over his belt revealed knuckles that, despite heavy calluses, were scraped and swollen from the beatings they had administered.

Despite her determination to remain in character, she shuddered.

His eyes narrowed. He followed her stare, then looked at her own hands. "Y' sure are skittish. Never seen a lick o' fightin', have y'?"

She resisted the impulse to hide them under the table. Ada had madeup the backs with crêpe hair and stain. She deepened her voice until it was as gruff as she could make it. "I'm new."

His leer widened. "I wouldn't rough y' up none," he promised. "Y' don't need to worry 'bout that."

Eyes like blue steel, she stared into his ugly face. "Good night, Sergeant."

He gave a bark of laughter before retreating to the far side of the room. Along the way he stopped at the bar to buy himself another beer. Tilting a chair back against the wall, he swigged and stared at her.

She could feel her skin crawl. He was convinced that she was effeminate. He would be at her room tonight. She was sure. What to do? He represented a subplot that she had never counted on. A new element of suspense had been added to the drama. Suddenly, a minor character had added a potentially deadly twist. As a result she would have great difficulty escaping detection for the next two days.

The original plan had been for her to get Shreve away from the fort where George and Ada would join them. The four would travel together to catch the train. Armistead's escort had changed all that. She had caught the quick expression of alarm in George's eye as they rode past him on the way to Fort Laramie.

She had not worried; she had great faith in George. A seasoned actor and improviser, he would have already figured out his next move. Undoubtedly he and Ada had set out for Cheyenne, checked in at a different hotel, and bought tickets for the same train.

The plan could still work if she could get Shreve on the train with her disguise intact. No one would pursue them because no one would know that they had escaped, unless Armistead should send a telegram to the U.S. marshal's office in Fort Leavenworth. By the time that unlikely event occurred, they would be far, far away going about their business.

Now this monster across the room was spoiling all her plans. If she could not keep him at bay, he would easily penetrate her disguise. He would know an escape was in progress.

She shoved the food into her mouth, chewing, swallowing, drinking the beer. If someone had asked her what she was eating, she could not have told him.

At last the plate was clean. She had finished and her throat was clogged with crumbs. She longed for a drink of cool water. She thought about asking for one but changed her mind. Going back to the bar, she paid for another bottle of beer and sipped it slowly.

Down the length of the bar, reared back in his chair, his third bottle of beer cradled on his hollow belly, Trask watched her. Once she glanced uneasily in his direction. Their eyes met. He grinned and tilted the bottle toward her. It stood at an acute angle in his lap.

Hastily, she dropped her eyes to her own bottle, studying the level of the liquid, the collar of foam, the tiny imperfections in the brown glass. She was exhausted. The day had been long, the ride from

Fort Laramie an odyssey of dust and heat. She wanted nothing so much as to take off her boots and loosen her clothing (she dared not think of undressing) and lie down to sleep. Instead, she was going to have to spend the night on guard against this stupid, bestial horror of a man.

Her temper flared, but she kept it tamped down. She would just have to outwit him. Setting the bottle on the bar still half full, she laid down a coin and strode from the room.

Once out of sight of Trask, she sprinted for the stairs, taking them two at a time. Outside the door to Shreve's room, she paused. Her inclination was to dart inside and use the prisoner and the soldier guarding him as shields. Surely, Trask would not follow her there.

The idea died almost as fast as it had been conceived. Suppose he did follow her in. Suppose he dismissed the guard and attacked her in front of the man who loved her. Shreve would undoubtedly try to fight him, chained and injured. The ensuing scene would be too awful to contemplate. Trask was a brute who would kill the prisoner as unconcernedly as he swatted a fly.

Her only chance was to lock herself in her room and refuse to let him in. If he made too much noise, witnesses would come. In their presence she could use her uniform and her position of command to drive him away.

At the door of her room, she made a horrifying discovery. The keyhole was empty. She could not lock herself in. The spindly straight chair she thrust under the doorknob was her one hope. Angry and trembling, she huddled against the headboard of the bed, her gun drawn.

She had not long to wait.

A knock and then the doorknob rattled. A heavy

body leaned against it. The chair scraped an inch, then its back legs dug in.

Through the crack a voice whined, "Hey, purty boy. Why don't y' open up and lemme talk to y'?"

"Go away, Sergeant Trask. You could be court-martialed for this."

"Maybe in Washington, but out here there ain't no females for a soldier. We've jes' had to make do with what we've got."

"I'll see you're brought up on charges."

"Hey, Lieutenant. There ain't no reason to talk like that. I'm jes' suggestin' a talk. Friendly-like. Get to know each other. Jes' lemme in." He pushed harder against the door. The chair creaked and edged an inch farther along the floor. It would not hold him long.

"Do you want a bullet in your belly, Sergeant? Get to your own room. Leave me alone."

Trask chuckled. "Hey, sonny, y' don't scare me none. C'mon. Y' ain't gonna shoot me. Why yo're way too purty."

"If you push that chair out of the way, I'll shoot you where you stand. This pistol will blow you all the way back across the hall. If anyone asks, I'll be terribly sorry, but I mistook you for a burglar. Now get the hell away from that door!"

The pressure on the door stopped, but the whining voice continued through the crack. "Y' know, y' could do worse. Don't hurt none. Makes y' feel real good. I don't care who does what. Hell, we'll just be sorta wrestlin' around. Like boys do."

She tried to make her voice sound bored as well as disgusted. "I don't wrestle with the boys. So go to bed."

"Yo're missin' a good time," were his final words. She could hear him leave the door and enter the room beyond hers. The thought that a single thin wall separated them set her to shivering again. The

42

next forty-eight hours stretched ahead of her interminably.

She leaned her head back against the headboard. She was so tired. Her room was hot and stuffy. How she wished she were standing watch in Shreve's room. She could lock the door and curl up beside him on the bed. The feel of his body would lull her to sleep. She could never sleep so well as when she slept beside him.

In another instant, her eyes had closed. The pistol slid from her limp fingers.

Trask's thin hand slid round the jamb of the door and lifted the chair. It creaked softly, but the figure on the bed did not move. The even breathing never changed. *Snores, does he,* Trask thought. *Any boy that purty don't snore.*

The moonlight revealed the darker form of the lieutenant huddled against the white sheets. Pushing the door farther open, Trask slipped inside and closed it behind him, being careful not to click the lock. On bare feet he moved across the floor. The shavetail was curled up dead to the world. Never send a boy to do a man's work. He could have told that U.S. senator a thing or two about sending someone who didn't know when to keep alert.

Beside the bed, he reached a hand down to feel himself. He was hard as a rock just thinking about that little nancy-nice. All them young purty boys kicked up a ruckus, but they all came around once he stuck it to 'em.

He unbuttoned his union suit and pulled himself free. As he did, the back of his hand encountered a piece of cold metal.

"Push it right back in your pants, Sergeant Trask."

He froze, his organ stiffened then began to go limp. "Now, listen here—"

"No you listen here. I told you I was a light sleeper." The figure on the bed rose on its knees.

Trask grinned as he realized the green lieutenant was off balance. "That's right, y' shore did. Guess I can't put nothin' over on a smart feller like you."

Trask moved like lightning. Twisting sideways around the gun, he drove his shoulder into the lieutenant's chest. His arms closed around the slender body and they sprawled onto the bed.

Trask half expected the lieutenant to fire, but the dern fool probably hadn't even cocked the weapon. "Yo're gonna love this, Lieutenant," he growled in the general direction of the young officer's ear. "Y' ain't never—What the hell!" His face encountered her breasts, loose beneath her military blouse. She had not been able to stand the bindings. "Yo're—"

The "lieutenant" brought the barrel of the revolver down with all her strength on the back of Trask's head. The force of the blow drove the man's forehead into the side of her cheek, but Trask collapsed without a sound.

For half a minute Miranda lay still, breathing hard. Her hand with the revolver was still poised above Trask's head. When she was certain that he was indeed unconscious, she pushed him aside, shoving at him with her feet and hands until his body thudded to the floor. She sprang up on the other side and lighted the lamp.

He was unconscious, but for how long? And when he waked up, he could be depended upon to remember that he had found her breasts. He was neither drunk nor a fool. Her disguise had been penetrated. She could not wait around with the troopers for the train. Injured or not, Shreve would have to move. She only prayed that she could find George and Ada.

Ripping the sheets off the bed, she tied Trask's hands and feet to the railings and stuffed a gag in his mouth. Still, he did not stir. She knew a moment's fear that she had seriously injured him, then remembered Shreve's face and ribs. Any minor bruising she might have inflicted was one the sergeant surely deserved.

Resisting an impulse to give the unconscious man a good hard kick, she took up her saddlebags, turned off the lamp, and tiptoed down the hall.

Three

I will not consent to die this day.

Sleepless and in pain, Shreve heard the faint grating at the lock.

He tensed as the door opened. By the dim light of the smoking lamp, he watched Miranda enter and close the door behind her. His eyes fastened fearfully to the guard, but the steady snores continued. Holding his own breath, he watched as she tiptoed to the bed. Her hand gently descended to cover his mouth. Then their eyes met.

With a small smile she stooped and touched her lips to his forehead. Even as she shook her head, she produced a second key. The chains slipped off in seconds. She pulled them to the end of the bed, careful not to let them clank. Shreve swung his bare feet out onto the floor.

Before the young guard could shake the sleep out of his limbs, he was gagged and the cuffs clicked onto his wrists. With bewildered eyes he offered no resistance when the "lieutenant" looped the chain that had connected the manacles to the leg irons around one of the rods on the iron bed.

After giving the chain a quick tug to test its security, Miranda closed her hand around Shreve's upper arm. "Can you stand?"

For answer he heaved himself upright, hanging on to the end of the bed. He tottered for a minute, then let go. "I can make it."

She nodded her head. "Come on. We've got a long ride ahead of us."

"Right."

But when she led him out the door, rather than head down the hall, she took him into Trask's room. "I've brought your clothes," she murmured, pulling the garments from the saddlebags. "Don't make any noise. The sergeant is tied up next door. We mustn't give him any clues."

Shreve's head pounded excruciatingly. The least movement sent shafts of blackness across his vision. In the end she had to help him step into his pants, button his shirt, and tie his shoes. "I keep falling over," he groaned, head hanging while he panted for breath. "Maybe you'd better leave me."

She caressed his cheek and dropped a kiss in his tangled hair. "You don't mean that."

He held her palm against his battered face. "No."

She smiled. "Then let's go."

The most difficult trick was getting down the stairs past the desk clerk, alert to guests trying to escape without paying their bills. In her best military manner, Miranda walked up to him and asked for directions to the marshal's office. The man gave them, but Miranda feigned hesitation. "Maybe you'd better show me. I get lost in the dark real easy."

"Glad to." The desk clerk stepped out onto the porch. Obligingly, he pointed down the street, counting the number of streets over, detailing the turns with hand motions. These Miranda mimicked leading him to the end of the porch. While they stood with their backs to the door, Shreve limped across the lobby and out, slipping the opposite way

47

along the veranda and dropping off into the dusty alley.

"I guess I've got it," Miranda said at last. "Thanks."

A minute later she found Shreve leaning against the side of the building, breathing shallowly and holding his ribs. "Maybe you'd better go and get the horses. I'll mount here."

"We're not going to ride."

"But—"

"That was just for our listener's benefit. Convincing, huh? I'm pretty sure George and Ada are over at one of these hotels."

"Pretty sure?"

"George is no fool. When he saw that I had an escort, he was certain to follow and be ready when I made my move. They can hide us. When the train comes through, we'll board it as a laughing foursome, returning to Saint Louis after a tour of the romantic West."

"We'll never make it," he prophesied direly. "You can put on your dress and the lieutenant will disappear, but my face—" He touched it tenderly. "Anyone can see that I've been beaten."

"Ada can fix it," she assured him.

"No. It's too bad. Now that I'm free, I could hide out—"

"Shreve." She closed his protesting mouth with a gentle finger. "I love you. And I know you're used to taking charge. But this time I'm the playwright as well as the director. We're going to follow my script. Now stay here while I check the hotels along this street."

He was wringing wet with perspiration when she half dragged, half carried him to the porch of the second hotel she tried—the Union Pacific. The sleepy clerk had not objected when she checked the register for Mr. and Mrs. George Windom. He

48

had gone back to his dozing by the time she brought Shreve into the lobby and left him to lean against the wall beside one of the leather chairs. "Stay here."

"No chance," he muttered. "Don't come back."

"You have to watch me," she flashed back. "Another great performance." She pulled the crêpe hair from her face and shed the lieutenant's coat. This time a guard's cap shielded her eyes.

"What d'ya think?"

"Schoolgirl play."

She made a face at him. "Just come in on cue." He managed a nod and a pained grin.

Squaring her shoulders, she slipped back to the door and made her entrance, reaching across the desk to shake the clerk awake. "Message for Mr. Windom."

Ada Cocks, clad in high-necked nightgown and robe, bent over Shreve's limp body. "Lord forgive us, Shrevey-boy. What have they been doing to you?"

Eyes closed, he managed a flick of one corner of his mouth. "They didn't like my performance."

She pressed one hand to her mouth. The other she placed on his forehead. "He's got fever," she pronounced. "And it's no wonder. His poor face."

"You should see his ribs."

"I can imagine," George remarked dryly.

"M' nose isn't broken," he whispered.

"Well, that's the only blessing."

"Hush, *ma bouchal*." Tears were trickling unheeded down Ada's cheeks.

Miranda bent over to touch her fingers to Shreve's neck. His skin was hot and flushed; his pulse beat strong, but fast. "You're right. He does have fever. It's sprung up suddenly. I swear, he

49

didn't have it when I first got him out of the hotel room."

"Something infected, I expect," Ada told her. "Or just the body tryin' to stoke a little heat in it to get the engine going."

Miranda looked sadly down into his bruised face. Her own face ached in sympathy. "Take good care of him. I've got to go back to the stable and steal two horses."

His eyes flew open. "NO!"

"No, Miss Miranda. Let me do that."

"Oh, no, dearie."

She blinked in the face of their united front. "It's the only way. They've got to think we rode out of town. If they don't, then we'll never get away day after tomorrow evening."

They stared at her forbiddingly. George shook his head. "It's too dangerous. You've got him away. Let it go at that."

"I found you on the second try. How long do you think it'll take a troop of soldiers to find us unless they have hard evidence that they should be out scouring the countryside? No. This was all foreshadowed in the previous act. I told the guard that we were riding."

"Stop her." Shreve reared up in the bed and made a grab for her wrist.

She whisked herself out of the way. "Don't make a fuss. I'll be back before you know it."

"Miranda!" he called. "For God's sake!"

George followed her to the door. "Miss. At least take me with you."

She hugged him. "George, you're the dearest and most loyal person, but you can't ride a horse."

"I could guard your back."

"Miranda," Shreve called imperatively. "Ada, stop her." He tried to rise, but the pain in his head exploded and he slipped back with a groan.

"I'll hurry," she promised and slipped out the door.

The livery stable was dark. Were it not for the distinctive odor of horses and hay, she could have been stepping into a subterranean cave. In the time since this whole mad adventure had begun, the wind had risen. A bank of clouds had rolled in from the west obscuring the moon. Lightning flickered in the midst of the thunderheads followed by ominous rumblings.

She shivered despite the humid darkness. The long ride to take the horses out of town and turn them loose was going to be a wet one.

She had planned to take the horse she had ridden in on and Sergeant Trask's horse, but the absence of light confused her. She could not remember which stall contained her mount. Better to take the first two and leave.

She felt her way to the first stall, encountered a dark head. The horse stirred, stamped, and whickered uneasily. Instantly, she clapped a hand over its nose. In the next stall another animal moved and snorted.

"Y'll have the whole kit-n-caboodle of 'em up in just a minute, darlin'."

The familiar voice spun her around. A match rasped; light flared. Glass scraped against metal as the chimney slid up. A lantern cast a pool of light in the interior of the stable.

Grinning like a rabid fox, Sergeant Trask stepped out from behind the ladder that led up to the loft. Almost casually, he hung the lantern on its hook and squared his shoulders. "I was hopin' you'd come a lee-e-etle bit farther down. If you'd jesta done that, darlin', you'd a walked right into my arms."

She did not bother to protest. Nor did she try to

run. Frozen at the sound of his voice, she stood blinking in the light, her mind forming and discarding plots for her escape. Outside the rain began to fall, not with a light preliminary sprinkle, but a sudden slashing flood.

A part of her noted the appropriate sound and lighting effects. After all this scene was the climax of the drama. All the action turned on it. She drew in a deep controlling breath.

"Now, I'm thinkin' that maybe we've been huntin' for the wrong thing all along." He slouched toward her. His Navy Colt was aimed straight at her belly, its hammer pulled back ready for use. "Seein' as how y' could fool me right up close, it makes sense that y'd fool all them people on Independence Day. You're the one plugged that general, ain't y'?"

"It was self-defense," she whispered, her throat dry. "He drew his gun."

Lightning flashed sending shards of light through cracks in the stable walls. A couple of seconds later the thunder answered.

Trask paid no attention. "The army don't see it thataway." He chuckled. "Kinda shortsighted of 'em, but they ain't the friendliest types around. And they purely don't like people shootin' down generals."

"He was a murderer. He was going to murder again." She did not expect her words to have any effect. She spoke them to buy herself more time, to make him—if possible—less sure of himself.

"Is that right?" Trask's eyebrows rose in mockery of shocked surprise. "Well, that sure don't surprise me none. Them generals are bastards from the word go."

"He killed my father."

Small hailstones struck the roof of the stable. The horses were all awake, stomping and whinnying nervously.

"Ah-huh. I might-a known. Shoot 'im or hang 'im?" He did not wait for an answer. "Well, if you was to be real nice t' me—real, real nice—maybe I could forget what I seen?"

Instantly, she was alert. Could it be possible that he had not told the guards of her identity? Would his own lechery cause his downfall? Who said life wasn't like the theater?

She smiled tremulously. "Oh, could you? Could you? You could say you never saw the lieutenant again. You could blame the guard for sleeping at his post. He was asleep. I'd be *so* grateful."

Her performance was a masterpiece. He relaxed with a wide grin. The muzzle of the gun left her as he raised it to scratch his temple with the gun sight. "Well, now, that'd be mighty fine. I'm sure gonna make it my business t' find out how grateful. 'Course there's yore pardner. What'll we do about him?"

She stared at the weapon, watched it come back to level at her. It was cocked. In that instant she knew that Trask had no intention of letting her go, no matter what hideous acts of gratitude she performed for him. She lifted her chin and reached for the top button of her shirt. Slowly, she slipped it free of the buttonhole. And the next. "What do you want him for?" she purred. "You've got me."

His mouth dropped open as the gun swung down on his finger. "That's right. That's sure as hell right."

"It's like you said, Sergeant, a man out here has so few opportunities he has to take what's offered. An opportunity like tonight doesn't come along often."

"Y're sure right." He advanced. The gun, still cocked but pointed at the floor.

She unbuttoned another button and arched her neck. The blood beat like a drum beneath her skin.

53

A flush rose in her throat.

"Y're sure purty."

This man had beaten Shreve's face to a shapeless pulp. He had offered to beat him again when she had said she wanted to question the prisoner. He had broken into her room intent on rape. He was lethal, deadly as a grizzly bear. She had never been more terrified during a performance.

He brushed her shirt aside and pawed at her breast. She could smell him, his body sour, his breath rank.

The lightning flashed again, lighting up the entire stable. The air crackled with ozone. Simultaneously, the thunder boomed with a force that she could feel.

Trask suddenly became aware of the gun still in his right hand. He made to stuff it into his belt. He missed, brought it up again.

"Now, girlie, gimme a little kiss."

She strained back away from him. One hand flattened against his chest, the other caught at his right wrist, tugged it upward.

He paid no attention. Her smooth white flesh had mesmerized him. He leaned forward. Black hairs bristled around his lips. He made an obscene smacking sound. "C'mon, girlie. Give."

The magazine of the Colt pressed painfully against her breast. He was leaning over the barrel. His lips almost turned inside out in their eagerness to reach her. Her left hand moved up his wrist, over the back of his hand, closed around the pistol, tilted it up at a sharper angle.

"Hey, now—"

Her finger slid inside the guard imprisoning his own finger on the trigger.

"What—?"

She squeezed with all her strength. The bullet plowed through the underside of his jaw. Blood spouted from his mouth and nose. He fell straight over backward, his hand clawing at her breast, dragging her down with him. The knobby fingers tightened in a final spasm, then finally fell away into the straw.

All along the shedrow of the stable, the horses neighed and stomped. From the stall nearest to her came a terrorized whinnying, a thunderous crash, and a splintering of wood as the animal tried to break down its door and escape.

Deafened by the blast in her face, she flung herself away from Trask's body and rolled up on her knees. Weak with reaction, she waited for shouts that would alarm the town and bring more people into the scene. The gunshot must have alerted the entire town of Cheyenne.

The lightning flashed followed by a malignant boom. No one came. The storm. The gunshot had been mistaken for thunder. A thin stream of water hit the back of her neck.

She cast her eyes upward to the leak in the loft. "Thank you, God."

Again, the lightning and thunder, but the hail had ceased. The heart of the storm had passed on.

Taking a deep breath, she struggled to her feet. Her hand left a bloody smear on the rung of the ladder.

The horse neighed again shrilly. From every stall came the stamp and clang of iron-shod hooves. Some dedicated stablehand might decide at any minute to come and see if the animals were all right.

She had to hurry, to get away taking the two horses as she had planned. By Trask's lantern she recognized the bald-faced sorrel she had ridden in on. The mount next to him must be Trask's.

Acting with feverish haste, she caught Trask's legs and tugged his body into the empty stall where he had been hiding. Rolling him over and over, she shoved him against the wall and piled straw over him. With luck he might not be found for hours, maybe even a couple of days. She dashed into the next stall, swept up an armload of straw, returned, and spread it over him. She added another and another disguising the mound of his body with a bank of straw.

᾿ Thunder rumbled as she backed away. She clasped her arms around her body. She had killed another man. Never mind that he was despicable, brutal, barely human. What lay in the darkness had been a man, and she had killed him with his own gun. She shuddered. Her teeth ached from clenching her jaw. She gagged and swallowed violently.

Like Shakespeare's greatest tragedies every turn of the plot seemed to end in blood. Her lips moved in a taut whisper. *"Thou wretched, rash, intruding fool, farewell!"*

A tiny hysterical giggle slipped out between her clamped lips. The drama of it all kept her from breaking down completely. But how angry Shreve would be if he could see her, standing here in the stable, blood on her hands, quoting *Hamlet*.

She stared about her, her director's eyes coldly checking the scene, then she swallowed tightly.

Macbeth's words leaped into her mind. *"Blood will have blood."*

The blood from the sergeant's ruined face had soaked into the hard-packed earthen floor. It left an incriminating trail. A bucket half full of water stood beside the sorrel's stall. She flung it over the stains, watching as they lost their bright color and soaked into the ground. Then she kicked dirt and straw over the whole.

When she was satisfied that no trail remained, she raised a shaking hand to her forehead. It was spattered with Trask's blood. A smothered sob burst from her as she ran to the leak and scrubbed at the dark smears on her skin. When dizziness threatened to overcome her, she turned her face up to the leak to let the cold water revive her. When she lifted her trembling hands to her cheeks, she could not bring herself to touch herself. *"What, will these hands ne'er be clean?"*

Setting her jaw against the icy shudders of shock, she dragged the sorrel's saddle from the side of the stall.

One mile! Two! She crossed Crow Creek and whipped the reins across the reluctant sorrel's withers. The rain slapped her face. The wet night wind chilled her to the bone. Unknown numbers of miles rolled away, and still she rode as if the entire U.S. Army was on her heels. Her horses were heaving and blowing when she judged they were far enough from Cheyenne to turn loose.

Heading the sorrel down into a draw, she rode a quarter of a mile. Out of sight of the road, she allowed the weary beast to halt. Sliding off his back, she leaned against his lathered side for support until her legs stopped quivering.

The night was at its darkest. She was exhausted and cold, but Shreve was safe. Even if she did not make her way back, her three friends would escape. Her vengeance would not take an innocent person down.

She pulled the tack from the horses and rubbed their blankets over their backs. Now they were too tired to move, but they would revive by morning. She gave the sorrel's neck a farewell pat before turning away to start the long walk back.

A faint pink began to grow on the horizon. The dawn was coming. Soon shadows would appear and then the light. She glanced at the dark sky above. The clouds were gone. The sun would dry the clammy uniform. Until then she would have to walk fast and set her teeth to still their chattering. Head down, fists thrust into her pockets, she hurried down the road.

By noon the sun was blistering her face. Her head throbbed. She had passed beyond hunger and would have given a great deal for a drink of the water that had soaked her the night before. The July heat rose in shimmering mirages off the land on all sides.

Too tired to go on, she staggered aside and sank down in the shadow of a tumble of rocks. No breeze stirred. The evaporation of last night's rain was like a Turkish bath. Pulling off her cap, she fanned herself before leaning back and closing her eyes.

She must have slept or lain in a stupor. At any rate she was unconscious of the passage of time. Gradually, the muffled tread of horses intruded on the edge of her dreams. Several horses. Her eyelids flickered. So heavy. Her head still ached. Her throat felt like sand. Horses. Riders. Perhaps someone would take her up behind him.

On that hope she managed to open her eyes. The shimmering mirages distorted the shoulders of the mountains. As if they waded in crystal waters, a band of Indians—Sioux or Cheyenne, Crow or Shoshoni, she could not tell—moved across the arid landscape. They rode naked except for breechclouts and fringed boots reaching to their knees. Eagle feathers wafted from the braids in their hair. Eagle feathers dangled from the rawhide hackamores knotted under the jaws of their painted ponies. In single file, they rode stirring no dust. Nothing marked their passing.

Lances clutched in their fists, their legs threaded through the surcingles around the horses' ribs, they rode ready for hunting or for war. Their faces were grim; their eyes, trained on some distant objective.

Miranda scrambled to her knees, her back against the rocks. If one should spot her—

From the southeast a troop of blue-coated cavalry, their faces shaded by buff campaign hats, trotted single file up a slope toward the advancing line. Like their counterparts, they came through the wavering mirages, their shapes merging and distorting. Jingle and creak of tack. Iron-shod hooves ringing on stone.

Mortal enemies converged in the center of the plain. The men exchanged no greetings, nor did they acknowledge each other's presence. No greetings, no hailings. No one raised his arm to parley. The captain at the head of the troop merely reined his dark bay to match the angle of the march. His Indian counterpart pulled his mount. The skewbald paint pranced, then settled into step so that the two rode shoulder to shoulder.

A column of twos, century-old enemies trotted westward side by side until they disappeared behind the shoulder of a hill.

Miranda sank back onto the ground. Her eyes had deceived her. Her headache, thirst, exhaustion, the supernormal heat had made her delirious. She needed water badly. Clapping her cap onto her head, she crawled out from the shelter of the rocks and headed for Cheyenne.

The rest must have revivified her because she walked rapidly, or perhaps the prickling of fear at the top of her spine added speed to her march. As a mile passed and then another, she thought about the riders. Had they been real? Did their spirits ride the plains as she had so often dreamed as a child? Had the violence she had perpetrated in their cause torn down the barriers between life and death for just a moment allowing her to see them united?

She halted on a rise. Before her, less than a mile distant, she could see the town of Cheyenne. Her shadow stretched before her as the sun reached the tops of the mountains. Slowly, she turned around, staring back the way she had come. The trail was empty. Her exhausted body and overcharged mind must have imagined it all. It had been a delirium dream. Yet, she could not leave this long, traverse without some sign.

There are more things in heaven and earth, Horatio, than are dreamt of in your philosophy. She raised her hand in silent farewell, then turned toward the town.

Tiny clear water blisters stood on her reddened nose and cheeks. Her lips were cracked. When Ada pulled off her boots, her toes and heels were bleeding where blisters had rubbed up and broken.

"God save us. She must have walked ten miles."

Shreve sat on the edge of the bed. To cover the tears sparkling in his eyes, he voiced his disgust. "She probably rode a lot farther than was necessary. She never uses any discretion. Always overacts for every performance."

"What do you need to take care of her?" George hovered at the end of the bed.

Ada shrugged. "I'd like to put ice packs on her face and neck, but cool water will have to do."

"Not some salve and some bandages?"

"Just cold packs. She's overheated. We need to cool her off."

Miranda's lips moved. "Cheyenne—"

"What did she say?"

Ada stooped to catch the next words. "Something about Ann."

60

"Sioux," Miranda breathed.

"She's talking about some women?"

"I think she's talking about Indians," George suggested.

"Indians!" Ada drew back, her hands on her cheeks. "Oh, mercy. Just let us get out of this god-forsaken country with our scalps."

Miranda's face contorted. She drew in her breath sharply. Her lips moved again, but her words were unintelligible.

Shreve put his hand on Miranda's shoulder and shook her gently. "You're dreaming, sweetheart."

She opened her eyes. Their blue was bluer than ever against her sunburnt skin. She looked around her, puzzled.

"Do you feel all right, dearie?"

"I—" Miranda cleared her throat amazed to find she could swallow. "I'm hungry." She pushed herself up in bed. "Oh, God. I'm so hungry."

The three exchanged relieved looks. Shreve chuckled. "That's the Miranda we've come to know and love. Can't eat a bite before a performance. Stuffs herself afterward."

"You look terrible," she told Shreve later between bites of steak and beans.

"You do, too," he replied equably. "Fortunately, we both feel better than we look."

Ada shook her head unhappily. "I don't know how I'll get the bruises and the blisters covered up enough to get us on that train."

"Maybe no one will be looking for us. Have they—uh—?"

"They've found Trask's body," Shreve told her.

"Along about sundown they rented that stall," George reported. "The horse wouldn't go in, acted crazy. They sent a hand in to clean it and found him. Pretty nasty sight, everyone's saying."

They all looked at her significantly.

"I killed him with his own gun." She laid the fork down in her plate and pressed her hand against her forehead. Suddenly, the headache had come back full strength.

Shreve put his hand on her shoulder. "He deserved to die. Don't have a moment of regret. No doubt you've saved a lot of young troopers from being abused."

Miranda lay back on the pillow, her face a tragic mask. "I seem to be saving everyone these days. First, the Indians, then the settlers, and now the soldiers. But I'm killing men to do it."

"Dark villains deserve dark deaths."

"Shreve, I don't want to kill anybody." Tears started down her cheeks. "I just—I just—"

Ada picked up the tray. George held the door for her. "Try to get to sleep, you two," she bade them. "Keep cold cloths on her face, Shrevey-boy. She'll be right as rain in the morning."

He nodded as he gently mopped at Miranda's cheeks.

The tears went on and on while he sat beside her. Finally, she managed to get herself under control. He handed her a glass of cold water. She drank it all and leaned back with a watery smile. "You know what? I'm thinking of applying for sainthood."

He nodded mock seriously. "Your emblems can be a pot of makeup and a false beard."

"Would something false be acceptable as the emblem of a saint?"

"Probably so. Considering the circumstances."

With a deep sigh she slid down in the bed and held up her arms to him.

Moving carefully because his body ached in so many places, he lowered himself into her embrace and laid his head on her breast. For several minutes they lay quietly savoring each other's nearness, holding each other close.

"I couldn't believe my eyes when you slipped into that room last night. I was terrified that he'd wake up."

"Let's not think about it ever again." She tapped him on the shoulder. "I want a kiss."

He groaned, but raised himself on his arms.

She tilted her head and kissed him. Her tongue slid between his bruised lips teasing him. The kiss went on and on until his muscles hardened and his breath came short. Then his tongue followed hers as she withdrew.

He shifted onto his side. "This is going to take some doing."

"Oh, well, if it's too much trouble—"

"I'll manage." His hands encircled her waist finding it slim as a wand then slid down over her hips that flared excitingly. She moaned and shifted herself toward him.

He pulled back, grinning into her face. "On the other hand—"

She caught her lower lip between her teeth. "Please."

"You're tired," he continued in mock solicitude. "You've walked and ridden miles. You haven't slept in twenty-four hours."

"More like forty-eight," she corrected him. "Please. I need you. I need you so much I ache." She slid one thigh over his hip opening the secrets of her body to him. "Please."

He ran his hand admiringly over its inner surface. Its muscles were hard and clearly defined. "You're more beautiful than ever."

Her face retained its strained look. "I don't feel like a woman. I don't feel like myself. Everything has gone so wrong. I never—" Her voice broke. "I never meant—"

"Sssh." He put his hand between her thighs, his fingers trailing through the moisture, insinuating themselves between the lips, tickling her throbbing nub of pleasure. She gasped in ecstasy. Her head arched back as her whole being contracted. A keening cry slid between her clenched teeth. Pleasure wracked her in a great explosive wave.

He laughed. "Are you ready?"

Tears of pleasure trickled down her cheeks. "I—I didn't mean to—"

"Don't apologize." He kissed her again. "That was just to warm you up."

"But—" She wiped at her cheeks.

He did not feel the pain of his bruises. Hot for her, he guided himself to her opening. She pushed forward, but the real power came from his hands. With all the strength of an aroused male, he clamped her buttocks and pushed her down upon him.

She gasped again, her leg tightening about his waist.

Overcome by a need so primal, he had not known it existed, he drove into her. One thrust, another.

"Yes!" She cried. "Oh, yes. Yes!" She was shuddering again, her mouth open in her cry of pleasure.

He rolled above her and drove in, deeper than he had ever gone before, filling her with elemental power. His shout of triumph mingled with her second ecstatic release.

Tenderly, he stroked the short blond head resting on his shoulder. "Have you saved everyone you're going to for a while?"

She pretended to think about her answer. "I suppose so. There don't appear to be any other groups around this area."

"Then I suggest we leave this dusty, primitive country and get back to where we're appreciated."

"My thought exactly." She yawned and stretched, then kissed the point of his shoulder. "While my performance has been thoroughly convincing, you must admit—"

"Girls' school theatrics," he murmured.

"—the audience was limited—"

"Limited in intelligence."

"—and the run of such short duration—"

"Too long for my taste."

"—that there really is no future here. I've done sufficient theater of the West to last me a lifetime. I want new worlds to conquer. I'm ready for our next engagement."

"We're too late for Saint Louis."

"Then what's next?"

"New Orleans."

"Perfect." She kissed his shoulder again. "I've always loved New Orleans."

Act IV
Scene 1
New Orleans,
1883

Four

> *All the world's a stage,*
> *And all the men and women merely players:*
> *They have their exits and their entrances.*

"Come hither, boy."

Orsino, Duke of Illyria, held out his arm clad in emerald velvet. Lace dripped from the wrist. A ring with a great glass emerald flashed in the footlights.

Clad in pale aquamarine tights and imitation leather jerkin of turquoise blue, Viola, disguised as the page Cesario, darted across the stage to kneel at his feet. Tilting her head back she stared upward, her expression adoring. She had cut her blond hair like a man's to perfect her disguise as Lieutenant Shaw. Now the style, like a Botticelli angel, lent realism to the role of Shakespeare's shipwrecked twin.

The ducal hand dropped languidly onto her shoulder. He looked into her eyes, frowned, then heaved a sigh of unhappiness. *"If ever thou shalt love, In the sweet pangs of it remember me."*

The audience listened intently. Every woman wished that Shreve Catherwood, Romantic Star of Three Continents, rested his hand on her shoulder. Every man, who had admired the slender figure of the Magnificent Miranda, wished she knelt at his feet.

"Young though thou art, thine eye hath stay'd upon some favour that it loves," Orsino continued. *"Hath it not, boy?"*

Instantly, Viola sprang from beneath his hand and hurried down stage. Her legs, long, slender, and shapely, had the men in the front rows leaning forward. She paused, to look unhappily out across them. Her blue eyes filled with tears that sparkled in the footlights. *"A little, by your favour."*

Orsino rose. His own muscular legs in tawny hose had every woman following his movement as he came across the stage to stand behind his page. At the top of his thighs, the masculine bulge, clearly defined in the tight-fitting knit, had them gripping the chair arms. He heaved a mournful sigh. *"What kind of woman is't?"*

"Of your complexion." She faced him fairly, her eyes scanning his face. She rocked forward slightly on her toes as if drawn against her will to his masculinity.

The women in the audience rocked with her.

He stared into their blue depths, then shook himself and strode away with a nervous laugh. *"She is not worth thee then. What years, i' faith?"*

The act continued. They talked of love in Shakespeare's witty dialogue, tripping around the problems of their own attraction for each other. Orsino's bewilderment was palpable at finding himself drawn to a boy. He put his hand upon her shoulder, let it linger a moment too long, then jerked it off and turned away.

When Orsino ordered her to present his suit to the Countess Olivia, Viola was a study in lovelorn longing. Forced to wear boy's clothes to protect her virtue after her ship was wrecked and she was cast ashore in a foreign land, she mourned her loss of identity now that she had found the love of her life. *"She never told her love, but let concealment, like a worm i' th' bud, feed on her damask cheek."*

He thrust the ring into her hand, drawing back his own and rubbing the fingers together as if they burned from contact with her. The look they exchanged on stage suspended the audience breathless. He shook himself visibly. *"To her in haste!"* he commanded, in an angry tone. *"Give her this jewel. Say my love can give no place, bide no delay."*

Turning on his heel, he strode off stage right, head down, his hands clasped behind him.

She stared after him, then slipped the ring onto her own finger. She lifted her face to the audience. The stage lights sparkled again on real tears that slipped down her cheeks. She held her hand up, staring at the ring with ineffable longing. Then sadly she slipped it off, dropped it into her purse, and ran off stage left.

The applause was thunderous.

"I'm getting too old for Viola."

"Nonsense. If you had gotten fat, I'd say maybe, but you're slim as a boy. In fact, you're too thin." Shreve turned Miranda to face the mirror and stood behind her. "See. I can put my hands around your waist." He demonstrated by placing his thumbs on her backbone and touching his third fingers together at the center of her midriff.

"I'm talking about the wrinkles." She sank back down on the stool and leaned forward to the mirror to study her reflection. Her skin had peeled on the journey down the Platte and the Mississippi. The result was a leathery look with a network of tiny lines around her eyes and at the corners of her mouth. She ran her fingertips over her cheek.

"Ada can cover them with makeup, and eventually they'll go away," he consoled her.

"I'm still too old."

"Next week, *Taming of the Shrew.* You're not too old for Katherina." He turned sideways to the mirror and studied his own slim figure. Appreciatively, he patted his flat stomach. "I've been too old for—ahem—several years, but I don't let that stop me. The audiences don't know how old these people are supposed to be. They just know that we look good on the stage. The only ones that really matter are Romeo and Juliet."

"We played them too long," she groaned.

He patted her head affectionately as if she were a child whose fears need soothing. "You look wonderful in your tights. Your legs are strong as a boy's. All that horseback riding around Wyoming did you a world of good."

"I'm glad some good came out of it." She rose and put her arms on his shoulders. With her thumb she smoothed the hair of his right eyebrow. He flinched despite the gentleness of her touch. Makeup, necessary to cover the red scar tissue, came away on her skin. "Oh, Shreve, your poor eyes. Do they still hurt?"

"Off and on." He grinned and presented her with his profile. "But they didn't get my nose."

She laughed. Gently, she turned his face back to her. "No, they didn't. It's still as magnificent as ever." She ran her palms across his temples. She would have died rather than tell him that a liberal sprinkling of white hairs had begun to appear in the raven black. She frowned at their number, faintly surprised that he had not noticed them and begun to cover them up. Then she smiled blindingly, pressed her body to his, and kissed him with practiced passion.

72

The door opened behind them. Ada Cocks hurried in. "The wig's finally dry, dearie." With no more than a quick glance in their direction, she set the piece on the wigstand and began to fuss with its curls. "This dampness is a horror. Nothing's dry when it should be. And I have to keep pulling things out of the trunks and pressing them to keep them from mildewing."

Reluctantly, the lovers broke apart. Shreve seated himself at the dressing table. His head was pounding, but he refused to acknowledge the pain. Resolutely, he leaned forward to retouch his makeup. He squinted at his distorted reflection, then opened his eyes wide.

Miranda sat so that Ada could put the wig on her head. She promptly took up the complaint. "On stage under the lights, you think you're going to drown in your own perspiration. It doesn't evaporate. And the mosquitoes breed like — like mosquitoes."

"But the audiences are grand." With that pronouncement Shreve overruled them both. "Ada, when you get through with her, could you help me a bit here? The light's so bad in here I can't seem to get it quite right."

In the mirror Miranda threw Ada a troubled glance.

"You're right about the light, Shreve-boy." Ada stretched her mouth into a tight smile. "It's hard for all of us to see. It's a wonder we don't have eyestrain."

"I want a detailed report of this entire affair within twenty-four hours. Every detail of the murder." Frank de la Barca's teeth bit the words off and spat them out.

"That's all in the report," Colonel Armistead protested.

"That!" The investigator slapped down the sheets of paper. His contempt for the official was explicit. "That is every bit of information you were able to extract from this prisoner?"

"He claimed he didn't know anything."

"Obviously, he lied."

Armistead's face turned a dull red. He swelled out his chest. "I know that. What I'm sayin' is that the witnesses all told the same thing. The rest of the report wouldn't be of any value."

"I'll be the judge of that." De la Barca's rage was tangible, heat lightning in the air between them. Yet his dark moon face never changed. He prided himself on never allowing any emotion to show, on never revealing his thoughts to anyone. Yet menace hung in the air around him. His black eyes glittered like shoe buttons from between the folds of brown skin.

With satisfaction he watched Armistead squirm. A good lead—the only lead—was gone. When he reported the fiasco to Butler, this fool would be lucky to get demoted to second lieutenant. "I'll want to question the two privates, too."

"Yes, sir. I've already done that. One was overpowered and tied up. The other was asleep."

"The first was probably asleep, too." The investigator sneered.

"I really can't say, Captain de la Barca."

"Just de la Barca will do. Tell me again what happened."

"It's just like I told you," Colonel Armistead repeated tiredly. He opened the bottom drawer of his desk. "This lieutenant had this courier pouch." He held it out to de la Barca, who looked at it disdainfully. "You can see it's old, and it looks just like the real thing."

"Probably it *was* the real thing once," the investigator sneered. He took the object in his square, blunt-fingered hands. They were unusually small hands for a man whose body was so bulky. He turned it over, then thrust it back to Armistead. "There are probably a half dozen of these lying around in every army post up and down the frontier."

Armistead slapped the pouch down on the desk. "That may very well be, but I opened it with my key. The orders were from Senator Butler himself. I didn't have any reason to doubt them. I knew that Miz Westfall had written to him."

For the first time de la Barca learned the name of Butler's source. He filed the information away for future consideration. "But didn't you think that her letter couldn't possibly have traveled clear across the country by that time? And the senator couldn't possibly have read it and dispatched someone through government channels so fast. Where were your brains, man?"

Armistead ground his teeth until the tendons in his jaw strutted like hausers. "I was told she sent a telegram."

De la Barca did not answer immediately. Armistead wiped his forehead. The man across the desk stood so still he might have been a statue. Then, the investigator cleared his throat. "Who told you that?"

"Adolf Lindhauer."

"Who's he?"

"A trader. He owns a whole string of trading posts up and down the state. Wealthy. Has lots of influence. Just the sort of man a general's lady would know and run to if she needed help." Ar-

75

mistead cleared his throat and shifted in his chair. "Go on."

"He and a lawyer came here wanting to get the prisoner released to them. Of course, I wouldn't let them have him. Civilians don't have any jurisdiction over army prisoners."

Suddenly de la Barca was alert. "Why did they want him?"

Armistead tucked his head. "They said Miz Westfall—er—wasn't satisfied with the way I was handling the investigation. I told them the guy would talk, but Lindhauer thought I was barking up the wrong tree. Said the murderer was probably clear to the Canadian border."

De la Barca scratched at his chin. "Could this Lindhauer have been the man we're looking for?"

Armistead's head shot up, then he shook it definitively. "He was on the platform with the general."

"Someone he knew."

Armistead rubbed his chin. "I doubt it. One of his sons was there beside him. And besides, why would he do something like that? He's been out here a long time. He's friendly with everybody. He wouldn't want to stir up any trouble."

"Why not?"

"Trouble would hurt his business. Years ago he got himself a Cheyenne squaw—sort of married into the tribe—and had a litter of half-breed young'uns. Since then he's been real friendly with the hostiles. He's fair and he has good prices. White folks like him for the same reason."

"Why would a general's widow go to a civilian?" de la Barca wanted to know.

Armistead had turned that idea over in his mind. "I guess he knew the Westfalls from Fort Gallatin," he replied promptly.

76

"A friend?"

Armistead shrugged. "Money always makes a lot of friends. Anyway. As I said before, he and his son were present on the platform right next to Mrs. Westfall when that trooper rode up and shot the general."

"Is that so?" For the first time since the interrogation had begun, de la Barca pulled a small notebook from his breast pocket. "Where can I find this Lindhauer. I want his business and home address."

"Frankly, I am not surprised that you have continued to suffer these headaches, Mr. Catherwood." The doctor's southern drawl lengthened every syllable and flattened every *r*. Slowly he pushed his physician's mirror aside and stepped back from his patient. "You were severely concussed, sir. Your right eye particularly shows a great number of ruptured capillaries in its interior. I am sure I do not have to tell you that you were lucky to get away with your life."

Shreve sat up and swung his legs over the side of the examination table. "I certainly was."

"You were attacked, you say?" The doctor's hand reached out to grasp Shreve's shoulder to steady him.

"That's right. Attacked and robbed." Shreve reached for his shirt. "On this riverboat in Saint Louis. The *Queen of Diamonds*," he added with an ironical smile.

Satisfied that his patient could see to his own dressing, the doctor turned away. "Those riverboats are bad business. They cater to a rough trade. New Orleans has them, too, to our shame."

"Well, I can promise you I'll never go near one again." Shreve buttoned his shirt and stood to stuff

77

it into his trousers.

The doctor sat at his desk. "I am giving you a prescription for the pain. Gradually, it will go away as all the damaged tissue heals. However, I must warn you." Here he pointed at Shreve with his pen. "The frontal bone as well as the orbit and temporal bones have all been badly bruised."

Shreve pressed his fingertips gingerly to the swollen surfaces beneath the scars in his eyebrows. "I didn't know bone bruised."

The doctor nodded. "Oh, yes. A bone bruises just as skin does. The difference is that while bruises on the skin disappear in about two weeks, bone bruises may take months to decrease in size. The structure is much denser, you see. It takes more to hurt it, to cause it to swell, but by that same virtue, it takes longer for the bone to resume its normal shape. Until that time the bone and all the tissue it touches, specifically your brain, will be extremely sensitive."

"How long?"

"I cannot say. Not knowing how thick the frontal bone of your skull was before you were injured, I cannot guess how extensive the swelling is." He slid his pen back into the inkwell and folded the prescription once, matching the edges of the paper precisely.

Shreve slipped into his coat. "What's in this prescription?"

"A very dilute tincture of laudanum, I assure you. I certainly would not want you to become addicted. It is a very useful medicine, but also very dangerous. I must warn you to use it only as needed and no oftener than twice a day." He handed Shreve the paper. "And do not engage in any strenuous physical activity until the headaches are completely gone. Calling upon your body to

78

perform will take energy that could be used in the healing process. Likewise, there is the danger that you might reinjure your head exacerbating the damage."

"I've got to perform," Shreve objected thinking of the rehearsals for *Taming of the Shrew.*

The doctor looked annoyed. "The human brain is protected from injury by a thick helmet of bone as well it should be. Behind it are the nerves which produce our senses—sight, smell, taste, sound. It appears that your sense of sight was the target of this attack.

"This helmet of bone protects the secrets of the brain as well. We cannot feel it, as we can a muscle on the leg. We cannot open it up as we would lance a boil on the skin. We cannot know what is going on inside the skull. Not only your skull, but your brain could be bruised as well.

"Simply put, Mr. Catherwood, your head will take a long time to heal; and, I state this uncategorically, we do not have any medicines to aid it in its recovery. All I can do is give you something to ease your discomfort while your body heals itself."

Hugh Butler puffed on the cigar. When it was lit and the waiter had carried the taper away, he leaned back and smiled at his colleague. "Now, Chester, no need to get in a dither. It's just a piece of bad luck."

"Goddamn it, Hugh," Waldron, the junior senator from Virginia, ran a hand over his thinning hair. "You said this was a sure thing. I've got tens of thousands of dollars already collected. I've had a string of Saint Louis investors practically begging me to take their money. You assured me it would just be a matter of a few months before the army would drive the hostiles out of the Powder River country."

"The delay will be minimal," Butler assured him.

"Who will you appoint now that Westfall's dead?"

Butler frowned. "I have several likely candidates."

"Several likely candidates." Waldron snorted. "Hugh, this is Chester. Who are we going to get to be the next director of Indian Affairs for the Mountain District?"

"I'm not prepared to name a candidate at this time," Butler admitted. "But very soon."

Waldron threw down his napkin and pushed back his chair. Face hard, jaw tight, he rose. "I've got some of my own money invested in this, Hugh. Money I can ill afford to lose. This thing had better get going soon, or we are both going to be up the proverbial creek without a paddle."

Blue Sun on Snow Lindhauer stared coldly at Frank de la Barca. "Mrs. Westfall is not seeing anyone."

"I think she'll see me," he replied, matching her impassive demeanor. "Just tell her Senator Butler sent me."

Her expression did not lighten. "I'll tell her."

She closed the door, leaving him to think about her. The dress she wore was silk and quite stylish. It would have been appropriate for a congressman's wife to wear to a tea in Washington. It was certainly a cut above the dresses he had observed on most white women on the streets of Cheyenne. Pearl earrings set in gold decorated her ears. A matching pearl bar pin secured her collar. He had no doubt that he had found the squaw of Adolf Lindhauer. But this woman was clearly a treasured wife—and no squaw.

His interest quickened. His heart stepped up its beat as his hunting instincts heightened. The trail grew warmer. With a wife like that, Lindhauer was more than just a trader of Indian goods. He was one who would have a vested interest in this territory. He would want to be among the men who controlled it.

The door opened. The black eyes dared him. "Mrs. Westfall will see you. You come this way."

The furnishings confirmed his estimate. A fine home with many expensive articles of gracious living. Senator Butler suspected a plot. Logically, Lindhauer could be a part of it.

"Mr. de la Barca." Three women came into the room. A slight older woman, whose blond hair was going to gray, held out her hand. "I'm Ruth Westfall. Did Hugh Butler send you?"

He took the soft small hand and inclined his head over it. As he did so, he searched her face. Her blue eyes had dark circles beneath them; her cheeks were hollow and quite pale. She had an air of sadness about her that he could not doubt. Ruth Westfall must really have sent a letter to Senator Butler. "Mrs. Westfall."

"May I introduce my hostess and dear friend, Blue Sun on Snow Lindhauer?"

"Mrs. Lindhauer." The Indian wife stared at him, her eyes as piercing as his own. He matched her look, recognizing in her the same wary estimating—the look of a hunter.

"And this is my daughter, Rachel."

A young girl of perhaps seventeen took his hand. Her eyes, as blue as her mother's, searched his face. They were speaking eyes. She pressed his hand with special fervency. His black eyes narrowed fractionally. This one wanted to tell him something.

81

"I'm very glad you've come, Mr. de la Barca. My father shouldn't have died."

"No, he should not have," he agreed. Actually, Westfall as a person and the fact of his death interested the investigator not at all. He hunted for the motive and the murderer. When he found them, Butler would pay him.

Rachel Westfall's skin flushed red, then white. Her eyes were very bright. Her voice was high and strained. "I hope you find the murderer very quickly. I hope you bring him to justice."

He made a mental note to find a way to speak to the girl in private. She had something to say that she could not say in front of her mother—or perhaps in front of the Indian woman. "I promise you I shall be very thorough in my investigation."

Ruth Westfall put her arm around her daughter's shoulders and led her to a sofa. "Please sit down, Mr. de la Barca. Rachel is terribly upset by my husband's death, as we all are."

He chose a straight chair where he could observe them all. "So is Senator Butler."

"Did you bring a message from him, a reply to my telegram?" Ruth asked anxiously.

The confirmation of the telegram still eliminated the possibility that the escape from jail had been engineered from Washington. Given the train schedules across country, no lieutenant in disguise with forged orders could have traveled faster than the investigator himself. Although the senator had not mentioned the telegram, de la Barca covered easily. "I guess I'm the reply."

"Oh, but—"

"That's wonderful," the daughter interrupted. "He sent you to find the murderer, didn't he?"

"That's what he did, miss. Senator Butler's very

anxious to find the murderer. Yes. He's afraid that the Indian problem will flare up again."

Ruth looked alarmed. "But my husband wasn't shot by Indians."

"You're sure about that?"

She nodded. "My husband was not shot by Indians."

His eyes never left her face. "You seem mighty sure. Had you ever seen his assailant before?"

She hesitated. "No."

De la Barca's muscles vibrated. She had lied. Not only did she not lie well, but he had studied the initial report of the assassination. As the riders had approached, Ruth Westfall had risen from her seat and called out the name "Francis."

"Can you recall what he looked like?"

Again the hesitation. "Not really."

"Then he might have been an Indian."

"The Indians had nothing to do with his death," she insisted desperately. "I'm sure you are mistaken."

"My dear lady, Senator Butler sent your husband out here specifically to handle the Indian problem."

Ruth wrung her hands. "There is no Indian problem. He was shot by a man in uniform."

"It might have been a soldier, but more'n likely it was someone dressed up like one, paid to do the job. Unfortunately, murderers are easy to hire. Lots of men out here would kill their own mothers if someone paid them a few dollars. They don't want the territory settled, either. Your husband's job was to settle it."

"I would know if it were an Indian," Ruth insisted.

De la Barca's eyes shifted to Blue Sun on Snow. "Probably a trader with a foot in both camps could make a lot of money especially if he could go freely back and forth where no one else knew what was going on in both places. He might pay a lot to keep this trouble goin'."

Ruth's face went white at the insult to her friend. She put her hand to her mouth. "Oh, no, Mr. de la Barca. You're quite wrong."

The Cheyenne woman's expression did not change. Only her eyes showed her hatred. She rose unhurriedly. "Excuse me."

Ruth began to stammer. Her hand went out to Blue Sun on Snow. "Oh, no. Absolutely not. Mr. de la Barca, you have gravely insulted my friend. I must ask you to apologize."

The investigator rose. "I do apologize for distressin' you, dear ladies. Unfortunately, my experience has proved that ladies are generally the last to know about their husband's plans."

Blue Sun on Snow left the room at a measured pace. Ruth Westfall rose stiffly. Her voice quivered with anger. "Leave at once, Mr. de la Barca! I have only one thing more to say to you. Your accusations will be reported to Senator Butler. I'm quite sure he did not order you to come here to insult decent women and their husbands."

He nodded coldly, his expression unchanged. "Report if you will, Mrs. Westfall. But be really sure of the facts you report. I didn't insult decent women and their husbands. I came out here askin' questions of people who saw a murder take place. They might be involved some way. In a murder everyone's a suspect."

She swayed where she stood, then rallied and held the door open wide. "Just go, Mr. de la Barca. And don't come back."

He took his time climbing into the rented buggy. Then he allowed the horse to amble slowly down the lane away from the great house. In a couple of miles the road dipped into the bed of a dry wash.

Her face triumphant, Rachel Westfall sat a horse at the bottom of the wash.

He halted the buggy and stared at her. The sun beaming on the vehicle's black top made the interior uncomfortably hot. Sweat trickled down his face.

"I wanted to speak to you," she began.

"I was pretty sure you did." He nodded. "You probably gave yourself away signalin'."

The look of triumph faded. "Do you think my mother noticed?"

"Most likely not. But Mrs. Lindhauer did."

"Oh." She looked around her nervously. "I didn't think—"

"Besides, you've taken a horse from their stables. Lots of people've noticed by now."

"I've only gone for a ride," she replied sulkily.

He did not point out that it was the middle of the day and much too hot to be riding for pleasure. The girl was clearly having second thoughts about meeting him. He made a conscious effort and smiled. "What did you want to tell me?"

She tightened the reins. Her mount shook its head up and down and stirred restively. "No one must know that I told you what I'm about to tell you."

Without comment he extracted a handkerchief from his pocket and mopped at his forehead. They all said that. "If you know who murdered your father, you're doin' the right thing in steppin' forward."

She looked past the buggy toward the house. She opened her mouth, closed it, then opened it again. "He wasn't murdered. At least not exactly."

85

De la Barca remembered the report. Westfall had indeed drawn his sidearm, an antique navy piece. He had not been able to squeeze the shot off, however, before the assassin, with admirable coolness, had shot him down. So much for Westfall's army training. Damn, it was hot. Why wouldn't the little idiot just spit the story out? "Maybe he was provoked."

"Oh, he was. Provoked and terrified."

"Terrified," de la Barca said softly.

"He thought the man riding toward him was a ghost."

Despite himself, de la Barca's iron control broke. He had driven along at a snail's pace in this suffocating heat, waiting for this girl to catch him. Now he found she was an idiot. He cursed vividly as the sweat trickled from beneath his hatband and stung his eyes.

The girl glanced at him uncertainly. "He did," she insisted. "He thought he saw the ghost of a man he had killed."

The investigator stuffed his handkerchief back into his pocket. "You mean he saw a—um—ghost. In broad daylight in front of dozens of people. Well, how about that?" He lifted the reins and made a clicking sound with his tongue. "Well, that certainly would terrify anyone."

The horse pulled the buggy slowly across the wash and started up the other side.

"You don't believe me?" She stared at him as he drove past her.

"Of course, I believe that you think he saw a ghost," he called. "I just don't believe that a ghost shot him."

A wheel caught on a rock. The horse threw its shoulder into the collar. She reined her horse alongside. "No, wait. You don't understand. He thought he saw a ghost! Don't you see? It was a plot to make him confess. It terrified him just like you said. He thought he saw a ghost, but it was my sister!"

The wheel bumped over the rock with a clatter. The buggy rolled swiftly up the side of the wash.

"It was my sister!" she called after him.

He whipped the horse up into a trot. "She's probably a ghost, too."

Five

The lady doth protest too much.

"Where have you been?"

Rachel dropped the bridle and spun around. Startled, her horse jerked away, its hindquarters thudding against the side of the stall. It whinnied and danced; its commotion caused the others to stir and stamp.

"Where have you been?"

"Oh, you scared me!" Face flaming, Rachel bent to pick up the piece of equipment. The reins were caught under the horse's hoof, so she had to disturb it again. Face hot, she threw the figure looming in the doorway a sidelong glance. Dreading what was to come, she straightened.

"I asked you where you'd been." Victor Wolf stepped over the sill, a dark silhouette against the brightness. His body fairly bristled with tension. His hands were clenched at his sides.

Refusing to look at him again, Rachel hurried to hang the bridle on its peg. Exercising elaborate concentration, she began unsaddling her horse. "I went for a ride."

"At high noon? In this heat? Think of a better story than that," he scoffed.

She flushed even darker at the contempt in his

tone. De la Barca had warned her she would not be believed. She picked up the comb and turned her attention to currying her horse's back. "I'd been inside all day. We're leaving soon. I won't get a chance to ride when I get back to Chicago. We sold off—"

His deerskin boots made no sound on the packed earth of the stable. Startled, she squealed and pulled away from the hard hand that closed around her upper arm. "Stop babbling! Tell me where you've been!"

"Let go! I've been riding."

"Don't lie. You went out to talk to that investigator."

"No." She clawed at his hand.

He swung her around to face him, catching her other arm. His blue eyes blazed out of his Indian features. "Surely to God, you didn't tell him about your sister?"

"Damn you!" She twisted against his hands and kicked at his legs. The horse whinnied and backed away into a corner of the stall.

He held her firmly, yet painlessly, as if she were a child pitching a temper fit. "Rachel, surely you didn't tell him that your sister killed your stepfather?"

"No."

His blue eyes, so startling in his brown face, stared into her soul. Then his face crumpled in anguish

She bit her lip. "Yes." Defiantly, she flung back her head. "Yes. Yes. I did."

"Rachel—" His hands dropped away. His color drained away leaving him white to the lips.

"Yes. I told him." She fell back a couple of steps, rubbing her arms where he had bruised her. She glanced up at his horrified face, then quickly

89

dropped her eyes. Sullenly, she flounced past him out of the stall. The man she loved was angry with her and it was all her sister's fault. "Victor, please don't be mad at me."

"Rachel, how could you do that?" He shook his head sadly. "When you saw—you heard—"

"Victor, he was frightened. He was a frightened old man. He was my father."

"Francis Drummond was your father."

"No."

"My mother was with you. She heard the same things you did. We all heard him. He thought he was seeing Francis Drummond. The reason he went for his gun was because he wanted to kill him again. He said so."

The girl in front of him hung her head.

Victor spread his hands. "Even if you don't want to believe what he did, how could you set the law on your sister?"

"Well, she had no right to do what she did."

"Even though she punished a man who'd caused the deaths of a troop of soldiers and gotten away scotfree?"

"It was a long time ago. My father—"

"Your stepfather."

"THAT DOESN'T MAKE ANY DIFFERENCE!" She screamed the words at him. The horse snorted and stamped.

Victor pulled her out of stable and shut the door. "Your father is blood of your blood. Your stepfather—"

She caught at his arm, pleading now for understanding. "He raised me. He was the only father I'd ever known."

"She's your only sister."

"Yes." She crossed her arms in front of her chest and lifted her chin. "Yes. She got her revenge.

Now I'll get mine. She's not the only one entitled to get revenge."

His expression turned incredulous. Then the blue hawk's gaze narrowed shrewdly. "Did you do this because you wanted to get your sister or to imitate her?"

Her mouth snapped to. When she opened it, rage spewed out. "Don't you dare say that I want to be like her! Don't you dare!"

"She's determined, she's clever, she's beautiful. She's a talented actress with a great career. Why shouldn't you want to be like her? Now you're trying to get revenge the way she did." His expression became sad. "I'll ask you the same thing I asked her. What will you gain from revenge?"

She swallowed. "Justice."

"You want to see her hanged?"

Rachel hesitated, her brow wrinkling as the thought took hold. "That's for the law to decide."

"How will your mother feel when her daughter's arrested?"

"She'll be upset, but she's already upset."

"She'll be more so when the family name is dragged through the mud, the family secrets exposed."

"Miranda deserves to be arrested," Rachel insisted. "It's only right that she should be."

"Your stepfather wasn't."

She looked away.

"Rachel." Voice low and intense, he strove to make her see the enormity of what she had done. "Your mother may very well be arrested, too. And my father and mother. I may be, too."

She stared back at him in disbelief. "Don't be ridiculous."

"I'm not being ridiculous. We were all party to the plot. We all heard what she was going to do.

91

We were all in the room when she planned it."

"But surely—"

"For God's sake! Think what we did. Adolf Lindhauer, my father, furnished the horses and the gear. Your mother Ruth Drummond called out your father's name in a loud, clear voice. Blue Sun on Snow and her son Victor Wolf heard the entire plot being hatched. We are *all* accomplices."

"You'll be safe," she offered. "Miranda would never implicate you."

He loomed over her. "Did you hear what you just said?"

She backed away another step. Her hands were shaking as she raised them in front of her—a futile barrier to his words.

He caught them and brought them together against his chest. "Not only that"—his words fell like darts of poison into her conscience—"you Rachel Drummond watched it all happen. And you did nothing."

She drew a deep shuddering breath. "I couldn't."

"You didn't," he contradicted. "You knew what was going to happen, but you didn't do anything."

"I—"

He hammered away inexorably. "You could have leaped out of the carriage and jumped up on the platform. You could have told your stepfather what was happening. You could have yelled at your sister. You could have—"

"Your mother—"

"My mother is fifty years old. She couldn't have stopped anything you wanted to do."

"I'm doing something now," she insisted sullenly.

"You don't know what you're doing. And you expect your sister not to implicate you as well."

"I want to see justice done."

"You're just a child."

The accusation stabbed her to the quick. "I'm a woman."

"You're a child, playing at imitating your sister." He caught her face in his hand. "Where are your tears, if you're so stricken with grief over the man you called Father? Your mother's been crying her eyes out."

"Guilt."

"Yes, and grief, and loss." His hand tightened on the beautiful face. He shook her gently. "Be honest with yourself. What really made you ride out to tell that man?"

Her eyes flashed angrily. His own were just as piercing. For an instant they traded stares, then hers dropped. She swallowed. "Let go. You're hurting me."

He dropped his hand.

She stepped out of his reach, working her jaw from side to side. "He didn't believe me anyway."

Victor relaxed somewhat. "What happened?"

"I started to tell him about the ghost thing— about how Father thought he was seeing a ghost, but the ghost was really my sister." She shrugged. "The detective just whipped up the horse and drove away."

Victor ran his hand around the back of his neck. His smile was rueful. "I hope for your sake and for everybody else's that he forgets about what you said."

Suddenly, Rachel flung herself against his chest. Her arms went around him. "Oh, Victor, don't let's fight. I love you. I really do. I want you to love me."

"Rachel." He tried to push himself gently out of her arms. The stable which had been warm became uncomfortably hot.

"I told you I fell in love at first sight. It's the way we do."

"Rachel!" He dragged her arms away from his body and stepped out.

"Victor." She reached for him again.

He held up his hand. "Stop right there."

Suddenly, she needed his understanding, needed to know that he still cared for her. She caught at his hands. "Nothing happened with the lawman. You didn't like the idea of what I did, but nothing happened, so you don't have anything to forgive me for."

"I'm not the one to forgive you," he said seriously. "Miranda and her mother would be the ones to forgive you. You may even have to forgive yourself someday."

She clasped him tighter, trying to wring acceptance from him. "I'll never forgive myself if this has made you stop loving me."

His mouth twisted in exasperation. "Rachel, I've already said this once today. But I'll say it again. You're a child. This stunt has convinced me, if I ever had any doubts. You need to go back to Chicago and finish your education and grow up. You'll meet a young man—"

"I've met him."

"I'm not young."

"You're younger than my sister. You're only a few years older than I am."

"Eleven," he reminded her dryly. "And I'm a lot older than that in terms of experience. Besides, I'm not the man for you."

"Because your mother was a Cheyenne."

"That's right. And because you don't know your own mind." He extricated his hands and crossed his arms over his chest. Staring down at her sternly, he might have been an Indian except for his blue eyes and blond hair.

She lifted her chin. "I do know my own mind. I-I just didn't plan carefully enough."

"Rachel," he chided. "Don't make any more excuses. What's done is done. Forget it and go back to school. In a year this will seem a dream. You won't even remember my name. You'll have changed."

She reached for his hand, but he kept them locked around his arms. "No, Victor—"

"White Wolf's Brother. Don't forget I've an Indian name."

"—I swear to you, that I will never, never change." Her eyes appeared luminous with tears.

For a moment he could do nothing but stare into their blue depths. His mouth twisted. Then abruptly he dropped his arms and backed away to the door of the stable. Voice hoarse, he whispered. "You will."

"Never." She flung herself after him and threw her arms around his neck. Before he could protest, she clamped her lips to his. His mouth opened and she drove her tongue in to caress his own. The kiss went on and on. At first, he pushed at her. Then as her innocent passion heated, he let his arms drop to his sides.

She was so soft, so eager, trembling, her blood racing hot beneath her smooth skin. He had never felt so much a man, nor so much a prisoner of his own body. Unable to remain calm with her body pressed against his, he put his arms around her waist.

"Tighter," she breathed into his mouth.

His heart stepped up its rhythm. She twisted and squirmed in his arms, her hands locked tight around the back of his neck. Her breasts were hard cones rubbing torturously against his chest. He had known only a few women carnally and never one of his own class. Never in his very limited experience had a girl touched him with her entire body. Never had anyone kissed him eagerly, pleading for his response.

His good intentions vanished in a tide of hot blood, pounding through his veins. "Rachel," he moaned into her mouth. One hand rose to shape the back of her head and tilt her face across his. The other hand cupped her buttock, lifting and pressing her to him to feel his maleness. "Rachel, stop."

She was already strung tight as a bowstring when the alien shape pressed through the layers of clothing. Liquid fire laved her between her legs. Swollen lips pouted and parted. Suddenly, the softest cotton became abrasive rubbing the throbbing center of her being.

She exploded. Frightened at the riptide she cried out, arched back away from him, pressing her lower body harder against him. Harder. Her eyes wide, transcending the dim stable, the heated July day, the man who held her in his arms. Her heart pounded. Her breath stopped. She could not suck enough air into her lungs. Lightning streaked across her vision, then all was black as she crumpled in his arms.

Aching and burning, he felt her lips leave his as her head fell back. She had become a woman in his arms. Through her own impetuous nature and no act of his, she had reached a climax. He could feel the tremors through his own clothes. With eyes of fire he took in the line of her arched throat, her mouth open, her lips pulled back.

Shivering in his arms, she was the essence of woman. He had created her but he dared not enjoy her. Cursing flatly, his body aching, he lowered her

96

to the bales of hay stored at the end of the shed row and stalked back to the door.

Her eyes fluttered open. At first she stared uncomprehending, the faintest hint of a smile on her face. Then she found him. A blush rose in her cheeks. Her smile became apologetic. She reached out her hand.

Ignoring it, his expression stony, he pushed open the stable door. Bright, blinding heat poured in. "Whenever you're ready, we'll go back to the house."

"Ay, to the proof, as mountains are for winds, That shake not, though they blow perpetually," Petruchio declaimed over the crashing and splintering of wood off stage.

The actor playing Hortensio stumbled back on stage and into Shreve's arms. Around his neck swung the remains of a lute, supposedly broken over his head by Katherina, the shrew.

Ordinarily, Shreve would have stood like the mountains as Shakespeare's lines directed the actor to bounce off him in a comic turn. Unfortunately, his distorted vision made him unsteady. When the other man careened into him, Shreve staggered back. The two almost fell together.

The audience roared with laughter while Hortensio caught his balance. "What the hell's wrong with you?" he muttered out of the up stage side of his mouth. "Are you drunk?"

Shreve propped himself on the doorjamb of Signor Baptista's house in Padua and shook his head trying to clear his vision.

Rising to the occasion, the actor playing Baptista caught the lute around Hortensio's neck and turned him around. *"How now, my friend? Why dost thou look so pale?"*

Hortensio described Katherina's behavior, while Shreve regained himself. Tonight was the worst night in a long time. His vision faded in and out. His head pounded. The laughter of the audience dinned in his ears. He pushed himself off, setting the scenery to rocking.

Baptista looked at him with realistic lack of confidence. *"Shall I send my daughter Kate to you?"*

Shreve cleared his throat. *"I pray you do—"*

Left alone, he walked carefully down stage to tell the audience how he planned to tame the shrew. At the end of his soliloquy, Katherina stormed in, brandishing the neck of a lute like a club. *"Good morrow, Kate; for that's your name, I hear."*

They traded insult for insult as the audience roared. Miranda delivered her lines for every woman in the audience. He spoke to the men in the audience drawing their laughter at Kate's expense until finally she could stand his bawdy jabs no longer. *"I am a gentleman,"* he insisted.

"That I'll try." Miranda drew back the neck of the lute, wound up broadly, and swung it at him.

Instead of his ducking beneath it, it caught him on the side of the head.

With audience, cast, and crew looking on in astonishment, Shreve Catherwood crashed to the floor and lay unmoving.

He awoke in the dark, disoriented, at first aware of nothing but throbbing pain. Then a faint buzzing penetrated his brain. It grew.

"Shreve!" Miranda's voice came from far away. "Shreve!"

"What the hell happened?"

"Is he drunk?"

"For heaven's sake, no. He's a professional."

"How hard did you hit him?"

"Not that hard. He must be sick. Shreve."

The conversation sounded as if they were speaking from deep in a barrel.

"Shreve." She was by his side. She shook him.

If she didn't stop shaking him, he was going to throw up. He waved his hand weakly in front of his face. But the room was too dark to see.

"What shall I tell the audience?"

Miranda's voice sounded desperate. "One of you step out and ask if there's a doctor in the house."

He must have been unconscious only a few seconds, but he had lost track of time. Yes, he was still in the theater. His head was lifted. A pillow slipped underneath it. They must have brought the house lights down somehow. He couldn't see a damned thing.

"Shreve!"

"Why'd you hit him so hard?" That was Baptista.

"He was supposed to step back."

"That's a hell of a lump."

"I've never hit him before. He's never missed his move." She sounded as if she were crying. He wanted to reassure her. He tried to move his lips.

"Now, dearie. Accidents will happen." Ada had been summoned.

"He's drunk!" This from Hortensio. "He almost dropped me through the scenery."

"He's not drunk." Miranda was cradling his head protectively. "He never drinks before or during a performance."

The theater manager leaned over him. "The audience is in an uproar! What shall I tell them?"

Ada hunched down beside him, her knees cracking painfully. "Here! Wipe his poor face. He's white as a sheet."

Shreve was sure his eyes were open, but he could

99

see nothing. "Turn up the lights," he murmured.

"Shreve!" Miranda wiped the cool cloth over his forehead and down his cheek. Petruchio's dark Italian makeup streaked. "Shreve, dearest!"

"Miranda."

"I didn't mean to hit you. I didn't. I'm so sorry."

He could hear the tears in her voice. He reached up and caught her wrist. "I know. Just help me up and turn up the lights. I can go on."

"The lights?"

"Turn the lights up," he repeated, his voice stronger. "It's dark as a damned tomb. We're not playing *Romeo and Juliet.*" He sat up gingerly, bowing over, his pounding head clasped in his hands.

She put her arm around his shoulders. "Dearest. The lights are up. Nobody's turned them down."

His breath caught in his throat. Carefully, he closed his eyes then opened them again. Once open, he began to detect a grayness. Fear lanced through him.

In his ear Miranda whispered, "What's wrong? Please, Shreve. Tell me what's wrong?"

"Nothing." He drew in a deep breath. "I'll be all right in a few minutes."

"What am I to do?" The theater manager wrung his hands. "They're getting angry."

"Dress the understudy," Miranda snapped.

"No!" Shreve raised his head and spoke in the direction the manager's voice had come from. "No! I'm all right. My leading lady was a bit too enthusiastic in her performance."

"Shreve!"

He turned toward her. Focusing all his powers, he conjured up her face. He could see her mouth saying his name, her straight nose, her beautiful eyes that he knew sparkled with the tears he heard in her voice. Taking another deep breath and managing a smile, he looked on where they had to be. "I'm all right, sweetheart."

She sobbed and threw her arms around his neck. "I'm sorry. I'm so sorry. I didn't mean to hurt you. I don't know what happened."

Her face pressed against his neck; hot tears wet the ruffled collar of his costume. "Easy, sweetheart. You'll ruin your makeup as well as mine."

"Oh, forget the makeup." She kissed his cheek and the line of his jaw.

"What are we going to do?" The theater manager was almost sobbing.

Shreve reached out a hand. Someone—he could not see who—grasped it. "Help me up. Announce to the audience that I'm able to go on. After all, that's the tradition. The show must go on."

"No!" Miranda hugged him tighter. "You can't."

With her hanging around his neck, they pulled him to his feet. "If you're sure—" The theater manager's voice reflected his doubt.

"You don't look so good," the actor playing Baptista remarked.

"My makeup's been washed off." Shreve kept his arm over Miranda's shoulders. "Ada!"

"Right here, Shrevey-boy." He could tell by her voice that she was somewhere to his right. He pivoted.

"Do I have a bad bruise?"

"More like a knot."

He could see her hand, a shadow flitting in front of his face, touching the throbbing pain, making him wince. "No sense worrying about that. The audience saw me take the blow."

"Shreve. You can't go on. You're hurt."

Someone shoved a chair against the back of his legs. He sat down thankfully. Ada—it must have been she—draped a towel across his chest. He could see the white. Shapes were beginning to form in front of him. He could see. He laughed shakily. "Think of the publicity, Miranda."

"Publicity." The theater manager's voice was brighter.

"Yes. Publicity. Go tell them that despite his injuries, Mr. Catherwood has elected to go on rather than disappoint his audience. Say he begs their indulgence."

The stage manager rubbed his hands together. "It'll be great theater. They'll tell their friends. Everyone will want to come and see you."

"Exactly." Shreve tilted his head back and closed his eyes.

Miranda struck him on the shoulder. "I could kill you," she snarled. "I don't believe you were really hurt at all. You just pulled this stunt because you made a mistake and didn't duck when you should have."

"Oh, Shrevey-boy." Ada used the wet cloth to remove the rest of the makeup and start over. Her touch was like a benison on his bruised, fevered skin. "Now you've done it."

He shrugged as Miranda stamped away. "I'm an actor. I turn things to my advantage." He shrugged as Miranda stamped away and opened his eyes, squinting upward into the lights. His dear old friend was a pale mask, her features barely discernible.

"Ah, Shrevey-boy," Ada murmured as she smoothed fresh greasepaint onto his cheeks and forehead. "What's going on?"

He kept his eyes closed, fearful of what his oldest friend would see if he opened them. "I zigged when I should have zagged. That's all."

"What can you see when you open your eyes for

102

me, Shrevey?" Her voice was gentle as his mother's.

He tried to bring her into sharper focus and failed miserably. Her face remained a dim blur in front of him. He spoke to the dark holes of his eyes. "I'll be fine, Ada."

She shook her head as she applied the dark greasepaint. "You're not fine, boyo. Can you see at all?"

He listened. They seemed to be alone in the center of the stage. "I can see," he whispered grimly.

"Enough to go on?"

"I'll take it easy. After what's happened, the audience won't expect a physical performance."

She rubbed darker color into his cheeks, creating the hollow-cheeked look that Petruchio, the penniless suitor after Kate's rich dowry, would have had. "Something's wrong with you. You haven't been right since Wyoming."

"I'm getting better. It's just a matter of time."

With infinite care she drew in the dark brows. "Your eyes are nothing to fool with, Shrevey."

Even her gentle touch made him wince. The bone-deep swelling did not seem to have decreased at all. It hurt as much as ever. More now that he had blundered and Miranda had struck him. He cursed.

"I'm sorry," Ada murmured.

"I'm not cursing you," he hastened to say. "I just thought of my own clumsiness."

"But you didn't tell her it was your own fault, did you?"

"No."

She whisked the towel off his neck. "I'll go find her and fix up the tears she's shed over you."

He fumbled at her arm.

She stared at his pawing hand, then grasped it and squeezed it with her own. Then she put it back

103

on his knee. "Ah, *ma bouchal,* that terrible pride. Bad as an Irishman for pride. Tell her yourself. In fact, you'd better sit down with her tonight and tell her the whole story."

He heaved a deep sigh. "She doesn't need to know. She'd feel like she was to blame. She'd cry and take on. No. It would only worry her."

"You want her to be your wife. She's woman enough to face the consequences of her actions. We all make wrong choices, Shrevey-boy. Women and men. And we live with them for the rest of our lives. You're not a little boy. Stop treating her as if she's a little girl." Then she stooped. He felt her lips brush his forehead.

Shreve sat alone in the middle of the stage. On the other side of the curtain the audience stirred restlessly. His fellow actors eyed him curiously. He put his hand to his forehead and struggled to remember not his lines, but his blocking. Under no circumstances could he be in the wrong place at the wrong time.

Six

Double, double, Toil and trouble.

Frank de la Barca walked down the gangplank at the foot of Canal Street. The wet heat of New Orleans in late July struck him like a steam bath. The numberless odors on the quay were dominated by the stench of rotting fish. A mosquito sang next to his ear. He paused to light a cigar and blow a cloud of blue smoke at the annoying creature.

His black eyes took in the activity around him, noting each person as he went about his business — riverboatmen, passengers, dockhands, bosses, idlers, and pimps. Toward one of these, he made his way.

The fellow tensed in alarm. De la Barca moved with fearsome purpose. Though his brown moon face revealed nothing, the carriage of his broad shoulders and the slight forward tilt of his heavy body ably conveyed his message.

His prey eeled away along the side of the warehouse, but de la Barca cut him off. "Hold it right there!"

"What you say? I don' do nothin'."

De la Barca pulled a coin from his pocket. A silver dollar glinted in his small brown hand. He held it up before the pimp's eyes.

The fellow instantly dropped into a relaxed pose,

yet his eyes remained wary. "What you want?"

"I want a hotel." De la Barca's piercing stare was heavy with meaning.

The pimp misread it. "You don' need no special hotel. I be willin' t' bring what you want where you stay."

De la Barca shook his head irritably. "No. Listen. I don't want your pitiful girls. I want a place where I can conduct any kind of business I want to and nobody will ask any questions."

The pimp propped his bony shoulders against the stained bricks of the warehouse. His dark eyes took on a knowing look. His heavy mouth curled insolently. "What kind of business you lookin' to do?"

"The kind that might hire someone for special jobs."

"Ah-hummm." White teeth flashed in a grin. "Pay maybe pretty good?"

De la Barca dipped the hand containing the dollar into his pocket and came up with two. They made a clinking sound as he rubbed them together. "A smart man could make it worth his trouble."

"I'm the smartest you ever did see."

"I thought so." De la Barca held out his hand. A dollar rolled from his fingers.

Swift as a snake, the other man dropped to catch it. Knees bent, back braced against the wall, he squinted upward. "Maybe more where that come from."

De la Barca flipped and caught the second dollar. "If someone carries my bags."

"You got 'im." With a lithe movement, he straightened. His feet never moved. He merely pushed up against the wall. Eye to eye, he matched de la Barca's height, but the bony body in flapping clothing looked small beside the compact one squeezed into the buttoned suit.

106

De la Barca led the way back to the gangplank. "Those three."

"You plannin' on doin' some huntin'?" The man groaned as he hoisted the long wooden box to one shoulder, shifted the square leather-bound case under his arm, and took the small grip in his hand.

"You don't need to know, boy."

The man deliberately let the box slide to the wharf. He straightened insolently. "I answer to Poteet."

De la Barca eyed him coldly. "Smith."

"Lots of yore brothers maybe roundabout here. Hardly a night go by without Brother Smith wantin' what I sell. Not so many hunters though." He stubbed his toe at the corner of the box.

De la Barca looked around him. Among the flotsam on the quay, he could not see a better choice. With a nod he capitulated. "Another dollar when we get to the hotel, Poteet."

Although the long box looked as if it outweighed him, the bony man hoisted it again. "We needs to get us a gig, I'm thinkin'."

"Don't press your luck, Poteet."

"You want to walk, we walk." The man shrugged.

"How far away is this place?"

"Too far." With an insolent grin he eyed de la Barca's black derby hat, his dark suit, his starched collar melting from his sweat. A couple of planters walked by, their cream cotton suits and broad-brimmed Panama hats a cool contrast to the Northerner's garb. "You walk after me, maybe you fall over dead with the heat."

At that moment a mosquito lighted on the puffy skin beneath de la Barca's right eye. Poteet grinned as he saw it. His grin faded as the newcomer to New Orleans did not bat it away. Instead, he deliberately extracted a handkerchief from his pocket as the insect positioned itself and sank its proboscis into his dark flesh.

Unhurriedly, de la Barca refolded the square of cotton into a pad. He took off the black bowler hat and wiped the sweatband, then wiped the perspiration from his forehead and his temples. At last he swept the handkerchief under his eye squashing the logy body and leaving a bloody streak down across his cheekbone. He turned the mess inward and put the handkerchief back in his pocket. "We will walk," he said deliberately. "Lead the way. I need to see the city."

Poteet's grin widened. "You big fool," he mocked. "You let that skeeter bite you, you get yellowjack."

"That's my lookout. Get on. We're wastin' time."

"What happened to you last night? Something's badly wrong and you're not telling me."

Clad in French blue silk-satin, Miranda paced around the bed. The sash of her robe had been loosely tied to begin with. Now the knot had slipped so the garment gaped open revealing her long bare legs beneath the edge of a French blue satin chemise. The heels of her satin mules tapped whenever her path took her off the carpet.

Shreve lay spread-eagled on his back, the swath of mosquito netting pulled back on one side and looped over the head of the four-poster. His body was bare except for a pair of thin cotton underdrawers. The black hair on his chest and thighs had curled into damp fishhooks. His skin glimmered through a coating of perspiration.

He leaned up and reached for the glass of water sitting beside the bed. After a sip, he dropped back down again and adjusted the wet compress to cover the upper half of his face.

108

Miranda stopped to watch him, then walked to the window. Angrily, she twitched the jalousies open wider. Then she swung around and tapped back onto the carpet.

Shreve let his hand fall limply back onto the bed. "Sweetheart, do stop pacing. You're working up a sweat and creating more hot air in this oven they call a room."

She put her hands flat on the bed and bent over him. Her breasts swung forward; their nipples made hard nubs in the smooth satin. "Shreve Catherwood." She spaced her words, each one pronounced with extreme care, each pitched for maximum projection. "I want you to tell me what was wrong with you."

This time his hand trembled as he raised the corner of the compress. His moan of pain would have wrung tears from a stone. "My head. Have mercy."

She caught him by the wrist. "Cut the scene and tell me the truth! You're trembling hard enough for the upper balcony to see you."

Instead, his gaze dropped and he leered at the effect of her nipples through the satin.

She followed his stare. Her eyes narrowed then dared him with her own to say something.

With a heartrending sigh he turned his face away. The compress slid off onto the pillow, presenting his profile, eyes closed, cheeks sucked in for a hollow appearance. "Ah! That I should hear such words from one to whom I have carefully taught the secrets of my craft."

"Shreve Catherwood!" She slapped the bed in frustration and pushed away to resume her pacing. "You are not being honest with me. I've lived with you for half my life. I've seen you sick as a horse, drunk as a hog, so exhausted —"

"Oh! My head!" He fumbled for the compress and draped it back across his forehead. "Those

109

similes. Those hyperboles. Terrible. Terrible. And where is the iambic pentameter? Spare me. No more. I pray you. *Speak no more than is set down for you.*"

"Stupid as a jackass." She smiled sweetly.

He groaned again, this time with great volume.

She came and perched upon the bed beside him, her arms on either side of his shoulders. "Shreve," she murmured softly. "Please tell me."

He opened one dark eye. The rest of his face remained perfectly still.

She could not help but note his lack of color, the paleness of his lips, the whiteness of his cheeks. The dark shadow of his beard and the dark smudges under his eyes stood out sharply in his face. "The heat—"

"No."

"Something I ate."

"No."

"The water."

"No."

"I give up."

"Is it your head?" Her fingers slid up his cheek into the damp locks at his temples. With infinite delicacy her thumb ruffled the thick eyebrows, to find the nubby scars underneath.

He lost his smile as the memory of that ordeal came flooding back. Only by exerting supreme self-control could he keep from shuddering violently. After a minute under her tender stroking, he mastered his thoughts and managed to regain his smile. "I've had a headache. But I've been to a doctor. He says it's going away."

"You've been to a doctor!" she exclaimed incredulously.

"Well, yes. I thought I should."

Her eyes filled with tears as real pain whitened her cheeks. "At various times over the last fifteen years, you've been stabbed, you've been burned, you've puked up everything but your toenails—"

"Iambics," he interrupted. "Iambics, please. You *have* been stabbed. You *have* been burned—"

She put her hand over his mouth. "—but through all that you've never been to the doctor."

He kissed her palm, teasing it with the tip of his tongue until she jerked it away. He grinned. "Miranda. You always exaggerate. I've never been to a doctor because I didn't need to go."

She shook her head. Tears brimmed over and trickled down her cheeks.

He reached up a finger to catch one. "Sweetheart, don't cry. It was nothing. He said it was nothing."

"Nothing." She choked on a sob.

"I told you. He said they'd get better."

"The headaches?"

He compressed his lips. "Yes."

"Is that all?"

"What else would there be?"

She looked at him closely. "Something you're not telling me about."

He made a sweeping gesture down his seminude body. "I have nothing to hide."

She placed her hand on his bare chest. "It was something Trask did to you, wasn't it? You wouldn't have had any of this if I hadn't been so obsessed. Something's badly wrong with you, and it's my fault."

He caught her wrists and brought her hands up to his mouth. "Stop that. I won't have you crying about something that's over and done with."

She sniffed unhappily and dropped her hot cheek onto his chest. The layer of perspiration made his skin feel slick. His maleness sent shivers through her. Beneath muscle and bone, his heart thrummed strongly.

111

He reached down and guided the rest of her body onto the bed, so she stretched out at his side. "Now just calm down. It's too hot to get so excited."

"I knew something was wrong." She turned on her side, sliding her thigh atop his. "You never in your life made a mistake in the blocking."

He said nothing. Instead one hand insinuated itself between their bodies to find her breast. His second and third fingers circled the nipple gently. The hiss of silk was matched by her sigh.

She arched her back, turning more to him, pressing her belly against his hip. Beneath his fingers her nipple grew taut as did the one that he had not touched. "Are you sure you feel like doing this?"

A chuckle rumbled beneath her ear. "I'm neither sick nor dead. I feel like doing this." His hand left her nipple and slid down over her belly and in between her legs. "You're hot," he teased her.

She rubbed the inside of her thigh over the top of his. His curling black hair made a scratching sound. "It's a hot day."

"Not this hot." He parted her and began to move his thumb in a slow circle over the hard nub of nerves between her legs. His fingers slid over satin skin slick with more than perspiration.

She gasped and twisted. Then involuntarily she tightened her buttocks, using the muscles to push herself against his hand. Her fingers curled; their nails scored over his collarbone and down into the hair on his chest. His own nipple was hard when she found it. She scratched it deliberately, the tip of her nail pricking him.

"Witchy," he cautioned. "Very unkind."

Her hand slid beneath his waistband. "If I'm so unkind, why are you so hard—and hot?"

"I live a hard life. It's a hot day," he mourned as he slid his hand down into the dark wet space between her thighs. His index and third fingers found her opening and curved inside.

"Shreve!" She arched against him. Her hand tightened over his staff.

"What?" His teeth set. His chest swelled as he took in a deep breath.

"Are you sure — ?"

"For the Lord's sake, woman. I'll tie a flag to it if it takes that to convince you."

She chuckled as she straddled him in one practiced move that did not even dislodge his fingers. Sitting back on his thighs, she unbuttoned the fine cotton underdrawers and exposed the engorged root in its nest of black hair. "You're the most beautiful man."

"Good, too." He smiled and twisted his fingers inside her.

The motion propelled her upward. She dropped her head back on her shoulders. The French blue silk spread around them. "It should be too hot for this."

He laughed. "You're going to hate yourself if you stop now." He pulled his fingers from her and let his hands fall limply to either side of the bed. "Ah, this is the life. I wonder if I can lie perfectly still, never move a muscle, and you — "

"Monster." She raised herself, guided him to the opening and let herself slide down, deliciously, slowly. Her sigh was pure pleasure.

He groaned in ecstasy. His fingers straightened on the sheet. "Take off your robe. Let me see your breasts."

Impaled on him, she allowed the robe to slide down her arms, then took the edge of the shift and drew it up and up, past her waist, past her breasts, past her arched throat. She lifted it to the full extension of her arms.

"Aphrodite," he whispered.

113

She let the blue satin fall and used her hands to pull the pins from her hair. The blond skein rolled down her back. She shook it free and clasped her hardened breasts.

The next few minutes were filled with the sounds of love. Their heavy breathing, their sighs of pleasure, the creak of the leather straps beneath the mattress.

His pleasure was more intense because her body moved with greater ease. The fashion was soft white women, with heavy pads of flesh on their hips and big pillowy breasts. Even her breasts were firm. He loved her for them.

He loved her muscles delineated under the skin of her thighs when she whipped her body up and back.

He studied her face through half-closed eyes, watching the play of passion, the fierce concentration that she devoted to her lovemaking. It was the same fierce concentration that she used to play her parts. In her acting, it transported her to hell. In her lovemaking, it took them both to heaven.

Suddenly, she raised her head.

"Yes," he whispered. "Yes." For the first time he moved, lifting his hips, surging upward, pushing himself impossibly into her.

Eyes closed, teeth bared, she sucked in her breath. Her nails tore at the sheet. A moment of absolute stillness, then a quake. Her entire body shuddered.

His own flesh answered hers. A fierce thrust upward of his hips bucked her upward, wringing a cry from her. She fell forward on his chest as they sank together.

She regained consciousness as her body slid slickly off his. Hot liquid gushed out onto her thigh. He moved over to give her room and she rolled onto her back staring upward through the folds of mosquito netting draped over its hoop. A long sigh of contentment escaped her.

They lay side by side for a long minute, only their little fingers touching. Gradually their heartbeats slowed.

He rolled away. She heard the splash of water. He had dipped his compress into the basin and wrung it out. She closed her eyes on a sigh of pleasure as he bathed her face and throat.

Following the cloth, his lips touched her cheek. "I got a marriage license."

Her eyes flew open. "When?"

He was not looking at her. Instead, he concentrated on dipping the cloth into the basin and wringing it out. "The day you ran away to Wyoming."

She searched his face incredulously. "After all these years."

"I got it too late." He spread the cloth over her breasts.

She closed her eyes against the shock of cool water on fevered skin—the shock of that and something more—a shard of pain so great her breath stuck in her throat. "I—I don't know what to say."

His smile was self-deprecating. *"Our wooing doth not end like an old play: Jack hath not Jill."*

She tried a smile in answer. *"Love's Labour's Lost.* But you never said a word about—"

He nodded as he stroked the wet cloth across her belly. "I didn't have any idea of marrying you. For years you were just a brat."

She snorted at that.

He lifted up the cloth and delivered a kiss to the tip of her breast. "I admit, a very attractive brat, but a schoolgirl, an apprentice."

"Is that what you thought I was?"

115

He ducked his head in embarrassment. "At first." He stroked the top of her thigh. "Oh, not for years. No," he said seriously, his black eyes fixed hard on her, "I hadn't thought of you as a schoolgirl—"

"You hadn't thought of me at all," she interrupted, a touch of bitterness in her voice. "You didn't even see me. I was the body in the dark."

His fist clenched, squeezing out drops of water that slid over her leg and soaked into the sheet. "That's not so. Never."

She stared into his face. It had frozen.

"You don't mean that. You know it's not true. I had just never thought about the future. It seemed we'd go on and on together. I never thought you'd even want to leave me. When I realized I didn't have any claim on you, I'd waited too late. You were gone. It was a shock, I'll tell you."

She looked away. "A marriage isn't supposed to be a prison."

She expected him to argue, but instead, he nodded shortly. The dark lashes slipped down over his eyes. He dragged the cloth down to cover her loins, slid his hand into the space between her legs, pushed up hard. His voice was rough and violent. "I waited too late."

She twisted against the pressure, arching her back and throwing her hips up to him. The other hand he clapped to her breast, squeezing, pinching the nipple. She caught her teeth in her lower lip, but he had caught her unawares. He had awakened her nerves with the cool water, the gentle caresses. She had been seduced as only he could seduce her, as he had always been able to seduce her from the first night they had come together. He had not known that she was only sixteen years old.

Since that night she had been his creature. Speaking, moving, acting as he bade her, loving

116

him as if he were her special saint, climaxing at his touch.

Only for vengeance had she found the strength to leave him.

She sobbed in ecstasy as he would not let the climax stop. One, two, three fingers pushed inside her, his thumb pressed hard. Her long convulsive shudder went on and on until she slumped unconscious.

His headache had returned full force. Wearily, he arranged her limbs, and stretched out on the bed beside her. He closed his eyes against the pain. For the first time he realized he had wept.

He loved her, but he dared not ask her to marry him. He blinked rapidly, then stared fixedly at the mosquito netting draped above them. Even now, slats of black broke the clear scene of his vision, and around the edge of his vision was a gray haze.

He would not marry her to a blind man. He knew her better than she knew herself. Faithful to a fault, she had never entertained a thought or a care about herself. If she knew—

He threw his arm over his eyes. He would wait. Perhaps the doctor was right. Perhaps the headaches would gradually cease altogether and he would be able to see as well as he always had. Perhaps last night was only a particularly bad spell. But until he could be certain, he would not speak of marriage.

What if things get much worse? his mind nudged. *What if—*

If things got much worse, he would drive her away. She could easily find someone better than an old, broken-down actor.

Miranda stared up through the swaths of mosquito netting, faintly surprised that her tears were

117

not trickling down her temples onto the pillow. More than ever she believed that she was the pawn of destiny. By a day, a few hours, she had missed being Mrs. Shreve Catherwood. For almost half her life she had wanted to be his wife. Now her heart ached. By such a little, she had missed being secure and safe with the man she loved.

As if her father's ghost had intervened to lead her to vengeance, she had boarded the train as Shreve was purchasing the marriage license.

The essence of tragedy — sterility. No marriage. No children. Only vengeance and death and now — She turned carefully in bed until she was facing Shreve. He was so beautiful. And yet the scars inflicted on him would be with him forever. She began to weep.

White hairs threaded through the thick black waves at his temples. His eyebrows ruffled over the ridged scars where Trask had beaten him. At rest his face looked exhausted. Deep creases bracketed his mouth and another bisected his forehead. Even in sleep, they did not smooth away. They revealed his pain. Even in sleep, he was hurting.

She had caused this. And she was a fugitive from justice. She could not marry him. Moreover, she must never allow him to get sentimental enough to ask her. Federal warrants had been issued for her arrest. Somewhere someone was searching for her, sifting through evidence for some clue to her identity.

The possibility of arrest was always there. Some clever investigator might put all the pieces together. Or someone would tell. And then she would have to flee again, or else be captured, tried, sentenced, hanged.

Her imagination well schooled in drama played the entire play while her muscles tensed and her stomach burned.

118

She should leave today, run away and hide herself so no one would ever find her, give up Shreve and the theater, Ada and George, her mother whom she had just discovered again, her sister before they could make their peace.

She cringed. Her stomach clenched.

She would take her chances for another day and another. A day at a time. But a day at a time did not mean marriage and a family.

Shaking, she rose and walked to the window. The day was ending. The sun had left the courtyard below. Almost time to wake Shreve and leave for the theater.

She turned back to look at him—her true love. What a fine piece of dramatic irony! Just when he was willing to marry her, the gods had played a cruel joke on her. And now she might never be able to marry.

One day at a time. She had not the courage for more.

Ruth Westfall stood on the station platform, her black widow's weeds blowing in the wild Wyoming wind. She smiled weepily at Blue Sun on Snow and Adolf Lindhauer. "I'm afraid this is goodbye again."

"Maybe not," the trader said, his eyes squinting against the cinders from the engine's smokestack. "You never thought you'd come back this time, but you did. Maybe next time you'll come because you want to."

Blue Sun on Snow nodded agreement. Her wise eyes took in the figures of her son and Ruth's daughter standing apart beyond the baggage cart. "The third time you will return because you want to come. You have friends here." She smiled. "Perhaps more than friends. A new life can begin close to where your happiest moments have been."

"Perhaps." Ruth looked beyond the depot down the dusty street. It was very different from Chicago. "I wouldn't go now if I didn't think I needed to go to Senator Butler. He has to understand what Benjamin planned to do. He has to know that the case should be buried and forgotten."

"Least said, best mended," Adolf warned.

"He's hired a private investigator. That man has to be called off," Ruth insisted stubbornly. "He can't be allowed to hunt Miranda down. Benjamin Westfall took her youth. He can't have the rest of her life."

The train whistle startled them all even though they were expecting it.

Casting a glance at the approaching train, Rachel caught Victor's hands. "Please don't forget me," she begged. "I'll be through with school in just a few months. Then—"

"Don't." He gently disengaged himself. "We've been all through this. We can't marry. I'll never marry."

She caught him by the shoulders before he could step back out of reach. "Just don't hate me! And think of me. Think of how I'll be next year." She swallowed painfully. "I'm Mirry's sister. Think of how much you love her."

"Rachel, please. This isn't any good."

"Well, you can't have her," she continued defiantly. "But you can have me."

"Rachel—"

"You don't know it yet, but I'm what you want. What you love." Her eyes were luminous with promise. Her lips trembled with the words. The train rumbled through, its bell ringing, its engine huffing.

"Damn you." She was going and he would never see her again. He caught her by the elbows and dragged her against him. One hard swift kiss he allowed himself, one swift taste of heaven. Then he shoved her away. With a violent twist of his body, he leaped off the platform and strode swiftly down the street.

"Rachel?"

"Coming, Mother." Tingling lips curved in a pleased smile, Rachel allowed the conductor to help her up the metal steps. One last look at the street, but he had disappeared. Still smiling, she followed her mother into the parlor car.

Seven

The sun's o'ercast with blood.

De la Barca lounged against the wall of the building directly across the street from the stage door of the Royal Orleans Theater. His appearance had changed considerably, so that he no longer looked like a Northerner suffering in the New Orleans heat.

In place of his bowler hat, he wore a Panama straw that shaded his face with its wide brim. Instead of the starched collar and tight-buttoned wool suit, he wore loose-fitting pantaloons and frock coat over a soft-collared shirt, all in cool cream linen.

Unfortunately, the frock coat was buttoned to the top button and the neckline of his shirt was covered by a cravat. The combination gave him a repressed look. Nevertheless, since he presented approximately the same look as the passersby, his garments allowed him to loiter unnoticed. They also concealed a veritable arsenal of weapons.

Sweat trickled down his cheeks and he batted at the ever-present mosquitoes with a weary hand. Perspiration soaked the armpits and back of his coat between his shoulder blades. He shifted restlessly as the steam rising off the cobblestones cooked his feet in their leather boots.

How could anyone exist in this New Orleans? In August people were required to walk the streets where moss grew between the cobbles, to breathe air rising off the Mississippi River flowing sluggishly on the south and Lake Pontchartrain gleaming on the north.

De la Barca stared at housewives and servants doing the daily shopping, at vendors moving along behind their pushcarts, at businessmen and planters wheeling by in their carriages and wagons. They seemed content, even oblivious in the heat that was threatening to consume him.

Finally, a carriage halted at the entrance to the alley. De la Barca pulled a newspaper from under his arm and consulted it. He moved back several paces pretending to scan the street numbers. From his new position, he could see a man alight.

The investigator blinked back sweat. The man was tall, dark, and unusually handsome. Obviously an actor, he thought contemptuously. He could be the man Armistead had described, but, so could more than three-quarters of the actors along the Mississippi.

Then he turned back to give his hand to a woman. The golden blond hair shone in the dying sunlight. Fresh in the investigator's mind were the two women he had spoken with in Wyoming. Rachel Westfall had the same color hair. Ruth Westfall probably had had the same before it had grayed.

"My sister," the younger woman had said. He had ridden off thinking she was crazy. She still might be. Women's word could not be trusted. For reasons of jealousy and spite, they were often found to have lied in accusing someone.

Coming to New Orleans had been a long shot. He had first returned to Chicago, where Benjamin Westfall had made his home. Somewhat to his sur-

123

prise, he had found Westfall had hired a Pinkerton detective, Parker Bledsoe.

Bledsoe had been hired to find Rachel Westfall's older sister Miranda Drummond. According to the reports, she had run away from home. A detective had located her with a theater troupe. She had been taken from the troupe by her stepfather, Benjamin Westfall, and subsequently she had died in a home for wayward girls.

The report must have been false. Rachel Westfall had clearly said "my sister."

He would have liked to question Bledsoe, but the man had been found murdered after turning in the Westfall report. His murderer had never been caught. Could Miranda Drummond be in some way responsible for the death of Bledsoe? And subsequently Westfall?

She had been only sixteen at the time of Bledsoe's death, but age, Frank de la Barca had discovered, had nothing to do with murder. A six-year-old could pull the trigger of a pistol. A ten-year-old could stab his mother in the belly.

The presence of a blond woman and a tall dark man in a troupe of actors had no link to the happenings at Fort Gallatin. Although somewhat unusual, Miranda could be the name of any number of women living in and around the country. The name Shreve Catherwood bore no resemblance to Mark Phillips. Still, his hunting blood was up at the sight of his first and most promising leads. He forced himself to remain coolly analytical.

The woman in all probability was not the daughter of Ruth Westfall and Francis Drummond. She was merely a blond actress who bore a coincidental resemblance to Rachel Westfall. Moreover, even if she were Miranda Drummond, she might have no connection to nor knowledge of the events that had transpired.

The man, on the other hand, might be the prisoner whose transfer orders had come in the old mail pouch carried by the bearded lieutenant. In the escape two guards had been overpowered and a sergeant, shot. Armistead had gotten no information from his prisoner, an unusual situation since criminals usually ratted on each other before the jail door had even swung to.

A man who withstood the extremely unpleasant tactics of the army interrogator was a determined man. Such a man might be smart enough to hide "in plain sight"? Without a positive identification, de la Barca was merely guessing.

He had to get closer, check his facts, make inquiries.

The woman was the approachable one, he guessed. She would be his target. Women were notoriously easy to confuse and frighten. First they lied and played dumb. Then they tried to use their bodies to distract. Finally, they wept and confessed. Sometimes, they screamed before they confessed. His tongue flicked out across his lower lip. But always they told him everything he wanted to know.

Some of it was even the truth.

From the back of the theater, de la Barca watched her move. He had hoped to see in her the possibility that she might have disguised herself as an army officer, but he dismissed the idea out of hand.

Although he did not understand the play, did not even pay attention to the foolishness, his black eyes followed her across the stage. She was dressed as a boy, but only a blind man would mistake her for one. Her limbs were long and curvaceous; her waist, tiny. Her melodious voice could never be taken for a boy's cracking tenor.

No. She was not the one, but the big one. Her partner. He might be. He scanned the rest of the

125

cast. A young man with blond hair, about the same color as the girl's, might have been the one. He studied him. The actor minced across the stage, his backside switching. De la Barca's mouth curled in disgust. That one would never have the nerve to climb on a horse and ride down to kill a man. Of course, all actors faced audiences. The presence of a crowd would have daunted none of them.

His eyes returned to the girl, woman actually. Under stage lights he could see the lines around her eyes and mouth. He stared at her. She moved with lithe grace. When she was called to wrestle with the leading actor, she put up a good job.

He must question her, he decided. She would lie. Then she would try to use her body. He stared at her smiling face as she fervently embraced the tall actor. He closed his eyes, for just an instant in the darkness. He would let her.

And then he would make her cry. He would make her scream. And then she would tell him everything about where she had been on the Fourth of July when Benjamin Westfall had been killed.

Some parts of his job were better than others.

"You were good tonight." Miranda watched Shreve carefully as he took off his makeup.

"I'm always good," he replied, peeling off the bits of crêpe eyebrows and placing them in a separate part of the makeup box.

"You were especially sharp tonight."

He pulled off Orsino's wig and placed it carefully on the wig stand. "Love in the afternoon." His reflection leered at her. "Nothing like practice for the real thing."

"So your head feels all right?"

"Never better." His voice was muffled. He buried his face in the towel to wipe away the greasepaint.

"I wish I could be sure you're telling the truth."

126

He jerked the towel away from his face and swung around in the chair. Fastening her with his most charismatic stare, he crooked a long index finger at her. "Allow me to demonstrate, madam. Assurance shall be yours and you will smile in the security of your knowledge."

She smiled at him, lazily, hectic color in her cheeks. "I believe you. You can demonstrate later."

"You're sure?"

"Sure."

He gave an exaggerated sigh and rose. "I'll be back. Think of me while I'm gone." He tipped her chin up and kissed her long and lingeringly on the lips. Then he patted her bottom. "And remember what can be yours."

Back stage was beginning to clear out. The crew had put the set and properties in place and gone. Cast members had changed out of their costumes and stripped off their makeup. Singly and in pairs, they were leaving. The men's toilet was empty.

In its privacy, Shreve sank down and held his head in his hands. He had been excellent tonight, but at what cost? His head pounded hard enough to nauseate him. If he had had anything to give up, he would have had to run for the alley between scenes. He doubted he would have made it.

How much longer could he continue his deception?

He knew the answer. He would keep it up as long as it took. As in all experiences, this one would make him a better actor. From now on he could lend real authenticity to a role if he ever had to play an invalid. He would heal leaving this all behind him. And then he could think about asking Miranda to be his wife.

He leaned his forehead against the cool bricks. He probably should not have told her about the wedding license. Suppose he did not recover. Suppose the swelling did not go down. Suppose the black lines increased in width until they became a solid black curtain—

He shuddered, a tiny whimper escaped through his clenched teeth. He would not live like that. If it happened, he would—

No more o' that, my lord, no more o' that! He pushed himself away from the wall. A few minutes rest would give him the strength he needed for the next deception. Back at the hotel, after supper, he could feign sleep. She would understand.

He studied his face by the small mirror, then frowned critically. His pallor was damned unhealthy looking. Unless he planned to confine himself to Banquo's Ghost and Hamlet's father, he was going to have to get more sun. This damned New Orleans heat made taking an afternoon in the sun uncomfortable.

Silently, he vowed never to book here again in summer. The best people were out of town on their plantations anyway.

Weary unto death, he pushed himself away from the mirror and straightened. He had stayed longer than he meant to, but the cool dankness of the place had actually eased some of the pain in his head. Perhaps he really wasn't suffering from his injuries, so much as the heat.

The passageway was dark. The lamp had been on when he had gone in. Now someone had turned it out. He must speak to the theater manager about employees clearing out while actors were still back stage. Gingerly, he moved along, feeling the fly lines that raised and lowered the scenery on one side and the bare brick on the other.

Scraping, clicking sounds. A slap, a grunt. The painful expulsion of breath. He stopped, blinking, trying to pierce the blackness, unsure whether the problem was with his eyes.

"Shre—!"

Miranda's voice, shrill, urgent, cut off. Something was terribly wrong. He lunged forward. The door to their dressing room banged open, striking him in the face. He staggered back, tripped over a rope, caught at the scenery, righted himself.

Still no light! The lamps in the dressing room had been extinguished. No wonder he had become disoriented. No light had spilled from beneath the door.

Heavy footsteps thudded down the hall, moving fast, but not running. He should be able to catch the intruder. No one knew back stage better than he. He took a couple of steps. His head whirled. He staggered, caught his foot in something on the floor, pitched down on his hands and knees, stumbled up again. "Stop! Help! Help! Thief! Murderer!"

The voice that could be heard in the upper balconies of the theaters of the world boomed out of the stage door as it was flung open. Silhouetted in it was a man's body with a burden over his shoulder.

"Miranda!"

The burden twisted, bobbed.

A kidnapping. Someone was taking her. He sprang to his feet. "Miranda!"

The stage door slammed to. At the same instant a dressing-room door beside him swung open. "What's going on?"

Light, blessed light flooded the passageway. Jerold, the second lead, stuck his head out. He was nude except for the towel he was trying to knot around his waist.

"Miranda's been kidnapped!"

"What! Are you sure?"

"What's happened?" An alarmed feminine voice called from behind Jerold's back. "Who turned the lights off?"

Shreve wasted no time in argument. "Send for the police!"

An instant's hesitation, then agreement. "Soon as I get m' pants on."

Shreve bolted out the door. "Help! Police!"

At the end of the alley a carriage door was closing. He dashed for it, but the driver laid the whip across the horses' backs. They sprang forward with a jerk.

"Help! Murder!" Shreve sprinted after them.

Inside the coach de la Barca slid open the window beneath the driver's feet. "Back streets and alleys as soon as possible, Poteet."

"Very much money to drive down back streets maybe," the pimp called laying on with the whip.

"I said the right man could make a lot of money at this," de la Barca responded.

"Help! Help!" Miranda's voice was muffled by the folds of the sack but nonetheless shockingly loud in the confines of the carriage.

"Here! Stop that!" De la Barca flung his arm around her struggling figure, fumbling for her head and her mouth.

Wriggling frantically, Miranda managed to get a hand under the edge of the sack. Still screaming, she jerked the edge of the sack partially out of the rope. She kicked and rolled half off, managing to free her other hand.

"Hold it right there." De la Barca was panting when he threw himself across her.

She screamed again as her body tumbled down on her face on the floor of the carriage. With the second length of rope, he threw a loop over one of her wrists. Instantly, she drew her other hand back under the sack.

The carriage swung wide to the left. The crack of the whip drew a shrill whinny from one of the horses. The occupants inside the cab were thrown against the side. Miranda's head banged against the door. It sprang open and only de la Barca's hand on her gown kept her from toppling out.

130

To his surprise she kicked at his hands. Even with her head only a few feet from the cobblestones and the whirling bouncing wheels, she fought his efforts to haul her back inside.

"Stupid woman! You'll get yourself killed. Get back in here."

She redoubled her screams. He cursed vividly. The whole city of New Orleans would be out on the street in a minute. He reeled back as she kicked him in the chest.

Poteet swung the carriage around another corner. De la Barca had to use one hand to brace himself to keep from going through the door.

"Idiot! Slow down!" he yelled to the driver. "She's—"

Looping her hand around the rope that bound her wrist, she pulled as she kicked.

For an instant, she felt herself falling, free of his hands. She set her teeth and braced herself for the impact.

But his hands caught at her skirts. The material ripped away at the waist but held long enough for him to drag her back in and slam the door.

"Go on!" her captor yelled.

"Slow down! Go on! Make up yo' damn mind!" The whip cracked and the coach jolted forward again.

Miranda tried to lift the sack. This time her captor did not try to stop her. In a few seconds she was free. Pushing the hair back out of her eyes, she saw the dark figure sitting across from her. She sucked in her breath to scream again, but he thrust the muzzle of his gun in her face.

"Scream again and I'll knock your teeth out."

She shrank back. "You'd better stop this carriage and let me out. You can't hope to get away with this?"

By the light of a street lamp she was able to see

131

his still, round face, his eyes gleaming from beneath puffy lids.

She shuddered. "You've let yourself in for a lot of grief, mister. Just what do you think you're doing?"

"I think I'm capturing a fugitive from justice," he said as calmly as the jouncing coach would allow.

The flat faintly accented speech alarmed her. So that was it. He was an investigator. She should have guessed. "You're mistaken," she replied. "I'm an actress."

"I don't think so." His eyes glittered as they passed another lamp, but more ominous was the gleam of the gun. Then they turned down a dark alley.

She pretended not to understand. "You're crazy. I'm an actress. I've given a few bad performances, but never one that would get me arrested."

The interior of the coach was absolutely dark. The rumble of its wheels prevented her from hearing his breathing. She could smell only the mustiness of the interior. So still did her captor sit, she might have been alone.

In a flash of inner terror, she saw Benjamin Westfall clutch at his chest as her bullet slammed into him, saw the blood spurt. With an effort she controlled herself and used her most authoritative voice. "I demand that you stop this coach instantly," said Lady Macbeth.

Miraculously, the horses began to slow.

Coincidence merely. On either side rose black walls of brick. They rolled through an alley or some dark side street in the rabbit warren of Vieux Carre.

She tensed waiting her chance. Shreve had taught her that life was not smooth and correct like a drama. Real people did not rehearse their movements, nor move with grace and precision. Her

132

captor would make a wrong move, shift off balance. And she would strike.

The coach swayed as the driver climbed down. He did not open the door as a trained coachman would do. She noted his rudeness immediately. Her captor leaned forward, hand outstretched.

She must have betrayed herself by her breathing. Shreve always said she could never get it right.

"Don't try anything foolish." He stabbed the gun into her chest. It hit in the center of her chest, bruising her breastbone as she lunged against it.

It drove her back against the cushions. Still she protested. "You'd better let me go."

"And you'd better do exactly as I tell you." His warning was dry and flat. "I hurt people before they hurt me."

Shreve's heart pounded against his chest wall. His temples throbbed like drums. Running on foot, he thought he would be forced to give up the chase when he spotted a gig on the lonely street. Without hesitation he leaped into it and wrested the reins from the driver's hands.

A hero would have been able to thunder to the rescue, but he was unused to driving at more than a snail's pace. When he laid on the whip, he had such difficulty steering the bolting nag that he tore the left wheel off in a sweeping turn into a narrow alley.

Leaving the owner cursing and shouting, he resumed the race, depending now on his ears to lead him through the steamy alleys.

"You are the daughter of Francis Drummond," de la Barca stated without emotion. His experience had led him to attack with his guesses calmly stated as facts.

133

This time he was doomed to disappointment. Maintaining the same icy demeanor, Miranda counterattacked. "Who are you, sir? I want to know your name, so I can report you to your superiors."

"My name's unimportant. Your name is more to the point. You are Miranda Drummond." He took a step toward her, rolling his shoulders, using his masculinity to intimidate her.

Miranda tried to match his lack of expression. "I don't use my last name. I hardly remember it — or my father. He died when I was a child."

At least he had verified that she was Miranda Drummond. Still de la Barca felt a flicker of uncertainty accompanied by frustration. Her unflappability disturbed him. She should be nervous, begging. He pointed a stubby finger at her. "Your mother married General Benjamin Westfall. He reported you were dead."

Miranda shrugged. "He was wrong."

"You hired a private investigator from the Pinkerton Agency to find your sister Rachel Westfall in Chicago only a few months ago."

"I thought we might renew our relationship. She attended a play at my invitation and we had lunch together. No crime there that I can imagine. But you — You have a lot of explaining to do to your superiors and to the police here in New Orleans. I want your name. I intend to report you at the first opportunity. I was kidnapped. People saw me carried out of the theater."

He pulled a notebook from his pocket and consulted it. "You left Chicago for an engagement in Saint Louis, but you did not keep your engagement. Your business manager and — I assume — partner reported that you were ill. The engagement was canceled."

The deliberate pause before the word "partner" brought Miranda's chin up. She tried to guess how the man could insult her with no inflection whatso-

134

ever. She tried to match him. Lady Macbeth to the life, she asked. "You didn't need to drag me out of the theater and gallop through the streets like a crazy man. You could have come to the theater and asked me these questions. I would have answered them. Your information is correct. I was ill. And I'm going to be ill again as a result of this bad treatment. Give me your name. I can't wait to report you."

"What hospital did you stay in?"

"No hospital. I stayed with friends."

"Friends in Wyoming?"

"No. Your name, if you please!"

"De la Barca," he dropped in irritably. "Then where did you stay?"

"Your full name."

"Damn you. Frank. Frank de la Barca. Where did you stay?"

"In Saint Louis."

"You're a liar."

She rose. "Mr. de la Barca, you have absolutely nothing in that notebook except the most basic biographical information and a great deal of supposition. You're the one who has committed a crime."

The investigator did not flinch. "What about your manager, that actor Shreve Catherwood?" His voice reflected his triumph. "What would happen if he were taken back to Wyoming to meet a certain General Theodore Armistead?"

"I'm sure the general would be very impressed to see such an important actor in such a backwater place." She lifted her chin. "Your superior officers would be impressed. Shreve and I are used to playing to very large audiences in Chicago, Saint Louis, New Orleans. In New York City. The entire state of Wyoming doesn't have as many people as one of those cities. Fort Laramie, probably doesn't even have a theater."

"How did you know Armistead was stationed at

135

Fort Laramie?" The corners of de la Barca's mouth twitched in what might have been a triumphant smile.

She allowed her own lips to twitch, though her stomach was shuddering uncontrollably and her arms ached with the chills that prickled them. "I did not know. I merely mentioned Fort Laramie as a famous military outpost in Wyoming. If you had said Texas, I might have said Fort Worth." She turned her shoulder haughtily to him. "I am merely using a metaphor."

De la Barca struck like a snake. Lunging from the chair, he caught her arm and pushed her against the scarred armoire. "You're lying! I want the truth. And I want it now!" The words were low but uttered with powerful emphasis.

"I'm not—"

He cuffed the side of her mouth with his fist. His blow knocked her sideways, and he deliberately let go of her arm so she would fall. He followed her body down and straddled her hips. His clenched fists hung above her. "Listen to me. You're goin' to tell me exactly what happened, exactly what all of this is about. And when you've told me everything to my satisfaction, then you're goin' to sit down at that table and write it."

Miranda's jaw felt as if it were dislocated. Flaming pain and shock were making her weak. Her own blood tasted sweet and salt in her mouth. She put a shaking hand to the bruise. "You're making the mistake of your life. I don't have anything to write."

He pulled her to her feet and hit her again. This time in the stomach.

She doubled over, paralyzed by pain, sick, gagging.

He hoisted her up by her hair. "Now you listen to me, Miranda Drummond. You've got some very powerful people mad at you. They've paid me a lot

136

of money to find out answers no one else can find out. They want to know why Benjamin Westfall was killed. They want to know who was behind his death and what they hoped to gain from his death."

Wracked with pain, she stared helplessly at him. "You're my link."

"I don't know anything. I wasn't even there."

He drew back his fist again.

"I wasn't! I WASN'T!" She put all her soul into her hysterics. Her very life depended on her making them convincing. Over and over she screamed the two words.

The door opened. "What you doin'?" Poteet lounged in the doorway.

"Nothing that concerns you."

"You maybe be too rough on that gal."

De la Barca drew his pistol again. "Don't come in here! What happens in this room doesn't concern you."

Poteet raised his hands. "Don't be mad. Just don't make her scream like that. New Orleans is full of men who don't touch women. Cut a man's heart out for a picayune, but don't touch women. Maybe you get one or two o' them in here. Maybe—"

De la Barca stabbed at him with the gun. "Get the hell out of here."

"Suit yourself. You too stupid to take a warnin', maybe you get hurt." Poteet cast an enigmatic look at Miranda where she slumped against the armoire.

De la Barca thumbed back the hammer, but Poteet slid around the doorjamb.

"Fool!" De la Barca slammed the door behind him. "Now!" He turned back to Miranda.

She pushed herself up. "He's right, you know. This isn't New York City. This is New Orleans. Women are treated gently."

He shrugged. "I don't care. I want that informa-

137

tion." He started toward her, but she had had time to think. Sweeping up the lamp from the table, she flung it straight at his chest. The well broke and spattered him with kerosene. Flame from the lamp wick set him afire.

"Goddamn you! Damn you!" He began to scream. Frantically, he batted at the blaze. The linen had soaked up the kerosene and the fire followed it. While he was trying to rip the buttons apart without burning his hands, she jerked open the door and ran.

Halfway down the narrow stairs, Poteet blocked her way. Their eyes met. He lounged away against the wall with a lazy smile. She darted past him, ran across the entrance, and flung out the door.

Into Shreve's arms.

Eight

He must needs go that the devil drives.

"I must be getting old. I'm supposed to save you." With a whoop of joy, Shreve threw his arms around Miranda and squeezed so hard that she squeaked.

When he immediately eased his grip, she tugged his head down and kissed him, her smile broad despite the swelling bruise on her jaw. "You're not getting old. You're just getting quicker. This time you didn't even stop to put on a disguise."

He touched the dark red blotch tenderly. "I wanted to burst into the room and punch him out."

"And now you don't have to. The difference is with me. I've grown up. You taught me to save myself. That works better. Saves you a lot of trouble and we still get to embrace in the end."

"Maybe y'all be better somewhere else?" Poteet's voice with a honey grin in it rolled over them. They looked around in time to see the pimp eel out of sight into a narrow passageway between the ramshackle boarding houses that lined the dismal alley.

"He's right." Miranda grabbed Shreve's hand to run.

"Hold it right there, both of you." In the doorway de la Barca aimed a pistol at them.

139

Shreve flung himself in front of her. "Run, Miranda!"

"I wouldn't advise that!" de la Barca called to her. "I'll shoot his leg out from under him and bring you down with the next shot." The investigator presented an awful aspect. He had torn off his coat. His shirt was black with smoke and his blistered flesh showed through holes burnt in the material. His chin and one side of his face were stained. His hair was singed off on the same side.

Despite the pain he had set his face in its implacable lines. A sheath knife and an empty holster hung from his belt. He looked as dangerous as a demon from hell.

Shreve pasted an idiotic smile on his face. He started toward de la Barca with his hand outstretched. "Now just a minute—"

"Shreve! No! Stay back!"

"That's good advice." The barrel of the gun dipped until it was trained at Shreve's knee. Eyes flickering between the man and the woman, de la Barca came down the steps toward them. Experience had taught him that nearly all people were cowed by the sight of a gun leveled at them. These two would be no exception. "Hands above your head."

Instantly, the actor threw up his hands. "Hey, don't point that thing at me. It could go off."

"It won't go off unless I make it."

"Shreve," the girl cried again.

"Really, old man, it's not the thing to do. Pointing guns. So uncivilized."

De la Barca's lip curled in disgust at the lisping voice.

"Besides, you don't want to shoot us." The actor took a mincing step toward him, then suddenly launched himself. Miranda's scream echoed down the alley.

Arms outstretched, Shreve flung himself bodily through the air.

With a surprised grunt, de la Barca jerked the gun up. Its bore was centered on Shreve's broad chest when he pulled the trigger.

The hammer fell with a metallic click. The gun had misfired.

Before de la Barca could squeeze off another round, the actor's shoulder plowed into his chest, level with his heart. His chunky body was slammed back across the steps. Cursing, he bucked upward trying to throw the other man off at the same time he tried to wrench his arms free.

"Run, Miranda!" Shreve yelled again. He tried to knock his head against de la Barca's chin.

The investigator jerked his knee up between the actor's legs.

The man on top grunted in pain but only tightened his grasp.

"Shreve!"

"Run! Damn you!"

Eyes wild, Miranda lunged toward the struggling men. Her fist connected with de la Barca's nose, snapping his head back against the weathered porch. Blood streaked across her knuckles.

Involuntarily, de la Barca squeezed the trigger again. Their bodies muffled the sound of the report, but a shriek of agony ripped through the steamy air.

"Shreve!" Miranda tugged desperately at his shoulders. "Shreve, oh, darling, oh, love. Oh, please God, are you all right?"

"I'm not shot," he groaned.

"You're not? You're not?" She ran her hands down his sides. "Are you sure?"

Beneath Shreve, de la Barca's body went limp. Only the shivering and twitching of his limbs and his groans and curses showed he had not lost consciousness.

Carefully, Shreve pushed up and looked down. The gun, a dark silhouette against the pale clothing, lay on de la Barca's stomach. The investigator's hand was still clasped around it. Shreve pulled it from the limp fingers and rolled away. Sick at the dark splatters of blood on his own clothes, he climbed to his feet.

"Sweetheart." Miranda threw her arms around his chest.

Burying his face in her disheveled hair, Shreve drew in a shuddering breath. For the first time in his life, he understood heroism. It was not heroic at all. It was the simple act of reckless abandonment of one's own life for another. No thought. No posturing. No great speeches. See! Act! Devil take loser! He could feel the hair rising on the back of his neck. In the hot steamy darkness he was chilled to the bone.

Finally, they turned to look at the investigator who lay limp, his body twitching in agony.

As they watched, he twisted so he could clasp his wounded thigh. Blood streamed between his fingers. He cursed steadily and with great fervor.

Miranda stared at him in dawning horror. "He shot himself."

"Yes, but he was this close to getting me." Shreve brushed at the black scorch marks on the front of his trousers. His fingers caught in a hole in the material. He grunted.

"Oh, dear lord." Miranda clasped her hand over his. "Are you sure you're not hurt?"

"Blistered from the feel of it, but otherwise all right." He looked down at her. "What about you? Are you all right?"

"Yes."

"Your face?" He touched the side of her jaw.

142

"Oh, it's nothing." She waved an unconcerned hand that came to rest on the revolver in Shreve's. Without his quite knowing what she was about, she relieved him of it, cocked it, and leveled it.

The wounded man suddenly grew silent except for his harsh breathing and suppressed moans of pain. His eyes narrowed. He clamped his lips tight together.

Miranda stared into the black eyes, glittering between folds of sweaty brown flesh. For all her reassurances, her jaw was throbbing and her midriff and ribs were aching. The sight of the blood, a black shining stream running thickly over the steps, was making her sick to her stomach. In that minute the full consequences of her revenge brought her close to tears. She swallowed heavily. "I don't know who sent you. I don't know why. But I hope he's paying you plenty for all this pain."

De la Barca made no move. He had clapped his hand over the wound. By the relatively small amount of blood and the lack of shock, he judged it to be no more than a crease. The chances of overpowering them, however, were slim. He discounted the woman, since none of her sex could ever shoot straight. His dark gaze flicked over Catherwood.

He must be hurt because he stood with head hanging dragging in deep shuddering breaths. The creases in his forehead testified to his pain. The investigator slowly started to sit up.

"Stay right where you are," Miranda warned him, "or I'll shoot you again."

"I'm bleeding," de la Barca answered, gasping and groaning for effect.

"Not a lot." With the back of her free hand, Miranda wiped her forehead. Both she and Shreve needed to be away from this steamy alley where they could rest. "Not nearly enough."

She stooped to bring the gun to within a couple of feet of de la Barca's face. "Listen to me," she commanded, Lady Macbeth's mantle of queenship dropping over her shoulders. "I answered all your questions. I and my partner are respected professional people plying our trade. We don't have anything to do with the U.S. Army in Wyoming."

She waited, but de la Barca made no reaction. "What you did to me was inexcusable — criminal. We could have you arrested."

De la Barca squeezed his thigh tighter. His eyes glazed slightly as pain made him woozy.

"We won't press charges of kidnapping — " Here she looked at Shreve, who raised his head and nodded. His face was streaming with perspiration and white with pain. He must have run all the way after the coach. She swallowed the painful lump that formed in her throat.

" — charges of kidnapping, assault, and attempted murder, provided you leave New Orleans as soon as you're able."

De la Barca slumped back on the steps. His head lolled. His blood had run down three steps and was dividing into rivulets among the flagstones of the narrow sidewalk.

"However, if we see you again, we'll turn your name over to the authorities. Don't for one minute doubt that we can do it. Our audiences are some of the best people in New Orleans. We're not unknown to city officials. You are. If you bother us again, I'll personally swear out a warrant for your arrest. You'll find yourself in very serious trouble." She leaned forward. The gun was less than six inches from his nose. "Do you understand?"

His eyelids drooped. He raised them with difficulty. His lips barely moved. "Yes."

Straightening proudly, she tried to thrust the gun into her belt. The effect was ruined when she

144

found she wore none, and her skirt was torn loose from her waist. She contented herself with dropping it into Shreve's pocket and slipping her shoulder under his arm. "Let's go, sweetheart. We'll take it easy walking back to the hotel. Maybe we'll find a carriage."

He shook his head blearily. "Not much chance of that at this time of the night."

"Night?" She chuckled wearily. "It's almost morning. With any luck we'll meet a milk wagon."

As they turned out of the alley, Poteet strolled up to the porch. "Maybe so I better give you a help up the stairs."

De la Barca let loose a virulent stream of curses. He pulled a filthy handkerchief from his hip pocket and tied it around his thigh. "Where were you? You were supposed to be guarding the front door."

Poteet shrugged. "What you mean guard? I stand down at foot of stairs. If anyone come up or go down, I watch 'em. I come tell you if you don't know. That guard."

"Why the hell didn't you stop her when she ran out?" He cursed again as his thigh was jostled as he hoisted himself to his feet his arm around Poteet's bony shoulder.

"I don' put my hands on no woman," Poteet muttered. "No two ways about that. I don'."

By the time de la Barca reached the stairway, he was putting some weight on his leg, but the pain was building to a crescendo.

"You maybe luckier than any man I ever see," Poteet remarked. "Damn fool thing you do, shootin' off th' gun when you don' see where you's shootin'. You damn lucky you di'n' shoot off Long John."

They had reached de la Barca's smoke-filled room. His coat lay on the floor still smoldering.

Weak from pain, the investigator tried to concentrate on something else. "The man—"

"He bigger than I am, maybe more'n six inches. What I s'pose to do? He knock you down. Why you don' shoot him then?"

"My gun misfired."

"Ah-huh."

"Then it went off accidentally."

Poteet laughed as he kicked back the door. "It sure do that. Maybe why I never use no guns. Anyway, you di'n' give me no gun."

"Never mind." De la Barca sank down on the narrow cot, his forehead clammy. His voice was much weaker. His consciousness was failing, his sight growing dim. "Get a shirt from my grip and make a good job of this," he commanded weakly. "Then go for a doctor. It's liable to get infected if it's not sewn up."

"I know a good *houngan*. He sew cheaper than a doctor."

"A what?"

"*Houngan. Obeahman*. You don't know him. No. But if you got enemy with magic, he turn it away." Poteet looked significantly at the self-inflicted wound. "Look like you got plenty."

"Damn you. No. Get a doctor."

"He maybe real steep."

"Get me a doctor!"

"Yes, suh." Poteet pretended to bow and scrape and then ambled indolently from the room.

Left alone, de la Barca managed to pull the pillowcase off the pillow and clap it over the wound. Then he lay back with eyes closed, pain throbbing through him, his teeth set. On the back of his eyelids was the picture of Miranda Drummond, pointing his own pistol at him with never a waver.

She was the one—the murderer. He knew it. Her eyes had been chips of ice. Her grip on the pistol butt, practiced. He had detected no fear, no hesitation. Likewise, her body beneath her feminine clothing had been strong and hard.

Not like a woman's. His limited experience with actresses had shown him creatures unable to draw a deep breath. Their corsets cinched in a seventeen-inch waist between a huge overblown bosom and pillowy thighs.

No, this woman's figure was more like a boy's. More than likely she had been the young lieutenant carrying the mail pouch with orders from Washington. An ordinary actress would have little knowledge of such things, but an actress who had spent her childhood at forts on the frontier would know.

Miranda Drummond was the one. Likewise, he was certain she was a tool, willing to do the job because it offered her a chance to get back at the stepfather who had run her off from home. The only question was who had hired her? That would be the answer Butler would want.

De la Barca winced as a particularly brutal twinge wracked him. He fumbled in the nightstand. From the drawer he withdrew a flask. Uncorking it with his teeth, he poured a restorative swallow down his throat.

Lying back, he resigned himself to waiting. His last conscious thought—in the nature of a vow that made his lips twitch upward in a smile—was that this wound would give Miranda Drummond and her partner Shreve Catherwood only a short reprieve.

He must have slept or slid into a stupor induced by loss of blood. He jerked awake to throbbing pain in his leg and a foul stench in his nostrils. "What the hell—"

Above him hung a face so black that only the white kerchief tied around the head and the whites

147

of the staring eyes separated it from the darkness of the room.

Behind it hovered Poteet, who raised the smoking kerosene lamp and grinned. "I bring Thoby-Cajigas. He good *houngan*."

"No! I told you—"

"No doctor come here. Too dangerous. Too dark."

"No! I'll pay—" De la Barca tried to move away from the spider-fingered black hands that reached for his wound.

"Maybe you not have to pay Thoby-Cajigas so much. Maybe you give some more to me." Poteet's face retained the shape of the grin, but the eyes carried a warning.

"Damn you. Ow! Goddamn—"

The *houngan* drew a packet from somewhere in the folds of his clothing and laid it on the cot. The long spatulate fingers unfolded it carefully.

De la Barca tried to sit up, but his muscles had stiffened and the blood loss had weakened him. He fell back, staring into the darkness of the high ceiling. "Damn," he whispered. He tried to make a fist, but his hand was trembling with weakness so he could not hold it.

He fastened his eyes on Poteet. "You'll get your money," he promised. "You'll get whatever you want."

Poteet nodded happily. "Maybe so. Maybe so."

Miranda lay flat on her back on her side of the bed with a cold compress on her jaw and a warm cloth on her stomach. Shreve lay flat on his side with a cold cloth over his eyes.

Ada hovered over them both. "Jesus Christ preserve the two of you," she scolded. "You're both old enough to know better. And I'm getting too old to take care of cuts and bruises from street fighting."

"Ada, I'm sorry." Miranda sighed pathetically. "I know we're a lot of trouble."

"That you are. A terrible lot of trouble," the woman agreed, her voice quavering with hurt feelings. "And I'm letting you know about it, too. I'm a makeup artist and wardrobe mistress, not a nursemaid. I didn't sleep a wink all night for worry about you and I haven't had a bite of breakfast. Not even a cup of that muck they call coffee down here. I've been that busy taking care of you two."

"Whatever you do, Ada, you're wonderful." Shreve allowed the last word to trail off wearily. He lifted the compress to manage a weak smile.

"Oh, you." She slapped his shoulder with the tips of her fingers. "Each one is worse than the other. And don't try any of that soft-eyed, silver-tongued acting with me. Don't think I don't recognize those looks. Stock and trade. I've seen the shows a hundred times."

Miranda pushed herself up on her elbow, but Ada hurried around the bed and pushed her back. "Now don't try to move around. You've got a nasty bruise on your poor face. And inside—We just don't know. Something could be damaged. Just tell me whatever you want, dearie?"

"I was going to get up and let you go to breakfast. I can take care of Shreve. He's not doing anything but lying there anyway."

"I wouldn't hear of it." The wardrobe mistress pressed her gently back onto the pillow.

"Really, Ada," Miranda protested. "I want you to. I need something to eat. I haven't had a bite since early yesterday."

"Of course, I forgot. Just you lie back down and the two of you rest. I'll be back with something in a few minutes."

"For me, too." Shreve crossed his hands over his distinctly concave belly.

"Just send a cart up," Miranda insisted as she lay back. "Eat your breakfast and get George to check everything out at the theater."

Ada looked doubtfully from one to the other. Neither one looked able to move to the bathroom. But they would go on that evening. They never missed. She patted Miranda's hand. "I'll not be gone long."

The room was silent for several minutes. Finally, Miranda sighed and shifted gingerly. The warm cloth felt wonderful on the bruise the size and shape of a man's fist spreading over her ribs. A smaller one but just as purple was swelled out on her jaw. To look at them in the mirror had made her sick at her stomach.

How many things that had happened to her in the last twenty-four hours had made her sick at her stomach!

A tear trickled from the corner of her eye. Another followed and another. Ashamed of herself and desperate to conceal her weakness, she dabbed at them. Her efforts had the effect of making them flow faster. They would not stop. Her nose and throat were clogged with them. She gulped for breath.

"Are you crying?"

"No."

"You sound as if you are." His warm hand dropped comfortingly on her thigh, rubbing the stiff muscles.

"I'm sorry. I'm sorry. I'm so sorry." Each short sentence was punctuated by a sob.

"I know."

"I shouldn't be crying. I never cry."

"No, you never do."

She rolled over on her side away from him, let-

150

ting the pillow take her tears. "I never thought that any of this would happen. Benjamin Westfall could have gone on forever—if I'd had the slightest idea you were going to be hurt."

Shreve's warm hand slid over the curve of her body as she turned. Thoroughly exhausted, he remained stretched out on his back, the compress covering his eyes. His voice was warm, too, as he said softly, "Life is never like a play."

She made a snubbing sound.

He patted her with his fingers only, his palm sitting on her jutting hipbone. "In a play once the villains are routed, the heros and heroines go home. In real life villains come back to haunt you."

"But how could what happened in Wyoming follow us to New Orleans, especially when Westfall confessed?" she wailed.

In the voice of Hamlet's father, Shreve answered. "Some things are better if you leave them to heaven. How could a murder that Westfall did half a lifetime ago rise to confront him on the day of his greatest triumph?"

"Oh, Shreve—"

"For murder, though it have no tongue, will speak with most miraculous organ."

"I didn't murder. I executed," she insisted defiantly.

"Of course you did. And that's why the executioner wears a mask, so people won't know who he is."

They lay silent for a long time. She was wracked with guilt. He was wracked with pain behind his eyes. When he raised the compress, he could see nothing but distorted bands of light and color. The wild race through the streets, the struggle with de la Barca had set back his recovery. Yet he would not mention his condition to Miranda. She was feeling bad enough as it was.

Likewise, a sense of his own helplessness wracked him. He could not help her. She lay there beside him flaying herself. He would not add his problems to her woes. Better to lie perfectly still and let his body martial its forces.

He had almost succeeded in falling asleep when the cart arrived. Miranda attacked it with a good-will. He picked at his food.

Over the "muck" that New Orleans called coffee but which was mainly chicory, Miranda began to talk.

"Why didn't he have the police there to arrest me?"

Shreve shrugged. "I'm sure he was a detective. They aren't exactly welcomed by police departments. He probably wanted to question you himself." He looked significantly at her bruised jaw. "He couldn't hit you like that in front of law-enforcement officers in a genteel Southern city."

"He said something peculiar, just before I broke away from him and ran. He said people were paying him large sums of money to find out who was behind what I did." She looked inquiringly at Shreve.

He gave up any pretense of eating and leaned back in his chair. His expression was grave. "We may have stumbled into something that's bigger than both of us."

"What's that?"

He shrugged again. "Did you ever wonder why Benjamin Westfall, an officer who had to give up his command in disgrace, was appointed to such an important position?"

"The army's a place where favors are returned as a matter of routine. It's the way the game is played."

"But he'd been out of the game for over a decade. Surely there must have been other men who'd earned favors in the meantime."

Miranda wracked her brain. "I think his first wife was the daughter of a congressman or a senator. I can't remember which."

"But he'd been married for years to your mother. Surely that connection must have been broken."

"Not necessarily. If Westfall had kept up—"

Shreve interrupted her. "What if the congressman or senator had some dirty work that he wanted done?"

"I don't understand."

"Sure you do. Think about it a minute. What if the congressman or senator had a dirty job? What if he wanted a man that he knew would do it? A man who wouldn't hesitate to do anything dirty or underhanded to accomplish his task?"

Miranda's mouth formed a thoughtful O.

"Someone so ruthless that he would send a troop of men to their deaths to kill one of them. A man ruthless enough to imprison his own stepdaughter in a house of correction for wayward girls where she would probably die—"

"—or murder a Pinkerton detective—"

"—or set fire to a theater full of people."

They looked at each other in dawning horror. Shreve's mouth curled cynically. "You've put a very untimely period to someone's schemes."

She pushed her plate back, her appetite gone. "This is all so horrible. This can't be true." One elbow on the table, she massaged her forehead. A frightening thought occurred to her. "What if that man was a U.S. marshal or someone like that sent to find the man who shot Westfall?"

"Not a chance. U.S. marshals work with local police. That detective obviously didn't want anything to do with them. He kidnapped you and took you to a building so deep in the back alleys

153

that we got lost twice trying to walk back here. Why did he do that if he were on a legitimate assignment?"

"I see your point."

"He'd already hit you twice by the time I got there." Shreve reached across the narrow cart and caressed her jaw with his thumb. "Imagine what you would look like if I hadn't come."

She turned her cheek into his palm and kissed it. "I think that that black man would have done something."

Shreve shook his head. "Not a chance. He was on his way out. That's not the point. The point is that someone wanted information and didn't care how much you were hurt."

She tried another tack. "Why would anyone believe a conspiracy was involved? Almost ninety men died in that massacre. Most of them have families that are probably just as angry as I am."

"They may be angry, although I seriously doubt that. Most people accept the fact that soldiers get killed in battle. They grieve for a few weeks and then pick up their lives. Only someone like you"—he tapped a long index finger on the tip of her nose—"could sustain her desire for revenge."

She flushed. "I'm not so unusual."

He leaned back with a sad smile. "You're the most unusual woman I've ever met, and I've met a lot of women. You've had this thing in your head since you were a girl. You've never let go of it."

She rose and began to pace the floor, her arms wrapped tightly around her body. At last, she stopped and faced him. "Then this is worse than I thought. I've brought this down on all of us. And I don't have any idea how to fight it, or who to fight."

Shreve rose, too, and began to strip for his bath. "We won't fight it."

154

"No, *we* won't. But I will if I can figure out how."

He poured water into the basin at the washstand and dipped a washcloth into it. "I don't think that investigator will be a problem before our run is over here. Ten days from now we'll be on our way to Veracruz."

"But we've been asked to extend the run. You always book so we can extend." She stared at him aghast. He never refused to extend a run. Indeed, he frequently demanded extensions.

"We'll just tell him we can't extend this time. It'll be the best thing for us anyway. We're both exhausted. A Gulf cruise will be just the thing. We might take the long way to Veracruz, via Havana." He was smiling as he scrubbed his neck and chest.

"This is running away from the problem. We have to come home from Mexico and South America in the spring." She tilted her head to one side, watching him. She knew every inch of his lean, muscled body, but the sight of it never failed to thrill her. He was so beautiful, so very, very dear.

"We'll cross that bridge when we get to it." He handed her the cloth and stood while she washed his back between his shoulder blades. "My guess is that once we're out of the country and nothing happens, the person or persons who hired him will become convinced that there was no conspiracy. We'll come home and it'll all be forgotten."

"People have long memories." She draped the cloth over the edge of the basin.

He unfastened his trousers and tossed them over the back of the chair. "You have a long memory. Ordinary people will let our faces, disguised as they were, fade from their minds. They won't see us on the stage, recognize us, and come up and confront us next year. Think how, day after day, we pass unrecognized down the streets. If someone should appear after a year, we'll simply deny everything."

"Shreve." Her voice carried all her doubts, all her regrets. "I still think —"

"Enough. It's over." He kissed her swiftly on the mouth and sat down on the stool to bathe his feet and legs.

Act IV
Scene 2
Mexico City and
Veracruz, 1883

Nine

Ser, o nada ser?

Shreve Catherwood looped an arm through the ship's ratlines and stared morosely at the gray water of the Gulf. Huge waves lifted the *White Hound* and dropped her into deep troughs as she plowed along. "Remind me never to take an extended cruise during hurricane season."

Miranda clung beside him, hanging on with both hands stretched comfortably above her head. Both her feet rested in the lowest rungs as she rode the movements of the ship like a child on a merry-go-round. Her smile was broad. Her hair, left to fall straight down her back for the duration of the voyage, blew behind her. "It's more exciting this way."

"Not if you're sick."

"You were only sick the first day."

"I've never been sick before," he complained bitterly.

She did not answer for a minute. More lightning branched through the clouds. Thunder muttered far away. "I think it might have had something to do with your headaches," she said tentatively. "Maybe your sense of balance is a little off."

Refusing to discuss his headaches, he bent his arms over the railing and rested his chin on his fists. "I should have asked about the weather," he griped. "We could have gone by train."

The horizon behind them was black. The ship was literally running before the storm.

"I think it's exciting." She took a firmer grip and let the ship's slide into the next trough swing her sideways. A great splatter of rain fell on the deck.

"Time to go below." He threw his arm around her waist and took her weight to lower her to the deck. They swayed and staggered. He transferred his grip to lines strung along the deck.

"It's such a shame to hide in our cabin. We'll miss the best part," she complained. "Look there!" A flash of lightning, forked out of the cloud. Thunder rumbled and crashed in no more than a second. The wind rushed through her hair. She squinted as more huge drops of water dashed her cheeks.

"It looks like a bloody hurricane."

"It's only a squall. Nothing to be alarmed about."

Several seamen scrambled up the ratlines and began to reef in the big sails. They paid no attention to the oncoming storm. In a few minutes the canvas was tied down to the spar. From the lee of the cabin Miranda watched them. "They aren't concerned at all," she reported over her shoulder. "And the ship has stopped heeling over so far."

"Close the door and come away. The floor's getting wet."

She did as he told her. "You're feeling better."

He stretched out as much as the cramped bunk would allow and held out a pathetic hand in her direction. "I'm in the middle of the Gulf of Mexico in a hurricane. My clothing is damp and my stomach is going to be upset any minute. Why do you say I'm feeling better?"

"Poor boy." She took the hand and raised it to her breast where it did not lie trembling and limp but rather turned and cupped her, gently pinching her nipple. She smiled. "You're feeling just fine."

He rolled his head on the pillow and sighed. "Perhaps I did feel a bit better today. Until this storm blew up."

"You feel just fine. Right now." She had to raise her voice to be heard over the steady din of the rain. The ship continued to make headway as the wind drove it. Miranda shivered deliciously at the sound.

Shreve slid his hand off her breast and around her side exerting an insistent pressure. "Come hold me in the bunk."

"Now?"

"Now is a wonderful time." He pulled her down so that his lips brushed her ear. Before his eyes the gooseflesh rose on her forearm. "If these are my last minutes on earth, I want them to be spent in the arms of a beautiful woman."

She laughed and climbed in beside him, snuggling against him, wrapping her arms around him, pressing her face against his neck. Within the hour they were both in a sound healing sleep.

"I always wonder about the audiences," Ada mused as she set the white blond wig on Miranda's head. "What do they listen to when they can't understand the words?"

Miranda waved a hand toward Shreve. "I've wondered about that myself. I don't suppose all of those people speak much English. We certainly have to have translators when they come back after the show. Yet most of the plays in this theater are in English. And Shakespeare isn't just in English, it's in old English."

He grinned. "They enjoy the sight of you in your nightgown, my dear. And me in my tights with my doublet all undone."

His costar made a disgusted sound. "They have

161

actresses with better figures than mine. Of course, they don't have actors with better legs than yours," she hastened to add when he looked at her with eyebrow raised in mock disapproval.

"Mexico City is an old city with a new regime of young, uncertain people. The Porfiriatos want very badly to impress the world with their cosmopolitan society. They don't care what they come to see so much as who sees them. You know that. For our parts we speak slowly and distinctly—"

"And spend a lot of time in sword play and dumb shows," Miranda finished for him.

"Exactly." He rose and held out his arms for Ada to slip Hamlet's black doublet on over the black shirt. "Except that tonight I have a special treat for them. I'm reciting the soliloquy in Spanish."

Miranda raised an inquiring eyebrow. "How is it going to sound without iambic pentameter?"

"They don't know iambic pentameter. Most people don't know iambic pentameter. Sometimes I don't think Shakespeare really knew iambic pentameter. I tell you what it'll do. It'll bring 'em to their feet. I'll probably have to do an encore then and there."

With a grin as irrepressible as a boy's, he bent over, hands braced against the dressing table, and pretended to study his makeup in the mirror. There his expression sobered. A frown drew his eyebrows together. Each time he stood so, he prayed. Unknown to even his dearest friends, he tested the extent of his eyesight.

In New Orleans the dizziness and swirling vision had been acute. Now it scarcely lasted a minute. He was getting better just as the doctor had said he would. The voyage to Havana and then to Veracruz had been just what he needed. He smiled at himself in the mirror.

Behind him, where she could exchange a knowing glance with Miranda, Ada buckled on his foil.

Miranda smiled back at his image. "You're terrible. No one has to pay you a compliment. You pay them to yourself every hour on the hour."

He straightened with a deep breath that swelled his chest like a bellows. He brushed at an imaginary speck of lint on the shoulder of his velvet doublet and adjusted the lace over his wrist. "A man can't look in the mirror without ringing down calumny on his poor defenseless head." He strode to the door. "I'll see you on stage. Don't be late."

Miranda sprang to her feet and grasped Ada's hands. Struggling to suppress their excited exclamations, they nodded ecstatically to each other. "Did you see?" Miranda hissed. "He's better. He didn't seem to be dizzy at all."

"He wasn't. Not a bit of it," Ada agreed. "Oh, the poor boyo. He's suffered so. I could see it in his face every time I put the makeup on. And feel it in his skin. The muscles in his jaw were strutted, he was hurting so bad. But he'd always try to smile."

"He'll keep acting that he's alive when he's been dead half a day," Miranda prophesied joyously. "I can't believe how well he looks. If you could have seen him that night in New Orleans. He was trying so hard to fight that investigator and he didn't have the strength of a child."

She shuddered. "And he launched himself right into the face of that pistol. I'm not worthy of that kind of love and sacrifice."

"Tush, now, dearie. Don't be humbling yourself. Shreve does what he does because it's in him to do it. No more, no less."

"If you could have seen him. He was a hairsbreadth from dying."

"A bad case of pride has my boy Shrevey," Ada mourned. She clasped her hand against her cheek. "He figures if he doesn't believe that a bad thing is about to be happening, it won't. You put adversity in his way, and he thinks that you're challenging him. It's what makes him a cut above the rest."

Miranda could feel chill bumps break out on her arms. Ada still had a great voice. She could deliver the most ordinary speech as if it were gospel. All her love and loyalty rang in her estimate of Shreve Catherwood.

"And it's what makes him able to stand on that stage before an audience that doesn't understand half of what he's saying and make them believe it."

Ada grinned then and shook herself free of her own spell. She gathered up Ophelia's outer dress, a rose velvet that slipped over the frilled nightgown. "Here, now, dearie. Put your arms through this and let me lace it up. Otherwise, you will be late for your entrance."

Shreve had had the curule chair moved down stage right. In the manner of Edwin Booth, he slumped back against one end of it and draped his arm languidly over the other. A dagger dangled from his fingers. Fixing his gaze in the middle distance, he drew his voice from deep out of his chest. *"Ser, o nada ser?"*

The audience as one collective body sat up in their seats. A few exchanged glances of appreciation. The tension grew in the house, as his noble voice rolled through a soliloquy that might have been written by a Spaniard, so nearly were the sentiments part of the dark Spanish character.

When he finished, stunned silence reigned. Then they rose to their feet, applauding wildly.

Smiling, Miranda held up her entrance while he rose in the manner of a man awaking from a dream as if the speech had somehow been his own. He bowed simply, without a flourish or a show of leg.

"Otra vez! Otra vez!" they shouted. The tragic

contemplation and rejection of suicide had spoken to the Spanish soul. They wanted, they demanded to hear it again.

The lights from the wings gilded Shreve's face. He was brilliant. He was magnetic, he was unchallengeable. He shone. With another bow of utmost humility, arms at his sides, eyes downcast, he resumed his place and repeated the speech, letter perfect, with excellent accent.

At the end, he switched to English. *"Soft you now! The fair Ophelia!"*

Miranda entered stage right with all her love in her eyes.

The green room was filled with people, richly dressed in the Spanish style, black suits with stiffly tied white cravats, black lace mantillas flowing over black silk dresses, gleaming gold watch fobs, and towering tortoiseshell combs.

A translator stood at Shreve's side and at Miranda's pronouncing the effusive compliments in English and answering in Spanish. He introduced Ignacio Vallarta, the minister of Foreign Relations in El Presidente Porfirio Diaz's cabinet. The young man bowed low over Miranda's hand.

In good English, he said, "I shall speak to El Presidente Diaz himself. He has little time for entertainment, but he must come to see and hear this. Never before has Mexico been graced with such a performance."

"You must pay your compliments to my partner," she replied, certain that Shreve was leaning in their direction taking it all in. "He is the one who deserves them. He took the trouble to have the speech translated into Spanish and learn it for your pleasure."

"He marks the beginning of our new international culture. His performance is a compliment to us all."

165

She gave him her most dazzling smile. "The audience was most appreciative and enthusiastic. We rose to greater heights for them."

"*Madonna.*" Vallarta bent over her hand with special fervency.

Through it all, though their hands were bruised and their feet ached, Shreve and Miranda stood. Finally, the last person moved away. Though the room was still crowded, the early arrivals had gone. Miranda leaned toward Shreve. "I'm going to try to get out of here for a minute. I need to find a bathroom before I have an accident."

"I'll keep up a front, but don't be too long. I'm in a bad way myself."

Smiling, nodding, she made her way out into the hallway.

Lifting her skirts, she hurried down the dark hallway. Suddenly, a man's figure limped out to bar her way. Her scream of horror was cut off as he lunged forward clapping a hand over her mouth. His weight carried her back against the wall of the narrow passageway. Before she could struggle, she was effectively penned by the weight of his body. "Don't make a sound," he hissed. "Don't move or I'll hurt you."

Her eyes were enormous over his hard hand as she recognized her tormentor. De la Barca! The man who had kidnapped her in New Orleans!

For an instant she went weak with shock. How had he gotten here? By what right had he followed them beyond the boundaries of the United States? But he had manhandled her, kidnapped her, struck her with his fists. The border of Mexico would not stop him. Viciously, she kicked at his legs. Coolly, he sliced at her legs with his cane. It ripped through her skirt. She twisted and scratched at his hands, screaming. But his hand muffled all but the faintest sound.

How could they struggle so violently without

166

someone in that room full of people hearing and coming to her aid?

At that instant a couple came out of the door. Light spilled into the darkness. She freed an arm, waving it frantically, but the man was holding a cloak for the woman, their heads were close. Talking excitedly, they hurried away toward the stage door without glancing at what might be happening just a few short yards away. Eyes wide with frustration and fear, she watched them go. All that came past his hard hand was a faint whimpering.

"If anyone looks, they'll think we're lovers," he sneered. His mouth was so close to her ear that she could feel the hairs of his mustache. His teeth grazed her lobe. To her horror he took it between his teeth and bit down.

Pain shot through her. She bucked up, but he was braced so she was caught in a vise.

"See! It won't do any good. I bit your ear so you'll know that I'll do what I say. Now you're bleeding." He licked his lip.

She could hear him swallow her blood. Nausea rolled in her. A warm trickle slid down her neck. For just an instant she went limp.

He chuckled, an evil sound. "Now listen to what I say. You're going back to the States with me. To Washington. There's a man who's real upset about what you've done to his plans." He leaned heavily on her. "Now, I'm going to take my hand away from your mouth and you're going to answer me in a real soft voice. If you try to scream, I'll hit you so hard, you'll never be able to cover it up." He moved his hand.

She did not scream. Instead she bit. Bit down with all her strength.

It was he who howled.

She bucked forward, planted both feet against the wall behind her, and thrust her whole body against his.

167

Down they went in a heap of thrashing limbs. She drove her forearms under his chin, so his head struck the floor with a satisfying thunk. He merely grunted before his hard hands closed over her shoulders. He rolled over on top of her. She tried to knee him in the groin, but his weight was too much.

His voice spoke again in her ear. "How much do you care about that actor?"

His weight on her chest had driven the breath from her lungs. She could not have struggled even a minute longer, but at the mention of Shreve, she went limp.

He shifted and grunted again.

The movement of his body ground her spine against the floor. She groaned.

"Not a sound," he reminded her. "Not a sound. Now listen to me. You like that pretty man. What about that sweet old lady that does your hair? And the old gent that handles all the money? What's his name? George Wisdom."

"Windom," she corrected dully.

"Right. Windom. He carries a lot of money around with him sometimes. Like tonight. That's real temptation to thieves. Someone could knock him in the head and the federales would think he'd been robbed."

"Let me up."

He pressed her harder, grinding his hips. His teeth closed over the lobe of her other ear.

"I swear I'll scream if you bite me again," she promised, the words tripping over one another.

He drew back with what might have been a chuckle. "Just wanted to make it a pair."

"Get off."

She could feel him shrug. Then he pushed up, awkwardly with both hands, and got his knee under him. Instantly, she scrambled out from under him and sprang to her feet. With a hint of satisfac-

168

tion, she watched him maneuver himself to rise. The wound in his thigh must have been very serious. She hoped it still gave him a lot of pain. Finally, he stood erect.

Breathing heavily, they faced each other, eyes glinting in the dim light, perspiration glistening on their faces. He pointed a stubby finger at her. "You're going back to Washington with me."

She stepped back out of his reach. "I have obligations. I can't just pick up and leave."

"You don't get it," he growled. "I could pick you up and take you right now."

"You'd never make it to the edge of the city," she contradicted him. "Didn't you hear the crowd tonight? Didn't you see those people?" She gestured toward the green room as more people came out. One man glanced in their direction, recognized her, inclined his head in respectful salute. "The minister of Foreign Relations was in the audience."

For the first time he took his eyes off her to throw a quick glance over his shoulder.

She pushed her advantage. "I think you'd better contact your superior in Washington. He won't thank you for creating problems for him here."

De la Barca swung his head back toward her. "You—You—"

She adjusted the shoulders of her dress and lifted her head regally. "I was on my way to my dressing room to fetch a souvenir fan for the minister's wife. You'd better not be here when I come back."

Behind her she heard him. "You're going to be sorry. You're coming with me to Washington."

"No," she said clearly over her shoulder. "No. I'm not." With that she darted into the bathroom, slammed the door, and locked it. Then she allowed her weak legs to let her slide down the door until she sat on the cool *azulejos* tiles. For a minute the fact that they were none too clean bothered her not

169

at all. She only wanted the blessing of coolness in the silent darkness. She was shaking so badly, she could not have moved had she tried.

Her body ached from the struggle. Her fingertips found the side of her neck and traced a sticky trail up to her stinging earlobe. Her quick intake of breath was a snubbing sound.

Monster!

The tears began to trickle silently down her cheeks. She should not be crying. She should not. She had faced him down. Called his bluff. Sent him on his way. She had bruises, her dress was torn, and she needed to go to the bathroom, but she had won.

But still the tears came.

She must get up and tend to her business and get to the dressing room. Ada would be waiting for her, or Shreve would come. She would tell them what happened. Warn them to be careful.

What if they were somehow hurt, here in Mexico, thousands of miles away from the scene of her vengeance? She was responsible for their danger. Was there no end? No end?

The tears no longer coursed silently. Full-throated sobs wrenched themselves out of her throat. Was this why God warned against man taking vengeance, because only God could handle the consequences?

Shreve found her sitting at the dressing table her back to the mirror. "Miranda!"

She turned her head away as he went down on his knees. The sight of her mutilated ear rocked him back on his heels. "My God. What the hell happened to you?"

"Oh, Shreve."

He caught her hands. "Were you raped? Who did this?"

170

She shook her head. "No. I wasn't raped." She allowed him to turn her face to the light. When their eyes met, she told him. "It was de la Barca."

At first he did not recall the name. Then his face changed. Anger changed to a sort of awful resignation. "I'm going to have to kill him."

"No. I'll kill him if anyone does."

"No one can treat you this way. I'll call him out."

"You can't do that."

"The hell I can't!" He sprang to his feet so fast that his vision swirled and blackened. He took a stagger-step to the right and clapped his hand against the wall as if he were venting his anger.

She was not deceived. "How will you do it when you can't stand on your feet?" The minute she uttered the words, she wished she could take them back.

Shreve's anger erupted in a vicious imprecation. "There's not a thing wrong with me."

"I didn't—" She stopped. Better to try to change the subject than argue. She raised a trembling hand to her forehead. "Shreve—"

"Do you think I'm not capable of taking care of you?"

"Of course not, but what I'm trying to tell you is that I talked the man out of doing anything."

"Did you do that before or after he beat you bloody?"

"During actually." She covered her ear. "I reminded him that he was in a foreign country and that we had friends in high places. I told him whoever hired him wouldn't appreciate an international embarrassment." She smiled winningly. "You would have been so proud of me. I gave the performance of my life."

"You fool. You don't seem to understand that it was the performance of your life." He came back across the room still scowling. She made no effort

171

to stop him when he pushed her dress off the shoulders. Darkening bruises stood out lividly against her white skin. He swallowed. When he found his voice, it was dark with promise. "I'm going to kill him."

She caught his hands. "You'll do nothing of the sort."

He closed his mouth like a steel trap.

With some effort she pulled her aching body to her feet. Her blue eyes shimmered with tears as she lifted his hands to her lips and kissed them. Then holding them between her own, she began. "I made a dreadful mistake, Shreve. I don't know how to correct it. I don't know how it will end. But it's not over yet. I haven't finished paying for it, but I have to be the one to pay for it."

"Miranda, sweetheart—"

"No, listen. Let me explain. I've brought you and Ada and George into danger. He threatened you."

"I'll kill him."

"No. He wants me. He doesn't want you. He doesn't care about you and George. He's not a lawman. He's something else." She shuddered. "He's something evil."

"Then nobody will miss him."

"Yes, they will. Somebody sent de la Barca. And if you kill him, whoever sent him will just send somebody else. Because my vengeance has started a chain reaction that's working against us all."

His heart turned over at the expression on her face. The weight of guilt had borne her down. Tears had streaked her makeup. Her eyes were swollen. The streak of blood had dried beneath her ear. She looked old and tired.

With a start, he realized she was thirty years old. When had she grown into a woman?

He took her hand and led her to the couch. "Miranda. I can take care of this."

"Shreve. I want you to know that I would give

172

everything that I possess if I had just listened to you. Back in Chicago you told me. You warned me. You did everything you could to keep me from going through with that awful thing. If I had listened to you—"

"You had more than personal reasons," he reminded her loyally.

"Did I really punish the guilty and protect the innocent?" she mused cynically. "Somehow I doubt that."

He pulled her into his arms and kissed her passionately again and again. "Don't hurt yourself," he begged. "Don't flay yourself alive."

She buried her face in his chest. "I should be flayed. But that won't do any good. Once these things are set in motion, nothing can stop them."

"Then you really couldn't have avoided it," he told her logically.

She raised drowned eyes to him. "Please take me home, love. I don't think I can take much more. When I've rested, I'll think about what to do. For now, please don't think about doing anything to him. He'll contact me again. Perhaps in a civilized manner. Maybe I can find out what he really wants."

"I'll take you back to the hotel," Shreve agreed sympathetically. "A good night's sleep will make everything seem better."

Ten

In all his dressings, characts, titles, forms,
Be an arch-villain.

"I'm beginning to gain weight," Shreve noted with a disgusted sigh. He stood sideways to the mirror, his belly sucked in, his chest swelled.

"I don't think it's noticeable," Miranda remarked tactfully.

He shot her an irritated glance. "Of course it's noticeable. I notice it."

"The audience—"

"I know what's happening," he interrupted. "And once it starts it gets out of hand in a hurry. It's all that rich food."

She smiled. "Being the beginning of Mexico's new culture carries with it some sacrifices."

He grinned then before he fixed her with a disapproving stare. "Such as being whirled around the ballroom pressed against the dress sashes of all the members of the cabinet."

She batted her eyelashes and made a show of rubbing her rib cage just below her right breast. "The sashes are no problem. Silk taffeta is smooth and slippery. It's the medals and stars of orders that are hard going."

He returned to his study. "I think I'll cut out

desserts and take a brisk walk every evening. Perhaps I'll walk to the theater."

"In this heat?"

He shrugged. "No worse than the gaslights behind the proscenium and in the foots. A healthy sweat will always take the weight off."

"You'll pass out and miss your entrance. We'll have to come and find you," she predicted.

"Nonsense." He slipped his waistcoat on and buttoned it. The material puckered a bit, but only a tiny bit. He sighed again and tugged the points down over his middle. "I've never missed an entrance yet. Besides, I'm in perfect health."

She smiled lovingly. "You really are, aren't you?" She came to caress his temple with her thumb. "No more headaches?"

"Not even a memory."

She held his coat for him to slip his arms through. "No more blackouts. No more dizzy spells."

"I'm solid as a rock."

She put her arms around his waist and rested her cheek against the back of his shoulder. "I'm so glad."

He accepted her caress with good humor. "Power is wonderful. I see why it's so addictive. A word in the right ear and Frank de la Barca disappears."

"He may be out of sight, but I can't forget his threats."

"He's just a street tough. I couldn't believe my eyes when he accosted us in front of the theater in broad daylight." Shreve shook his head. "What did he expect me to do? Pat you on the fanny and pass you over to him?"

She shivered. "You got so mad I thought you were going to kill him."

Shreve checked his appearance in the mirror one more time. "I would have, but I took one look at

175

the situation and realized that the police could handle him for us."

"A good choice," she said dryly. "He looks solid even if he is shorter than you."

He grinned at her. "I'm above getting into a brawl."

She nodded, smiling inwardly. Shreve would always be the consummate actor conceiving the grand gesture but whenever possible avoiding the action of real life. In the theater he was a hero. Off stage, he was a wily negotiator.

"I just hope he's gone."

Shreve tilted his hat at a gallant angle atop his head and smoothed the carefully combed hair back from his temples. "Wish me success. I'm off to meet with George and the theater manager. De Guzman isn't offering nearly enough to extend the run. Especially since we constitute the beginnings of a new cultural era for Mexico."

"You're so clever. You'll get whatever we want." She poured herself another cup of chocolate and returned to studying her lines. Ophelia's mad scene had been translated into Spanish for her. She intended to garner her own share of applause tonight. Her performance could very well draw return audiences. Certainly, Vallarta would return to hear her.

Shreve bent over. She lifted her face to receive his kiss. Their eyes met and held for a long moment. "When we get this run behind us," he promised solemnly, "I have something to ask you."

She dropped her eyes in confusion. "I—Don't be late."

"No." He squeezed her shoulder and left.

She sat for a moment staring into space. Her heart thudded in her chest. How could she refuse him? And yet how could she accept him when this cloud still hung over her? If she were a decent person, if she cared about her friends at all, she would disappear. The thought made her stomach clinch. She should leave him and Ada and George. They were constantly being inconvenienced because of her. They had been in danger. They had lost money, canceled a booking, and turned down a chance to extend a run. Worst of all, Shreve had almost died.

She knew why she stayed. She loved Shreve Catherwood. Loved the man who had seduced her and bullied her—and made her a famous actress. From the first time Romeo had smiled at her from that stage, she had loved him.

She squeezed the bridge of her nose between her thumb and third finger. She would not cry. She would put these thoughts aside and study Ophelia. For the first time she felt a certain kinship for the pathetic creature. *"Lord, we know what we are, but know not what we may be."*

From the other side of the *avenida,* de la Barca lifted his cane toward two men loitering in an alleyway. Dressed in peasant garb, they looked like simple farmers rather than *soldados* of the rebellious Madero party. At his signal, they took up positions with their backs to the wall.

Dusk was falling, the hot, still day giving way to a warm night.

Shreve Catherwood walked briskly toward the theater. The last night of their extended performance had arrived all too soon. The applause, the praise, the reviews in the Mexican newspapers had combined to make an engagement to dream of.

Never in his memory had *Hamlet* been so well received. Five major speeches had been translated. Other actors had learned some of their lines in Spanish. Members of the audience had returned as

177

many as five times to hear the new additions. One night Porfirio Diaz and his entire cabinet had filled the presidential box.

Next year he and Miranda would play a return engagement with *Macbeth*. The contracts had already been signed. He had promised to work with a translator who would do all the major speeches of the thane and his villainous lady.

He was looking forward to a triumph in Rio de Janeiro next month and Buenos Aires the month after. The fact that Portuguese was the language of Brazil bothered him not at all. He would work with a translator when he arrived there. He could foresee a tour of Spain. His billing as the romantic star of three continents would be a reality. He would be able to demand and get huge fees for his performances.

His train of thought was not interrupted by a flurry of footsteps as he passed the alley. Then rough hands grabbed him and jerked him into its relative darkness. "What the hell—!"

"Silencio!" The word punctuated a blow to the pit of his stomach. He doubled over clutching at his middle. His assailant grasped one wrist and grappled for the other one.

Fighting off the paralyzing blow, Shreve pivoted, cursing. His attacker tried to twist the imprisoned arm up, but Shreve moved too fast. Dropping onto one knee, he dragged the would-be captor over his shoulder and into the chest of the one who had hit him.

The agony in his solar plexus was still making him want to retch, but he lunged to his feet, his legs like water under him, and staggered around the two flailing bodies. The space in the alley was too narrow, and he was too slow. An arm locked around his ankle and tripped him. He fell on his face but rolled over and kicked viciously. His attacker yelped as Shreve's heel crushed and scraped at his fingers.

"Help! *Socorro!*" Shreve yelled. "Help! Damn!" The high walls were trapping the sound, so that it echoed back on itself.

He scrambled backward with all his strength, dragging the assailant who held on tenacious as a bulldog. If he could just get out of the damned alley, passersby would see the struggle and come to his aid.

The man whom he had thrown rolled off the first and climbed to his feet. He launched himself at Shreve, who met him with his free leg, punching his boot into the man's stomach. With a grunt and an expulsion of breath, the attacker went sailing back across the alley.

Shreve kicked again, now at the face of the man who was crawling hand over hand up his leg. A couple of feet, inches really, and he would break out into the street. He hit the climber's nose with his heel. The man yelped and let go with one hand.

Shreve twisted free, rolled over to lunge upward.

Legs in black wool trousers barred his way. He looked up with a smile of relief into the face of Frank de la Barca.

The investigator's impassivity never faltered. The gold-headed cane rose and slashed down on Shreve's temple. The blow drove the actor against the wall of the alley. Stunned, but still conscious, pain like a knife shooting through his temple, he clawed at the rough limestone.

Single-minded, he staggered on his knees, reaching for the light that was the street beyond.

Stolidly, de la Barca stepped after him, raised his cane again, and brought it thudding down at the base of Shreve's skull.

Ada Cocks twisted a handkerchief in her hands. Tears trickled down her cheeks as she appealed to the other two. "He'd never be late if he could help it. He never would. Something's happened."

Miranda could feel her own control cracking. She clinched her fists at her sides as she turned to George. "You'd better check the streets again. And the hospital." Ada did not quite stifle a sob. "I'm afraid he's had an accident."

"There, there, old girl." George patted Ada's shoulder. To Miranda he said, "I'll do it, but I don't think we'll know anything more."

Miranda shuddered. "Then take the stage doorman with you. He speaks Spanish and English. He can ask the questions and translate the answers. There's probably some place we haven't tried."

De Guzman mopped at the perspiration trickling down his face. "What shall I tell the audience?"

Miranda could have screamed at the man. Wasn't he the theater manager after all? Instead she replied patiently. "What about the understudy?"

De Guzman gave a frantic squeak. "He didn't even come in tonight. I told him—That is, he's never been needed."

"Laertes?"

"Laertes? *Quién es?* Who?"

She rolled her eyes in exasperation. "The actor who plays Laertes. He should know Hamlet's lines."

"I'll ask him." The man rushed away.

Ada rested her forehead in her hand. "Oh, Shrevey-boy, where are ye? Where are ye?"

"Ada." Miranda dropped to her knees in front of her friend. Ada's face was paper white, its cheeks sagging pathetically. Looking up at her, Miranda realized that Ada, like Shreve, had grown old. She took the trembling hands. "Ada, I'm sure everything will be all right. Shreve is tough."

Ada shook her head. Her Irish brogue thickened as her grief stripped her of her training. "Oh, the poor boyo. He's not tough. He's gentle as a spring lamb. Surely, ye know that now. You're the tough one. He's not nearly the man ye are. Away from the stage he's just a boy."

"But, Ada—"

"Sure, dearie, an' he'd do anything ye asked of him. Don't ye know that now? He loves ye. Oh, he loves ye so much." She put her soft hand on Miranda's cheek.

The theater manager rushed through the door. "He can do it. We'll set up prompters in the wings. *Señora,* will you assist him?"

Miranda shivered. "In every way I can." He started away; she called after him. "You must send for the police. They must search for *El Señor* Catherwood."

"*Sí,* you are right. Something bad has happened."

When he had closed the door, Miranda dropped down in front of the mirror. The sight of her own face shocked her. She had lost all her color and her eyes were swollen and red. She had been crying without knowing she did so. "Ada, you'll have to help me."

The older woman raised her head. She nodded as she wiped the tears from her cheeks. "Ye'll have to be going on without him?"

"It's what he would want. You know that."

"Aye, he would." Ada rose and tottered to the dressing table. She steadied herself against the chair back. "If some rapscallion tried to rob him, he got nothing for his trouble. The boyo never carries any money. Oh, if he's been knocked in the head—murdered—for a pocket full of these worthless pesos—"

181

Miranda's hands were trembling so hard that she could not lift the comb. "I'm afraid to think. Maybe it isn't what I think might have happened. But if it is, we'll know very soon."

Shreve awoke to pounding pain and darkness, darkness so impenetrable that he knew he must be in a dungeon or some sort of underground cellar. He listened, but heard nothing. He took a slow, careful breath. The air was stifling hot but not particularly stale nor fetid.

His hands lay at his sides unbound. His fingertips tested the surface beneath him. Cloth—rough wool by the greasy prickle of it. By the rank odor of it. He closed his eyes since they were useless to him and worked his hands crabwise. Almost immediately they encountered the edges of the pallet on which he lay. His right touched a wall; his left, dropped away into space. A cot. He lay on a cot.

He had investigated as much of his prison as he could without moving. He had to sit up. The first movement of his head unleashed claws of pain that pulled him back into unconsciousness.

"We have instituted a general search." Ignacio Vallarta's voice shook with anger. "That such a thing should have happened on the streets of Mexico City. To one who has brought so much to her people. It is infamous."

"I'm certain the man you want is Frank de la Barca," Miranda told him. "He would have taken Shreve to a boarding house in the very poorest part of the city. Someplace where he could t-torture—" Her voice broke. She could not finish her sentence.

"My dear lady." Vallarta put her hand on her shoulder. "We will find him. This I promise you.

For now allow my soldiers to escort you back to the hotel."

From out of the darkness came a voice. Some-one turned his head roughly from side to side, slapped him. Slapped him again. He opened his eyes. But the darkness was the same. How could anyone see to hit him in such blackness?
"Wake up!"
He managed the word "No" through dry lips before oblivion dragged him down again.

"No word, George?"
"No, ma'am."
"Is Ada asleep?"
He hesitated. "I really don't think so, ma'am. The Irish take their grieving and worrying very seriously. I think she's just turned herself inward."
Miranda pressed her hand against her forehead. "Why haven't we heard something? Oh, God. Suppose Shreve fought de la Barca and de la Barca hurt him. K-killed him."
"Don't say it, ma'am. He wouldn't be any use to him dead. It really hasn't been so very long."
"Twelve hours, George. Twelve hours is a long time."

The third time the pain did not seem quite so bad.
"You will sit up and write for me." The voice was vaguely familiar, but he could not place its owner. He batted at the sound.
" 'Sit up,' I said. Here."
Shreve felt himself pulled around and straightened up. His legs were dragged over the edge of

a bed. A short stick was shoved into his hand. "Write."

"Light a lamp," he croaked. He licked his dry lips.

A moment's silence. A palm slapped down on a table. Paper crackled. " 'Write!' I tell you."

Nausea was roiling up in him. In a minute he was going to be violently ill. "I'm about to be sick," he informed his tormentor. "And anyway I can't write anything in the dark."

He felt the faintest of breezes slide by his face. A muttered exclamation. The scrape of a match. Heat close to his face. He could see nothing. Heat very close to his eyeballs. His eyes were open, but he could see nothing.

He sucked in his breath as horror washed over him. Purposely, he blinked rapidly. Despite the fierce pain, he rubbed at his eyes. Massaged his temples. Looked again.

"The light's on, isn't it?" he asked.

No one answered. The pen was taken out of his hand, he was pushed back onto the cot again. He could hear paper being crumpled. Footsteps limped across the floor. A door opened and closed.

He lay in silence for a long time. He did not know exactly when the tears started. Trickling down his temples onto the pad beneath him. He lifted his hand to his face. The center of his palm touched his nose. He could see nothing. Nothing at all. His head began to pound.

The doctor in New Orleans had talked about swelling. The blow to his temple. He touched it, found the long welt, traced the dried blood that streaked down his face. He had been struck a terrific blow. Perhaps if he could sleep for a few hours —

* * *

"No sign of him, *señora*." The doorman shook his head apologetically.

"He can't have been whisked off the face of the earth." She pressed her fist against her mouth. "George, what do the police say?"

The old actor exchanged a look with the doorman before he shrugged. "That they've looked all along the route. They didn't find a thing."

"They can't have looked very hard. Wait outside for me." Even before the doorman was out of the dressing room, she had whisked behind the screen. There she stepped into men's breeches, boots, a shirt, and coat. Her hair was not so long that it needed to be tucked up. She set a hat upon it and turned to George. "Let's go."

"Now, Miranda, where can you look that the police haven't already done?"

"Lots of places." From the drawer of the dressing table, she pulled a pistol. With practiced hands she loaded it. Giving George a tight smile, she slid it into the pocket of her coat. "Lots and lots of places. And the most important thing is that I won't give up until I find him. And that will make the difference."

He must not lie here any longer. He needed water. He needed a bathroom. Mostly, he needed to escape. De la Barca had undoubtedly kidnapped him to use him as a hostage to get Miranda. He needed to get to her.

Steeling himself to withstand the pain, he dropped one leg over the edge of the cot. Holding his groans between clinched teeth, he slid the other leg over and let its weight level him up.

While he sat there, sick to his stomach, reeling with dizziness, he concentrated on checking his clothing. Everything seemed to be in place. Even his money was still in his breast pocket.

Gradually the pain eased and he leaned forward, feeling cautiously in front of him. As he had expected, a small table stood only an arm's length away. De la Garza must have had some place to lay the piece of paper that he wanted written.

With a wide sweep of his arm, Shreve found that the cot was in the corner of a room. The door must be directly opposite, if his hearing and memory were still serving him. Placing his hand on the wall at the head of the bed, he rose and leaned painfully against it. When his head stopped reeling, he shuffled along until he came to an obstacle.

A washstand, his fingers told him. He edged past it and then found the wall again. Slowly, his senses throbbing with the pain in his head, he found the jamb of the door, and then the knob.

His hand trembled. His fingers closed around it, tightened in a death grip. He was afraid to step outside. *Makes us rather bear those ills we have than fly to others that we know not of.* Hamlet — or rather Shakespeare — knew what he was talking about.

Deliberately he turned the knob. It opened with a clear grating sound. de la Barca had not bothered to lock his blind captive in. He took a deep breath and stepped through.

His terror became extreme. He did not know where he stood. In another room? In a hallway? If, as he suspected, he were in a sleazy hotel room like the one where de la Barca had taken Miranda in New Orleans, then was he on the first or the second floor? And where was this room in relationship to the hallway? To the stairs?

He could very well kill himself falling down stairs. A kind of desperate anger struck him. At least it would be a quick clean death. No pitiful, feeble meanderings.

Outstretching his arms before his waist, he pat-

186

ted the floor tentatively in front of him with his foot. He took a step and repeated the process. A third and a fourth time and he had come up against another wall. At least he had found he was in a hall. If he kept his arms outstretched, he could touch both sides of it at the same time. As he had guessed, his prison was a cheap hotel or boarding house with narrow passageways.

One side of the wall was hotter than the other. It must be an exterior wall, he reasoned. Perhaps he was closer to getting outside than he thought. A thrill of fear shot through him. He would be outside before he knew it — and then what? At least with walls he could feel his way in a certain direction. Without walls, he could wander aimlessly. He wanted to scream, to weep, to curse. A good choice. He spat a curse from between his teeth.

He passed another room on the same side of the hall as the one he had left. The rooms were very close together. The hall could be very long. He tried to relax the muscles in his neck and back. His head was pounding so hard, he might be in danger of passing out.

He thought about his lack of facility with Spanish. He could barely ask for a drink of water. When he met someone, how could he make that person understand where he needed to go? *Por favor, I need to go — take me to —* He didn't know enough words.

Still he kept walking. Suddenly, his fingers found a corner. Had he come to the head of the stairs, or was the hallway merely turning. Swallowing nausea, he placed both hands on the corner and followed it down.

A newel post! He tapped one toe along the edge of a stair. A strained smile curved his mouth. So far so good. Accomplishments were measured in inches. Or in this case thirteen steps. His hand found the post at the bottom. His toe discovered a flat floor beyond.

"*Señor?*" a woman's voice inquired.

He turned in her direction. "*Sí!*"

"*A dónde va?*"

He took a deep breath. "*Voy a el teatro.*" He felt very proud of himself. He had spoken a sentence. Even if it was grammatically incorrect, it was understandable.

"*El teatro?*" Was there a suggestion of laughter in her voice.

"*Sí! Soy un* actor." Damn! He could not remember the word for his profession. He held out his hand toward the voice. "*Por favor, señora. Socorro.*"

Another woman's voice answered. Her hands closed around his arm. She tried to turn him around. "You—are—sick, *señor.*" Each word was separated as if she did not know English well. "*Vamos*—we go back to bed."

He pulled away. "No. I must go to the—er—El Teatro Real." He swung his head toward where the other woman had been. "Please. *Por favor.*"

"No, *Señor* Catherwood. You will not—"

She knew his name. She must be hired by de la Barca. This time he caught her wrist. "Get me out in the street, *señora,* or I'll break your arm."

She screamed and struck at his face. The pain was worse than anything he could have imagined, but he managed to push her around and twist her arm behind her back. Suddenly, the room was full of women's voices, chattering in Spanish. A couple of them pulled at his coat.

"Get back! I'll break her arm!" he shouted.

His captive screamed and chattered at them in Spanish. The heavy odors of perfume and women's bodies assailed him powerfully. A brothel. He must be in a brothel.

188

His voice was hoarse, but it was still strong. Stronger than any of theirs. *"Silencio!"*

The chattering stopped instantly. The woman he held stopped screaming and trying to get away. But rather than ease his grip on her arm, he tightened it. "I have — *Tengo* — er — money — *dinero.*" He thought carefully. His eyes strained to see, to pierce the blackness. How could he judge the effect of what he was saying? "I — *yo* — will pay — pay — one hundred — *cien* — pesos. No! *Cien* dollars. American. To anyone who will take me to El Teatro Real."

A storm of Spanish rose around him, spoken so rapidly that he could not separate a single word. Women argued, chattered. His head pounded. The woman he held began to push violently against the others, slapping at them. *"No. Vamos! Vamos!"*

Finally, they became quiet.

His captive spoke again. He could feel as well as hear her panting. "You pay one hundred Yankee dollars?"

"My business manager will pay you at the stage door."

"Pero el otro — the man who brought you said he would pay for two nights. He promised *más.*"

"Has he already paid you?" Suddenly, the performance was everything. Shreve laughed, and the pain lanced through his head. "I'll bet he hasn't paid."

"He paid," came the sullen reply.

"Not one hundred dollars."

"He pay more to keep you."

"He's gone. *Vamos.* He doesn't want me anymore. *No quiere.* You will have to throw me out sooner or later."

Another woman's voice, older, huskier interrupted. From the height he would say she was descending a staircase. The one down which he had just come. "Concha, *Quien es?*"

A rapid-fire Spanish return. A long conversation containing his name. Then the older voice spoke at his side. "We will take you to the theater, Mr. Catherwood. For one hundred dollars."

He let out his breath in a long sigh and allowed himself to relax. *"Gracias, señora."*

She guided him to one side. "Sit down."

His legs touched the edge of a piece of furniture and he lowered himself onto a upholstered chair. He was so tired and he hurt so badly. His next question was almost a groan. *"Dónde* — Where am I?"

"You are in La Yegua Blanca."

"Where?" He pressed his hand against his temple. "My Spanish — *Mi español no es bueno. No bueno.* No good."

"La Yegua Blanca is The White Mare." Her voice was deep.

He could imagine the sort of deep-chested figure that would produce such a voice. The picture gave him an idea of where he was. "What time is it?"

"Morning. Very early."

He had missed the performance. He closed his eyes, thinking he could not have gone on anyway. Miranda must be frantic. De la Barca had undoubtedly contacted her. He licked his parched lips. "I am — I need to go as soon as possible."

No answer. Then another voice spoke. *"Aquí, señor"* A glass was pressed into his hand.

He could have cried with gratitude. *"Gracias,"* he murmured, then added politely. *"Gracias.* Whom do I have to thank?"

"Celestina," was the terse reply.

A man spoke in Spanish from across the room. Celestina smiled. "You promise one hundred dollars?"

190

Shreve felt in the direction of the voice. A small warm hand found his. "I swear, Celestina. One hundred dollars."

"Then go." She pulled him to his feet and guided him across the room. "El Teatro Real," she told the driver. *"Cuidado."*

"Yes," Shreve said. "Quickly."

The deep voice had a smile in it. "I tol' him 'Carefully.' "

He rose to the occasion. "Then I thank you doubly." He bowed stiffly though the effort almost cost him his balance.

"Do not thank me. Just watch out for that man," she called as the driver led him to the carriage. "He don't like you very much."

Eleven

*A man may see how the world
goes with no eyes.*

The carriage was really a dray wagon. It lumbered through hot and dusty streets for what seemed an eternity. The sun beat down fiercely on Shreve's aching head, lolling as the vehicle's unsprung bed jolted him unmercifully. He draped his arm over the side and rested his forehead on the back of his hand.

The roads seemed to grow worse and worse, but his headache was so bad that he was not conscious enough for their condition to register. Nor did he rouse enough to fight the swarms of mosquitoes that buzzed and lighted on his unprotected neck and face.

The driver of the wagon looked over his shoulder at the semiconscious man from time to time and whistled a little bit between his broken teeth. Finally, he pulled the wagon to a halt. Climbing down, he came around to the end and pulled his passenger out.

"Are we here? *Dónde es—er—estamos? El Teatro Real?*" Shreve's throat was so dry that every syllable rasped.

The driver answered not a word. With frightening efficiency, he slid his hands over Shreve's clothing, dipping into every pocket, checking his waist for a money belt.

"Here! What the hell are you doing? I told you George would pay." Shreve pushed himself away and punched at the man's shoulder. His efforts to defend himself drew a single grunt from the thief who in quick order lifted his passenger's wallet, stripped him of his watch and fob, pulled out his pocket knife.

Shreve batted at the hands. "Get the hell away! Help! Thief!"

Hard hands slapped against Shreve's chest and shoved. The blind man stumbled and fell sprawling. Even as he got his feet under him and struggled up, the wagon began rolling away.

"Wait! At least point me in the right direction." Shreve swung his arms around him trying to find something in the steamy darkness. "For God's sake." His voice rose to a frantic shriek. "Wait!"

He lunged after the wagon. His outstretched hands encountered the rough bed, but it rolled out from under him. He tripped and fell forward, his face down in the road.

"Wait! Stop! For God's sake!" He scrambled to his feet.

The wagon rumbled on, getting farther and farther away until finally it faded entirely. Even before it was gone, Shreve heard the sounds that told him he was not in the city at all. Actually, the lack of sounds drove him into a panic. No coaches rumbled by. No iron-shod hooves clanged on cobblestones. No booted heels clicked along sidewalks. Only swarms of singing mosquitoes darted at his head. He batted at them weakly. Where had he been taken?

He lifted his head and stared at the sky. It was totally black. He could not see the sun even though

193

he knew it was directly overhead because of the heat falling on his face. The mosquitoes buzzed in his ears and lighted on his cheeks. Their stingers sank into his skin. He was helpless and deserted.

"Help! Help! *Socorro! Socorro!*" The words bawled with all the strength of his lungs vibrated into a void. Nowhere were there walls for the sound to bounce off. With an actor's trained ear, Shreve pivoted a quarter turn and howled, another quarter turn, another, and another.

He froze. Goaded by the painful stings, blind panic gripped him with claws so fierce that he could not think. *Run! Find someone! Something! Keep running!*

He almost did it. Almost.

But what if he ran over a cliff? What if he plunged into a river? What if wild animals—?

Sweat trickled through his eyebrows and stung his eyes—his useless eyes. He forced himself to relax his muscles. He could not run. He would not run. He would stand very still and take stock of his situation. He would force himself to think.

With a conscious effort he drew in deep controlling breaths. The blood ceased to thunder in his ears. His heartbeat slowed. He put his hands to his cheeks to protect his stung flesh for a few moments.

For a time his thinking was muddled and disjointed. He had been tricked and lied to. He had been a damn fool. He should have expected treachery in a brothel! Celestina and Concha and the rest at the White Mare were probably toasting their cleverness in getting rid of him without a struggle and making a profit at the same time.

Time! How much time had elapsed?

He cursed his own stupidity as he batted at the mosquitoes. They had been tricking him while he had been thanking them for their kindness and generosity. Like a village idiot, he had leaned back in that cart, smiling foolishly, while the driver took him out of Mexico City to abandon him. He had made no effort to listen nor to keep track of the way, nor the time.

He felt at his waist. And now his watch was gone. He cursed again. Miranda had given him that watch. It was gold and valuable. The damned thief had taken it first.

Of course, it might be of no use to him anymore. Immediately, his heart began to pound. Panic sent another spurt of adrenaline racing through his veins. He resorted to the old stage technique of clasping his hands together in front of his chest and pushing hard. By simultaneously drawing in deep breaths he pumped his diaphragm to make the muscles work out the fear.

Gradually, he began to feel the technique's effects. He reminded himself that thinking of what he could not change was no help. He must concentrate all his energies, all his senses on just one thing. How he was going to get back to the city.

He tried to remember the trip. For several seconds his mind was a blank. He could remember nothing except bumping along in the sun, his legs dangling over the end of the wagon.

The sun. Had it hit him on the right side or left side, in the face or on the back of his neck? He struggled to remember. The driver had made several turns; but, primarily, it had struck him in the back of the head.

Therefore, he had been driven west of the city.

He congratulated himself as if he had worked out the most important problem of his life. Then ruefully he told himself it might just well be. If he had been driven west, then he must walk east keep-

195

ing the sun in his face. Except now that the sun was directly overhead, he would have to walk toward the sun which would go down in the west.

He put his hands to his head. He felt like an idiot. But the pain was turning the simplest deductions into extraordinary achievements. He really should make notes of this. The next time he played a hero, he damn well wouldn't cavalierly brush off a blow to the head. This experience would really deepen his performance.

He pushed aside the thought that he might never perform again and tried to remember. He had touched the wagon as it moved away, actually fallen down between the tracks of its wheels. Carefully, he patted his toe in a semicircle. The soles of his boots were too thick. Stooping, he felt with his hands. His fingers were actually trembling when he at last was able to locate the ridges and indentations of wagon tracks.

His sigh of relief was audible. Shallow as they might be in the dust, they were a line, a ribbon, a rope to lead him to safety. All he had to do was follow them. No matter how much time he would spend, no matter how slowly he had to move, he would follow them.

If he did not, then he had nothing else to do with the rest of his life anyway.

"Get back in that room. I don't want to be seen." De la Barca shoved his way past Miranda and strode into her bedroom. Spinning, he pushed the door closed and locked it. When he turned back into the room, he was looking into the muzzle of her pistol.

"Put that down."

"Not in a million years."

"If you want to see your lover alive, you will." The death threats sounded strange uttered in a monotone and issued from an impassive face.

Color drained from her face. Her mouth twisted. She could not control her emotions as he did.

He nodded at the sight. "You come with me and I'll leave instructions for your friends to tell them how to find him."

Miranda stared into the impassive face. "No. Tell me now."

Quick as a striking snake, he wrenched the weapon from her. A backhanded blow knocked her across the bed. She rolled across it and came up on the other side where she watched him, break it, empty the bullets out, and drop them into one pocket in his coat. He stuffed the pistol in the other pocket and faced her again. Despite the extreme violence of every action, his expression had never changed.

Still uncowed, she pointed her finger at him. "You'd better tell me what you've done with Shreve. Otherwise, I'll send for the police and have you arrested."

He grunted. "Don't waste time trying to bargain. You don't have a card. If you don't hurry, you'll never see Catherwood again."

"Where is he?"

"He's where I put him. And if no one comes for him in forty-eight hours, he'll be dead."

Equal parts of nausea and tension burned her stomach. "How do I know he isn't dead already?"

De la Barca shrugged. "Why should I kill him? He's not important. And then there's the problem of the body to be disposed of."

She shuddered at his coldness. "It doesn't bother you that you'd be guilty of murder?"

"Me? Who says I murdered someone? Where's

the body? Even if they threw me in jail, I'll only be there a few weeks before diplomatic letters come from Washington to get me out."

"You're lying. You're not important."

"But you are. You're important." His black eyes measured her reflectively. "You've sure fooled me. I thought for a while this assignment was going to turn out to be a wild-goose chase."

"It is. I told you—"

He cut through what would have been her explanation. "But I can see that it's not. I've got eyes. You're staying in a fine hotel. A policeman's on guard in the lobby. At least a half dozen others are out searching for your lover. In a foreign country you're entertained and protected by important people."

"I'm an actress. We are—"

"Save that for people you have to convince." He pointed to the big steamer trunk. "Take what you need. I'll write the directions—"

French doors behind her opened onto a balcony above the entrance. He had said she had a guard in the lobby. Whether or not he was there, she could make herself heard.

Shaking her head, she backed away. "No! No! You can't take me!" It was a very bad performance. Her voice sounded emotive rather than natural. She was supremely glad that Shreve could not hear her. "I've done nothing."

Did his eyes narrow slightly in amazement?

One hand groped behind her for the brass latch. She raised her voice hysterically. "Please! Please!"

She caught him flat-footed. She would swear as she whirled around and threw herself out onto the balcony that he had no idea what she was going to do. Leaning far over the rail, she drew her breath in and let it out in the most piercing shriek she had ever uttered.

It blasted like a trumpet down into the court-yard. Not only the doorman, but two porters as well popped out from beneath the arcade. "Help!" she screamed. "There's a man in my room. He's broken in. Help!" When their upturned faces looked puzzled, she switched to Spanish. *"Socorro! Un hombre."*

Behind her she heard de la Barca curse. She threw a frightened look over her shoulder. Eyes blazing, he had followed her to the doors. Now he pointed her own pistol at her head.

She screamed again, real terror making her voice weaker than her practiced sound.

But de la Barca turned up the barrel. "He's dead," he promised. "Your lover's dead. You've killed him." With that final threat he whipped around and ran.

Clutching the rail to keep from falling, she screamed. "Help! *Socorro! Socorro!"*

A small crowd had gathered beneath her, but the original trio were no longer visible. With a small prayer she pictured them running up the stairs, followed by the policeman. "Help!" she screamed again for effect before she raced back inside. Her room was empty, the door to the hall standing open.

She made the hallway in time to meet several men in different uniforms. "Did you catch him?"

"Who?" *Thank heaven the policeman spoke English.*

"De la Barca. A stocky man. Black hair. Black eyes. Heavy mustache. Wearing—" *What had he been wearing!* "—a dark suit," she finished lamely.

"Where is he?"

"He ran out of my room."

"He didn't go by us."

"But he must have." She could feel her momentary triumph dissolving in alarm. "He must have. Does this floor have another way out?"

The policeman consulted with the other men. *"No, señora."*

"Then he's still in the hotel."

They looked at her reproachfully. "Who, *señora?"*

"My God, you don't believe me."

Only the policeman looked around him suspiciously.

The manager came hurrying up. "What has happened? What has happened?"

The doorman turned and answered him in Spanish. Immediately, the manager's expression changed from alarmed to unctuous "Where was this man, *señora?"*

She turned to the policeman. "I know he was here. You must search the rooms on the hall. He's probably hiding in one."

The policeman looked at the manager, who shook his head. "We cannot have other guests disturbed." He turned to her again and tried to herd her back into her room without actually touching her. "Please, *señora,* perhaps you would like to resume your nap."

At that minute she saw what they were all seeing and damned her luck. The costume did not fit the performance. She stood talking to five men in a confusion of lacy petticoats and a silk-satin wrapper. Her feet were bare. They guessed that she had been asleep — therefore, she must have had a bad dream. She started to protest. "I wasn't dreaming."

Their eyes lost the last traces of alarm. The policeman relaxed. The manager smiled at the hotel employees. A couple of them began to drift back down the hall.

She could have screamed in frustration. She had said the wrong thing. Shreve was right. Life was not like a play where the lines were written with precise meanings. Now these men were sure she was making excuses for her own foolishness.

The consequences of her failure smote her so that her stomach clinched. It felt on fire. Shreve would die if she could not find someone to help her. The hero would die. The villain would triumph. She drew herself up tall and scorned them with a look. "Send for Minister Vallarta," she directed the policeman. "He'll want to know."

"Señora," the manager protested. "You must not disturb so important a man."

"I won't, if you will believe me and institute a thorough search of this hotel. You must search every room on this floor." She was Lady Macbeth ordering her thanes. "He probably ducked into one of them."

The manager's mouth tightened, but he managed a cool smile. "Of course, *señora*. If you will please to go in and rest from your ordeal. We will conduct the investigation and make the proper report."

Shreve thought his back would break. The only way to be sure he was following the tracks was to touch them with his fingers. He dared not walk along upright for fear of straying off the road. Every time he considered that possibility, a smothering feeling contracted his chest. The darkness became a tangible blanket, cutting off his air.

He was sure that if he lost those tracks, he would wander forever.

As he crept along, bent almost double, his fingers sweeping the dust, his head reeling from the

201

heat and the pain, he made himself think about what to do when he finally found someone. He must get someone in his grasp and under no circumstances let that person go until he had been taken to the theater.

Whatever happened he must not let people find out he was blind until he had taken a hostage for himself. He hoped it would be an adult. A small child would be frightened. Besides, children always messed up an act. They froze or they forgot their blocking or their lines. A teenager might be all right.

Quite suddenly, he became aware that the sun was no longer striking the back of his neck with punishing force. A cloud? A line of overarching trees? He raised his head, then straightened his stiff body. He listened.

Did he hear chickens? The faint clucking of a hen? A brood of chicks peeping?

He tried to turn his ear toward the sound. It seemed to come from up ahead. A breeze blew across his face. A new terror struck him. It smelled of rain. "No," he murmured. "Don't rain. For God's sake, don't rain."

He stooped again, groaning. The wind gusted stronger. He could feel the dust blow across his hand.

"Oh, God! Don't rain."

A drop of water struck the back of his head. He howled as if it had been acid. His fingers scrabbled at the disappearing tracks. He ran forward, fell, and lay there body sprawled, arms outstretched, as the tropical shower, lasting no longer than a few minutes dissolved his lifeline.

"*Señora,* Minister Vallarta cannot come himself,

202

but he has sent me to help you. I am Raul Calderon, at your service." The young man clicked his heels and bowed. "I understand you have been threatened."

"Yes." Miranda extended her hand. At the same time she produced her most dazzling smile. As he raised his eyes, it smote him full force. "I was terrified. I am terrified. A man broke into my room, *Señor* Calderon. He threatened me with the death of my dearest friend, the man who has brought a new cultural life to Mexico, Shreve Catherwood."

She had carefully chosen her costume for meeting this man. Her black dress was buttoned to the neck with jet buttons. Only white linen collar and cuffs relieved its starkness. Ada had wound her hair tightly on top of her head in a golden crown and applied makeup to look as if she wore no makeup at all but had suffered from many sleepless nights.

With professional detachment she listened to her delivery. She was using just the right amount of anger and shock that such a thing could happen. As she prefaced Shreve's name, she strengthened and deepened her voice, so by the time she pronounced it, it was a swelling hymn of praise.

For a conclusion, she dropped her eyes to her hands in which she clutched a white lace handkerchief. "If we don't find him, Shreve will be dead in less than forty-eight hours."

Calderon was impressed. The beauty of the lady before him touched rich chords within his Latin heart. He would seize this opportunity to serve her. If he found her friend in time to save his life, he would be rewarded. If he arrived too late, he would be on hand to console her in her grief. He drew himself up to attention. "This man must be found."

"I told the policeman and the manager of the hotel. They searched all the rooms on the floor, but somehow he slipped away. I truly don't see how. I stood in the hallway the entire time."

Calderon's eyebrows rose. His eyes narrowed as he studied the woman with new eyes. "Possibly he ran upstairs and waited. When they had finished their search and found nothing, he strolled down and easily left the building."

"Of course. I should have thought. How simple. Oh, I'm a fool." Miranda could have kicked herself. Her distress was so real that Calderon put his hand over her doubled fist.

"*Señora,* do not blame yourself. The man on guard should have thought. I will call his mistake to his attention before I leave."

"Oh, thank you." Miranda flashed an honest smile for the first time since Shreve's disappearance. At last, a man was actually putting his mind to work. "I'm so glad *Señor* Vallarta assigned you to me, *Señor* Calderon. At least you believe me. The men who came when I screamed discounted my story. I could not convince them that anything had really happened. Oh, if only you had been here, de la Barca would undoubtedly have been caught."

The young man bowed again in acknowledgment of her compliment.

"Where can we begin to look?" Miranda asked urgently. "Shreve has hours only."

Calderon withdrew a small notebook from his pocket. "I would not be too sure of that. If this man—"

"De la Barca."

"—De la Barca kills *Señor* Catherwood, then he has lost his only chance of getting you to do what he wants you to do." He poised a short pencil over a fresh page. "What does he want you to do?"

She did not hesitate to answer. "He wants me to leave the country with him."

"Ah. Why?"

"Because important men in the United States want to question me about a supposed conspiracy."

"And is there one?"

Again she could answer with all truthfulness. "None that I know of."

He studied her. The silence grew between them. Then he nodded. "Men who have much to hide think everyone is like themselves. Is there anything you know about this man that might give you some idea as to where he would take your friend?"

"A rundown hotel in a poor section of town. One where he could keep him locked in a room under guard. I don't believe that he did this by himself. In New Orleans he had a driver."

Calderon mentally shrugged his shoulders. The man could be anywhere. "We might send soldiers throughout the city with pictures of your friend. If you have one."

She selected one from the drawer of the steamer trunk. "Actors always have photographs of themselves."

He looked at his rival. "This is a very handsome man. Is he very tall?"

"Over six feet—two meters."

He grimaced, then smiled. "He will be easy to find."

"I will offer a reward."

"Wait. Plenty will recognize him. Someone will come forward and tell us. *El Señor* Catherwood is too unusual. He cannot be hidden long."

"But, do we have time?" She twisted her hands in agony.

"I think we do, *Dona* Miranda. I do not think this man de la Barca will get rid of the thing that makes him powerful."

De la Barca arrived at La Yegua Blanca in a foul mood. The problem with blackmail was that it only worked if the person allowed himself to be blackmailed. If he or—in this case—she did not allow herself to be, then the entire thing became cumbersome.

A shock would be best. She was a tough one, this Miranda Drummond, capable of anything. Hiding in the third-floor stairwell, he had heard her voice as she directed the policeman and the hotel employees. She had gotten them to check the rooms easily.

He was lucky she had not thought of the third floor. Her mistake was common. Who would expect that someone would hide on the floor above, effectively trapping himself? People trying to escape ran in the most obvious direction and people in pursuit followed in that direction.

His shoulders set, black eyes glittering, he strode deliberately into the brothel. At the foot of the stairs, a heavily built man barred his way. "Celestina wants you gone."

De la Barca measured him. "I want the man I brought here."

"He's gone. You go, too. "

The investigator looked around him for the brothel keeper. The woman was no where in sight. He put his foot on the first riser, but the guard seized his upper arm. "You go."

De la Barca looked pointedly at the offending hand, then back at the owner. The guard did not change expressions. Finally, the investigator stepped back. "Where did he go?"

The guard shrugged. "Who knows? He's gone. You go, too."

"Let me speak to Celestina."

"No."

De la Barca's hand brushed his coat aside to clear his pistol, but the guard dropped his hand to a huge bush knife. In a mirror over the guard's shoulder, the investigator could see a second guard moving in behind him. Drawing his pistol, he pivoted and faced them both. "This could become very bloody, very fast, my friends. I suggest that you let me talk to Celestina."

"Talk," her voice barked from behind him.

He could not face all three of them. He hoped the men were the only real danger, but he suspected that she also had a gun. He threw a quick glance over his shoulder. "Where did the man go?"

"Shreve Catherwood."

He took a chance and turned slowly to face her. Her voice should have come from a big woman. Instead, she was very small, her chest obscenely large. He stared at that chest. "How did you know?"

She shrugged. Her breasts heaved with the movement of her shoulders. "He's very famous in Mexico City. Even whores know about famous people. You could have gotten me into trouble by bringing him here. If Vallarta had found out, I would have been closed."

"He was hurt. I was helping him."

She shook her head. "You lie. Get out. La Yegua Blanca is a place for entertainment. Not to conduct dirty business. If you're not out of here in ten seconds, the boys will make you very sorry."

He could have screamed with frustration. Everything seemed to be going wrong with this case. He had been unable to depend on anyone. He could see his chances of getting Miranda to leave Mexico with him disappearing. "Just tell me where he is?"

She waved her hand. "He's gone. I had him carried off. He was too dangerous to keep around. And you—you have about five seconds to go off under your own power."

"Tell me—"

She threw a look at the man who flanked de la Barca on the right. With one practiced motion, he drew a heavy club from his belt and swung it at de la Barca's head. The investigator ducked, but still the weapon struck him a glancing blow that knocked him into the man on the left.

His arms were pinioned and he was held so he could not avoid the next blow. It came as the club was rammed into the pit of his stomach, pitching him forward against the hands that held him. He never saw the third blow coming when it fell on the back of his head.

The assailant thrust the club back into his belt, stooped, and grasped de la Barca's ankles. Like a sack of flour, he hung between them as they carried him out.

"George, will you go with me?"

The old man looked at her with doubtful eyes. To him she looked exactly like what she was—a woman in men's clothing. "It's late, ma'am."

"I know, but I can't sleep. If you won't go, I'll ask—"

"I'll go," he murmured. "Give me a few minutes to get dressed and drink a cup of coffee."

They hailed a carriage in the street, and Miranda gave a street address. George looked at her questioningly. "I asked one of the maids who speaks a little English. She didn't know, but she found a bellman who did. It's a section of Mexico City famous for its bordellos. According to her, every building on the street is one. It's where he directs hotel guests, and where he sends for women to come to their rooms."

"Ma'am, I don't think you ought to know about such things," George said, his tone disapproving.

"I don't think I should, either." Miranda smiled sadly. "I'll try to forget as soon as we find Shreve."

The street was well lighted, its sidewalks clean, its houses well kept. Brass or wrought-iron lanterns hung on every gatepost. Some walks even had flowers blooming along them. Some houses had their windows open. Music and laughter issued from several.

"Cheerful place," Miranda remarked. She directed the carriage to traverse the entire street. At the end she ordered the driver to let them out. "Wait at the opposite end."

"Miss Miranda!" George protested.

"I'm going to find him, George. Or die trying. He's done the same for me."

A woman with the most enormous breasts Miranda had ever seen opened the doorway of the first house. There she posed, the light behind her, silhouetting her tiny waist and her shapely legs. *"Ola,"* she called. *"Bienvenidos, señores, a La Yegua Blanca."*

Twelve

No, no, my heart will burst.

He could hear chickens. Before he remembered, he raised his head and looked in the direction of the sound. The blackness remained, a bitter blow that made him close his eyes and grit his teeth.

Still, somewhere near him off to the right, a hen clucked softly. Several baby chicks peeped. He pushed himself up until he knelt, turning his head slowly, brushing away the eternal mosquitoes, trying to pinpoint the direction of the sounds.

The steaming air bore primarily the scent of vegetation, perhaps flowers, but also manure. A house must be nearby. A hen and baby chicks would not have wandered far from their coop.

He listened to the hen, heard her scratch the earth somewhere nearby, heard the excited peeps as her babies ate the insects and seeds she turned up. Surely, the owner must be nearby. "Hello," he called tentatively. "Er-*Ola?* Hello? Is anybody there? *Quíen es?*"

He thought at first no one was near. Time passed and the hen continued her scratching. Then he heard a soft, *"Ola, señor."*

A woman's voice! He started to his feet arms reaching in the direction of the sound. *"Por favor, socorro, señora."*

He had been rehearsing those words over the exhausting trek. He had muttered them under his breath, practicing the inflection and accent until he was sure they were correct. He listened desperately for her reply.

When none was forthcoming, he took a couple of steps in the approximate direction the voice had come from. "Please, help me," he begged, lapsing into English. "Please. I'll reward you. *Dinero. Tengo mucho dinero.*"

A child's voice shouted. *"Padre!"*

"Yes," Shreve said slowly and clearly. "That's good. *Está bueno.* Call your father. Get him out here. With a wagon preferably. Ask him if he'll take me to the theater, or at least into the city where I can—"

"Padre!" Another child's voice.

"How many of you are there?" he asked trying to sound friendly even though his voice trembled. *"Cuántos niños?"*

He heard a soft giggle and a shuffling of feet.

The movement must have startled the hen. With a cackle she brushed against his leg. He grabbed for her. His hands closed around her scrawny body. With an angry squawk she began to flap mightily. Her wings struck his face. Dimly, he realized that he had his eyes open because the feathers flicked across the corneas.

Shreve staggered on his feet and held her head down. Still she squawked setting up a noise loud enough to wake the dead and certainly to bring a farmer out of his house to investigate. He ran a frantic hand over his face and hair. He must look like a crazy man. He might even look dangerous.

He could hear the scrunching of shod feet coming fast. He thought of the heavy knives he had seen at the belts of most Mexican peasants. He put

211

a pleasant smile on his face and held out his hand in their direction. *"Señor, por favor, socorro.* I will pay if you will take me into the city."

No one answered. He listened, turning his head in an attempt to pick up something. He heard nothing. Even the hen had relapsed into resigned silence, no doubt expecting to have her neck wrung for the pot at any minute. Likewise, someone might be sneaking up on him preparing to strike him down.

He shuddered. He was an actor, thrust onto a stage without lines. He took a deep breath, trying to rid himself of strangling terror. *"Voy a ciudad. Por favor."*

"You really can't go any farther, can you, George?" Miranda scanned the exhausted face of the troupe's business manager.

The old man stiffened and sucked in a breath between his clenched teeth. "I'm fine. Just resting my eyes. Are we there?"

"No."

He looked out the window of the carriage. Another seamy hotel, an open door with boxes for rooms. They had left the street of relatively fine establishments and were now in the most dismal part of town. At every place they had asked questions and shown Shreve's picture. No one had seen him. In fact, no one appeared to have seen anything at all—ever.

George reached for the door handle, missed, and had to grab again. Miranda caught his hand. "We'll go back to our hotel and rest, George. We can't do any more tonight."

He looked as if he might protest. Then his shoulders slumped. "I guess you're right."

She rapped on the top of the carriage and gave the directions to the driver in execrable Spanish. While George slumped back on the seat, his eyes closed, she leaned forward fingers curled over the window ledge, staring with burning eyes at the buildings. Somewhere inside one of them, she was sure de la Barca had imprisoned Shreve. Somewhere in one of those miserable rooms, he was locked up, perhaps abused. She did not want to give up without finding him. But there were so many.

Her stomach burned and tears pricked the backs of her eyes. She was every bit as tired as George. "I'll try again as soon as I've rested," she promised. "I won't stop until I find you."

Miranda sank onto the bed in their hotel suite and stared at her dusty boots. Useless and exhausted, she wrapped her arms around her body and rocked back and forth. Try as she would, she could not summon up the power to do anything. Still she did not think that she would cry.

She had been shocked at George's condition when she saw him in the good light of the hotel lobby. George—loyal, practical, indefatigable— George, who handled all the business, who made things work for them all. She had somehow forgotten that he had grown old in the fourteen years that she had known him. And George was not so very much older than Shreve.

What rough treatment, what abuse, what privation was he being subjected to? She rose and began to pace. The tears started a slow trickle at the thought. He had been so happy when he started out the other morning, so proud of his triumph, so enthusiastic. Had he really only been gone three days? His absence seemed interminable.

213

The bastard de la Barca had deprived him of his last night on the stage in Mexico City. He should have had his last night. They should have traveled in serene security toward Veracruz, bound for greater triumphs.

She dabbed at her eyes. What if he did not return? What if de la Barca ordered him killed?

"No," she whispered. "No, no, no."

She began to tremble all over. She flung open the door to the balcony and stepped out, drawing in deep breaths, staring up into the moonlit night. Fingernails cutting into the palms of her hands, stomach burning, she barely controlled the urge to shout his name, to scream with all the strength of her lungs.

Back in the room, she set the top hat on her head. She could not rest. She must go back out and look for him. She would find him.

She could barely see the doorknob through her tears. Angrily she swiped at her cheeks. She was being stupidly melodramatic. She could hear Shreve lecturing her on the difference between life and theater. In the theater the heroine would find the hero by the middle of the last act. Together they would thwart the villain.

In Mexico City she had little chance of finding him. But what could she do? She could not even speak the language well enough to ask intelligent questions.

Perhaps if she sent for Calderon—?

The knob turned in her hand. She jumped back, startled. A key grated. The door opened. Before her stood the hotel manager and the policeman and—

"Shreve!"

"Miranda!" he cried hoarsely.

214

She launched herself into his arms. The tears that she had tried to control now fell freely wetting his collar, the side of his neck, his cheek. She kissed his mouth, rubbing her lips raw on the black stubble of his beard. "You're safe. You're safe," she cried wetting his cheek with tears. At last she stepped back, nearly blinded with emotion. Her hands patted his shoulders, his arms, his chest. "Are you all right?"

"Yes," he croaked.

She threw her arms around him again. This time without the support of the other two men, he grunted and swayed where he stood.

Both had stepped back from the room to allow her a little privacy. Now the policeman who had been in charge in the lobby stepped forward and took Shreve by the arm. "Let me help you into the room, *señor*. A doctor has already been sent for, *señora*."

"A doctor! Oh, *gracias*." She took Shreve's arm on his other side and helped him to a chair. "Oh, yes. Do so. Immediately."

His handsome face was swollen and fiery red. A hand on his cheek told her that he must have a fever. The skin felt knobby. His lips were swollen also and distorted. His eyelids flicked open to reveal bloodshot whites.

"Shreve, darling. What's happened to you?"

He waved a careless hand although his face was strained, the jaw set. "Same old problem."

"What?" She knelt in front of him. And then she knew. His eyes did not follow her down. They were still directed where her face had been. "Oh, Shreve. Darling."

Instantly, he "looked" at her. "A couple of knocks on the noggin." He grinned thinly. "Looks like they set me back a bit."

The spurt of acid to her stomach doubled her over her crossed arms.

"Miranda?"

She swallowed and cleared her throat. "You do look pretty beat up."

He grinned again. "I'm surprised you recognized me. I've been dragged from pillar to post, ridden in the back of at least two farm wagons, crawled through a forest, rolled in the mud, caught a chicken. But mostly I've been chewed on by mosquitoes."

"Sounds exciting. All but the mosquitoes." That explained the terrible swelling, and probably the fever.

"I could do without that kind of excitement. In fact, I never want to be excited again." Wearily, he leaned his head back against the chair and closed his eyes.

"You need a bath and a good night's sleep."

"And something to eat and drink. Lord, I'm thirsty."

"A bath and a hot meal are on the way, *señor.*" The hotel manager stepped forward with a glass of amber-colored liquid. "Here is a restoring drink. I have taken the liberty of having a bottle of the hotel's best Napoleon brandy sent up."

Miranda took the glass from him and guided it into Shreve's hands. "Thank you. *Gracias.*"

"If I can be of any further service—"

She rose and escorted him to the door. "You've thought of everything."

He looked at her doubtfully. "Perhaps a valet to help you with his undressing?"

"Shreve, do you want a valet?"

"Christ, no." He took a healthy swallow of the Napoleon brandy, licked his upper lip, and smiled.

"Maybe just a little more of this."

The manager smiled also. "Brandy, *señor.*"

"*Sí.* Brandy."

Before she could close the door on the manager, the bath arrived. While the maids were setting up the screen, she stooped over him and kissed his forehead while she began to unknot his tie. "Your skin is salty."

"It's probably a lot more than that. Even though I love your kisses, I'd advise against them. Like my mother used to say, there's no telling where those mosquitoes had been."

She hugged him, tears trickling down her face. "Your collar's filthy."

"Indicative of the skin beneath."

"You have an awful wound on your temple." She touched it just with the tip of one finger.

"That's the knock that did it." His knuckles turned white over the arms of the chair. "Hit me with a cane. The bastard. I'd like to take a swing at him."

She unbuttoned his mud-stained shirt. "Where did he take you?"

"To a whorehouse."

She was choking on her tears. "I knew it. I knew it. George and I hunted for you until we couldn't go any farther. I was just getting ready to go out again."

"Are you crying?"

"Yes."

He caught her wrist and carried it to his lips. "Don't cry."

"I can't help it."

His head rolled on the chair back. "Don't cry. I'm back. More or less in one piece."

She dropped down on her knees and pressed her face against his chest. Beneath her cheek his heart

217

beat with its dear familiar rhythm. "I love you so much."

"Miranda." His hand caressed the back of her head. "I love you, too."

She felt the hand drop away. His legs fell open. Frightened, she lifted her head. His eyes were closed, his breathing steady. She smiled. He had fallen asleep.

"The bruising is severe," the translator told them. "But *El Doctor* Ramirez says there is a possibility that the sight may return after the swelling has decreased."

"Only a possibility?" Shreve inquired bitterly.

The doctor shrugged. *"Es possible, pero quíen sabe?"*

"Yes," Shreve agreed. *"Quíen sabe?"*

Miranda could have slapped the man. His lack of consideration for his patient was obvious. She turned to the translator. "Is this the best doctor in Mexico City?"

The translator looked uncomfortable. "Yes, indeed. He ministers to *El Presidente.*"

"Well, *El Presidente* is running a big risk."

The doctor's eyes narrowed. Lips curled back beneath his heavy mustache, he rattled off a spate of instructions. From his bag he took a small vial and handed it to the translator, who in turn handed it to Miranda. "This is laudanum for the headache *El Señor* Catherwood will have."

"I'm not going to take the stuff," Shreve declared.

"Is that all that he can offer?" Miranda demanded aghast. "What about the fever? He's burning with fever."

The translator relayed that piece of information. The doctor replied.

218

"He says he believes that the fever is the result of the mosquito bites. He thinks it will lower as the poison sweats out of his system."

"But he's so swollen and so hot. Should he have to suffer through that? And what about the poison? What about malaria or yellow fever?"

Again the conversation and the translation. "If he contracts either one of those diseases, he will be a very sick man."

Miranda clenched her fists to keep from screaming with rage. "Is that all he can say? And do?"

"That is all, *señora*." The doctor answered for himself.

"You speak English?"

"Yes, but not well enough to practice medicine in it, only to hear and understand your insults. Good day." The doctor picked up his black bag and left.

The translator, looking more upset than ever, hurried after him.

From the bed Shreve spoke. "Don't be too hard on them."

She thrust her fists toward the ceiling in a melodramatic gesture. "I can't believe that's the best doctor in this hellish country."

He cleared his throat, but the rasp remained in his voice. "They don't know what to do beyond laudanum."

"But—"

"On the other hand, what would you expect them to do? Would you want them operating on me?"

"Dear God, no."

"Then forget about them." He closed his eyes and composed his breathing.

She waited for several minutes. "You're not asleep."

"Yes, I am. I got the breathing exactly right."

She came to the foot of the bed, to stare down at him. She felt the tears start again. She was turning into a damned watering pot. "What do want to do?"

He stirred wearily, reaching for the glass of water beside his bed. Instantly, she was beside him, guiding his hand. He took a sip, grimaced, and put it away. "Even the water tastes funny."

"The hotel manager's bottle of brandy was a very small one."

"Too bad." He sank back wearily on the pillow already damp with perspiration. He lay quiet for a few moments marshaling his strength. "There's no reason to stay," he said at last. "I want us on the next ship that leaves this country. I don't care where it's going. I want us on it."

"But, are you strong enough to make the trip to Veracruz?"

"No. But I'll make it anyway. I don't want another visit from de la Barca."

She bowed her head. "I don't want another visit from him, either. And if he comes near you again, I'll kill him."

He smiled then, opening his eyes, sighing, and closing them again. "Come here, you bloodthirsty creature."

She stretched out on the bed beside him and laid her hand on his chest. His skin was dry and hot. "I have only one goal in my life now. To get you safely out of this mess."

"How nice that our goals coincide!"

She leaned over and kissed him tenderly, letting her tongue linger in his mouth, drawing caressing fingertips across his chest, but he caught her hand. "Not now, darling, I have a headache."

* * *

The instant he hit the water, de la Barca snapped his body into a curl and dragged off his boots. His own natural buoyancy coupled with the air in his clothing lifted him to the surface. As his footgear drifted away, he struck out, swimming strongly.

His hand dipping into the water, snagged strings of weeds. Bits of flotsam brushed against his body. A nauseating odor filled his nostrils. The sharp sting of ammonia made his eyes water.

The bastards had thrown him into an open sewer. He trod water and looked around him. Suddenly, he realized his situation was serious. Limestone walls rose precipitously on either side. A couple of quick strokes and his hand slid over its surface. It was slick with algae, impossible to climb.

He tossed the hair back from his eyes and swam to the other side. It was the same. Flattening himself against the wall, he raised his arm as high out of the water as it could reach. Only vertical stones slid beneath his questing fingertips. He looked from back and forth, but he could see only a few feet in the gloom. He hesitated, his clothes weighing him down. If he stopped moving for very long, he would sink.

A slow current moved him along the wall. Mentally, he cursed the whore Celestina. She would pay for this.

A large body bumped against him. He turned in the water to find a dog's carcass, feet sticking straight up, belly like a white drumhead, exposed to the pale moon. It bumped against him again, then swayed around him and moved lazily down the sluice.

He shrugged. The walls could not last forever. It emptied somewhere, and when it did, he would have a chance. Stupid idiots. They had walked

221

away without seeing whether he was alive. They wouldn't have a chance to be stupid again.

"There's only one ship setting sail today, miss," George reported. "She's the *Pride of Narragansett,* bound for Portsmouth."

Miranda touched Shreve's dry forehead. His head lay in her lap, his eyes were closed. Often his lips moved, muttering aimlessly. Sometimes, his mouth hung slack, dribbling saliva onto her skirt. Sometimes he stirred and batted at imaginary mosquitoes. Ada would reach across the seat to restrain him, but he quickly settled back again.

Ada pressed her handkerchief to her eyes. "He doesn't even have the strength to be out of his head, dearie. He's that bad off."

"We'd best take it, George. I don't want to stay a minute longer than necessary in this country. I don't know what's happened to de la Barca, but Calderon said he's disappeared. I keep expecting him to swoop down upon us any minute."

"Then I'll book passage for four and we'll sail with the tide."

"Do it."

"But he's so sick," Ada protested. "What if he takes a turn for the worst?"

Miranda wiped the sweat from his forehead. "We'll get laudanum and quinine before we leave. That's all these fools that call themselves doctors have prescribed anyway."

They looked at her doubtfully.

She could have screamed with exasperation. She was still the little girl she had been when she joined the troupe. She had grown up with them telling her what to do, dressing her, leading her around, handing her spending money. The change was too much for them both.

She held out her hands to them, George where he stood on the ground in the door of the carriage, Ada where she sat across the seat from them. "Please don't worry. Please don't be afraid. I love him so much. I wouldn't do anything to harm him. I'd harm myself before I'd harm him."

"We know you would," Ada murmured. "We know you would. It's just that he's so very precious. He's the dearest boy."

George echoed her. "He puts on a good show. More talent than most of them that's in the big theaters in New York right now."

"I know. And I promise I won't give anything to him unless he absolutely needs it. He's strong and healthy. He'd be the first not to take medicine if he didn't need it."

The three held each other tightly, then pulled apart.

"I'd check into a hotel and wait right here until he's better, but I'm afraid for him," Miranda said. "Almost the last rational thing he said was that he wanted to make the trip to Veracruz so he could get out of the country."

Ada snuffled unhappily into her handkerchief. "He was too weak to make this trip. We should have stayed there in the hotel until he was completely well. Lord knows, they were willing for us to stay."

"I know," Miranda agreed. "But he was afraid for us. I know him. He was afraid of what de la Barca would do to me while he was flat on his back." The acid in her stomach burned as the words came out. "He pretended that he was afraid, but I know he wasn't. A man who's brave enough to stay in a burning theater chopping away at a rope to bring the fire curtain down, isn't afraid of a swine like de la Barca."

Ada shook her head. "Lord love him. I'd forgotten about that."

"I haven't." Miranda smiled. "So, George, book passage for us on that ship, the *Pride of Whatever-She-May-Be*. And tell them that we want to come aboard and get settled immediately." She bent and kissed Shreve's forehead.

He murmured softly, but his eyes did not open.

"Captain Ward presents his compliments, ma'am. He's heard you've got a sick man. He wants me to have a look at him before you bring him aboard." The man wore sailor's garb and carried a very shabby medical bag.

"My God, you can't expect to examine a sick man in the confines of this carriage," Miranda protested. "Let me assure you that what he has is a fever from mosquito bites. It's not contagious."

"That's as may be, ma'am, but I have to have a look."

"Would I be looking after him if he were dangerous?" she went on, her voice shrill with exasperation. Sweat was dampening her clothing and standing out on her face. The prevailing breeze from the Gulf did not counteract the broiling heat of the Veracruz docks.

The man looked at her dourly. "Women do terrible odd things, ma'am. That's why I went to sea. Never could stand odd things."

"Well, this is not an odd thing. I'm holding him here on my lap, with my hand on his chest because I know it's perfectly safe. He is quite ill from this awful heat, and I am about to collapse from it. I demand that you let us on board the ship immediately."

"Can't do that, ma'am. Not till I examine him."

"Oh, very well."

The doctor set his medical bag on the floor and climbed in. He sat on the seat across from them and folded his arms. "Now if you'll get out, ma'am."

"No."

"Ma'am, I can see you're not his wife. You're not wearin' a ring. I don't believe in a woman havin' carnal knowledge of a man who's not her husband. If he wants that and you're willin' then shame be on both of you, but I don't condone it."

Miranda flushed to the roots of her hair. "Damn you."

He set his jaw at the oath and gazed toward the ship's masts where they towered stiffly upright over the glassy water. "The captain's given me my orders."

Throwing him a look that would have set stone asizzle, she gently eased Shreve's head onto the seat.

He stirred, opened his eyes, and fumbled for her. "M'randa."

She bent over him. "It's all right, dearest. A doctor is going to examine you. Then we'll take you aboard a ship. We'll be out of here and on our way in just a few more hours."

"Ship?"

"It'll be just like when we came to Mexico. You'll rest and get better. You'll be well by the time we dock in England."

"England?" He fell to muttering.

She stepped down from the carriage but remained standing in the door. "Be quick," she advised him. "And you'd better make the right diagnosis."

He hooked a pair of wire-rimmed glasses over

his ears and looked at her over them. "That's as may be."

"No." Katherina the Shrew thrust the upper part of her body into the cab and pulled a silver-plated derringer from her handbag. "No. That is not as may be. Doctor, I'm a very determined woman."

"Ma'am!"

"I love that man very much. I swear to you on my father's grave that Shreve is no danger to anyone on board your ship. You may check him to your heart's content, but you will discover that he has nothing that the crew or any of the passengers could get. He's had a terrible ordeal, but all he needs is time to rest."

The man gaped at her.

She tilted the pistol, so that it trained directly on his heart. Her voice was soft and breathy, a sweet contrast to the deadly looking weapon. "He is feverish, but it's nothing to be concerned about. Just a jungle fever, probably malaria. Isn't that correct?"

The doctor was brave, but not foolish. Under the gun, he took out his stethoscope and listened to the rattling breaths coming out of Shreve's chest. "He has a great deal of congestion."

She nodded.

He pulled back an eyelid. The great well of the pupil stared at him. "Probably had a blow to the head that gave him a severe concussion."

"On the temple," she advised him dryly.

"Yes, ma'am. I can see that." He listened again to the chest, checked the pulse. "Could be pneumonia."

"Which is not contagious."

"No, ma'am."

She shoved the derringer back in her handbag. "Then I'll bring him aboard." She flashed him the

Magnificent Miranda's most dazzling smile. "I'm glad you're the ship's doctor, Doctor—"

"Clinton." He folded his glasses in their case and regarded her sourly.

"Doctor Clinton. It relieves my mind to know that medical help is available should Mr. Catherwood require any before we get to England." She turned from the carriage and signaled to Ada to watch Shreve, while she made arrangements with the captain.

The doorman of *La Yegua Blanca* never saw the muzzle of the gun as the man strode across the porch. When it rammed into his big belly just below the heart, he thought he had been hit with a stick.

Before his victim could react, de la Barca pulled the trigger. Blood spurted over the investigator's hand as he stepped back. The light died in the doorman's eyes. His body toppled sideways across the door.

"Qué paso?" One of the guards who had manhandled de la Barca and thrown him in the sewer stepped out and knelt at the doorman's side. *"Qué paso?"* he repeated.

"This pass-o's," de la Barca said and shot him, too.

The guard was made of stronger stuff than the doorman, he staggered to his feet and lunged back into the hallway. Blood flowed over his fingers where he gripped his belly. With his murderer in pursuit, he stumbled into the living room.

A whore in black underwear and red satin wrapper had her hand inside a client's fly. At the sight of the guard, she screamed. The client took one look and bolted for the window.

The whore screamed again as de la Barca appeared in the doorway, hot blood dripping from his wrist.

"Where's Celestina?"

The woman screamed and waved a frantic hand toward the stairs.

De la Barca nodded. He raised the muzzle of the gun and stepped back into the hall.

"Rogencio!" The second guard came from behind the stairwell.

"He's dead," de la Barca said as he squeezed the trigger. The man spun around and sprawled over the foot of the risers.

The house came alive. On the second floor women began to scream. Men cursed. Doors slammed.

"CELESTINA!" de la Barca bawled. "They're dead, Celestina. And I'm setting the house on fire."

Suiting action to word, he shot out through the door of the living room. The kerosene lamp on the table exploded. Fiery coal oil spattered everywhere. The whore in the red satin wrapper screamed and scrambled out the window.

Enjoying himself, de la Barca flung open the door of the room across the hall. In it a man and a woman struggled to get their clothes on. He shot out their lamp.

A shot whizzed by his ear. He ducked.

At the top of the stairs crouched the whore with the big breasts. Celestina aimed her pistol at him again.

He plunged across the hall into the blazing living room. Her shot splintered wood on the wall behind him. He waited a minute, then crouched low. Smoke was rising swiftly in the old house. People were running screaming down the stairs and past the door.

He coughed. It would get thick in just a few minutes. Already the air must be unbreathable on the second floor. Another man and woman staggered past, coughing.

Celestina would not be able to get a clear shot. He bolted out the door, gun trained on the head of the stairs. She had disappeared.

He leaped over the sprawled body, but then stopped with a curse. More people tumbled by him, screaming. The hallway was thick with smoke. The rising heat created a draft from the open doorway.

He leaped back down and holstered his gun. Let her cook.

He joined the crowd in the street. By the time the flames had reached the second floor, he had hitched a ride in a patron's carriage and was rolling away down the street.

Thirteen

I am a fool
To weep at what I am glad of.

The *Pride of Narragansett* slid gently through the smooth waters of the Gulf of Mexico. The sails billowed and the sun blasted anyone not standing in their shade, but the wind over the water brought a cooling breeze.

In the stuffy cabin Shreve moaned and tossed the wet cloth off his forehead. Wearily, Miranda replaced it. He moaned again, then began to shake. His teeth began to chatter. Suddenly, he wrapped his arms around his body and groaned between his teeth.

Miranda flew to the door of the cabin. "Send for Doctor Clinton," she demanded of a passing sailor.

The man eyed her dishabille, then shrugged and strode away.

Self-consciously, she caught the edges of her batiste wrapper together at her neck and ducked back into the cabin where she had little time to worry about her state. Shreve was trying to sit up, bawling orders to an imaginary cast of actors at the top of his lungs.

She threw herself upon him pushing him back onto the bunk.

In some odd way he recognized her. His arms

closed around her. "Sweetheart." He cupped the back of her head and tried to lift his mouth to hers. "Sweet, sweet Miranda."

"Shreve. Umph! Let go! You're sick."

"Kiss—Kiss me. So cold. Warm me right up."

"Shreve." She pushed futilely. "Stop. You'll—"

He pulled at her skirt, hiking it up past her thigh. His fingers splayed over her partially exposed buttock.

The door opened. A dour voice inquired, "You sent for me?"

She twisted in Shreve's arms, horrified to see Dr. Clinton standing in the doorway, bag in hand. "Help me. He's delirious."

"A man does in his delirium what he's accustomed to when he's sane," he remarked, looking pointedly at the ceiling of the tiny cabin. He rocked back on his heels. "Shall I come back at a more convenient time?"

"No!" Thoroughly disgusted and embarrassed, she wriggled out of Shreve's arms, by pushing herself down his body. Because he was much stronger than she and used to having his way, she ended by falling out of the bunk onto the floor. In a welter of clothing and naked limbs, she rolled over to face the doctor.

That pious professional gentleman met her eyes, his own lip curled in distaste, then returned to his study of the beams overhead. She stared down at herself and moaned. Beneath the lace edge of her wrapper, she had exposed naked knees and thighs above the rolled garters of her hose.

She scrambled to her feet and tried to shake her clothing down. Unfortunately, she succeeded in shaking her wrapper open at the bosom, so the dour doctor was then treated to a view of her

231

cleavage.

His own face was puce by that time. He turned on his heel.

"Doctor." She hurried to catch his elbow. "He's really truly ill. He had a chill just now and he's delirious. He was trying to get out of bed. That's—um—that's how I happened to be —that's what I was trying to do. Put him back in the bed."

Dr. Clinton pulled himself to his full height until he rose several inches above her. "I don't hold with unlawful carnal knowledge."

She jerked her hand away. "For God's sake, the man is sick and I am nursing him. Practice medicine now and preach later."

He snorted eloquently. "That's as may be."

She put her hands on her hips. "Will you help him?"

He looked as if he wanted to refuse. "I'll help him. He sounds as if he needs a dose of quinine."

"I brought some."

His mouth pursed as if he had swallowed some of the bitter draught himself. His eyes narrowed. "If you had some, why did you send for me to witness your shame?"

She wanted to fly at him and beat him with her fists, kick him in the shins, and generally wreak mayhem on his body. She drew her breath in so deep that her nostrils pinched together. "If you will show me the proper amount to administer, Doctor, I will be very greatly obliged."

In hostile silence he checked Shreve's pulse, thrust a thermometer into his mouth. He read it irritably, then threw her a look as if the patient's temperature were somehow her fault. He touched the bruise on the temple, then thumbed back the

232

eyelid. This time his face sobered. Rather than angry, he looked concerned. He thumbed back the other eyelid.

"Serious," he muttered. "Very serious. Extreme dilation."

Finally, he took out a small beaker, measured a draught into it. He showed her the level mark on the side of the glass before he held it to Shreve's lips.

Miranda waited for the man she knew and loved to spit the quinine all over the dour face leaning above him, but nothing so appropriate happened. Instead, Shreve swallowed the bitter dose without so much as a grimace. His head lolled to the side, and the doctor gently brought it to rest on the pillow.

Replacing everything in his bag, Dr. Clinton turned. His steely eyes pricked over her unbound hair, her thin cotton wrapper that did not conceal the fact that she wore only a chemise and drawers. He cleared his throat authoritatively. "Now, ma'am, I would suggest that you avail yourselves of the captain's prerogative."

"The captain's prerogative?"

"He can marry you, ma'am. And make an honest woman out of you." He crossed to the door. "I suggest you think about it very seriously."

Miranda stared a long time at the quiet figure on the bed. She had denied herself the joy of marrying him until she was free of the shadow that hung over her. She knew he had not asked her to marry him in New Orleans because he feared he would be blind. But now—

What if he were blind?

What if he were doomed to live the rest of his

life in darkness? Because of her?

He needed her now, not when all the problems were solved. They could remain in England. She would work on the stage and take care of him. He would be her husband and she could protect him. She could make up to him for all the pain she had caused. In her own heart she was satisfied that if he lived three lifetimes, she would never be able to make it all up.

She was also satisfied that he would never marry her without his sight. He would flatly refuse—if he were conscious. The perfect opportunity had presented itself.

He moaned and turned over. His hand dangled over the edge, his fingers drooping languidly. She slipped down to sit on the floor and touch her cheek to the back of them.

She loved him so much. She could say with Othello's adoring Desdemona, *I loved him for the dangers he had passed. And he loved me that I did pity them.* She kissed his hand, then raised her eyes to his face.

The bruise made an ugly stain on his temple. She guessed that if she opened his eye, as the doctor had, she would see the great well of the pupil, the iris disappeared, unresponsive to light. The tears began to trickle down her face. She must find some way to help him, or she would die of grief and guilt.

The captain's prerogative.

She rose and kissed his face, his cheek, his temple, touching the bruise with the softest brush of her lips. Then she wrestled her trunk into the middle of the cabin to select her wedding dress.

* * *

234

George and Ada stood beside his chair.

"Wha's goin' on?" Shreve muttered. The quinine had broken his fever for a short time, but it had begun to climb precipitously after about an hour. A bright flush sat on his cheeks and his sightless eyes glittered.

Ada bent over and kissed him on the cheek. "It's what should have gone on a long time ago, Shrevey-boy."

"Congratulations!" George reached for his hand and shook it.

Shreve turned his blind eyes from one to the other. The crease between his eyebrows deepening, a sure sign to Miranda that he was getting a headache. "Wha's happenin'? George. Ada." He ran his hand around the back of his neck. "Lord, I'm hot. George, tell them to put some ice back here? We're going to cook in these costumes."

"I'll do the best I can."

"Miranda." He groped for her. "Aren't you hot?"

"Yes, sweetheart." Miranda took his hand. "I'll put you back to bed in just a few minutes with cold cloths on your head. For now just say yes when I nudge you."

"Yes?"

"That's right."

"Wha' for? Wha's goin'—?"

She laid her arm across his shoulders. "You're getting married."

The frown on his face deepened. He looked around him, thrusting his face forward as if he could push it through the blackness that he lived in. The muscles around his eyes squinted and twitched. "Who? Can't see."

She kissed his bruised temple. "It's just a formality, sweetheart. I had to agree that we would marry

235

before they'd let us on this ship."

"What? Wha' 're you talkin' about?"

"This ship is the *Pride of Narragansett*. The captain and crew are strait-laced Puritans from Massachusetts. They don't hold with us having unlawful carnal knowledge of each other."

He struggled to rise from the chair, but the fever had left him too weakened. "Wha' in hell's goin' on? Ada, my makeup's going to smear. What show are we doing tonight? George."

"I'm here, Shreve."

"Wha's goin' on? Can't think. Is ever'thing all — " His words trailed off till they were unintelligible.

His head lolled. His facial muscles relaxed.

The business manager slipped his hand under Shreve's right shoulder and tugged him gently to his feet. "Everything's right as rain. It's the right thing to do. She promised them you'd marry her. I heard her myself. She promised. You wouldn't want her to go back on her word."

Shreve shook his head. The motion made him stagger a step. Miranda caught him on his right side. "No."

"We'll be all right tonight," Miranda assured him. "You'll get some more medicine in a little while and then you'll sleep."

Shreve frowned at her. "Marry," he said slowly. "Marry?"

"It's for the best, Shrevey-boy." Ada came up in front of him and adjusted his collar points. Her eyes shining, she bestowed a tender kiss on his cheek. "It's time you made an honest woman of the girl."

He stood solidly enough, his face sunk in gloom. "Can't make an honest woman out of someone I can't see." He looked around him again. "Why's it

236

s' dark in here?"

Ada turned his face back to her. "Now, laddie, you'll be right as rain in a few weeks. You know you will. It's happened before. It'll happen again. Just give it time."

"Ada—"

"You've had your way with this dear, sweet girl for half her life. You owe it to her."

"Miranda—"

"You owe it to me, Shreve." She turned to Captain Ward and Dr. Clinton. "If you will please, sir, we're ready."

"Who giveth this woman to this man?"

Ada, George, and Dr. Clinton all replied, "I do."

They had left the Gulf of Mexico and were sailing up the coast of North America when Shreve was finally free of fever. By tacit agreement the three conspirators kept his newly married status to themselves. They had more to worry about with the condition of his spirit.

Miranda watched his face each morning as he awakened. His breathing would quicken, his chest would rise and fall more rapidly. He would turn himself over on his back, face up, and open his eyes.

The ritual broke her heart. He lived on the hope that a burst, a beam, the tiniest, faintest ray of light would pierce the everlasting blackness. When nothing did, he would close his eyes again.

For the first few days, he waited a bit and then got up. Later, he stopped trying to get up. Only when she actually invited him to get up, would he go through the motions.

The day came when he merely shook his head.

"Shreve."

"What's the point, Miranda?" he muttered.

"The point is that we're going to be docking in England soon. You need to be exercising."

"Why?"

She swallowed hard. "Because we'll have to find an engagement and start rehearsals."

"We?"

She injected just the right note of heartiness and matter-of-factness into her voice. "Well, of course, we."

He looked in her direction, his eyes turned toward her mouth. "Don't."

"Don't what?"

"Don't pity me."

She came and sat down beside him. "I'm a woman and pity's my job. I'm supposed to pity you. You've been sick. But now you're getting your strength back. You've lost weight, but it will come back once we get on shore and get fresh meat and—"

"*Stop it!*"

"Shreve."

"I mean it."

"You will gain weight and strength," she promised, as if those were the only things bothering him.

"Don't put up a covering dialogue!" he stormed. "And for God's sake, don't act a scene. I can always tell when you're acting."

"You can't."

"Of course, I can. That's what you're doing right now. You know I can't act. I'm blind."

She smoothed her fingers over the white knuckles on his hand. "I don't see why you can't. You know your part. You have to learn different blocking for every theater. It should be simple for you."

"Romeo cannot be blind," he snorted. "Can't you just hear the audience? *O Romeo, Romeo! wherefore art thou Romeo?* And I stumble in and fall through the set. They'd laugh themselves to death."

She bowed her head in silent acknowledgment. Unless he could see again, she very much doubted that he would ever be able to stage a duel. His favorite parts—Macbeth and Hamlet—might be forever beyond his scope.

"No answer?" he asked savagely.

"You're too old for Romeo anyway."

He lay there silent for a moment. When he spoke, his voice was low. "Is my hair white?"

"No. But it's grayer." She smoothed it back from his temple that was still showing the faintest traces of de la Barca's blow. "We're going to have to touch it up. But Ada can do that in a minute."

"This is ridiculous."

"She's the greatest makeup artist around. You know that. She can—"

"She can't make me new eyes. Don't even think about it, Miranda," he warned. "It's over. Macbeth cannot be blind. Hamlet can't be blind. They both have to fight duels."

"You never touched anybody with your sword anyway."

"That's exactly the way I want to keep it." He let out his breath on a long sigh. "Anyway, no actor would duel with a blind man. He'd run the risk of getting killed."

"You could play King Lear," she suggested hopefully.

"I'm not old enough."

"Or Othello."

"Not dark enough."

239

"Or Brutus."

"That wimp."

"Or Prospero." She smiled suddenly. "That's it. We'll do *The Tempest*. Miranda has always been one of my favorite roles."

"Will you forget it?" He rolled over and turned his face to the wall. "I can't act now. I can't see. I'd trip over the furniture. Or fall through a flat."

"You've never fallen or tripped when you've taken your place on a dark stage."

"That's different."

"How?"

He rolled back over, his expression anguished. "Jesus Christ, Miranda. How can you expect me to act? I can't even dress myself without your handing me my clothes."

She rose from the edge of the bunk, walked to the tiny porthole, opened it to allow in a breeze, and walked back.

He tracked her movements with his eyes, even though he could not see her.

She put her knee on the bunk and sank her weight. He "looked" where her face would have been if she had sat down. "How did you do that?" she asked softly.

Instantly, he adjusted so that he "looked" directly at her. "Do what?"

"You followed me with your eyes."

He shrugged and flopped back on his back. "Automatically. I didn't even think about it."

She leaned forward and kissed his chin. "Don't you think you can do that on the stage? You haven't lost your skills." She kissed his cheek. "You can still make the audience believe the part."

"And get laughed at. I'm not going to try."

She kissed his nose.

240

"Quit that."

She blew in his ear.

"I said quit that."

She slid along the bunk until she was pressed against him. Even though they were in the middle of the North Atlantic, the ship still rode the Gulf Stream. Shreve was wearing only fine cotton shorts and a thin undershirt with no sleeves.

She ran her hand over his body. His organ rose up to meet her clasp. "Here's another skill you haven't lost," she whispered, her breath tickling his ear.

He groaned, involuntarily lifting his hips. "No. I haven't lost that. I suppose if I were deaf and dumb as well, I'd still have that."

She cupped his sex, feeling the shape and weight of it through the thin white material. "I'm glad."

He did not put his arms around her. Instead, he stared sightlessly at the ceiling. He had lost weight, so that her arm slipped freely beneath his waistband. Indeed, his hipbones jutted up sharply. While his sex responded with a will of its own, the rest of his body lay still.

"Shreve," she whispered uncertainly.

He turned his face to the cabin wall. "For God's sake, Miranda. I'm a dead man. Don't waste time making love to a corpse."

"Shreve."

"I mean it." His bitterness was palpable. His organ went limp in her clasp. "Leave it. Leave me. Go out on deck and enjoy the voyage. Go find a sailor if you've got a yen."

"Shreve Catherwood!"

He caught her wrist and hauled her hand out. "Leave me alone. Do you hear me?"

"Please—"

241

"Damn it! Leave me alone! I don't see any reason to get out of this bunk. I don't see any reason to act. And I sure don't see any reason to make love."

"Now, dearie, don't take on so." Ada held Miranda's shoulders as she wept. "You'll make yourself sick."

"He wouldn't even let me touch him. He pushed my hand away and told me to g-get out." She began to sob afresh.

"Oh, that poor dear boy. He's having a terrible time." Ada's voice broke as she laid her forehead on Miranda's shoulder.

Miranda nodded. "I know."

Ada proffered a handkerchief. "What brought all this on?"

"I was trying to get him up to eat some breakfast and take a walk around the deck. He's lost so much weight and most of his tan. But he got mad at me. He wouldn't get out of bed. Then I said that he had to get his strength back so he could perform in London."

Ada raised her head. "You told him what?"

"I told him he had to get his strength back so he could perform in London."

"But—"

Miranda hurried on. "He could. I know he could. He couldn't do Macbeth or Hamlet. But he could do Lear. I suggested that we start with Prospero in *The Tempest*."

"*The Tempest?*"

Miranda sprang up. "Don't you see? It'd be perfect. It doesn't require much movement. Just walk around the stage majestically and recite lines."

"But he can't see."

She caught the older woman by the shoulders. "Don't you start. He doesn't have to see. He can still talk and move. He's still got his voice. It's as wonderful as it ever was. Better really. Because he's rested it for several weeks now."

Ada put her hands to her cheeks. "Oh, Miranda, dearie. I don't think it was a good idea to suggest that."

"Why not?"

"Well, you know, with Shrevey-boy it's his pride. He's proud as a demon. He couldn't bring himself to be on stage"—she swallowed with difficulty—"the way he is."

"Ada!"

"Well, miss—"

She stepped back and opened her arms wide in a grand gesture. "Shreve would be a sensation. When he thinks about it for a while, he'll see the possibility of it. The fact that he's blind could be an asset. And besides, he needs to keep his name in front of the public. He won't always be blind."

"Now, dearie—" Ada put out her hand.

Miranda shook it off. "It's pressure, Ada. Just like it was before. Swelling. When the swelling goes down, he'll be fine—just like he was before. Until then he can act as he is. He'll be an overnight sensation on the London stage."

Ada stared at her as if she had lost her mind, but Miranda paid no attention to the shocked look. She was caught in a dream of her own making. "As Prospero, he'll be a sensation. Maybe the best Prospero ever. And he could do Oberon, King of the Fairies, *Midsummer Night's Dream*. Can't you just see him now, all blue and silver paint with fairies pulling his silver chariot."

243

Ada shook her head. Her mouth spread in a smile. "I have a little trouble with a silver chariot, but I can see who reared you, right enough. You're his greatest creation."

Miranda smiled in return. "He can do it. He's just having a low moment right now. And when he gets his sight back, he can go back to Macbeth and Hamlet."

"You'll have to convince him first."

"I will. It's just a matter of making him see the possibilities. He's afraid now, but later on he won't be. He'll treat it the same way he's treated everything else. It'll be his greatest role." She brandished her fist in triumph.

Ada laughed as she went to the door.

"Where are you going?"

"I'm going to get George in here. He needs to hear this. With the three of us working on him, he can't back down."

Alone in the cabin, Shreve sat up on the side of the bunk.

All that talking had made his head ache abominably. It ached more often than it did not these days. He put his hand on his thigh and felt the muscle. It was soft, his leg thin. In the weeks of his illness and recovery, he had turned to jelly.

And he had no way of getting back what he had lost. A blind man could not exercise. A blind man could not walk along the street. He could not visit a gym and box a few rounds. A blind man could do nothing except move from the bed to the chair and the chair to the bed with a few obligatory turns around the deck on the arm of a long-suffering woman.

244

He had seen invalids with their nurses before. He had pitied them. Now that he was one of them, he adamantly refused to be pitied. Miranda was crazy if she thought he would step out on a stage when he could not see.

He would not be a laughingstock.

Nor would he be a burden to her. More than the invalids, he had pitied the nurses. Hired servants or once-loving wives, it made no difference. They were doomed to the same tiny world as the invalid. Only their pain was worse, for they could see the world as it swirled by them — and left them behind.

He pushed himself up from the bunk. The roll of the ship staggered him. He righted himself and knew the disgust of his own condition that he had to sweep his arms around him to find the chair, the table, the trunk.

His clothes were hung neatly on the rails. He felt the soft materials, recognized the shirts. He swung one over his shoulders, and pushed his arms through. A minute and it was buttoned. His suits. The gray cutaway with the brocade vest. He could recognize it by the texture of the vest.

A wry thought. Suppose Miranda had not hung them together. Suppose he was putting on the tan cutaway with the brocade vest.

He stepped into the trousers and buttoned them. Good enough fit, although a bit loose. And next the coat. He shrugged into it. He felt in the bottom drawer for socks, but could not find them. Perhaps Miranda had moved them.

He did not care. He thrust his bare feet into his Córdoban leather half boots. A shame about these boots really. They were very expensive. He loved them. He spared a caress for the smooth soft tops.

"To be or not to be," he whispered to the silent cabin. *"Whether 'tis nobler in the mind to suffer . . ."* He crossed to the door. *"Or else take arms against a sea of troubles and by opposing end them."*

He smiled to the empty room. "Goodbye, sweet Miranda."

His mind concentrated on the distance to the companionway. He found the steps just as he had estimated. They numbered eight. Back straight, one hand controlling his body against the roll of the ship, he mounted them.

The sea breeze struck him immediately. The sails snapped above him. He lifted his face to the sun. He would take a dozen steps to the rail.

"Good morning, sir."

An unfamiliar voice greeted him. He smiled vaguely. "Good morning."

He listened. The sounds of the sea were in his ears, but also the pad of the man's feet and the swish and slap of a mop. The man was swabbing the deck. He shivered. God forbid that he should slip on a wet plank and end up ignominiously on his backside.

And so he would if Miranda had her way and drove him onto the stage. He would end up flat on his backside with the audience falling down in fits.

— the slings and arrows of outrageous fortune —

The sun was warm, but he shivered in it. He had always loved the sun. It was one of the things he had missed when *The Sons of Thespis* had stopped touring by wagon.

— take arms against a sea of troubles, and by opposing end them.

The sea would provide the way. He could feel it

rushing beneath the ship.

The sailor was on his right. The mop was slapping the deck beyond the voice.

Adopting a casual air, Shreve strolled to the rail. His lips caressed the words he had spoken so often. *"To die — to sleep — no more."*

Fourteen

All dark and comfortless!

Shreve clutched the smooth, damp wood of the rail with both hands. The salt breeze stung his eyes. He had forgotten they were open. With agonizing deliberation, he closed them and prayed for a miracle.

When he opened them, all he saw was blackness.

Blackness. Open or closed was the same. Rage and pain rose in his throat. An *agon* worthy of Macbeth filled his mouth. It was bitter. Bitter. The punishment of the gods. He knew it. *Tomorrow, and tomorrow, and tomorrow creeps in his petty pace from day to day to the last syllable of recorded time.*

Hamlet and Macbeth. The words of his oldest and truest friends filled his mind with tragic wisdom.

Act Five had arrived. Where was vengeful Macduff come to Dunsinane to end his misery? Where was Claudius, the fratricide, to drop a poisoned pearl into a cup?

He could hear the rush of water beneath the hull of the ship. He was standing on the edge of the ocean, the bottomless gulf, the abyss. A swift tilt forward and blackness would be nothingness.

He shuddered. He must make a good job of it. Without rehearsal, without his eyes to orient him, to block his movements, he might easily botch the job. Was he close to the bow or the stern?

Better to go over near the stern. There in the wake, he might escape notice. A clean, quick, and total disappearance. The only problem was making his way to the stern.

Again the rage boiled up in him. He was so helpless that he was in danger of failing at his own suicide. What a fantastic piece of dramatic irony! He ground his teeth at the thought that someone might see him and sound an alarm.

A bit player with no direction, acting through ignorance of the high purpose of tragedy would drag him back onto the set in an act of misplaced heroism. The picture of his body being hauled dripping from the sea at the end of some rope made him squirm with humiliation.

He considered returning to the cabin and waiting for nightfall. To his total frustration, he confronted the damnable problem that he really did not know when night would fall.

Moreover, Miranda would be beside him, touching him, holding him, crooning to him, spinning her impossible schemes. Go back to the stage, she said. Act again, blind as a bat, pitiful, stumbling. Absolutely not!

He turned resolutely in the direction of the stern. His left hand alone rested on the rail. His suicide would be his last performance and his most important. On cue, he had to get this exactly right. Elaborately casual, he made his way along the deck.

"Good to see you out of your cabin, Mr. Catherwood."

The deep voice froze him in his tracks. He looked toward it. "Do I know you?"

"Perhaps not. I'm Doctor Clinton."

Damn and blast! Shreve put on a pleasant smile. "So you're the one who's been taking care me. Well, as you can see, you've done your job well."

The man seemed to hesitate fractionally before he answered. "Aye. I'm very gratified. You were a very sick man when you came on board. It was touch and go."

"I had a fever," Shreve acknowledged.

"That you did. My guess is you had a case of malaria, one of the worst I've seen." Again the fractional hesitation. "It's a bother, but it won't kill you. Of course, it will probably come back on you. Best carry quinine with you as your wife has taken to doing."

"Yes. Good advice. Thank you, Doctor." Shreve held out his hand and it was immediately wrung heartily. He smiled. "Well, I'll continue my stroll." He started forward, willing the man to continue about his business.

To his disappointment, the doctor turned and matched his steps, even being so damnably companionable as to slide his arm through Shreve's. "You're a very brave man," Clinton remarked, "to be out here alone on deck, walking along the rail this way. A blind lady sailed with us once before. She never came out on deck at all."

"Oh, and why is that?" Shreve knew the answer before he asked the question. The rolling of the vessel was making him distinctly queasy. Without sight to fix his bearings, he could not compensate properly for the motion. He swallowed. His mouth was dry. The salt breeze blew in through his nostrils and stung his throat.

"Fear of falling overboard, I should say."

Shreve faced the water. "But the rail is always here."

"Aye." The doctor's voice was gentle in his ear. "And lines, too, strung all along the top. When the sea gets really rough, some without good sea legs would pitch right over."

Shreve raised one hand. Sure enough less than a foot from the rail was a line. "Most efficient," he remarked. "I'm sure it saves many lives."

"Aye, that it does." The physician resumed his place beside Shreve. Their shoulders brushed when a wave tilted the actor over. "You're having a bit of trouble with your blindness. Mind telling me how you came by it?"

"A blow on the head."

"Ah. Quite a recent one."

"Very. This is the second time it's happened. The first was a few months ago. I was partially blind for just a few hours. This time it's—it's—"

"Total."

"Yes." Shreve clutched the rail, his knuckles turning white with frustration. "Total."

" 'Tis a sad thing, man. But if it cleared up once—"

"This is total. I can't see anything but blackness. Not a ray. Not a glimmer. Not a shadow." His voice rose in his panic. His teeth bit off the word as if it were a curse.

The doctor put his hand on Shreve's shoulder. "Steady there, man. You can't be sure."

"I'm sure," Shreve told him bleakly. "I could see before. I had trouble picking out fine details,

251

but otherwise I could see. And the vision got clearer all the time."

"Is that so?"

"Yes."

"Did you see a doctor?"

"Yes. In New Orleans. He told me my bones were bruised and when the swelling went down, he thought I would see again."

"Aye. That sounds reasonable."

"But this is something different. I know it. I can feel the difference inside my head. I can't see at all now."

The doctor waited so long that Shreve thought the man might not respond. Finally, he said, "Still, I think I'd wait awhile if I were you before you do what you were contemplating."

Shreve swallowed. He blinked in the direction of the voice. Of course, blinking did no good. He bowed his head. "Can't a man just take a stroll around the deck undisturbed?"

"A stroll. To be sure." The doctor's voice went on implacably. "To take one's own life is a sin, man. Man's life belongs to God—"

Furious, Shreve turned away. Keeping his right hand on the rail, he walked what he judged to be a sufficient distance. He had not counted the steps because he had not expected to walk back. He hesitated, listening. The slap and rustle of the swabber was farther away. But he estimated that the man would be farther on down the deck.

The water was behind him, gurgling against the hull, but he could not get over the side now. No doubt the interfering doctor would be watching him as if he were crazed and must be protected from himself. He ground his teeth.

He dreaded the few steps necessary to cross to

252

the door that led down the companionway to his cabin. He would miss it and fumble, perhaps bang into the wall, perhaps stumble and fall over something left in his way, a coil of rope, a bucket. If the deck were wet from the swabber's efforts, he might go down on his tail with his feet in the air, rolling around like a great clown.

He would have to sweep his hands in front of him and feel with his feet. He would have to walk tentatively. Damn! He wanted to weep.

"Shreve!" Miranda spoke directly across from him.

Thank God. "Here." He abandoned the rail in an instant and walked into her arms. At the same moment the ship rolled and his weight flattened her against the bulkhead. She grunted as the breath exploded from her lungs. He groaned. He had almost knocked her down. "Sorry."

She steadied herself. "That's all right. I'm just glad to see you here. I couldn't find you. I came back to the cabin—"

"I was just taking a turn around the deck."

He could hear her smile. "Why that's wonderful. And you did just fine, didn't trip over anything or—"

"Oh, I was wonderful," he interrupted bitterly. "The wind was blowing, the sun was shining, a man was swabbing the deck. But I didn't see a damn thing. On the other hand, if I'd had a cane and a tin cup, I could have collected enough for our passage."

"Shreve—"

"Take me back to my cabin."

"Of course." She slipped his arm through hers. "You must be exhausted. You've been so sick."

"So I've been told."

"I see Doctor Clinton." Her voice had warmed. She must be smiling and nodding to the interfering bastard. "Did you and he talk?"

"Yes."

They descended the short companionway and reentered the cabin. Once through the door, he flung off her arm and staggered across the floor. It tilted, bumping him hard into the table. The pewter water pitcher and tankards went clattering.

Cursing vividly, he dropped into the chair. For a minute he sat, waiting for his heart to quiet and the sweat to cool on his body. Not surprisingly he found he had a headache. He looked in the direction of the door. "I hear, by the way, that we are married."

"Yes."

She had moved to sit on the bunk. He had been talking to empty space. The knowledge set him to cursing again.

"Are you very angry?"

"No. The pretense is probably a good idea. The voyage could be most unpleasant if you were shunned as a scarlet woman."

She braced herself and cleared her throat. "The captain married us a couple of days out from Veracruz."

"What!"

"George and Ada and Doctor Clinton were witnesses."

He rose from his chair. "You and I are married? Really married?"

"Yes." She actually hunched her shoulders against the eruption that was sure to follow.

"NO! I don't remember. I didn't know what was happening." Two steps across the tiny cabin brought him to tower over her.

254

"You did. You just don't remember."

"Damn you!" His face was dark with anger.

"Shreve, we're married. You even signed the logbook. We have a certificate with the witnesses' names on it. Please be glad about it. You bought me a license once."

He caught her by the shoulders and dragged her upright. "But — I'm — blind!" The bitterness and anger in his voice slammed into her. "How could you do this to yourself?"

She twisted to get away. His hands bruised her. She wrapped her arms across her stomach as jets of acid burned inside her. "I love you."

"You pity me."

"No. I love you. I love you."

"Goddamn you!" He flung her backward.

She cried out as the chair tipped back, then slammed down again. "Oh, Shreve, please don't be so angry. We had to get married."

He drew in a shivering breath of his own. "What do you mean? Are you pregnant?"

She sat stunned for a moment. "No. Oh, no. Of course not."

He stumped back to his chair and threw himself into it. "Thank God for small favors."

"Amen."

They had been together so long, shared the same home, the same work, the same bed, that they thought as one. In the silence that came between them a kind of horror grew. They were praising God that they were not giving birth to a child. Like a measure of their lives the realization grew. Miranda spoke first, her voice a harsh whisper. "Oh, Shreve, what have we come to?"

He laughed. "Why, don't you know? Don't you realize?" He pushed himself from the chair as if

255

he were freeing himself of it. "When you went after your revenge, you became Hamlet. You had his character to life. You gloried in it. You created the opportunity and you avenged your father's death."

She was weeping softly. He could picture the tears trickling down her cheeks. She always looked so beautiful when she cried. "Yes."

His voice lowered, became calm, a sermon, a lesson to be recalled. "I said those old dramas weren't like real life. But the end result is the same. Shakespeare knew what he was talking about. Hamlet saw his mother and his lover die. He killed his uncle and then died himself. The end of the ruling house of Denmark. Sterility. The death of a line. And the play's over. No one but Horatio left to tell about it.

"What is much worse about all this is that we didn't die, did we? We're still sailing along. Messy, untidy, loose ends with nothing but misery ahead of us. Misery. Now the play's over and we're still alive."

Miranda could not stem the tears. They fell like a flood into her lap.

"And because of what's happened to us, we don't dare have children. We're glad that we're not going to have them. The house of Denmark, the house of Macbeth, the house of Catherwood. Sterility."

He lay beside her in the dark, drained of all his wrath. Drained of all desire as well. He wanted only one thing. To die. To go over the side into the clean black depths of the ocean. To feel it close warmly over his head. To suck the salt into his lungs like blood. One deep breath and he would know nothing else.

He swung his legs out of the bunk and sat up. Then he listened.

Miranda did not move. She had cried until her tears were all expended. Still fully clothed, she huddled in the bunk. When he climbed in beside her, she had not moved except to put her hand on his thigh. Within a minute her even breathing told him she was sound asleep.

He put out his hand to touch her shoulder. She did not stir. Her breath was deep and faintly stertorous, as if she had a cold.

He rose and found the clothes he had stripped off. Thank God, she had not put them away as she usually did.

In the companionway he turned and with sure stride mounted the steps at the end. No wondering and wandering around the deck this time. He would march straight to the rail and put his face down on it. The space between the stanchions was wide enough that he could swing his legs over one at a time beneath the rope. A quick roll of his body and he would drop over the side. He had rehearsed the blocking in his mind. It should play without a hitch.

Outside on deck he lifted his face to the breeze. It was cooler with a touch of rain in it. He hoped the moon was down. The blacker the night, the better.

Surefooted, purposeful, he strode across the deck. As he had rehearsed it, he laid his cheek against the wood. One leg up.

"Wait," came a soft voice. "I'll come with you."

He dropped his leg back onto the deck and spun around. "I thought you were asleep."

"No. I'm dead."

He wanted to scream at her. She had made her entrance too soon. Instead, he controlled his voice. "I'm the one who's dead. Or I will be shortly. Go away, Miranda. Go back to sleep. You'll wake to a brave new world."

She came up beside him. Her shoulder brushed his. She was looking out over the ocean, too. Was the wind lifting her short pale hair? Were her eyes slitted against the spray? "I imagine one sleep is just like another. If you go, I go."

Her presence annoyed him above all things. "Don't be stupid. You have your life in front of you. A great career. You can take all the things I've taught you —"

She pushed herself between him and the rail and clapped her hand over his mouth. Her body was pressed against his. "Answer me this, love. How can I live if I've killed you?"

He tossed his head pulling away from her hand. "Miranda. I can't live the way I am."

"You can." She caught his shoulders. "You have to. You have to because we're all depending on you. You're Shreve Catherwood, Romantic Star of Three Continents."

"And you're the Magnificent Miranda. You can walk into any theater in London. They'll hire you without a reading."

She pressed her cheek against his chest. "I can't do it without you. No one wants Katharina without Petruchio."

Their names sobered him. How ironic that comedy should make him feel uneasy. Suddenly, he wanted to be Petruchio again and bury himself in his wild Kate.

No! He pushed at her body. When she balked,

258

he stepped to the side. "You'll do fine on your own."

"What about George and Ada?" Her voice accused him.

He hesitated. "What about them? You need them. Ada takes care of your costumes and makeup. George takes care of the business."

"What if there isn't any more business?"

Ruthlessly, he brushed aside her question. "If you don't want them, they'll still survive. They're troupers. They'll find other work."

"They're old." She transferred her grip to his upper arm. "They've followed you for years."

"A quarter of a century." He could feel himself turning to mush inside. Responsibility was weakening him. His throat was aching. Tears were starting at the back of his eyes. But no longer could he be responsible for them all. "Damn you, Miranda, don't you understand? I can't see. I can't act if I can't see. This is best for everyone. You can go on with your careers without a millstone around your necks."

She stepped away from him leading him with her voice. She paced in patterns across and up and down the deck. "It's dark out here. The moon is a sliver, the stars are tiny candles miles away. To me, you're only a shape. Yet you're following me with your eyes right now. Anyone looking at you would think you can see me perfectly."

He turned away instantly and faced the open sea. "But I can't. And what happens when you stop talking?"

She laughed. "In a play, whoever stops talking?"

"But I can't just stand still." He pivoted, threw

out his arm, and slapped his hand into the line stretched above the railing. "Now I'm tangled up in a rope. You see. I'd be a laughingstock."

She swooped toward him, caught his hands, and brought them together beneath her chin. It was her favorite position for a coquette. "I'm not laughing. No one else would be. You've been too careful for that. You've been all over this ship. You've staged your blocking yourself. If I hadn't made an unexpected entrance, you'd have blocked yourself right off the stage."

He felt a tiny flicker of pride. It swelled inside him. All the more reason to end it here, in triumph rather than defeat.

"Confess, Shreve," she mocked him softly. "You didn't commit suicide earlier today because you couldn't get the staging right."

He grunted.

"Am I right?"

He hung his head. "I wasn't going to fail and be hauled back over the side and humiliated."

"Right." She kissed his knuckles.

"You can help me."

She sighed elaborately. He could tell she was acting. "I can go with you if you insist. That's all I'll do."

He jerked his hands away and turned back to the rail. "You're acting. I can tell it. Don't deny it. I taught you everything you know. You may be able to fool everyone else, but never me. You don't want to kill yourself. There's no reason."

"The same with you. There's no reason for you to die, either."

"This is a ridiculous conversation to be having. Any fool can see that I can't live the way I am."

She put her arms around him and laid her head

260

against his shoulder. "Shreve, you're giving up too soon. I don't think you're going to be blind always. But even if you are, you're one of the few people in the world who could be blind and function normally."

"This conversation has passed the bounds of ridiculous. It's insane."

"No, I mean it. Think about it." She shook him gently. "First of all, I think the situation is pretty much the same as it was in New Orleans. You've got terrific swelling inside your head. And that malaria made everything worse. But there's a good chance that it isn't permanent."

"No. It's permanent. It's different. I know."

"You don't know. A sea voyage cured you before. Give this one a chance."

"And when you're wrong, I'll have to have a cane and dark glasses the minute we set foot in England. I don't want to wait for that." He shook himself and gripped the rail. So long as he held tight to it, he retained the right of self-determination. "I'll grow complacent. I'll never be able to see, but I'll get used to being blind. Used to compromise. Used to being a burden. I'll like it. It'll be a treat to have you and Ada wait on me hand and foot."

"It won't—"

"The hell it won't. You'll come to resent me because I can't pull my own weight. You'll think that I'm pathetic. Oh, you'll try to get me work for a few times. They won't hire me. They'll hire you, of course. I'll sit in the hotel room. Or Ada will steer me into the wings—well back, of course, so I can hear, because I don't need to be able to see."

"Shreve—"

261

"Say I could stumble around the stage, maybe playing Lear or Prospero, how long do you think you'd want me as a partner?"

"Shreve—"

"*Shreve,*" he mocked. "I won't be able to exercise. My body will get fat, my eyes will sink back in my head. Oh, I've seen blind people. I know how they look. How much will you love me with greasy hair and a potbelly? I'll forget to shave. After all, I don't have to look at myself."

"Shreve Catherwood, you'd never—"

"And then your leading man or maybe the theater owner or the producer or the director will realize you're beautiful and unattached. They'll take you out for dinner—"

"Shreve, for God's sake—"

"—and you'll fall into bed with them or in love or both. And you'd be right to. They're young and strong and can pay compliments to your beauty. I'm—" He shook his head. "I don't want to wait for that."

She stood silent on the deck for so long he thought he might have convinced her. At last she began to clap her hands, slowly, then with gathering speed. "Bravo. Bravo. What a performance! What a script! Bravo! One thing's for certain. When you get too old to act, you can write great dramas."

"I'm not acting."

"Well, I certainly hope not. It was much too frantic, too forced. Too much melodrama." She began to emote. "*I renounce the fair Elizabeth for I am not the man for her.*"

"Damn you to hell!" He left the rail and took a step toward her.

She laughed and caught his outstretched hand.

"Come back to bed. You've talked yourself out it."

He jerked his arm out of her grasp. "I—I—"

"Have you run out of lines? Too bad. But then life is never like the theater is. If this had been a production, you would have stepped gracefully and gallantly over the balustrade onto a mattress back stage. I would have run to the edge, screaming, then turned to face the audience and fallen to my knees as the curtain swished to."

"I'll never step over a balustrade again." He continued to argue, but his words held no conviction. "I won't be able to find it."

"You found this. Not only that, but you found it twice." She caught him by the arms. Her voice rang with joy and optimism. "Shreve! Shreve! You can do it. You've always memorized your blocking the same way you've memorized scripts. Once the sets are built and the props laid down, you won't fumble. Believe in yourself."

"I can't."

She kissed him hard on the mouth, wrapped her arms around him, rubbed her breasts against his chest. The inside of her thigh slid up over his hip.

Suddenly, he wanted her very much. And—God help him—he wanted to live. He caught her behind the knee and pulled her hard against him. "Miranda."

She jerked her mouth away. "Yes. You can do it. You're alive. Your whole body is singing with life and pleasure. You're hot and wanting me right now. You don't want to be cold, wet, dead, food for fish—"

He clamped his mouth down on hers.

She kissed him with all the strength of her

263

arms, her body, and her thrusting tongue.

Just as she had said, his passion rose. His body turned to steel, denying death, denying icy water with a blaze of desire. The ship dipped as it crested the waves.

Locked together, they staggered across the deck. Her back came up against the hull of a lifeboat. She whimpered but could not protest. Mouth still drinking from hers, he lowered her to the sun-warmed planks.

He was bursting, his blood pounding in his temples, his breath coming hot and heavy. "Miranda."

"Monster! You hurt me!" She bit at his lips at the same time she pushed up against him, digging her heels into the deck, thrusting against his hardness.

"Lady Macbeth!"

"But screw your courage to the sticking place, And we'll not fail."

He clamped his mouth to hers again, taking her words deep in his throat. His need was painful, terrible, torturing. He had never known such desire.

Her fingers curved into talons. She dragged up her skirt.

He reached for her, expecting petticoats and drawers. Her thighs were bare. The silken nest at their jointure was hot, damp, swollen. "Oh, God!"

Lightning sliced through his body. She had followed him to seduce him. If her words failed, she had come prepared to save him with her body.

She was a — He was saying the words. "Vixen. Shrew. Succubus.

"Love."

264

Her mouth smiled beneath his words. She tore at his buttons, freed him, then gasped at the size of the rod that sprang free into her hand. He lifted himself. She guided him to her opening, spread her thighs, brought her legs up along the sides of his body to grant him the greatest access.

He rammed into her. As he slid into the slick, hot darkness, he exploded. Exploded. Exploded. Throwing back his head, gritting his teeth. Every muscle in his body swollen with hot blood driving his life into her.

She accepted him, rocked him in the cradle of her hips, took his length and breadth into her, tightened her grip. The muscles of her sheath closed around the root of his manhood.

He cried out again, this time in ultimate pleasure.

His voice set her vibrating, her heels pushing against the backs of his legs, driving him deeper until they could be no closer together. Neither could move. Stasis in darkness.

And then with a sigh, as he began to relax. "Miranda."

Her nails dug into his back. "Again, Shreve," she demanded. "You're not through yet. Again, my love."

He shuddered. His mind told him he could not. Men did not—

She arched her hips and rubbed her mound against him. Hot, slick, rubbing against his belly. Holding him. Keeping him inside her.

"Sweetheart—"

"Ssssh. You must. I have to have you. I can't wait another day, another hour." Her breath scorched his ear. She took his earlobe between her lips, sucking, biting delicately. "Feel how

265

much I want you. Don't leave me wanting. Please, Shreve, please, please."

He shook his head or tried to, but she held him, with tiny pains sharp as her white teeth. Her hands slid through his clothing, around his hips, pressed his buttocks hard. "You can't get away from me. Not until you please me."

His heart stepped up its beat a bit. His breathing increased to bring oxygen into the blood that had cooled. He could not. He could not. Men did not.

Miranda's hips followed when he would have pushed away. Her buttocks left the deck as she pushed the sensitive center of her being against his pubic bone. The pressure was painful, but something would come, something she needed.

"Shreve," she pleaded. "Shreve." Her lips slid across his cheek, pricking through the beginnings of his beard. Her breath blew hot in his ear, her tongue traced the shape of it.

He groaned. Already he was filling her, hardening. "Witch."

"Yes."

"Shrew."

She hunched herself upward. Rubbing, seeking, hot, wet. "Yes."

"Love." He moved within her, began a slow, seductive rocking, pulling out, sliding in.

She lost control. Her head fell back against the deck. Her back arched taking him in impossibly deeper.

Out and in. Hard again. Pleasure.

She began to shudder. Tiny cries turned to sobs. Pleasure.

Out and in. Pleasure in his movements. Pleasure.

266

Again the shuddering. The stiffening. The convulsion of her muscles, of her womb. "Don't. Stop. Don't stop."

Out and in. Pleasure building, building.

They cried out together, pushed over an edge into an abyss of stars and light. In darkness, yet blinded by light.

Act V
Scene 1
London and
Washington, D.C.,
1884

Fifteen

'Tis time to fear when tyrants seem to kiss.

"Senator Butler. Hugh!"

He looked around to see who had called him, an affable smile ready for his constituent. One look and the smile swiftly faded. He tipped his hat, using it to shield the upper half of his face, and lumbered down the steps.

"Hugh. Wait. I must see you." Ruth Drummond Westfall, dressed in a widow's unrelieved black hurried after him.

His carriage was too far away. He plastered the smile back on his face and turned to extend his hands. "Why, my dear Ruth. What a pleasant surprise! I didn't recognize you at first."

She gave him her hands clad in black kid gloves. Staring up into his florid face, she searched his features. "I've put on mourning out of respect for Benjamin."

"Of course. Terrible thing. Shocking. The western frontier will never be safe until every one of those savages is eradicated like the vermin they are."

"Hugh. Benjamin was not killed by Indians."

He frowned. Then his expression became bland. "My information—"

"—was wrong."

"Really." He heaved a sigh. "My staff is usually

271

so accurate." He pulled his watch from his vest pocket and snapped it open. "Ruth, it's so good to see you. And you're looking so well. Especially after the terrible shock. If there's anything I can do—anything at all, I want you to let me know immediately. Now if you'll excuse me—"

She blocked his way. "Hugh. I need to see you. There are things you should know about what went on out there in Wyoming. The persecution of the Sioux and Cheyenne must not go further."

Trying not to look at her, he motioned vigorously to his carriage. "Perhaps you could set up an appointment—"

"I've tried to see you for several weeks now. Your secretary says your appointments are filled every day."

He nodded. "He's right. Besides the time in the chamber, there are the committee meetings. You know how busy a politician can get."

"Yes, I understand," she replied, looking squarely at him. "Maud Mary understood, too."

He stopped at the mention of his long dead daughter, Benjamin Westfall's first wife. The frown lines deepened between his eyes. His lips twitched as if he were trying to frame proper words. Finally, he settled for, "She did, indeed."

"Hugh. I must talk to you."

He consulted his watch again. His carriage had finally pulled alongside him at the curb. He threw the driver a poisonous look, then smiled down at Ruth. "I have it. Let me buy you a cup of coffee. I have a few minutes before my next appointment. Of course, I had planned to devote those to study." He looked hopefully at her, but her expression did not waver. With a shrug he capitulated. "Would you care to come with me now?"

"Where?"

He looked up and down the street. "Just a block away, my dear." He offered her his arm. To his driver he said, "Follow us."

The cafe looked out on Pennsylvania Avenue. He seated her, then allowed his enormous frame to drop into the chair. Once the waiter had taken their order, he leaned back, hands wrapped around the lapels of his frock coat. "You're looking very well, Ruth."

She smiled. "I have recovered from the shock of Benjamin's death, but I cannot forget how needless it was."

His eyes narrowed. "Needless. Yes, I'm sure it was needless. Cold-blooded murder is certainly the most needless of crimes."

"It wasn't cold-blooded murder. It was self-defense. He drew his pistol first."

"Ah, but it wasn't loaded."

"He didn't know that. He only thought to shoot the man." She paused as the waiter served their coffees.

Butler took a drink of his immediately, oblivious to the steam. "That's exactly why he was so valuable. He was a soldier. And a good one. He was prepared to defend himself. Hostiles—"

"Hugh. I was there. So were several hundred people. We all saw the man who killed Benjamin in self-defense. He was dressed in a soldier's uniform. He had blond hair."

"Undoubtedly a disguise."

She paled. Her hand trembled as she spooned sugar into her cup. "I've come to you to implore you to make sure that this terrible tragedy will not be used as an excuse to persecute innocent Indians."

He met her gaze sternly. "No one innocent will be persecuted. The United States government is not

273

in the business of persecuting anyone. But when one of our own is murdered, we will leave no stone unturned in our efforts to punish the guilty parties to the full limits of the law."

Ruth dropped her eyes to her cup. Carefully, she poured in cream and stirred the concoction.

Convinced he had closed that conversation, the senator drained his cup.

She met his eyes as he set it down. "Why did you send him back there, Hugh?"

He choked slightly. Touching his napkin to his lips, he regarded her balefully. "He was the person for the job."

"Only if the U.S. Government wanted to become embroiled in another Indian war."

"Now, Ruth, I'm sure you're putting the wrong complexion on—"

"Hugh, I was privy to his plans on the long trip out by train. He planned to rebuild Fort Gallatin. He talked endlessly of the numbers of men and supplies that he would need in order to control the territory. More young men would have died. Weren't Clarendon and Custer and all their men enough?"

"The West must be safe."

"It *is* safe. Colorado is already a state. Wyoming is about to become one. Montana. Idaho. The Dakotas. They're all being settled peaceably. You should have seen the hundreds of people that drove up to the monument that July Fourth. Young men with their wives and children. They wouldn't have brought them to that land if it hadn't been safe. My husband was out for revenge. He would have stirred up the Indians."

"My dear." Hugh Butler reached across the table and patted her hand. "You don't have the entire picture. My staff supplies me with the very latest

274

information from all over the West. The Indians constituted an omnipresent threat. Benjamin was the logical person to handle the situation. He had experience."

She looked at him squarely. "You had dozens, maybe hundreds of officers as experienced, some more experienced. Why send Benjamin back to the scene of his shame and disaster?"

The senator leaned forward in his chair. His huge hands clutched the edges of the table. His jowls sagged forward. "My son-in-law deserved a chance to absolve himself."

"Maybe ten or fifteen years ago, but not when he was an old man. Hugh, he was sixty-four years old. He should have been sitting in a rocking chair reading a good book. Or writing his memoirs."

The senator cleared his throat. "He was not old. I am old. Eighty-five is old."

"The fact is that Fort Gallatin killed him. And I want his death to be the end of deaths associated with that horrible place."

"That place was most recently consecrated to the memory of the gallant men who died there." He straightened in his chair. "Your first husband Francis Drummond was among them."

"I know that," she said softly. "I was left a pregnant widow."

He flushed at her frank speech. "Ruth —"

She rushed on. " — with a thirteen year old girl to rear. I had nothing but a small pension. Had it not been for my mother and father's hospitality, which was offered grudgingly, I might add, I would have been in dire straits. I probably would have suffered."

"I would think you would want revenge on the Indians who made you a widow."

"I don't want revenge. I want peace. And so

does every woman from the Atlantic to the Pacific." Her eyes flashed latent fire. She debated telling him that she knew that Indians were not responsible for either of the tragedies in her life. Initially, they had been pawns of Benjamin Westfall. She shivered slightly.

Hugh's sharp eyes caught the movement of her shoulders. His hand closed over her wrist before she could withdraw it. "Go back to Chicago, Ruth." His voice was stern. "You're expending your frail strength unnecessarily. Go home."

She shook her head. "I can't go home until this thing has ended. It's been going on for nearly twenty years."

His grip tightened.

She flashed him a look of alarm.

Abruptly he released her, letting her hand drop back onto the tablecloth. Reaching into his pocket, he extracted his purse and threw down a silver dollar. "Go home." Rising, he towered over her. "This doesn't concern you anymore. Go home where you'll be safe. Start your life over again."

"For the third time," she remarked bitterly to his retreating back.

He left the cafe and climbed into his carriage. She watched him through the window. The vehicle swayed as he settled ponderously into it.

He was a giant, she thought. A giant of a man in stature and in power. She drank the rest of her coffee in one gulp. The caffeine would steady her nerves that hummed and vibrated beneath the force of his implicit threat.

"Victor!"

Only by a dint of willpower did White Wolf's Brother manage to keep from groaning at the sight of her. Rachel glided across the lobby

276

toward him, her hand outstretched.

Rachel Drummond Westfall, as beautiful as ever. More beautiful really. In the few short months since he had seen her, she had bloomed. Her skin was like the petals of a white rose, her eyes were the clearest blue, he had ever seen. Her hair, no longer hanging down her back like a schoolgirl's, was pulled back from her face into a cascade of ringlets that spilled down her neck. Wisps of hair, like spun gold waved around her temples and in front of her ears.

He took the hand she extended and drank her in. He could not return the smile that lit her face. For him it spelled disaster. "Rachel," he said through stiff lips. "You're looking well."

"I finished school," she told him proudly. "They allowed me to take all the classes I needed for graduation. I studied hard. Really hard. My grades were excellent."

He nodded. "I'm sure they were."

She lifted her chin. "Are you satisfied?"

"Rachel, I—"

She stepped closer to him. Their bodies almost touched. He could smell the toilet water she wore, see the play of light in the luminous eyes. He felt his heart step up its beating.

"I haven't changed my mind, Victor. I never will. Are you going to pretend that we aren't in love?"

Looking around in alarm, he retreated. His arm stiffened holding her at its length. "Rachel, you know what I am. I've told you."

"Yes, I know what you are. You're an American. You're more American than I am. And I love you."

A man crossing the lobby raised his eyebrow in Victor's direction. One corner of his mouth lifted in a congratulatory smirk.

"God! Rachel. This is a hotel lobby. You're

going to disgrace yourself."

"Then promise to meet me."

"RACHEL!"

"Or we can go up to your room right now." She made a move to put her arm through his.

He backed away from her so fast that he stumbled over a hassock in the center of the lobby.

"Careful." She caught his arm, as he flailed to keep his balance.

As he righted himself, he caught the desk clerk eyeing them suspiciously. He could feel heat rising in his cheeks. Inwardly, he cursed his fair complexion. An old man in a wing chair by the window, lowered his paper and peered at them over the top of his glasses. They were a spectacle for the entire lobby.

"I'll be careful. Just let go of me," he snarled under his breath.

"I just didn't want you to get hurt."

He pulled his arm out from under her hands. "I'm not going to be hurt. You're the one who'll be hurt."

She clasped her hands in front of her over the brass handle of her parasol. Her smile was sweet innocence personified. "If I'm hurt, you'll make everything right."

"You don't understand. Not at all."

She stepped close again. "Where shall we meet? Your hotel room?"

"God! No! Someplace public."

"Where?"

He struggled to turn his mind to coherent thought. "The Smithsonian. That's it. The Smithsonian Institution. On the Capitol mall."

She made a disappointed face.

"Take it or leave it," he said. "We can look at the exhibits."

She nodded. "Among other things."

"Rachel."

"At two, this afternoon, then."

He stared after her. Sweat had started on his forehead. The starched collar felt tight. More important, he was excited. His body had responded to her like wild fire.

The desk clerk smirked as he handed over the room key.

Hugh Smith Butler sifted through the papers on his desktop. "There are entirely too many loose ends in this thing. It could turn nasty overnight. Investors flee scandal like the plague."

De la Barca scowled at the senator. His thigh still ached from the gunshot wound. His shoulders ached where the guards at La Yegua Blanca had twisted his arms. The right side was worse than the left. Gingerly, he probed into the heart of the muscle, testing for the source of the pain. He regretted that he had shot them dead. They should have hurt longer, the way he was hurting.

"Are you listening?" the senator boomed.

With elaborate care de la Barca settled his arm at his waist before he looked up at the figure leaning forward over the wide desk. "I'm listening, but so far I haven't heard much that's any of my business."

Butler's hands clenched into hamlike fists. His shoulders humped around his head like an old bull buffalo. "I need to know the number of people involved in this plot. At first, I thought that they were large. But when Ben's wife confronted me today, I began to get an idea that this might have been nothing at all."

De la Barca watched the man stalk back and forth across the office. The senator's big body

279

sweated profusely. Its acrid odor filled the room. The front of his coat had food spots.

Butler swung an accusing arm at the investigator. "If you had done your job and caught the girl, we'd know."

De la Barca did not allow his eyes to flicker by so much as a centimeter. "It's hard to bring someone out of a foreign country when she doesn't want to go. Especially someone who has friends in the government." Neatly, he shifted the blame back to the senator. "If you'd given the order, I could have eliminated her at the same time I got rid of her lover."

Butler flared as he resumed his seat behind the desk. His breathing was loud in the room. His breath heaving out of his great bellows of a chest was rank, rotten. The old man's health was deteriorating rapidly.

"If I could only be sure. Hostiles are ultimately to blame for all this, but those fools on the committee have taken Westfall's assassination by a soldier or a disguised civilian as a sign that people do not want the army on the Powder River."

He had fallen to mumbling more to himself than to the man seated before him. De la Barca climbed to his feet. "Let me know what you want me to do, Senator. I'm at your service."

"What? Wait." Butler started up. "Wait. Er— Ruth Westfall. She mustn't continue to spread her stories around Capitol Hill. Send her back to Chicago. Her and her daughter."

De la Barca's lips tightened. "Easy or rough?"

Butler wiped his hand across the lower half of his face. "Rough. Rough. I warned her. I told her to go home. She's still in town. Still talking to people. A general's widow in trailing black veils. She gets their ear."

"Maybe her daughter might have a little accident — nothing really serious, but knocked about — maybe a couple of mugs — "

"I don't want to know about it!" Butler waved his hand in dismissal. "Just let me hear about it after the fact."

"It's the sarcophagus Andrew Jackson refused to be buried in." Victor straightened from reading the sign near the base of the carved stone box.

"I can't say that I blame him. I don't think I could fit in it. And they'd have to cut you off at the legs." Rachel looked her escort admiringly up and down.

"They must have stuffed people in sacks and buried them all bundled up in those days. I think that's what shrouds were actually."

She shuddered. "I really don't care to see the inside of that building if that's what we're going to see."

He shrugged. "Perhaps you're right. We could just stroll down the mall toward the Capitol. Did you know Washington is laid out like a giant wheel to defend against attackers?"

Rachel accepted his proffered arm. "I think we need to talk about what we're going to do about the next thirty or forty years."

His mouth tightened. "I've told you. We don't have thirty or forty years. We have now. Today. And that's all."

"Victor Wolf!" She planted herself firmly in front of him. "This is the third or fourth time you've said that to me. Don't you think you'd better give it up?"

"White Wolf's Brother," he argued. "My name is White Wolf's Brother."

She caught a strange note in his voice. His eyes

281

stared beyond her. She threw a quick glance over her shoulder. People were all around them. Some strolled up and down the mall seeing the sights. Some milled in groups in front of various government buildings. She looked up at him inquiringly. His arm had gone tense under her hand. "What's wrong?"

He gave his head a quick shake. "I don't know." He turned her around and led her purposefully down the street away from the Capitol. "Something—"

Behind them a pair of men detached themselves from a group. One nudged the other and signaled to a man farther up the street. He pushed himself away from the side of the building and stepped out in front of the couple.

A delivery wagon rattled up the street.

"What's wrong? Victor—"

He pushed her toward the single man. "Go on, Rachel," he encouraged softly. "Walk on. I'll join you there later."

She froze, trembling. The color drained from her face.

The man in front of her grinned. He held out his hand to her as he would a dog. "Come on, lady. Do like the gent says."

She shook her head.

"Go on, Rachel," Victor urged. He pivoted, his eyes shifting to the other two men, hurrying toward them. His hand dipped beneath his coat and came up with a hunting knife. Its nine-inch blade glinted in the sunlight.

The men slowed. But still they came on, balanced on the balls of their feet like dancers. As they neared him, they separated circling him.

"HELP!" Rachel's scream turned heads the length of the mall. Then the man behind her sprang and clapped his hand over her mouth. The delivery wagon halted. The man dragged her toward its back door that suddenly swung open.

"Rachel!" White Wolf's Brother lunged toward the struggling pair.

The two men jumped after him. One grabbed his knife arm.

Lithe as the wolf for which he was named, Victor whirled. His knife slashed like a saber.

The man screamed as the blade sliced through the clothing and skin of his middle. He fell back.

The Cheyenne's blue eyes blazed at the other, who held up his hands and backed hastily out of reach.

Rachel struggled violently, beating her assailant around the head with her parasol. The brass knob on the head caught him above the eye. He cursed and flung her against the tailgate of the wagon. Her bonnet fell off and her hair cascaded down her back.

"Hey! Leave that lady alone." A young man hurried to cross Jefferson Drive.

The man in the wagon, caught Rachel by the shoulders.

She screamed again, kicking angrily as her feet left the ground.

"Drive!" her captor yelled over his shoulder.

The wagon jumped forward as the driver whipped the horses. Victor leaped for the tailgate. The man whom Rachel had struck made a dive for the back of the wagon at the same time. They collided. Victor knocked him aside, and made a grab for the vehicle, but it gathered speed.

The young man in the middle of the street shouted to people ahead. "Help! Stop that team. They've taken a woman."

From the group in front of a building farther

along the way, a couple of heavyset men sprang down, and grabbed the bridles.

The driver swung his whip, lashing at them furiously.

Other men gathered around.

The two men who had first tried to hold Victor scuttled into the crowd. The one who had collided with Victor also scrambled up and disappeared.

Suddenly, the driver of the wagon realized he was surrounded. Lowering his whip, he stared at the stern faces around him. From the back of the wagon came Rachel's squeals. Then the bystanders heard the thud of a fist against flesh followed by a shriek of pain.

The man at the horses' heads scowled blackly at the driver. Hand over hand, he came up the reins, set his foot on the wheel's axle, and hauled the unfortunate man down by the scruff of the neck.

Victor tore through the people encircling the wagon and pulled on the door. When it resisted his first efforts, his face contorted in anger. With a war whoop that lifted the hair on the necks of the crowd, he caught hold of the bottom edge of the door and heaved. The wood cracked and the door broke open.

Rachel had crumpled to the bed of the wagon. A man stood over her, his fists clenched. At the sight of Victor, he bared his teeth in a snarl.

"Get the hell outta here! This ain't none of yore business."

Knife drawn, Victor vaulted into the wagon.

The man reached for Rachel to lift her body to use as a hostage. "I said—"

What he would have said died with him. Victor's knife tore into his belly and ripped up through his heart. The man's eyes glazed even before Victor twisted the knife out of the wound.

Not really conscious of what had happened, Rachel knew only that she had to escape. She dived for the door opening, falling headfirst into the arms of the men gathered around.

"Rachel!" Victor pushed the dead man aside like a sack of moldy grain and scrambled after her. "Rachel!"

"Here now, little lady, you're all right."

She fought them, scratched and clawed at their faces, screamed for help, twisted violently when they tried to hold her.

"Rachel." Victor spun her around and caught her by the shoulders.

Her eyes were glazed but not with terror. She had bared her teeth in a feral snarl. From out of her chest came deep, gasping, grunting sounds as she fought to be free.

"Rachel." He shook her.

"Let go! Let go!"

"Rachel! It's all right. You're safe." He ducked his head trying to catch her eyes.

Dimly, she recognized him. But all around her were men's faces. They looked stern, forbidding, angry. "Victor! Run! Run!"

"Yes, dear. Yes, sweetheart."

She looked fearfully over her shoulder into the depths of the wagon. The dead man lay limply in the opening, one hand dangling over the edge. Blood dripped from his fingers. She looked down at her skirt. It was spattered with red.

Her eyes sought Victor's. "You killed him."

"Yes." He waited, not certain what she would say or do.

Suddenly, she relaxed, slumped against him. "Take me home," she whispered. "I—I must change my dress."

He put both arms around her to support her

285

against his side. A reporter for the *Washington News* appeared at his elbow. "What's the young lady's name and why were they after her?"

Before he thought, Victor answered. "She's Rachel Westfall. Her father was General Benjamin Westfall."

"Westfall." The reporter scribbled hastily. "Westfall. Westfall? Would that be the man assassinated out in Wyoming in July?"

"Assassinated." The word spread out in ripples. "Who? When? Her father was assassinated. Do tell."

The driver of the vehicle took the opportunity to swing his fist into the gut of the man who held him and scramble away through the crowd.

Victor watched his escape helplessly. No policeman had yet appeared. The crowd was sympathetic but unprepared to hold a felon.

The reporter did not let the escape bother him unduly. "And what's your name, sir?"

Victor hesitated, but Rachel lifted her head proudly. "He's my fiancé, Victor Wolf from Wyoming."

"From Wyoming?" the reporter prompted excitedly. "A real western hero."

"More than that," she replied.

"Rachel," Victor warned.

The reporter's face was alight. "Let's hear it."

"Victor's part of the territorial committee for statehood."

"Let me get her back to her home." Victor tried to drag her away, but Rachel dragged her feet and the reporter matched his steps with hers.

"He's from Sheridan," she insisted. "And—"

The reporter scribbled frantically. The crowd pressed close.

"He's a Cheyenne warrior."

Sixteen

A braver place
In my heart's love hath no man than yourself.

"Fools! Idiots!" Hugh Smith Butler shook his huge fist at de la Barca. "I pay you an outrageous sum to ensure that everything—everything will go off without a hitch. And you hire blunderers."

"They'd worked for me before." The investigator defended himself. "The plan was good. It should have worked perfectly."

"Well, it didn't!" Butler's breathing was stertorous. His jowls were puce. Tiny red capillaries snaked through the oily skin as if the bottom of his face were cracking and about to fall away. "Abduction in broad daylight! On the mall! What kind of plan is that, for God's sake?"

De la Barca raised his hand. "If it had worked, you'd be the first one to applaud."

"But it didn't work!" The senator's fists thudded down on the desk top. He pushed back his chair and strode across the room.

"She fought."

Butler's hands shook as he poured a glass of whisky and tossed it off. He returned to the desk and leaned across it, huge and intimidating. "Of course, she fought. What woman wouldn't have?"

The investigator stared up at him implacably. "Most women."

Butler damned him to hell.

De la Barca rose. "Look. The plan was virtually foolproof. Push over her escort, grab her, throw her in the back of the wagon. If the guy tries to get tough, punch out his lights and run for it. Lots of gangs milling around the mall, complaining about stuff. They get into scuffles all the time in front of the buildings. You know that."

Butler refused to acknowledge that he did.

"We were going to tie her up, drive her around a bit, put a couple of hands up her dress—"

"My God! Not rape!"

"Naw! Just tease her, you know. Nothing serious. Get her good and hungry, bawling her eyes out, scared out of her wits. Then tell her we'll be watching her and throw her out on the street. The police pick her up, take her home safe to mother, and mother's on the next train back to Chicago." De la Barca shook his head. "It should've worked."

Butler sank back in his chair. He pulled an extra large handkerchief from his pocket and mopped his perspiring face.

"Instead she fought like a wildcat. Screamed her head off. Scratched, kicked. Hit Billy a real knock on the side of the head."

"She might as well have finished him off," Butler snarled. "He's no use to anyone."

"The guy she was with turned vicious," de la Barca went on. "Pulled a knife. Ripped Tolly's belly open."

"What a pity!" Butler looked at his hireling with distaste. He picked up the newspaper lying on top of the desk. "The incident could not have turned out worse. The fool girl gave the whole story to a blasted reporter, who turned it into something out

288

of a dime novel. The 'vicious guy she was with' was identified here as a Cheyenne warrior. He tore the door of the wagon open with a wild war whoop.' Damn! Damn! Damn!"

The senator flung the paper down on his desk top, then snatched it up again. With trembling hands he folded the picture to the artist's sketch of Victor and thrust it into de la Barca's face.

"Look at him. Damn you! 'Victor Wolf, White Wolf's Brother.' Read it. He's blond, for God's sake. A member of the Wyoming delegation. Some romantic idiot'll introduce a bill to accept Wyoming for statehood immediately. God! A blond Indian."

He flung the paper across the room and buried his face in his hands. "The investors will pull out. I'll be ruined."

De la Barca stared at the balding dome, red and shining with grease.

Butler raised his head. "Get out. Get out. I'll send for you if I can think of anything for you to do. Just get out of my sight."

"You've got to take your daughter and leave Washington. Back in Chicago she'll be safe." Adolf Lindhauer stared sternly at the three women arranged before him in the hotel suite.

After a moment's silence, Ruth Westfall shook her head. "I can't leave. Hugh Butler sent the general to Fort Gallatin to give Benjamin a chance to redeem himself. Now Hugh's angry. He believes Indians killed the general. I kept explaining that they hadn't had anything to do with his death. I told him a soldier shot in self-defense, but he wouldn't believe me. You know I've got to set the record straight. And you know why."

"Mother—" Rachel began, but Adolf interrupted.

289

"We know how you feel, Ruth, but you may be beating your head against a stone wall. Probably the senator doesn't believe your story because his facts don't jibe with yours."

"That's exactly why I've got to—"

"Or maybe they do," Adolf interrupted. "And he doesn't want them known. You've said yourself that Westfall was planning to start a war. Butler must have known that. He and Westfall went way back. There's a lot of opposition to statehood for the western territories. Politicians—senators especially—don't want more senators in the Congress. It threatens their power."

Ruth's mouth quivered. "Hugh Smith Butler is one of the most respected men in Washington."

"Then he won't want you telling your story and calling him a liar," Adolf said shortly.

While Adolf had been speaking, Rachel's expression had become more serious. In a truly horrible way, what the Westerner was saying made perfect sense. And if it were true then her father had been involved in a plot to destroy Victor's people. "He's a U.S. senator," she objected weakly. "No one's calling him a liar. He's just mistaken."

Adolf looked at her pityingly. With uncharacteristic emotion he put his hand on her shoulder.

Her eyes bore dark circles, the evidence of a sleepless night. The left side of her jaw showed a scalloped bruise where the assailant's hand had clamped on her tender flesh.

"Ruth," he asked gently, "why would someone pick out Rachel to abduct? And in broad daylight?"

Ruth shook her head. "I don't have any idea. I've never heard of such a thing."

"Nobody else has, either. She wasn't the only young lady on the mall that day, nor yesterday, nor the day before. Women of all ages, some without male escorts, stroll down the mall in front of the Capitol every day. The streets are always full of people. No one's ever been abducted."

"You're saying it was deliberate," Ruth whispered.

"Of course deliberate. I'm suggesting it was a warning."

"To me?"

"Yes."

"I think my husband is right." Blue Sun on Snow spoke for the first time. "If Rachel had been taken, she would probably have been set free eventually. She might have been allowed to escape. But she could just as well have been killed."

Ruth wrapped her arms around her body to control her shuddering.

"Victor saved me," Rachel declared.

Adolf picked up the paper. "Actually, he didn't save you. There were too many men for him to fight off. The way the newspaper account reads 'The crowd surrounded the wagon and pulled the driver from the seat.' You were already being taken away."

"Victor broke open the door to the wagon. He used his knife," Rachel insisted loyally. "They wouldn't have gotten very far."

"My son is a very brave man and a very strong one," Blue Sun on Snow agreed, "but he could not have fought off two men and caught a wagon on foot."

"He was a hero," Rachel insisted.

Adolf put the paper down and smiled at Rachel. "You are an angel. Any man would fight to save you, but" — his pale blue eyes sought out Ruth's — "you must take her out of danger."

"No." Rachel rose to her feet. "Victor and I are

291

going to be married," she declared proudly.

They all looked at her in amazement.

"Has he said something to you that he shouldn't?" Adolf rumbled. "I'll tan his hide. He—"

"He hasn't. But I've already made the announcement. It's right there in the story."

Ruth picked up her own copy of the paper. "Oh, sweetheart. I thought that might have been a romantic notion that the reporter inserted to make the story more exciting."

Rachel fairly beamed. "No. I was the one who made the announcement. I wanted Victor to get credit for saving me. Actually, the reporter wasn't nearly so excited about our being engaged as he was about Victor's being a Cheyenne warrior." She leaned over to study the article. "The sketch doesn't do him justice. He's much handsomer than that."

"Ye Gods and little fishes," Adolf groaned.

Ruth shook her head. "Oh, Rachel. What have you done?"

Her daughter lifted her chin. "I fell in love with Victor the first time I saw him. I think he fell in love with me at the same time. But he's afraid to marry me. He thinks I'll be shut out of society."

"You could very well be," Blue Sun on Snow told her quietly. "Most white men hate and fear Indians." She looked at her husband. "Just as most Indians hate and fear the white men."

"I don't care. Victor's wonderful and I love him."

Adolf threw up his hands. "Another reason for you to leave, my dear Ruth. You've got to take your daughter back to Chicago where she can find someone suitable to marry."

"No!" Rachel exclaimed.

"No," Ruth said at the same time. "That's not a

reason, either. I would be pleased and proud to have Victor for my son-in-law if he and Rachel can come to a mutual agreement."

"Oh, Mother." Joyfully, Rachel flung her arms around her mother's neck. "We will. We will. Just wait till I tell him you approve."

Ruth frowned at her daughter. "You're eleven years younger than Victor, my dear. He's a grown man with a well-established business and political aspirations. He may want someone more his own age."

"That's silly. You're much younger than Daddy was."

"Not your real father. He and I were only a few years apart. We started life together. He was just a shavetail lieutenant fresh out of West Point and I was barely out of finishing school in Chicago. Victor has a rich life and opportunities to be an important man in Wyoming." She looked at his parents. "Perhaps in the United States Government."

"He'll need the right woman," Rachel agreed. "And who would be better than a general's daughter?"

Adolf rolled his eyes at Blue Sun on Snow. His wife giggled. He threw up his hands. "However that may be, the fact remains that you both have to leave town. Someone's gone to a lot of trouble to scare you. They've hurt you. Maybe the next time they might even try to kill you. Ruth, you've got to face facts."

The woman paled. Her eyes sparkled with tears. She nodded. "I suppose you're right."

"Mother!"

Ruth took a deep breath. "But this has gone on so long. Adolf, I ran away before. I should have stayed and told the truth to the court-martial about

293

Ben Westfall. I should never have married him when he came back into my life in Chicago. I should have refused to go West with him in June. I should have done so many things. I didn't do them. I let my older daughter be persecuted for what he did. Now maybe I've endangered the lives of countless Cheyenne and Sioux. I can't run away again."

"Most of that was a long time ago." Adolf interrupted the flow as it threatened to turn hysterical. He looked at his wife for support. Blue Sun on Snow moved to the divan beside Ruth and put her arm around the other woman's shoulders. "A lot of water under the bridge since then. And the Sioux and Cheyenne have other friends besides you."

Ruth raised her head. "Nevertheless. I didn't do the right thing. I have to do it now."

"But what can you do?"

"I'm a general's widow, dressed in black. That counts for something. Look what Libby Custer's been able to accomplish. I'll go everywhere, be seen everywhere. I'll talk to congressmen and senators and reporters. I'll tell everyone the truth. I can be sure that the Cheyenne and the Sioux don't get blamed for Benjamin's death. And while I'm doing that, I can be a force in getting Wyoming statehood."

Rather than give her energy, the determined speech seemed to tire her. She slumped back against the divan. Blue Sun on Snow rose and walked to the bellpull. "We need some coffee or maybe tea. Which would you prefer, Ruth?"

"Coffee, please." She pressed her fingertips against her temple.

Adolf stared from one woman to the other. He shook his head. "You are both crazy." He glanced over at Rachel, whose eyes were shining with pride. "All three of you."

When White Wolf's Brother walked into the dining room of the hotel, a dinner guest recognized him. He whispered to his companion, who began to fan herself excitedly.

The maître d'hôtel recognized him and instructed the waiter—a bit louder than necessary—to "give Mr. Wolf the best table."

A slow flush rose in Victor's cheeks as at every table people craned their necks and began to whisper. His progress was interrupted when a distinguished man in a dinner jacket rose and proffered his hand. "Allow me to tell you, America needs men like you. I'm proud to shake your hand."

Victor shook it, mumbled his thanks, and tried to move on. His progress was barred by another, who repeated much the same thing. Finally, seated at his table, he raised the menu and tried to hide behind it.

The waiter approached with a bucket of champagne. "Compliments of the management, sir."

It was too much. Victor laid down the menu and pushed back his chair. His color high, his eyes straight ahead, he hurried from the dining room.

He stood with his fist poised before the panel. Should he confront her? As he hesitated, the door opened.

Rachel beamed up at him. "I saw you coming," she whispered excitedly. "I was watching for you from the window. I calculated the time it would take you to get upstairs and here I am."

She wore a dress of dusty rose moire taffeta. It

brought out the roses in her cheeks and made her eyes bluer by contrast. Its collar was trimmed in an upstanding frill of tiny pleats. They covered her nape and framed her face. She looked incredibly fragile and totally desirable.

He swallowed uncomfortably. "We have to talk."

Her smile seemed to light up the entire hallway. "Yes, we do. Where shall we go?"

Her perfectly natural question stopped him in his tracks. He could have wept with frustration. Why had he charged over here without a plan? He could not take her into the hotel dining room, especially in light of his recent embarrassing experience.

They could not go for a walk. Who knew what might be waiting for them on the streets of Washington?

The idea of going into the suite that she shared with her mother made him distinctly uncomfortable.

He should not have been with Rachel yesterday. He had given in to his own feelings, his own desires. She was the woman he had dreamed of all of his life. He wanted her. He loved her. And he should have renounced her utterly. But he had not.

"I suppose we could sit in the lobby."

She wrinkled her nose. "I didn't notice any place to sit except for a round divan. If we sat there, we wouldn't even be able to face each other. I'd be looking in one direction and you'd be looking in the other."

He looked up and down the hall seeking inspiration. Finally, he groaned, "Forget I came."

He strode away, but she closed her door and dashed after him. "We could go to your room."

"Are you crazy?"

"Who's to know?"

"I would know."

"And I would, but we wouldn't tell anybody."

"My father would skin me alive and shoot me. And *then* he'd turn me over to my mother."

"Victor." Her eyes had shadows under them, and the bruise on her cheek stood out starkly beneath the gaslight. "We do need to talk."

"What about your mother?"

"She's gone to bed early. This whole business has just about made her sick." She put her arm through his and allowed him to lead her up the stairs to the next floor. The Lindhauers had taken rooms on the fourth floor at the back.

As they walked along the hall together, each was fearfully silent.

He cleared his throat. His voice still sounded hoarse. "We shouldn't be doing this."

Rachel nodded. "You're wrong. It's the very thing we should do."

He stopped at his door. "I can't seem to do what's right when it comes to you. I don't want to hurt you."

"You won't. You could never hurt me."

"Let me take you back. This is stupid."

She put her hand around the doorknob. "Let's not stand in the hall. Someone might come along and see us."

His mouth set like his father's, he unlocked the door and allowed her to step inside. He closed it behind him and pointed sternly to the straight chair in front of the small desk. "You, sit down there."

Hands folded demurely, she tucked her head down and did as he commanded. Her lips quivered trying not to smile.

He placed his hands behind him and stationed himself across the room. Still it suddenly seemed very small. He cursed mentally. He should never

297

have brought her here. He should never have come to her room. He should never have taken her to the mall.

She looked up at him expectantly. His face was quite red. The beautiful fair skin he had inherited from his father showed his blush. No doubt their children would be lovely, all very fair, with blond hair and blue eyes and the same tendency to blush when they were excited.

"—to stop. I've told you why you can't be seen—"

He had started speaking and she had been so entranced that she had not heard him. His shoulders were so broad in the well-cut suit. He was so incredibly handsome.

"—brought you here tonight, but I didn't want to hurt your feelings. You're very young. You have such tender feelings. Are you listening to me?" She had had a glazed look.

She blinked and smiled. "Go on, Victor."

"Because you're very young, your mother can take you back to Chicago where you'll meet someone suitable. You think you're in love with me, but you'll find that I'll just be a memory. The attack will help you to forget me. You'll forget it and me at the same time." He paused, rather proud of himself for thinking of that.

"I think you've said most of this before," she murmured.

His nostrils dilated as he sucked in an irritated breath. "I'm a half-breed Indian. That's worse than being an Indian. It's like being a mongrel dog."

"You're a hero in the newspapers."

"I'm already forgotten," he lied.

"I want to marry you."

He gulped. His skin turned redder than ever. "Rachel."

"You think I'm too young to know what I want. You think I'm just a child with a romantic infatuation."

"You're fresh out of school."

"Ah, but I graduated with honors from Miss Wilcox's School for Young Ladies of Good Families. We're taught from the first minute we walk through the doors how to be a credit to the men we marry. We're also taught how to pick those men."

He gaped at her.

"You're going to be an important politician for the state of Wyoming. 'A politician is an excellent choice for a husband. With the proper family connections, he can very well turn into a statesman,' she quoted. A politician needs an excellent wife. I can be that, so we'll be very successful."

She held up her index finger. "Plus—" She held up her third finger as well. "I love you very much, so we'll be very happy. And, finally—" She held up her ring finger. "I'll be a good mother, so we'll have beautiful well-behaved children." She wiggled the three fingers at him as she started to rise.

He held up his hands as he backed away from her. "Don't get out of that chair. Stop! Sit right back down. I won't marry you. I'm not going to ruin your life."

She subsided and pressed her hands over her knees. She reminded him of a cat ready to pounce. "Did your father ruin your mother's life?"

"No, but that was different."

"How?"

"He loved her."

"Don't you love me?"

He shuddered. "Yes, but times are different."

"Thirty years has made a difference," she agreed.

299

"Our people are no longer at war."

"Rachel, I can't marry you." His expression was anguished.

She rose deliberately, smoothing down her skirt. "Wolf. White Wolf's Brother. Victor Wolf. Wolf Lindhauer." With each name, she took a step toward him. With each name, she unbuttoned a button on her dress.

"Rachel!" His voice dropped on the second syllable. He had backed away into a corner. Now he could not get to the door to let himself out. His eyes were drawn to the pure white column of her throat. His mouth twisted in anguish. She was all he had ever dreamed of having.

"You say your father loved your mother enough to marry her despite the problems. Well, I want to know why a man is more loving than a woman."

"He's not—that is—" She was less than an arm's length away.

"Ah, so you agree a woman can be just as loving as a man."

"Of course." She was only a foot away. Her dress was completely open to the waist.

"Then don't you think I'll be able to endure any slurs against me as well as your father did—or your mother for that matter?"

He wiped the perspiration from his forehead. She was standing only inches away from him now. She unfastened the buttons at her wrists and raised her arms to pull the pins from her hair. Her breasts rose, pale crescent moons above the lace and ribbon of her camisole. He could see the nipples, like pink shadows beneath the thin silk.

"Don't do this," he begged. He was backed against the wall, his hands spread wide against it, his head turned to the side. Still his eyes would not shut. "Please. Just button up your dress and leave."

300

She shook her hair down, turning her head so the long skein fell over her shoulder. The ends curled around the nipple of her breast.

He groaned as if she touched fire to his body when her fingers opened the buttons of his coat. Then she put her hands together in front of his chest and slid them inside. Her palms slid slowly over his ribs. He groaned again, so intense were the sensations that shot through him. Blood throbbed painfully in his lower body, engorging him, until he could no longer move. He had to stand still and endure this torture.

She raised her lips and kissed his chin. "Wolf." Her voice was shaking, too. "Please love me. Please." Her little teeth nipped his skin. Their touch sent chills rippling down his spine.

Involuntarily, his arms went around her, his hands clasping her buttocks with punishing force, dragging her in against him. "For God's sake!"

She felt glad tears start in her eyes. He was going to love her. He was trembling as if he hurt. She knew she hurt. Hot pain curled in her belly and made her legs ache. She was afraid, yet not afraid. She shuddered as waves of pain and excitement swept her. "Please, Wolf, love me."

He looked down into her face, her cheeks blushing, her eyes luminous with tears. "Rachel. I do."

She put her arms around his neck as he transferred his holds and lifted her high on his chest. She could not get her tongue deep enough into his mouth. He tasted so good. His taste made her wild. A gasping, moaning sound tore out of her throat and poured into his. She clawed at his shoulders with her fingernails.

Her feet dangled against his knees as he leaned backward, letting her body rest against his. The sweet weight of her hardened him until he was sure he could not wait to have her. From deep in his being, a cry was born. More like a howl, primeval, feral, it erupted from his lungs, into his throat, and from his mouth to hers.

He straightened and lifted her higher until her hair almost brushed the ceiling. He set his mouth against her flesh at her waist. His teeth closed on the thin lawn and tore it.

"Victor," she whimpered, afraid of him.

He flung his head back. "I want you. God! How I want you!" His voice was hoarse. On stiff legs he bore her to the bed. "I've had no woman to love. Never thought to have. Because of what I am, all my life I've been alone."

"Victor, I've had no man."

"I know." He laid her down and covered her with his body. He was too heavy, but the weight between his legs felt heavier. It rode between her thighs, while his hands tore the camisole away.

While his mouth suckled her breasts, she stroked the thick mane of blond hair. "I'm afraid," she whispered. "I'm terribly afraid. You're different. Suddenly, you're—so different."

Struggling for control, he raised himself up on one elbow to look into her eyes. "I'm a man. I've a man's needs. I've denied them a long time, I guess for you."

She stared at him. His face hung above her, so dear and so passionate. "Then this is right, isn't it?"

"No."

She patted his cheek in what was a tiny slap. "Yes, it is. I want to hear you say it."

His blue eyes were almost black. "Yes. It's right."

Her smile was like a light. "Then do what you want to do. It'll be wonderful."

He pushed himself from the bed and stripped out of his clothes. Then he unbuttoned her waistband, unfastened her petticoats, and slid her out of her skirt and underwear in one swift, efficient motion. Below her waist and camisole her belly was flat, her hipbones slim ridges on either side of it. At the top of her thighs was a nest of palest gold ringlets.

He fell upon them and kissed her, fiercely, inhaling her scent.

"Victor," she wailed in embarrassment.

"Your body is so beautiful," he moaned. "And your scent is so—" He could not finish his sentence.

"Victor—"

He parted her legs and stroked the lips of her sex. She was slick with desire. And embarrassed because she was. He touched his tongue to the slickness.

When he licked the throbbing pearl her lips concealed, she screamed. "I don't know—I don't understand—"

"You're ready," he told her. "Ready for me. Your body knows I'm coming."

She closed her eyes, but he shook her gently. "Look." Lifting her hips, he brought their bodies together. "Look. This goes into you."

He was shuddering with the anguish of restraint. Now was not the time for an instruction, but he did not want to hurt her, more than necessary.

She stared fascinated at a drop of clear liquid oozing from the tip of his staff. "I'm ready for you."

Her eyes flew upward to his face. "Then do it."

With surprisingly little pain, he put the tip into her. The virgin shield stretched and tore with only a little bit of pressure. She gasped and bit her lip.

He slid farther in, giving her time to accommodate herself, stretching her, shivering with his own needs until he touched her womb. "Ah."

"Is that all?"

He chuckled. "No. There's more." He began to move on her. Her own body lay limp for only a moment, then it, too, began to respond. She drew her legs up, then tilted her hips up. Her legs went naturally around his back.

His whole body contracted as if he had been shot. Every muscle, every nerve, every tendon, his very bones combined to experience and give intolerable ecstasy. His whoop of triumph echoed in the room.

And she held him inside her with her heels, riding out the storm, her own climax building and building until it vibrated through her.

Seventeen

*Come, sit you down every mother's son,
and rehearse your parts.*

"The Beresford Players are mounting a production of *The Tempest*," George reported. "It's perfect for you, Shreve. They're auditioning right now."

Shreve lay on his back on the chaise longue. "Yes, perfect, except that I can't find the bloody theater, let alone the bloody stage when I get to the theater. Let's face it, George. Nobody's going to hire me. Hell. They won't even let me read."

"I don't think you'll have to read." The business manager threw a quick look at Miranda who mimed further instructions. "I've—er—already talked to the producer. He's—er—heard of you. And he's overwhelmed that you'd be interested in his production."

"Well, of course," Ada chimed in loyally.

"As well he should be," Miranda added.

Shreve flashed a wintry smile toward the ceiling. "Ever my faithful audience, but I'm afraid it's not going to work."

"Why not?"

"Goddamn it! Surely, *you* can see. Even if I can't. Whatever your fantasies, I'll never act again." He wiped his hand across the lower half of his face. "My whole world's black as the bottom of a well. My sight's gone."

"Ah, Shrevey-boy, you can't know for certain. It's only been a few weeks," Ada protested, her voice breaking.

"It's been three months. Or at least I think it's been three months. Morning after morning, I've opened my eyes, hoping. Until I can't stand it anymore. It's too hard to live in hope. So I'm not going to do that anymore. I've given it up."

"You can still act," Miranda said.

Bitterness etched his voice. "Maybe I could let someone beat me over the butt with a slapstick, but the chances are that they'll want someone they don't have to lead around on a string." He rolled over and sat up abruptly. "The truth of the matter is, dear friends. You should leave me and go on about your business. I'm finished."

Miranda heaved a mock sigh of resignation. "Perhaps you're right. Ada, what do you think?"

The old woman completely misinterpreted the tone of the question. Tears trickled down her cheeks. "Oh no, he's not. Oh no, dearie. He's just going through a bad stretch right now. He'll think about it today and come to a different conclusion. Won't you, Shrevey-boy?"

Like a tiger he turned on the woman who was the nearest thing he had to a mother in the world. "No! Goddamn it! No! What do I have to say to you people? How many times do I have to tell you? I'm blind and I'm not going to see again. So leave me alone."

Ada's cheeks paled and she swayed where she stood.

George put his arm around her. "Steady, old girl."

Miranda hurried to her side and hugged her tight. "Ada, please don't cry."

"Monster," she threw at Shreve, who hunched on the edge of the chaise, fists pressed into the cushions, face red with anger and frustration.

She turned back to Ada. "Why don't you go have some tea, dear? George, take her downstairs. I'll join you later."

"Right away. Come on, old girl." The business manager shook his head as he opened the door and guided the weeping woman out.

Miranda closed the door with a little more force than necessary and swung around. Her heart almost broke at the sight of Shreve. The fight had gone out of him, like air from a balloon. He had slumped. His head drooped, his hands dangled between his knees.

The sight of his hands hurt Miranda the most. They were such beautiful hands. They could do such wonderful things — brush a tendril of hair from her cheek, caress her breast, wield a sword to thrill an audience. They gestured with such expression to add the perfect nuance to each of Shakespeare's mighty lines.

She longed to drop down before him and catch up those hands. She wanted to bathe them with tears and cover them with kisses. Sternly, she caught herself up. Pity was a debilitating thing. He had had enough of it. Likewise, her love now had to be tough, a towering oak, not a weeping willow. She drew in a deep breath.

He heard her and raised his head. His black eyes stared uncannily, warily, not just in her direction, but at her face. She could not believe that he could not see her. His mouth twisted. "Out with it."

"You should be ashamed of yourself."

"Not a very original accusation."

307

"Oh, stop it!" She crossed her arms over her chest and began to pace.

He followed her progress unerringly. "Your performance lacks originality as well as script."

"I'm not acting, Shreve Catherwood. You make me so mad. I'm pacing back and forth to try to cool down. I want to fly across this room and slap you silly. Why did you hurt that dear old woman? Ada's the best friend you have in the world."

He rose, his fists clenched at his sides. "Her tears are beginning to wear on my nerves," he said brutally. "I can't stand any more. It's time for people to stop pitying me. I don't need pity."

She came to a stop in front of him. Head thrown back, she aimed her words into his face. "That's right. You don't need hers or George's or mine. You have more than enough of it for yourself."

His face whitened. His lips curled back from his teeth in a snarl. He caught her by the shoulders. No fumbling, no stumbling. Again he might have been fully sighted. His fingers dug in, squeezing, hurting.

"Let me go. You're hurting me," she said evenly.

He opened his mouth, then closed it. Abruptly, he released her.

"That's it," she jeered. "That's as far as you're prepared to go. No comment. No defense. Talk about me with no originality and no script."

"Shut up." He dropped back down onto the chaise.

"I'll not shut up." She stood over him raining fury on his head. "You're a member of the troupe. You're more than a member. You're the lead actor. You're Shreve Catherwood, 'Romantic Star of Three Continents.' We've taken care of you because we love you, but also because it's what we're supposed to do. We're protecting you until you're well enough to go on. You wouldn't have abandoned us. We don't abandon you."

She paused trying to gauge how he was taking this. He stared straight ahead, his eyes open, his face impassive.

"But now you turn on us. You tell us to go on and get a job without you. And then what?"

"I suppose you do what you want to do," he suggested nastily.

"And leave you here?" Her voice rose in volume until she was shouting. "Is that what we're supposed to do? Simply pack our bags and leave you here in a hotel room to be thrown out into the street? Do we leave you a few dollars to pay the bill? Do we take you to the door of the state asylum, ring the bell, and run away and leave you?"

"Do what you want to do," he shouted back, after just a fraction of a second. She grinned. He had hesitated. Clearly, he had not thought about that.

"Is that what you want us to do?"

"If that's what you want to do." He crossed his arms over his chest.

"What we want to do is go back to acting before our money runs out."

"Well, do it. I don't care."

"But you want us to support you."

"I never said that."

"No, but you implied it. 'Leave me alone,' you said. Until suppertime, you meant."

His face darkened. Bitter anger was being replaced by pain and his own helpless frustration. His voice softened. "Damn you, Miranda. I can't work. If you and the others want to leave me, go ahead."

She wanted to weep for the pain she was causing him, but weeping would not make him whole again. Lady Macbeth forced mockery into her voice. "You don't mean that. You can't bring a convincing reading to that line and you know it."

He raised his hands and let them drop limply between his legs. "I can't work."

"You can. And you will. The free ride's over. Remember what you said to me in Saint Louis when you told me not to pick the troupe to be my second family. You said, 'We're professionals in a tough business. We don't run a charitable organization.'"

He was silent, hurting under the force of the words he had hurled at her when she was hardly more than a child.

"Well, this is no charitable organization. And you're no charity case. You're going to start pulling your own weight. You're a valuable commodity and we're going to exploit you."

"Damn you!"

"So you're scared. I was absolutely terrified. You didn't have any mercy on me. You needed an actress. I was handy."

"Damn you!"

"I'm going to march downstairs right this minute and send George out to make arrangements with the producer for a private reading. Then I'm coming back upstairs with a pot of coffee and a playbook and you are going to learn Prospero's part in *Tempest*. You're getting a little old for Ferdinand anyway. I will review Miranda's at the same time."

She expected him to argue, but he did not. Instead his mouth shut like a steel trap. He lay back down on the chaise and resumed his blind stare at the ceiling.

She was shaking so hard she could scarcely totter

to the door. Outside in the hall, she allowed the tears to flow, but only until she got to the head of the stairs. She had given Shreve good advice about self-pity. She should take it herself. She had no time for tears. She had her work cut out for her.

"He wants to meet with you," George told her. "His name's William Beresford, but he asks everyone who knows him to call him Billy."

"Did you explain that Shreve was the Romantic Star of Three Continents?"

George looked hurt. "I gave him the whole song and dance. I produced credits and clippings, the whole portfolio with pictures."

"And you told him that I would act Miranda."

"He was clapping his hands and rummaging through his desk for contracts. The money was nothing. He's serious about this production." George paused.

"And then you told him."

"And then I told him. And I made it clear that Shreve's looks just the same and sounds just the same and would act just the same."

"And what did he say?"

George spread his hands wide and let them drop limply to his sides. "He stuffed the contract back in the drawer so fast, he tore a corner. He got up and started for the door. I told him nobody would know. The audience would never be able to tell."

"And—"

"He stopped. He looked at the portfolio again. Mostly, the pictures of you." George looked miserable.

"I don't want to know what he said next, do I?"

He shook his head. "He wants to see you. Alone."

She shuddered. "Dear God!"

"We'll find something else." George patted her shoulder.

"No. This would be perfect. I'll meet with Mr. Beresford."

"I won't let you. Shreve would never forgive me."

"No." She put her hand over his. "I won't meet with him alone. But I will meet with him. And I'll convince him — somehow."

She felt like opening night in Saint Louis. Miranda's stomach clenched and burned as if she were sixteen years old again. She was playing Ophelia in a nightgown on stage in front of hundreds of people. In all her years in the theater, Shreve and George had conducted all the business. She had never even met the producers of her plays except socially.

To all practical purposes, she had been isolated from every other person who worked in the theaters where she had performed. George and Ada and, of course, Shreve had kept her in a playhouse like a child. She had signed where they told her, dressed the way they told her, spoken the way they had told her. She had been their little girl for half of her life.

Now circumstances were forcing the little girl to grow up suddenly. And if she failed — But she could not fail. The prospects were too awful to be considered. They would have to separate. Without this job or one like it, where would George go? Where would poor Ada go? Both were getting on in years. They only knew the theater. The jobs they would find would be very hard for them both unless they were very, very lucky.

Could they live away from the theater? She did

not know whether either of them had anything put aside. For that matter, she did not know whether she did. Shreve kept all the money. Or George.

She must ask him about it as soon as this meeting was over.

The theater was dark and very cold. London was cold after the heat of Mexico. She left her navy blue coat buttoned up to her chin.

George led her through the lobby to a suite of offices on the mezzanine. The carpet was worn on the stairs, the chandelier dusty, with swathes of spider webs draping the crystals.

The cold seeped up through her boots. She began to shiver. George looked at her apologetically. "It's not what you're used to, ma'am."

"It's not what any of us are used to."

His thin lips flicked up in the hint of a smile. "Believe me, I've seen much worse than this."

"But it's been a long time."

He nodded. In an uncharacteristic move, he put his hand on her arm detaining her on the landing. "You don't have to feel responsible if this doesn't work, ma'am," he told her seriously. "You don't have to do anything you don't want to do."

Her teeth began to chatter at the very suggestion.

He faced her squarely while he chafed her hands. "Just remember, he's most likely bluffing. Most likely he's just trying you out. The bastard. Probably he just wants to see if he can get a roll in the clover for the run of the play."

"George—" she quavered.

"But you just face him down. Give him your best Lady Macbeth performance. She wouldn't put up with any of his shenanigans and don't you do it, either. Tell him right straight just exactly how it's going to be and get on to business."

313

"Suppose he tells me that he doesn't want us."

George hesitated, then shrugged. "There's other fish in the sea, ma'am. And I'll jump right in and tell him so. None of us—not me, not Shreve, and sure not Ada—would want you to—"

She interrupted him. "George. I can't forget that you did what you didn't want to for me. Let's not talk about this anymore. I'll do what has to be done."

His eyes dropped. He nodded. "Yes, ma'am. You'll do what has to be done. We all know that."

"Mrs. Catherwood," George announced as he escorted her into the office.

The man behind the desk started up. His eyes opened wide.

"May I present Mr. Beresford," George continued, his tone implying *noblesse oblige.*

She allowed George to bustle around her as if she were very much a *grande dame* of the theater. The illusion she hoped to create was that of Mrs. John Drew, or Mme. Vestris, or the Divine Sarah bestowing a favor by her presence.

Mr. Beresford wiped his hands on his pants. "Miss—er—"

"Mrs. Catherwood."

"Of course, Mrs. Catherwood." He came from behind the desk. His pale blue eyes surveyed her with growing interest. His thick blond mustache brushed the back of her gloved hand as he bowed above it. "Won't you be seated?"

George pushed the room's most comfortable chair into position in front of the desk. Beresford seated her in it. She crossed her hands over the brass handle of her umbrella.

He retreated. "May I send for some refreshment,

314

perhaps some tea?"

"No, thank you," she replied in clipped British tones. She looked first at him and then around her with an air of disdain.

He followed her look suddenly aware of his office. It was a shambles of books and papers, playbills and programs. His furniture was shabby. His floor none too clean. His radiator banged and hissed beneath the grimy window. Two coats, a sweater, and an umbrella hung from his hat tree in the corner. He flushed as his eyes rolled upward. He stood in his shirtsleeves, his hat on his head.

Embarrassed, he jerked it off and hurried across the office. The hat took the coat's place as he shrugged into the garment. "Excuse me." His face had turned bright red, his expression murderous. "I wasn't expecting you quite so soon."

Be gracious, Miranda. Forgive. "I am always prompt when it is a matter of business," she said, her British accent becoming more pronounced. She might have been a governess with a particularly simple student. "Although, I must confess, I seldom deal in business myself. Mr. Windom always takes care of these details. He is very efficient."

"Thank you, ma'am." George fell immediately into his part.

"Of course. Of course." Beresford retired behind his desk and picked up a piece of paper. He dropped it immediately and scrabbled for another. "Well, I — er — that is, I can't seem to find — "

"If you cannot find whatever it is you require, perhaps Mr. Windom could come back at a later date." Miranda leaned forward slightly in her chair as if she were going to rise."

"No. No. Please." He gave up the search. "I'm sure that won't be necessary." He stared at her perfect face for a minute. Then he took a grip on

315

himself and remembered why she was here. "The fact is that I can't possibly hire Mr. Catherwood."

"And why not?"

"Because of his—Because the man's blind." He blurted out the last sentence.

"Well, of course, he's blind. Now. But the condition is only temporary. The doctors have assured us of this. Furthermore, that particular circumstance should not inhibit his performance." Miranda continued the governess tone.

He gaped at her. "For God's sake! Of course, it would. He couldn't see where he was going. He'd fall all over the stage. He'd be talking to someone and the person would be standing behind him. I'm sorry for him, but I'm not going to have the audience laughing themselves silly in the middle of a romantic drama."

Miranda regarded him coldly. "I believe you misunderstand the situation, Mr. Beresford—"

He grinned then. "Call me Billy."

She allowed her mouth to flick up at the edges. "I believe you misunderstand the situation. Mr. Catherwood is merely blind. He is not lame, so he will not fall. Nor is he feebleminded. If an actor speaks to him, he will speak back, directing his voice and his face in the same direction you or I would."

"Well, maybe. But what about moving around the stage and picking things up and so on?"

"He will memorize his blocking as any good actor does. We all have to take our places when the theater is dark. We don't fall over the stage—"

"Listen, Mrs. Catherwood, I've heard the greatest fall. Believe you me—" Billy interrupted.

"—and if we fall," she interrupted in her turn, "we pick ourselves up in the dark and find our places."

316

"Suppose he did it out in front with the lights up."

She shook her head. "He is a professional. To move about the stage is his life. He has been at it for twenty years."

Beresford leaned back. His face took on a bull-dog expression. "Maybe it's time he quit."

Miranda's look would have cracked stone. "He will play Prospero. It is a part for which he is perfectly suited. He has presence. He has height. He has a voice to hold an audience spellbound. You need have no fear because Prospero does not have to move around the stage to any great extent. Cast members scurry around his feet. He is always in command." For just a moment she broke her character to lean forward. "It's a part he was made to play."

Beresford blinked at the change in her, then his mouth curved in a sly smile. "Well, well, Mrs. Catherwood."

Instantly, she saw her mistake. She straightened. George flinched.

Beresford leaned still farther back in his chair also and surveyed them. His hand rose and cupped the back of his head. "You really had me going there for a minute."

"I don't know what you mean, Mr. Beresford."

His smile was wolfish. "Yes, you do. You want something from me, Mrs. Catherwood. I can give it to you or not. It all depends on you."

She stared at him, her eyes narrowing to blue slits. She could almost hear Shreve cursing from the wings. She had broken character. No help for it now. Stomach clenched and burning, she played her last card. "That is right, Mr. Beresford. It all depends on me. I am prepared to offer you my services free for the first week of the play."

"What's that?" His arms dropped. He leaned forward.

"You heard me. You will provide contracts for Shreve Catherwood and for Ada Cocks, my personal dresser and makeup artist. I will work for free. You will essentially have two stars for the price of one. At the end of the first week, should Mr. Catherwood's performance prove outstanding, which I'm sure it will be, I will sign a contract for the run of the play."

"One week's not very long."

"That includes three weeks' rehearsal time before opening," George reminded him quickly. "Plus public appearances to publicize the production."

Beresford frowned. "What happens if he can't perform?"

"He will," she declared unequivocally.

"No, what happens to you if he can't perform?"

She sat nonplussed. She had not thought of that possibility.

"She gets his salary from the time he's let go," George improvised smoothly.

"Pay an actress as much as an actor!" Beresford scoffed at the idea.

"She's your headliner, no matter what," George reminded him. "Even if he leaves the play 'for reasons of health,' you've still got her."

"That's right." He studied her narrowly. His mind worked furiously, thinking about the money he would save for a month. "Two for the price of one?"

She nodded.

He grinned. "What have I got to lose?"

"Exactly." She felt as if she had stepped off a cliff in the dark and discovered that the bottom was only a foot down. She wanted to grin and hug herself and jump up and down so great was her elation, but she did not. She lifted her chin.

Lady Macbeth would now depart. She rose majestically. "I will leave the details for you two gentlemen to work out."

Beresford sprang from his seat and shouldered George aside to open the door. "I'll see you to your carriage. Be back in a minute, Windom."

Miranda nodded frostily. Past Beresford's shoulder, she saw George raise his fist in triumph.

The lobby was even colder, if such were possible. Through the beveled glass doors, she could see a light snow beginning to fall. She had to set her teeth to keep them from chattering.

"You're quite a woman, Mrs. Catherwood." Beresford dropped his arm across the theater door effectively barring her way.

She looked straight ahead. "Thank you."

"A class act. And quality. I've got to hand it to you."

"Thank you again." She could feel the spurt of acid in her stomach.

"You look like a girl." He allowed his eyes to roam over her face. "But you're no girl."

She could feel her skin crawl. "Let me pass."

"Sure. But understand me. You owe me. I didn't hire your husband because of who he was. As far as I'm concerned he's finished. I hired him because of who you were."

"Mr. Beresford, Shreve is not finished. You will not be disappointed with either one of us."

"I know I won't with you." He raised his hand. She watched it leave the door, saw it rise, felt it touch her cheek. He turned her face toward his. "I expect you to pay up."

"Then the deal is off."

"No. No, it's not." He rubbed his index finger along her jawline. "You came here to find work.

You're not going to walk away."

Anger erupted inside her. No one touched her this way except Shreve. "I suggest you take your hand away instantly."

The steel in her voice made him stop his stroking. He had never heard that note in any woman's voice before. He dropped his hand. "Now listen to me, Miranda—"

She stiffened at his use of her name. "Open this door."

"—your clippings say you're a pretty good little actress, but you've got a lot to learn about humility. Right now, you're tied to an old blind man. Get smart. Get a new man. I'm on my way to the top. I could take someone like you with me."

She looked him up and down. "I am already at the top. Shreve Catherwood has taken me there."

Beresford's face hardened. He did not move.

She opened the door herself.

As she brushed past him, he caught her arm. "I always get the birds I want," he sneered. "Billy Beresford knows what kid-gloved ladies like you want."

"Billy Beresford does not have the slightest idea what I want," she denied as she passed out into the street.

She sat in the dimness of the hansom cab and wept. As she wept, she scolded herself for weeping—thereby making herself weep harder.

She should just brush aside the entire experience. She had dealt with much worse than Billy Beresford, Bastard. Why Big Hettie at Mrs. Mortimer's had humiliated her until she had thought that she would die of shame. And Billy Beresford was nothing compared to Sergeant Trask. At least the producer wore clean linen and brushed his teeth.

She tried to brace herself by remembering the way she had come. She had run away from home and joined a theater troupe at fifteen. She had killed men who deserved to die. Billy Beresford had better watch his step with her. She was lethal.

She cried harder.

"Shreve—Shreve—Shreve. Why, oh, why? Oh, God, why?"

The hanson stopped in front of the hotel, but she rapped on the top of the carriage. "Drive on!"

"Are y' all right, mum?"

"Drive on!" she sobbed.

Helpless, she huddled in a corner of the cab. Overwhelming guilt and grief rolled over her in waves that weakened her with each successive blast. The loss of Shreve's precious sight had been like the loss of a part of herself.

Nevertheless, she had put herself together to be strong for him. She had taken the leadership of the little troupe upon her woefully inadequate shoulders. She had taken fear and pain and loss and tamped them deep inside her and tried to forget them. But they had festered.

Beresford's insulting proposition had cracked the dike and now the tears would not stop. She was hurting, so badly that she could barely move. She did not want to leave the carriage. She felt she could not go back to the hotel in tears to face Shreve and Ada. She wanted to go on driving forever. She wanted the cabbie to drive to the Thames and let her throw herself into its gray waters.

And still she cried. Her hands were clenched in fists pressed tight against her cheeks. Her throat was a raw wound. But her stomach—usually burning—bothered her not at all.

Finally, when she had no more tears to cry, she

321

managed to control the snubbing and hiccuping. She pushed herself out of the corner and looked out the window of the cab. The snow was falling harder. A lamplighter was coming down the street, leaving tracks behind that quickly filled.

She tapped on the top of the carriage and named the hotel.

The driver gave a sigh of relief and turned the cab around in the street.

Poor man.

As she alighted, she pressed a guinea into his hand. He stared at the gleam of gold, then smiled. "It's sorry I am fer yer trouble, mum."

She managed a watery smile. "Thank you. You've been a good coachman."

Eighteen

'Twas caviare to the general.

"*As you from crimes would pardon'd be, Let your indulgence set me free.*" With an elaborate flourish Shreve recited the last words of the epilogue.

"Letter perfect. Bravo! Bravo!" Miranda clapped enthusiastically and threw her arms around his neck. "You'll set the standard for all Prosperos to follow."

He kissed her hard on her smiling mouth, his smile more like Romeo's than it had been for many months. "Did you have any doubts?"

She shook her head vigorously. "Never. Never."

"I practically had it anyway." He disengaged himself from her arms and pushed himself off the chaise. "I've heard the play so many times, I probably could memorize Ariel or even Caliban in a couple of tries." So thoroughly familiar with the room that he moved without fear of stumbling or bumping, he wandered to the bureau and then to the window. Standing facing it, his fingers fiddled with the inner curtain. The noises of the street rose to his ears. "What does Ferdinand look like?"

She laughed watching him. "Are you jealous?

323

You should be. He's a splendid youth of twenty-two, the perfect pretty boy for a famous actress like myself."

His fist closed around the curtain.

"He's frightfully handsome with a superb voice, strong straight legs that fill out his tights to perfection. And he has the dearest boyfriend you've ever seen who sits in the back of the house and watches him like a spider."

"Minx," Shreve muttered. He had played opposite her for so long. He had been her lover—Hamlet to her Ophelia, Macbeth to his Lady, Benedict to Beatrice. He had played Ferdinand to her Miranda in two productions. For him the upcoming ordeal had a special significance. It left his passions raw, his nerves screaming. How could he face playing her father?

He squinched his eyes tight closed and prayed. When he opened them, the blackness was the same.

"Shreve?"

"Don't tease me," he begged humbly. "Don't."

Alarmed at the break in his voice, she hurried across the room and put her arms around his waist. "Oh, sweetheart. I didn't mean to tease. But you mustn't worry. You know actors. They don't care anything about actresses. Actresses are people they work with every day. The few couples like us are the exceptions. You don't have a thing to worry about."

He remained stiff in her arms.

She rubbed her cheek against his shoulder. She could not allow his unhappiness to become magnified by jealousy. He was having a hard enough time accepting the part of the magician. Shreve had often said that the role was mostly posturing and proclaiming.

"Shreve," she whispered. "Thank God for Prospero."

"Why?"

"Because it's a perfect vehicle for you."

"It's not the romantic lead," he snarled.

"Ferdinand's a sissy anyway. All he does is play chess with Miranda. You get to wear a fantastic costume. You get a magnificent staff all of gold. You get to stand on stage and make sweeping gestures and call down thunder and lightning. Everyone else runs around and does your bidding. I kneel at your feet and beg for your mercy. And you've got some of the very best lines Shakespeare ever wrote."

He walked away from the window, his face bleak. "If only I don't deliver them to the back of the stage or knock down the set."

His hands were icy inside his gloves. Nothing he had ever done in his life frightened him like the prospect of walking into the theater to meet the cast and crew. He began to shiver. He realized that he was breathing hard, his heart beating like a triphammer.

Which would be worse? Laughter or pity? His very soul cringed at the thought of having to appear before them like this. He should have flatly refused to go along with the entire project.

The cab slowed then halted. It swayed as the driver leaned down to open the door.

Miranda waited breathless, hands knotted in fists, teeth clenched.

"All clear," Shreve asked.

"A long step down, but the cab is right at the curb, so you'll step down onto the walk."

"Good." He took a deep breath, pulled himself

325

up, and stepped down into the biting air. Turning he held out his hand. She gave him hers and allowed him to assist her to alight. Slipping the cabbie's money from her glove, she allowed Shreve to lead her to the door.

Inside the theater he could hear the voices from the stage. People recited their lines. Someone hammered on wood. He could smell paint and turpentine. And greasepaint. His heart thudded painfully.

Suddenly, the speakers broke off their rehearsal. Immediately afterward, the whispering began.

"Damn!" he muttered aside to her.

"It's all right," she whispered. "Mr. Beresford—" She let go of Shreve's hand and extended hers. "Dearest, this is the producer of the show, Mr. William Beresford."

"Call me Billy," a harsh voice demanded.

Shreve plastered a cool smile on his face. Unerringly, he looked directly at the source of the voice and extended his hand. "A pleasure."

Automatically, Beresford wrung it. "Right, it's a pleasure." His voice took on an uncertain note.

"I'm looking forward to working with you," Shreve remarked pleasantly.

"Say, what's going on here?" Beresford had moved, the sound of his voice moving with him.

Shreve followed the sound, directing his sightless eyes to look at the spot a few inches above the source. "I assure you, Mr. Beresford—"

"Billy."

"Billy." He paused for dramatic effect. "I cannot see."

"Then how'd you know where I am? You act like you're looking right at me." Beresford bobbed over to the opposite side of the aisle.

"Your voice. If you stopped talking, you'd probably leave me appearing to stare at space."

The man stopped talking and tried again. Unfortunately, for him, his breathing was heavy from a lung congestion, and his breath smelled powerfully of onions. Automatically, Shreve tracked him again.

"Hey. You can see! You followed me again." Beresford glowered at Miranda. "Are you pulling my leg?"

She smiled. "I told you. No one will ever know."

Beresford waved his hand in front of Shreve's face. The stir of the cold air caused the actor to draw back. "You're lying. Did you see that? He jerked his head back."

Shreve shrugged.

The director came up behind them. A thin, gray-haired man, with stoop shoulders and glasses set far down on his nose. He looked like a bookkeeper, but when he spoke his enunciation and tone were exquisite. "The name's Boatwright, Mr. Catherwood. I've heard of your work. I'm glad we're going to be working together." He reached around Beresford to shake Shreve's hand.

Shreve hesitated. In the tiny silence Beresford stared at the director's hand. Then Shreve thrust his in the direction of the voice. He missed. The director immediately adjusted, but the botch had convinced Beresford. "Say, you didn't do that so well, did you?"

Eyes damning the man to hell, Miranda thrust herself between the producer and Shreve. "I'm Miranda Catherwood, Mr. Boatwright. We're anxious to meet the cast and get started with the rehearsal."

He interpreted her look correctly. "Then let's begin. I suggest we do a run through of Acts One and Two while I explain the way I see the play."

"Is the set constructed?" Shreve wanted to know.

Miranda took his arm as they followed the director up the aisle.

"Just about." They climbed the temporary stairs from orchestra pit to the stage. A hush had fallen over the rest of the cast and crew.

Shreve paused on the apron of the stage, the object of all eyes. Miranda felt the shiver that ran through him. She saw his Adam's apple bob. He spoke to the director. "I'd like to be taken over every inch of it."

"It's pretty rough." The director sounded skeptical.

"You wouldn't want to trip over something and break your neck." Beresford's voice was overloud as he came out of the pit. No one on stage could help but hear.

Both Shreve and Miranda froze. Then slowly Shreve turned. His sightless eyes raked the producer. And Macbeth answered in his most regal voice. "No. And for that reason I need to learn it now. I shall go over the stage at the beginning of every rehearsal and before every performance. To make sure that nothing so unlucky will happen.

"Frederick Franklin?"

" 'Allo, Miranda."

"Freddy? Freddy Franklin?"

The man nodded. He twisted his head on his shrunken shoulders and managed a cocky grin. It looked misplaced in the raddled face.

She peered at him in amazement, struggling to recognize the bright young comedian, dancer, singer, and Shakespearean actor she had known. Then she realized she was staring. "Come in."

"Thank you. Don't mind if I do."

He could barely hobble. His back was bent, his frame gaunt.

"Ada," Miranda called. "Look who's come to see us. Freddy Franklin."

The wardrobe mistress stared at him. "Good Lord, Freddy. What's been happening to you?"

He shrugged. "Oh, same as always."

Miranda frowned. "I don't — "

"Shame on you, Freddy," Ada interrupted. "One sissy-boy too many."

He chuckled nastily. "Three or four too many."

No one had anything to say for a minute. He cleared his throat. "I heard that Shreve Cathcrwood and the Magnificent Miranda were playing Shakespeare for Billy Beresford. So I thought I'd toddle over and find out what sort of hard times you'd fallen on."

Ada clamped her lips together. Miranda took a deep breath. "We haven't fallen on hard times."

"Beresford's is not exactly in Piccadilly Circus," Freddy pointed out.

"The fact is — " Miranda began.

"Whatever it is, it's none of y'r business," Ada declared. "So very glad you could drop by, Mr. Franklin. If you'll come by the box office on opening night, there'll be a ticket there for you."

"Same old Ada," he snarled. "Still protecting little Shrevey-boy. Or is it this bird? You never could act."

"Goodbye." Ada opened the door.

Miranda found her voice. "Wait." They both looked at her. "What did you come for, Freddy?"

He glanced at the open door, then heaved a deep sigh. "I thought you might find a job for me. For old times sake."

She threw Ada an amazed glance over his shoulders. "You have a funny way of asking for it."

"I hate asking." His eyes were pale blue with a

network of red veins that seemed to run into the broken capillaries on the sides of his nose.

"Are you sober?"

His eyes damned her, but he nodded. "Yes."

"We're here on sufferance," she told him frankly. "I don't know whether I can get you anything or not." He turned away. "But I'll try."

Ada looked critically at his clothes. "Is this the best you've got?"

"Yes."

"Want me to be pinching something out of the wardrobe?"

"I'll do that. You make up that face."

Freddy made a concerted effort to straighten his back. "I'll make you proud," he promised as she walked out. "Just see if I don't."

"Just be we don't regret it," Ada said. "Now, Freddy, m'lad, sit yourself down here and let's lay it on with a trowel."

THE TEMPEST
Act I

The perspiration dripped from Shreve's body. Even in his boots the soles of his feet felt wet. Thank God, he was wearing a robe instead of tights. Otherwise, the audience might think he'd pissed in his pants.

Seeking reassurance, he pressed his right foot against his first mark. It was a six-inch-long ridge of wood the set builder had nailed to the ramp. With the side of his foot against it, he was facing the audience and more important the proper lights for his first appearance. Carefully placed about the set were eight other marks, each set at exactly the angle that he should stand when he delivered a certain speech or performed a dialogue with another player.

Miranda. Miranda!

Goddamn, her. He wanted to scream her name, but the curtain was already up.

On the stage below him, the shipwreck was taking place. The actors' voices rose over the thunder and wind being produced behind the scrim. *"All lost! To prayers, to prayers!"*

Where was she? Where was she?

He could hear nothing over the din. She could be standing beside him or be back in the dressing room fiddling with her hair. Damn her! Her entrances had driven him crazy from the first day he had put her on stage. She was never where she should be on cue. He should never have put her on stage.

No! She should never have put him on stage.

He could not play this part. He could never act again. Even Prospero was beyond him. He was going to fall down or walk through the scenery or stumble over a brace or a floor plate. If every inanimate thing was as it should be, he could still blunder into some fool of a bit player off his marks. Any back stage was a cramped maze. And he could not see!

The secret had been poorly kept. Originally, only the producer and director were supposed to know. Then the set designer and builder had had to know. Then Beresford, the idiot, had announced it on the first day of rehearsal. Undoubtedly, half the audience had come mainly to see the blind man make a fool of himself.

"We split, we split!—Farewell, my wife and children!—"

"Miranda," he whispered. His voice would be drowned in the creak and groan of the ship's tim-

331

bers and the screams of the actors. He called again with more force. "Miranda!"

"The wills above be done! but I would fain die a dry death."

The actors fled the stage as the scenery was pulled away as if blown by a storm.

Thunder rolled. At that precise instant, her hand slipped into his. He shuddered through all the length of his body.

"I love you," she murmured. "Here we go."

He took a deep breath and led her out of the cave. The two took their places center stage on an elevated ramp. Again a roll of thunder. On a catwalk above, stagehands pulled covers off shaded lanterns. Their lights flashed in his face. He could not have seen them under any circumstances. His eyes were closed, his eyelids covered with gold sequins three-quarters of an inch in diameter. They reflected the light eerily.

The audience gasped at the effect and gave a spontaneous burst of applause that quickly grew in acknowledgment of their entrance. He wore a long white wig into which Ada had lovingly woven hundreds of strands of gold. He dropped Miranda's hand and raised his arms wide. His robe, trimmed with gold braid and cabalistic symbols fell from his wrists to the ramp. In his right hand he brandished a gold staff with carved flames rising out of its top. He raised it above his head.

The thunder rolled. Again the lights flashed.

Miranda, her blond hair hanging long down her back, and one bare shoulder sprinkled with gold dust, slipped to her knees at his feet. *"If by your art, my dearest father, you have put the wild waters in this roar, allay them."*

He lowered the staff and looked down at her. With a blink the sequins fell from his eyelids and when he raised his head, his black eyes stared sightlessly at the audience.

Act III

A disaster occurred not of his making. Standing in the wings, Shreve and Miranda listened as the actor playing Caliban botched line after line.

His old directorial fervor reasserted itself. "Where's Boatwright? What the hell's the matter with that man?"

Miranda's voice carried a world of distaste. "He's drunk."

"Drunk!" Shreve snorted. "Where's the director? Who allowed him to go on?" He swept backstage with his blind eyes, looking for the culprit. "Do you see him?"

Miranda looked across the stage into the opposite wings. "Actually, I do." Lawrence Boatwright was literally tearing his hair out. His usually calm face was a mask of angry frustration. "But I don't think he wants to hear from us right now."

"I should think not. The audience is dead in their seats out there. Listen to them. Nothing but an occasional cough. Lord! What did you get us into?"

Miranda patted his arm reassuringly. She thought it prudent not to tell him that the audience did not care whether Caliban acted well or poorly. They were waiting for Shreve. Like fire the news of his blindness had spread among them at the first intermission. Beresford had seen the quality of his star's performance and had spread the news himself.

Unfortunately Caliban's botched job had put Shreve in such a mood that he charged on stage, knocking his staff against the scenery in his next speech. Standing off stage, Miranda saw his mouth

333

tighten. He made the gesture again, this time lowering the prop to accommodate the set and covering the mistake with an improvised line all in good iambic pentameter.

The actor facing him, playing Ariel, grinned in encouragement. "That's the way, guv'nor."

Entr'acte

The actor playing Caliban was hustled away and stripped of his costume.

"I'm your man, Mr. Boatwright." Frederick Franklin accepted the green canvas covered with scales.

"Report for makeup. Hurry," the director growled.

Freddy practically skipped into the star's dressing room. "Ada, old girl, I'm going on."

She looked at him suspiciously. "Did you get him drunk?"

"Ada." He clasped his hand to his heart. "Would I do a thing like that? I couldn't get a man drunk that didn't want to be that way, now could I?"

She slapped the green greasepaint onto his cheeks with punishing force.

Act V

In the climactic scene for Prospero, Shreve's magnificent voice was hoarse, a sure sign of the enormous strain he had placed on himself.

Ada stood beside Miranda in the wings. She mopped at her eyes with her handkerchief. Her rosary beads were wrapped around one hand. "Oh, the dear, dear boyo. He's doing it, Lord love him. And in such a grand style."

George laid a comforting arm around her shoul-

334

ders. "Sure he is. I never doubted that he could for even a minute."

Miranda dared not streak her makeup. With the tips of her fingers, she caught the tears as they brimmed over onto her cheeks. Her doubts had never been for him. She had known he would give his heart and soul to perform. Shreve was a trouper. He could not turn in a bad performance. But had she been wrong to bring him back on stage? The work was killing him. He was sweating through his makeup and his clothes. His gestures were every bit as sweeping, his movements as sure as if he could see, yet she knew he completed each as a test of fortitude.

"This rough magic I here abjure—"

The passion in his voice carried its own message to her. He was sick with strain, dying of trepidation.

"—And deeper than did ever plummet sound I'll drown my book."

At the side of his right foot was his seventh mark. With his foot against it, he was supposed to fling the magic staff away into the wing where a stagehand waited to catch it.

Shreve knew the possibilities for failure were numberless. If he threw it with too much force, he could hurt someone back stage. If he threw it without enough force, it would crash to the floor, vibrate noisily, and roll around. If he threw it to the right or left, it would strike the wing curtains and bounce back into the scene. Hell, if he hurled it straight but with too much force, he might hurt the catcher.

After Act I, the terrible sweating had stopped. His skin felt clammy and the costume chafed him beneath the arms. Now the sweating began again. He ran his hand across the staff. It slipped. He gripped it firmly. He bent his head. His hand rose to his face as if to mourn the loss of power.

Every person back stage held his breath.

The music crashed. The thunder rolled. The lights flashed again on the sequins he had placed on his eyelids. Then he brandished the staff above his head and flung it away. The tip of it caught the wing curtain, but the stagehand managed to catch it and bring it down.

The audience went wild with applause.

"Mr. Catherwood, we are delighted to have you in our fair city."

"Such a performance. I have seen nothing the equal of it."

"I've always said that Americans can never do Shakespeare, but now I have to take back every word. And glad to."

"We are having a small supper afterward. Just forty or fifty of our best friends and patrons of the arts. We'd love to have you and Mrs. Catherwood attend."

"Why you're much too young to be playing Prospero! Your makeup must have been extensive."

Preening like a peacock, Shreve acknowledged every compliment. His smile was broad. His answers picked up the cultured British accent and imitated it perfectly. Standing next to him, Miranda smiled. If his head got any bigger, he was going to float off the ground.

"I've never seen anything like it," a gentleman with a regimental tie leaned into Shreve's face to stare intently. "I've known men who can see perfectly well who can't see as well as you do."

The remark, intended as a compliment, sobered the actor instantly. Beside him Miranda put her hand on his sleeve. "Really."

"Oh, yes, indeed. Quite remarkable the way you do it. Dashed good show. I know a lot of fellows who'd give a great deal to see you and hear you talk about how you've managed to go on with your work. You're an example for us all."

"Thank you."

The bulk of the crowd began to depart. Shreve put a trembling hand to his forehead. "I think I've had about enough," he told Miranda behind it.

On cue she signaled to Beresford, who had been grinning like an ape all evening, watching them receive the compliments. "We must retire," she told him in her best formal style. "I am not feeling well."

"Well, you go right ahead, Mrs. Catherwood." His solicitude was overdone. "When the time comes, I'll escort our star back to his dressing room."

"No. We'll go together. Shreve will take me."

The audience waiting to meet them had thinned out considerably.

Beresford's grin faded. "He stays until the last one of 'em's gone. Word of mouth'll spread this story. We'll be booked solid till the end of the run. I can already see we'll extend." He rubbed his hands together, his grin wider than ever as he thought of his prospects. "We might even need to hire a bigger theater and move the whole show."

Shreve took Miranda's arm. "We'll leave now."

"Hey, wait just a minute."

She caught up her skirt and bowed and smiled to the people waiting in line. "So sorry, but I'm feeling dreadfully fatigued. Thank you for your lovely tributes. Thank you."

Though disappointed the remaining people applauded warmly.

"Yes, thank you all for coming." Shreve raised his hand and nodded to each as he passed down the line.

When the dressing room door closed behind him, he staggered to the cot and fell upon it. It rocked with his weight, and Miranda had to steady it to keep it from spilling him out.

She dropped down on her knees beside him. "Oh, sweetheart, are you all right?"

He flung an arm over his eyes. "Yes. Just tired to death."

"Well, of course." She climbed to her feet and pulled up a chair. "You were magnificent."

"Was I? I thought my performance was merely adequate. Yours—on the other hand—was masterful."

She leaned forward and put her palm to her forehead. "Shreve Catherwood, have you got fever?"

"You were." He caught her hand and brought it down to his lips. "You were everything that Miranda should be and more. And do you know why?"

"Because you couldn't see my mistakes."

"No. You didn't make any. You really acted. For the first time in your life, you acted. Miranda Catherwood maintained herself as a separate entity from Miranda of the Tempest."

"Did I really?"

"Yes. For the very first time, you were thinking, calculating. You have been since the rehearsals began, but I wanted to wait and see if you did it on stage in front of an audience. And you did? You're an actress."

She could feel tears starting in her eyes. "High praise from the master."

"The king is dead. Long live the queen."

"Don't say that. You know what you were. If I'm queen now, you are a god. You heard what that man said. He knows men who can see, who can't see as well as you do. Think of it. Think of what you did. You were an inspiration to them all."

He was silent for a long time. "I can go on. I know that now. And it feels good. But I'd give everything I have if I could open my eyes right this minute and see your face."

She slipped to the floor beside the cot and laid her wet cheek against his.

Beresford rapped on their dressing room door and barged in without waiting for an answer. The silent tableau stopped him only for an instant. He hunched his shoulders and started forward. "Listen, when I say you're supposed to stay, you're supposed to stay."

Shreve roused and sat up, swinging his legs over the edge of the cot. Miranda tried to scramble to her feet, but her legs had gone numb.

"My wife was tired," he said mildly as he rose.

"I told her she could go on back to the dressing room, and lie down, but you—" The producer stabbed his finger into Shreve's chest. "From now on you're going to stand right there and shake hands till they're all gone."

Furious, Miranda pushed herself up on her knees. "Mr. Beresford—"

"I took a chance on you."

"Yes," Shreve agreed. "You surely did. However—" His right hand clutched Billy Beresford's finger and bent it back.

"Hey! What're you doin'? Hey! Ow!"

Shreve's voice rose. "I'm grateful for what you

339

did. However, you do not pay me for after the performance. Nor do you pay my wife."

"I don't pay her at all. Ow! Damn! Let go!"

Shreve frowned in Miranda's direction. "What's he talking about?"

"I made a deal with him."

"Ow! Ow!"

"What kind of a deal?"

"Leggo!" Beresford was down on his knees, his face contorted in pain, tears spouting from his eyes.

"You're hurting him, Shreve."

"What kind of a deal?"

"Ow! Oh, God. Stop! Ow!"

"I agreed to work for free for the first week of the run. Then if you couldn't perform, you were out and I would stay on."

"You didn't get paid for performing tonight? Did you work free through rehearsals?"

"Yes."

"For God's sake! Leggo!"

"Did George and Ada get paid?"

"Oh, yes."

"Thank God for small favors." He turned his attention back to the sobbing Beresford. "Now listen, Billy. I'm sending George Windom around in the morning for the moneys owed Mrs. Catherwood. He'll have her contract in hand and I expect you to sign it. Agreed!"

"Agreed! Agreed!"

"Good!" Shreve let go of the man's hand and lifted him to his feet by an arm under his shoulder.

Beresford's face was bright red. His breath was coming in great gasps. He held his injured hand in his other one. "You're going to be sorry for this. I'll —"

"No, Billy," Shreve interrupted. "I'll never be

340

sorry for this. We're going to forget this ever happened. It will be a secret among the three of us friends."

"Friends?!"

"Friends." Shreve shoved him away. "Because we each have something the other needs. Therefore, we can't hurt each other. I—for example—cannot beat you half to death for trying to cheat Mrs. Catherwood out of her lawful wage."

"Here now—"

"Mrs. Catherwood sterling woman that she is— was raised on the frontier in America. She cannot—as she would undoubtedly like to do—shoot you right between the eyes."

"Oh, I say—"

"You cannot fire either one of us because you have a certifiable hit on your hands. Clever man that you are—you have capitalized on the fact that your lead actor is blind. People who have never seen a Shakespearean production will come to this one to see me perform. You stand to make a great deal of money. Am I not correct?" Shreve flashed his best, his more seductive Romeo smile.

Miranda had never been so proud in her life.

"Well, there's a bit of truth in what you say." Beresford straightened his coat and tie. He bent to brush dust off the knees of his trousers.

Shreve nodded. He reached out his arm, and Miranda went into it. He hugged her against his side. "Billy, this is the only woman in the world for me. She's been with me for more than half her life. She's more than my partner and my friend. She's my wife. So long as I'm alive, no one is going to hurt her. Now, I can't see your face, but I can find you anywhere, anytime."

"Are you threatening me?"

"Absolutely. I didn't think you would take so

long to figure that out. You've got a wonderful thing here, so go home and dream of all the money you're going to make. Get out, Billy."

Mr. Beresford got — slamming the door behind him.

Shreve swept her around and bent her back over his arm. He kissed her as Romeo had kissed Juliet, as Benedict had kissed Beatrice. Long and passionately and deep.

"Now what's all this about your working for nothing?"

Nineteen

And death's the market place, where
each one meets.

The howl of a wounded wolf issued from the interior office. As Raymond, Senator Butler's secretary, sprang from behind his desk, the senator came charging out, the latest edition of the *London Times* crumpled in his hand.

"Get me that bastard de la Barca! Tell him to get himself over here at a dead run." His face was puce. His jowls shook and trembled like wattles on a turkey.

Raymond stared in horror, sure his employer was going to have a stroke.

The senator pulled open the newspaper, reread a few words, and howled again.

"Yes, sir." The frightened secretary did not even sit down to write the note. He bolted down the hall, yelling for a messenger.

When de la Barca arrived, the senator thrust the paper under his nose. "Eliminated, was he? Eliminated, you said! Well, this is the way you eliminated him."

De la Barca smoothed the page and began to read.

Butler dragged in his breath in great sobs as if he had run miles. "You said . . . she had disappeared. You said . . . they wouldn't be a problem again. I only have . . . your word for what happened in Mexico. Now . . . answer me this. Did you ever go?"

De la Barca's control broke. His emotions swept across his face in ugly waves. Fury at the senator's insult. Disbelief at the content of the article. Anger at himself because he had failed.

"He was dead," he insisted stubbornly.

"Dead — huh! But you didn't see his body. You didn't feel his pulse."

"No, but —"

"Get out!" the senator thundered. He braced himself on his desk while he pressed one hand against his heart. "You'll never work in Washington again. I'll see to that. I have paid enormous expenses for you to travel all over the Western hemisphere and you have produced nothing."

"I swear —"

"You swear! YOU SWEAR! Much good that will do. I see now that you can't be trusted. Get out!"

"Listen here —"

"GET OUT!"

The secretary opened the door for de la Barca to charge through it. Then he hurried to Butler's side. "Senator, please. Sit down. You'll hurt yourself. You'll make yourself sick. Please."

Like a punctured balloon, Butler sank into his chair. Sweat had wilted his collar and darkened his shirtfront. The secretary bent over to loosen his tie and then reeled back as the man's rank breath struck him forcibly. His own eyes watering with the stench, he plucked his handkerchief from his pocket and thrust it into Butler's hand. Pivoting,

344

the young man went for water and brandy.

When he returned carrying a carafe of each, Butler had loosened his own tie and was sitting with head tipped back in his chair.

"Senator?"

Bloodshot eyes fluttered open. "Shouldn't let m'self get so excited."

"No, sir. Would you like a glass of water? And then maybe a brandy?"

"Yes. Good." Butler's words were uttered in a dry whisper.

"I'll pour them both."

"Good lad." Butler closed his eyes again. "Good lad. Not enough good lads."

The secretary poured the water. Then while Butler drank it in one gulp, he poured the brandy. "Shall I call a doctor, sir?"

"No." Butler swigged down the brandy and leaned back again with his eyes closed. His chest felt as if a band of iron encircled it, squeezing tighter with every breath he drew. "No. Just close the drapes. I'll sit here in the dark for a while."

His mind raced. Of course, the actor and actress might have no connection to Westfall's death, but he had come to believe from de la Barca's reports that they had. Now he did not know what to believe beyond the obvious fact that de la Barca had evidently failed in his mission and lied to cover up the failure.

No, he did not know what to believe. And his lack of knowledge frightened him most of all.

Frank de la Barca's composure appeared to have returned. Outwardly, his face looked cut from stone. But his volcanic eyes betrayed the rage within him. He might have been an Aztec idol with a fire blazing behind it, a god whose assuagement demanded human sacrifice.

He sat unmoving as the boat train to Baltimore rumbled along. Across his lap lay a case identical to the one he had had to leave behind in Mexico. And overhead in the luggage rack lay another long box. His clothing, stuffed untidily into a small metal locker, was checked through to the London packet that sailed at dawn.

They would not know he was coming. They would never see him until he pulled the trigger that sent the man into hell. He would take the woman back to Washington with him, unless she resisted.

If she fought and scratched, then he would send her to hell, too.

Shreve rubbed his cheek against Miranda's belly. The enticement of cool silken skin made his sex heavy and warm. With a sigh he smoothed his palms up and down her flanks. His thumbs slid over her hipbones.

Against the windows rain pattered lightly, then with redoubled force, driven by wind gusts. The fire glowed red except for occasional licks of golden flame.

When she moaned softly, he turned his head and pressed his mouth into her soft curls until he found the lips that they hid. The scent of their lovemaking filled his head.

"Shre-e-eve." Her hands stroked his disordered hair.

"Mm-m-m-m."

"I'm chilly."

He raised his head dreamily. She lay on the pillows across the head of the bed. Her hair hung down halfway to the floor. He lay lengthwise, the covers pulled up around his waist. "I'll have to warm you up again."

"No. I'm cold. I'm really cold."

He sighed and kissed her again, his tongue flicking back and forth across the nub of nerves between those soft, scented lips. She drew up one knee, more a reflex action than a conscious act of will. "We're not going to get any sleep at all tonight."

He slid his hands under her buttocks and held her still. "Not at the rate we're going."

She shivered.

He touched his tongue to the skin below her navel. It was covered with goosebumps. With a sigh he left off his lovemaking and raised himself on his knees. "Oh, all right. Come down here with me."

When they were snuggled spoon fashion, the blankets pulled up to their ears, she sighed with pleasure. "You must have been very happy tonight."

He kissed her ear. "I was. I am. And I can't get enough of you."

"Even after making love twice." She giggled contentedly. "I thought you were too old to do it twice in one night."

He popped her bottom.

She gasped and made a show of rubbing the spot tenderly. "Well, it has been a long time."

"I've had other things on my mind."

"But not tonight."

"My mind is clear. I feel whole again. And insatiable." The last word was growled in her ear just before his tongue stroked around the inner curve of the helix.

She laughed and protested and tried to squirm away by rubbing her naked bottom against him. "No. No. No."

347

"Yes. Yes. Yes."

"Monster." She arched her back and thrust herself onto him with a squeal of pleasure.

"Monster, am I?" he chuckled. "I thought you said no." He wrapped his arm around her waist and held her tight while she twisted deliciously.

"I did, but I meant yes."

"That's what I thought."

They began a slow dance that drove them both to ecstatic heights. One hand splayed over her belly, his index and third fingers squeezing and pressing against the tingling nerves buried between her nether lips. His other hand squeezed and pressed the nipple of her breast. From her arched throat came soft cries and groans.

"Are you in pain?" he asked softly, applying more pressure to the throbbing nerves.

"Yes. Oh, yes." She groaned and twisted, bent like a bow, his staff boring deep into her. "Oh. Shreve."

Her climax began like a ripple caressing his staff. It spread from that point in waves, beneath his hands where they touched her belly and breasts, against his belly where her buttocks pressed. It ululated from her throat out of her open mouth.

Quite unexpectedly, he felt his own release inside her. His heart slowed, his breathing almost stilled.

Only in sleep did she roll over on her stomach and break the connection between them.

"What are you thinking?" She climbed back into bed after putting a scuttle of coal on the fire.

He lay on his back, his eyes closed, his hands clasped across his waist in an attitude reminiscent of prayer. "That I have to thank you for my life."

"Nonsense," she said softly.

"And that I love you more than than life itself."

She slid over beside him, their shoulders touching. She closed her eyes too. "You make me sound like a saint. I'm ordinary. I'm human. I'm just what you made me."

After a moment's silence, his rich voice rumbled out of his chest. "What are you thinking?"

"That you gave me my life a half dozen times over. I love you more than you love me."

He frowned. "That might have been true once, but not now. Not ever again. You couldn't."

"I'm sorry for—everything."

He dismissed her apology with a wave of his hand. "Surely not for everything. And besides, think what this has done for my career."

"Shreve Catherwood." She levered herself up on her side facing him. "How can you say a thing like that?"

"Why, sweetheart, would I be the toast of London if I weren't blind as a bat? No indeed. I'm smart enough to know that I'd probably be playing second lead, or even third to some of Britain's finest. The critics would be condescending toward my performance if they didn't pan me out of hand. No, I'm getting the opportunity to perform with a sympathetic press."

"But it's a terrible price to pay."

"Not a bit of it, as our British friends would say. I've started a new style. Actors will be standing in line to get knocks on the head, so they can't see. Actresses, too. There'll be whole schools dedicated to teaching the Catherwood technique." His voice bore no tinge of bitterness.

She pretended to consider the matter as she flopped back on her back. "Possibly you exaggerate."

"Possibly I do," he agreed mock seriously, "but

349

the fact remains that I have become a wonder. George tells me that he has received several very impressive offers from producers in New York City, in Paris, in Washington, in Madrid. In fact, wherever that review in the *Times* went, the offers have come back."

"And so you're happy."

He hesitated only a moment. "As happy as I'll ever be."

She reared up again to regard him thoughtfully. "Why don't you visit a doctor here in London? They have some of the best—"

He laid his finger over her lips. So unerringly did his hearing direct his hand, that she could not believe that he could not see. "If the swelling goes down and my sight comes back, it will happen when it will happen. If something worse is wrong, if something is broken, then it's broken."

"But an operation—"

"Never." His voice had a note of steel. "Let them cut into my head! Not ever. Don't even think about it. I might get my sight back and lose my brain. Let's not talk about it anymore. We go on from here."

She knelt up above him and kissed him reverently on the cheeks, on the forehead, on the chin, on the lips. "I love you."

He kissed her back and then pushed her playfully away. "And I want food. I have to eat if I'm going to perform—on the stage tonight—and elsewhere. Hop out of bed, woman, and order the whole lunch menu from room service."

George Windom made his way cautiously down the spiral staircase from the dressing rooms. For some unknown reason, back stage tonight was dark

350

as a hole. *Who the hell had turned out all the lights?*

He heard someone moving toward him. He could see a rectangular outline of light around a lantern shield. "Open up that light there," he called. "It's —"

A club whistled out of the dark. It struck him across the temple. He dropped like a stone.

Frank de la Barca flipped back the lantern's cover and directed the light onto the huddled body of his latest victim. For assurance he played it in the direction of the door where the nightwatchman's feet could be seen sticking out from his cubicle. The old man had somehow sensed de la Barca's presence, for he had turned and ducked. The investigator had had to hit him again before he had fallen. Now the feet were unmoving.

He directed the lantern back to the body at his feet. Stooping, he felt for and found the pulse in the throat. The fewer dead bodies the better, he believed. Survivors told conflicting stories that sent the police on wild-goose chases and confused the issue.

He played the lantern up the iron framework of the circular staircase. His eyes burned like anthracite. Shreve and Miranda Catherwood were up there alone, except for the old woman.

Leaving nothing to chance, he had stationed himself outside the stage door on three successive nights. The cold and dampness had been so terrible one night, that his feet had almost frozen to the pavement. However, he had conducted a thorough investigation. He had counted the number of people back stage and noted when they left. Because the Catherwoods were the last to leave the green room, the stars and their business manager and wardrobe mistress left the theater last. Then he

351

had gone in and prowled the building, taking care to avoid the Beresford's nightwatchman. He had seen only two lights burning. One on stage and one in the guard's cage. He had found the dressing rooms up in the loft.

Now with set face, he mounted the stairs.

His eyes on a level with the landing floor, he stared down the hall. Light beamed from under only one door—their door. Behind it he could hear the actor's voice—cheerful, energetic.

Damn him to hell!

He heard Miranda laugh. The old woman murmured something. Again she laughed, joined by his deep rumble.

Damn them all.

He tightened his grip on his revolver. He had tested it in his mattress. This one would not misfire. He would open the door and shoot twice. The old woman first, then the blind man. In a bottle in his pocket, he had chloroform to keep the girl from making trouble.

He had already booked passage for himself and his insane sister-in-law on a ship sailing on the morning tide. No one in London would ever know what happened to her. He would leave the man at the bottom of the staircase to try to explain what had happened. Since he had seen nothing, he could do no more than delay the police.

Scotland Yard would never close the case.

He set down the lantern beside the stairwell and walked noiselessly to the door. Easing back the hammer on the revolver, he twisted the knob and pushed the door open.

It should have swung back to give him free access to the room. Instead it caught in less than a foot. Its lower corner dragged and stuck in a quarter circle groove worn white into the floor. Through the narrow opening the only person he could see was the woman reflected in the mirror.

Their eyes met. She screamed.

With a curse de la Barca lunged forward, throwing his shoulder against the door. It groaned and scraped another inch or two, but to the purpose he might have run into a wall.

Miranda sprang to her feet and flung the first thing at hand at his head. The metal powder box caught him in the temple. A white cloud covered his face, blinding him. He drew a breath, choked on it. He began to sneeze and cough violently.

Shreve leaped to his feet. "What's happening? Miranda!"

"For mercy's sake!" Ada spun around and saw the man jammed in the doorway, the gun wavering in his hand. Darting across the room, she stabbed the hot curling iron into his cheek.

He howled and backhanded her. The blow knocked her down, but she twisted around and crawled toward his legs.

"Miranda! What the hell is going on?"

"It's de la Barca," Miranda screamed. Stuffing the pound jar of cold cream into a stocking, she swung it with all her might at the side of his head. She hit him at the same moment Ada reached his legs and threw her arms around his knees. He went down, the gun underneath his body.

Miranda followed him swinging the stocking for another blow, but he rolled over and pointed the gun at her middle. "Stay back."

She froze.

"Let go, old woman," he shouted. "Or I'll shoot her."

Ada's grip relaxed and he scrambled back. His path took him out into the hall. "Now." He climbed up on one knee, keeping the gun leveled at the figures in the doorway. "Now—"

The door slammed shut.

The next instant the light went out beneath it, and the hall was plunged into darkness.

He stared nonplussed. He could see nothing, absolutely nothing. His eyes accustomed to the light had not had time to adjust. He heard the door open again. He fired at the sound.

A high-pitched scream, probably from the old woman reached his ears. Then the door closed. He heard the lock click.

Cursing vividly, he lowered the gun and wiped at the powder in his eyes. His head was throbbing savagely where she had hit him with the cold cream jar. Those damned women. Not only the girl, but the old woman as well, fought like tigers. He shook his head and cursed the bitches.

He started to fumble back toward the spot he nad set down the lantern. He would get it and break in. It would take longer, but the outcome would be the same.

Just as he turned, a fist came at him from nowhere. It connected with his chin and drove him back down the hall toward the spiral staircase.

He dropped the gun. His heel struck the lantern and sent it clattering. A flash of light revealed Shreve Catherwood, blind eyes open, face twisted in rage. Then the lantern rolled into the stairwell and crashed to the stage far below. Its light went out.

Groaning, reeling in pain, de la Barca sucked in a deep breath.

The fist came out of nowhere again, hitting him in the ribs under the heart. He doubled over, his breath rushing out in a whoosh. Another fist caught him on the mouth and straightened him up.

He could not even curse. He stumbled back and

fell through the well. Tumbling, bumping, clawing weakly for a handhold, he rolled down the stairs. Just before he hit the stage floor, his right foot hooked into the railing as he went over. His weight twisted his ankle. Muscles, ligaments, blood vessels ripped apart. Finally, the bone itself snapped, the jagged edges bursting through the skin.

His agonized shriek filled the theater to the upper balcony.

When he regained consciousness, he was standing on his neck, one knee in his face. The lights were on. Stiffly, he tried to move. He felt as if he were bound in this position, his whole body racked with torment.

People's faces filled his circle of vision. A policeman by the look of his uniform bent over above his face. Another man had his thumb in de la Barca's eye in the process of pushing back the eyelid.

He opened his mouth to speak, but hideous pain burned up his leg as someone extricated it from the railing with ungentle hands. His intended speech became a shriek.

Miranda stood in his line of vision, her face white and angry. She had wrapped her arms around the waist of Shreve Catherwood, who was nursing a pair of badly scraped knuckles.

When they had finished straightening out his body, de la Barca tried to speak, failed, moistened his lips, tried again. "—blind—" His voice took on an incredulous tone. "You're supposed to be blind."

The actor's face turned in his direction, seemed to be staring down at him. "Oh, I'm blind, all right. You didn't get that wrong." Satisfaction was pervasive in the voice. "But once you're used to the

355

dark, you can manage."

"What the hell's going on here?" Billy Beresford came storming in through the stage door. His overcoat flapped open to reveal he had stuffed his nightshirt into a pair of trousers. "Who's that?"

"Someone tried to murder us," Ada told him. "He hit poor George and came up the staircase with a gun, but Shrevey-boy knocked him back down again."

"Your nightwatchman's dead," the policeman declared. "Poor blighter had his skull smashed in."

"This man's got a compound fracture of the tibia and fibula," the physician reported. "We need to move him to a hospital immediately. This foot's going to have to come off."

Even through his pain de la Barca heard the diagnosis. "No!" His voice should have been strong, but it was only a weak whisper. "No. Don't cut my foot off."

"You knocked him down?" Beresford stared incredulously at his leading actor. He gravitated around to whisper in Miranda's ear. "Is that the truth? Did he really knock that bloke down the stairs?"

"Yes," she hissed.

"For God's sake. You can't cut my foot off. Listen to me," de la Barca repeated but his voice was barely a whisper.

The physician had already closed his medical bag and was moving away to direct the transfer of the body. Shreve heard the plea. "Doctor, he doesn't want you to take his foot off."

The man swung back around, bumping into Beresford, who bolted for the stage door. He threw the producer an irritated look, then addressed Shreve. "What's that you say? He doesn't want his foot off. Well, he's not got much choice in the

356

matter. If he doesn't have it off, he'll die."

He knelt back at the injured man's side. "Listen, man, you've got splinters of bone sticking out of the wound. Your ankle's gone for all practical purposes. It'll never bear your weight again."

"No." De la Barca's face was a gargoyle mask stretched and contorted scarcely recognizable as a human being's. Two great knots stood out on his cheekbone and his temple where Miranda had hit him. His nose and chin were swollen where Shreve's fists had connected, and all these were beneath a covering of white powder. "Don't."

The physician patted his shoulder. "You're lucky. You've still got your knee. We can fix you up with a peg, attached a shoe to it. Nobody will ever know. Practically as good as new." He tried for a little humor. "Except it won't have corns."

"Waste of time," the policeman observed under his breath. "He'll swing for sure."

"No!" de la Barca's voice was weaker. "You don't know who I am. You can't do that to me."

"Nonsense. Won't hurt a bit more than it hurts right now — and you'll be alive this time next week." The physician rose to his feet and gestured to two orderlies. Ignoring the injured man's weak protests, they loaded him onto the stretcher.

Frantic, de la Barca grabbed Shreve's hand as they lifted him. Tears and sweat cut streaks through the white. "Tell them," he begged. "Tell them. They can't cut off my foot."

The actor raised his face, no longer maintaining the pretense of looking at the weeping man. "I can't see how bad it is. If I could, I might be able to tell them whether or not to do it."

"Ah, God!" de la Barca began screaming, weak, pitiful, threads of sound. "Help me!" He stretched out his arm to Miranda. "Tell them."

She looked instead at the gun lying ominous and black at the foot of the stairs. The orderlies had just returned from carrying out the nightwatchman's body. "You were planning to kill us all, weren't you?"

"No. No! Not you. I was going to take you back. Butler wants to see you. I was going to take you back to Washington."

The physician motioned to the orderlies, who bore the man away. He screamed agonizingly.

The police inspector picked up de la Barca's gun, looked at the gash in George's head, and began to take down their stories.

"Now do any of you know the man?"

"His name is de la Barca," Shreve supplied. "He's evidently a paid assassin."

The policeman wrote the name "Della Barker." "Now did he take a fall?"

"Yes —"

"No," Miranda interrupted Shreve. "Mr. Catherwood fought him. De la Barca killed the nightwatchman, doused all the lights in the theater, knocked out Mr. Windom, and came up to our dressing room to kill us. I saw him in the mirror when he opened the door. I screamed. Mr. Catherwood slammed the door in his face and then fought him and knocked him down the stairs."

While she was speaking, Billy Beresford, red-faced, gasping for breath, returned dragging an older man with him. He whispered in the man's ear and pointed at Shreve.

"I see," the policeman wrote in his notebook. "And you're —"

"He's Mr. Shreve Catherwood," Beresford interrupted, striding forward, enunciating every word in a loud clear voice. "He's an international star of the first magnitude and the leading actor of the

358

Beresford production of *The Tempest*. I know he wouldn't want me to say this, but unfortunately, he's blind."

The policeman's mouth dropped open. He moved his head from right to left, watching to see that Shreve's eyes did not follow him. "Blimey! He's right. You can't see. And you duked 'im out and knocked 'im down the stairs and broke 'is leg?"

"That's right." Ada put her two cents in. "He would have murdered us dead, but Shreve told us to lock the door and he went out and fought him. He's as good as an Irishman with his fists."

The reporter from the *Times* was scribbling as fast as his pencil would move. "How many times did you hit him, sir?"

"I don't recall," Shreve replied. "It's not important."

"Probably five or six times," Miranda said, then squeaked when he pinched her.

"And why did he try to kill you?"

"I have no idea."

Miranda could feel him begin to tremble. She slipped her hand into his and held up the bruised knuckles. One was bleeding. "I think all these questions can be answered in the morning." She looked at the producer. "Don't you think that would be best, Mr. Beresford?"

An odd look crossed Billy Beresford's face. He straightened his shoulders and nodded. "Absolutely, Mrs. Catherwood. Gentlemen. Gentlemen. I'm going to call for a cab right now and send my stars back to their hotel. They need to rest and recuperate if they're going to be able to turn in their usual sterling performances tomorrow night."

"But—" the *Times* man began.

"You've got your story." Billy Beresford held up his hand as Miranda led Shreve away. "Just see that you write it well."

"The bloke must have been on his way out of town," the policeman supplied helpfully. "Found tickets in his pocket for the *Pride of Portsmouth* due to sail in a couple of hours. And he planned to take the lady with him. Heard him tell her so."

The reporter whistled thinly between his teeth.

"Let me help you, Mr. Windom." Billy Beresford actually stooped and helped George to his feet. "Mrs. Cocks." He turned to one of policeman. "Would you climb up to the dressing rooms and get their overcoats?"

"Right-o."

Miranda kept her arm through Shreve's. She could feel him shuddering and feel her own control stretched as her reaction matched his. She held out her hand to Billy. "Thank you so much."

He took it and found it ice cold. "I'll take care of everything," he promised gravely. "Just take him home and both of you get plenty of rest."

"You're a hero," Miranda told Shreve. " 'International Star Bests Would-Be Murderer.' "

"Oh, lord." He stretched his arms toward the ceiling. "They'll all be back again. The show will never close."

"Tsk! Tsk! Poor little boy."

"I know. Trouping the boards is a tough life."

They lay side by side grinning at the ceiling.

Then she rolled over and propped herself up. "I think you're ready to do *Macbeth* again."

"Play Macbeth." He dropped his arms. His black eyes stared sightlessly at her. Hope flickered like a light across his face, then faded. "I can't play Macbeth."

"Anyone who can beat a man half to death in

360

the dark can duel on a stage with fake swords."

He snorted. "Nobody bothered to point out that you'd already blinded him with powder and knocked him half silly with the cold-cream jar. And before that Ada had stabbed him with a curling iron and wrestled him off his feet. I just had to push him and he fell."

She lifted the bandaged knuckles to her lips. "You hit him hard and at least twice. Don't try to play down what you did."

"I'm not. I hit him. I heard him cursing and groaning. The fool couldn't see in the dark, so he thought no one else could."

"Exactly."

"You mean the actor playing Macduff could make noises?"

"Probably."

He slowly rubbed his chin. "It's a thought. For later."

"Later?"

"Yes." He transferred his hold until he was gripping her hand. "Miranda, we're going back to Washington."

"Shreve! We can't." Fear made her voice lose some of its timber. "You heard the man. He came to kill us."

"That's exactly why we have to do it. The four of us have a stake in this. For the first time we have a name. Butler. It's either face this Butler person, or spend the rest of our lives dodging assassins. I, for one, want to get it over with."

"No." She shook her head violently. "No. Before I let this happen, I'll go alone. I'll turn myself in."

"You'll do nothing of the kind." He sat up on the bed and crossed his legs tailor fashion. He captured both her hands and stilled their fluttering by stroking his thumbs over their backs. "I don't think that's what's wanted. I think this Butler means to kill you."

"You don't know that."

"Sure I do. And so do you if you think about it. He wouldn't slaughter all of us back in London, kidnap you, take you to America, question you, and then leave you alive to tell about it?"

She was silent. Finally, she said in a low voice, "He wouldn't, would he?"

"No. The play is not yet ended. Not half enough the corpses yet. Rosencrantz and Guildenstern may be dead, but Claudius and Laertes await us. We have to go and face this head on."

She pressed herself to his side and laid her head on his chest. *"If it be now, 'tis not to come; if it be not to come, it will be now; if it be not now, yet it will come."*

He clasped her hand. *"The readiness is all."*

Act Five
Scene 2
Washington, D.C.

Twenty

They offend none but the virtuous.

"Why does he weah those smoke-tinted glasses, Cassie?"

"Why haven't you heard? He's a famous sportsman. He's just passionate about it. He thinks he has to save his sight for hunting."

As she listened to her hostess's answer, Phyllis Lee Merritt's blue eyes widened. Worshipfully, she scanned the tall, exquisitely garbed figure of the Englishman standing straight-backed and smiling across the room.

No question about it. He was certainly the handsomest and the most exciting man in attendance at what was otherwise the same old Washington party. Posed in the arch, a smile on his face, white teeth gleaming from beneath a small black mustache, he drew every feminine eye in the room. From his wavy black hair with its attractive sprinkling of gray to his shining patents, he was the epitome of English nobility — or at least Mrs. Merritt's idea of English nobility.

"And what did you tell me his name was again?" Phyllis drawled from behind her fan. He was looking in her direction. She waved at him and smiled dazzlingly, then frowned when he did not appear to notice.

"Lord Edgemont-Canfield, Maurice Francis John," her hostess recited triumphantly, taking note that Phyllis had been passed over. "He prefers to be called merely Lord Edgemont."

"And how did you manage to make his acquaintance, Cassie deah?" Mrs. Merritt's Southern drawl was more pronounced when she was sulky. She snapped her fan closed and looked around at the other guests. "Oh, Ah can't understand how you do it. It's too, too bad when you have the only new people in town at yore pahty."

"Oh, now don't be upset." Cassie Waldron smiled sweetly. "Chester has connections everywhere. As a senator, he's expected to entertain so many more important people than a mere congressman is."

Phyllis Merritt ground her teeth. "That's as may be, but tell the truth now. How did you land him?"

"Actually, his wife's a very distant relative of that tiresome Ruth Westfall."

"No, she can't be." Phyllis turned her attention to Lady Edgemont who came from the doorway and took her place at his side. If Lord Edgemont was the handsomest man in the room, the woman standing next to him was certainly the most beautiful lady. Even the small strawberry mark on her left cheek looked endearing rather than disfiguring.

Phyllis's mouth drooped even farther and her forehead knitted in a scowl. "She cain't be any kin to Ruth Westfall," she sneered. "That li'l ol' frump must have made that up."

Cassie registered her own displeasure. "I'm inclined to agree with you, but I never look a gift horse in the mouth. Mrs. Westfall's enlisted Chester's support in her crusade to help the Indians. So when she told him her cousin was coming to town and told him who she was—" The senator's wife shrugged. "Even though I told him he shouldn't get involved, he went ahead and did it anyhow. He says she's a general's widow and the press likes her."

"No soonah does that awful Libby Custer retiah from town than Ruth Westfall rides in. You'd think the Congress would get enough of weepy ol' women dressed in black."

"Well, I know I am. But Chester has to think of his constituency. And at least she did produce Lord and Lady Edgemont-Canfield. So her connections can't be all bad." Cassie smiled warmly at an acquaintance across the room.

Lord Edgemont offered his arm to his lady. With a practiced movement, she bent to catch up her train. Phyllis caught Cassie's arm. "Mah goodness."

"I know."

"Mah stars! How does she walk in it?"

Lady Edgemont's gown was of midnight blue silk taffeta, its cap sleeves draped off the shoulder points to frame her beautiful neck and bust. In a straight pure line, the skirt fell from her tiny waist to the floor in front and was caught up in back to just below the waist in an enormous bustle. From beneath it, knife-edged pleats in the same material cascaded to the floor and spread behind her in a foot-long train. To create the effect of impossible straightness in front, the underside of the skirt must have been tightly tied at the hips and knees.

"I, for one" — Cassie's voice was harsh with envy — "hope she trips and falls." She plastered a gracious smile across her mouth and glided forward. "Lady Edgemont. Yoo-hoo. My dear, so good of you to come. And you, too, Lord Edgemont."

"We are delighted to be here." The couple smiled restrained but warm smiles. Lady Edgemont allowed her fan to move languidly in her white-

367

gloved hand. It was a full circle of pleated white silk in the Spanish style with an ivory handle. Its center was decorated with lace and fresh white roses. Both ladies thought they would die of envy.

"Such a beyoo-ti-ful dress," Phyllis simpered as she closed her own handpainted half-circle fan with a snap.

Miranda smiled frostily as she answered in her very best British accent. "So kind."

"Yes, indeed. We are most pleased to be invited." Shreve's black eyes behind the smoked lenses stared directly into those of his hostess.

Crimsoning beneath his direct stare, Cassie put her hand on Phyllis's arm. "Lady Edgemont, may I present Mrs. Merritt?"

Miranda nodded and smiled graciously, if a trifle frostily, at the woman who had addressed her without an introduction.

"Phyllis is my dear, dear friend," Cassie continued. "Her dear husband is Congressman Merritt of the Alabama delegation.

"Charmed, I'm sure." Miranda's British accent was so clipped as to be barely comprehensible to the Alabaman.

"Lord Edgemont, may I present Phyllis Merritt?"

"Utterly charmed, my dear." Her husband's accent was also clipped, but his deep voice sent shivers down both women's spines.

Giggling and blushing, Mrs. Merritt extended her hand. Miranda took it first, not what Mrs. Merritt had intended at all. "Your dress is lovely too, Mrs. Merritt. Isn't it lovely, Maurice?"

She passed Mrs. Merritt's hand to her husband, who bent over it in a formal bow. His lips did not touch it, but his breath was warm. "Lovely."

At that moment Ruth Westfall entered the room behind them.

368

"Ah, Cousin Ruth," Miranda said to her mother, "what a lovely party you have brought us to."

"I thought you would enjoy it, Cousin Miranda."

Both Mrs. Merritt and Mrs. Waldron extended warm welcomes to Ruth, who allowed a small ironic smile to play about her lips. Mrs. Waldron went so far as to embrace her.

"Lord Edgemont, Ah understand you are a sportsman," Phyllis caroled. "Ah hope you'll considah hunting in Alabama. Mah fathah's plantation is jus' alive with whitetail deeah. We'd love to bring you down theah and let you hunt to yore heart's content. Why you could take home a rack that'd be the envy of everyone in London."

"I thank you for your kind invitation, Mrs. Merritt." Shreve smiled his most seductive smile. "But my time in America is somewhat limited. Actually, my fascination is with the West. I long to hunt buffalo."

"Oh."

His voice took on a serious note. "But I'm sure that whitetail are equally exciting. I'm familiar with the deer hunt. Our English deer do provide good sport. I have a box in Scotland, of course. The shooting's perfectly splendid. But when an Englishman comes to America, he wants the one thing that England cannot provide. Buffalo. The great beast of the prairies. The shaggy monster of lore and legend. The ground shakes where they move. The thunder of their passing can be heard for miles. The experience of a lifetime."

The guests listened, mesmerized to the beautiful voice describing the magnificent creature few of them had ever seen.

Senator Waldron made his way up behind his guest. "That's exactly what I told my friend Senator Hugh Butler that you'd want." He clapped

369

Shreve on the shoulder familiarly. "The three of us must get together."

Shreve glanced pointedly at the intrusive hand, then moved deliberately away. "Are you a sportsmen, sir?"

Waldron instantly dropped his hand to his side, then shook his head uneasily. "Not really. No, not in the usual sense."

His guest's black eyebrows rose in inquiry.

"Oh, not along the lines that you are," Waldron continued. "A few days 'tramping Virginia woods,' as the poet says, is all I can fit into my busy schedule. Isn't that right, dear?"

His wife smiled brightly. "Oh, yes, he's very busy. Attending to affairs of state."

Shreve pretended to consider. His timing was impeccable when he inquired, "Then this Senator Butler must be a sportsman?"

"Him." Waldron laughed. "No. He's eighty if he's a day."

Shreve frowned. "I fail to see—"

The senator raised his hand to pat the Englishman on the back again, then thought better of it. He smoothed his own thinning hair. "You'll just have to meet with us and learn all about some very intriguing opportunities. What about lunch next week?"

Shreve appeared to hesitate. He looked in his wife's direction. Waldron barely managed to conceal his irritation. Men who consulted their wives disgusted him because they were so unpredictable.

Lady Edgemont-Canfield shrugged. "I think you should take advantage of everything."

"Then, perhaps—" he began reluctantly.

"Good. Good." The senator held out his hand. Shreve made no move to grasp it. Waldron looked questioningly into the handsome face.

"My husband does not shake hands," Miranda informed him with a smile.

"Sorry about that," Shreve explained equably. "But I've had my hand wrung so many times at royal receptions that it's been swollen to twice its size. Just decided that I wasn't going to do it anymore. When the hand is injured, it has a deuced effect on the shooting, don't you know? Timing is all off."

"I never had any idea." The senator withdrew his hand. "I can understand your feelings though." Looking around at the rapt circle, he laughed heartily if a bit nervously. "Handshaking can be a nuisance and a pain. It's a wonder a politician's hand isn't wrung off."

"Exactly."

"We did it," Miranda whispered aside as they strolled away. "The news will spread like wildfire. No one will ever offer his hand again. You'll be safe."

Shreve smiled as their progress around the room continued. "It's all very easy if you put your mind to it."

"I kept expecting someone to recognize us. I've never been so afraid."

"People see what they expect to see. You know that. I'm Lord Edgemont-Canfield with a beard and dark glasses. I bear only the slightest resemblance to an actor—what was his name. You're Lady Edgemont-Canfield, a perfect English rose, with an unfortunate strawberry mark on your left cheek. It's all anyone sees."

"Ada can do anything." Miranda squeezed his arm. "You're the hit of the party. The senator's wife was ready to kill me and carry you off to an assignation."

He chuckled under his breath. "Was she the one

371

with the Southern accent you could cut with a knife?"

"No. That's Phyllis Merritt. She and her husband are from Alabama. She invited you to go 'deeah huntin' on her fathah's plantation.' "

"Sounds intriguing," he murmured. "But I'm invited for lunch. Unfortunately, I won't be able to make that, but when they send a message with the time and place, I'll send it back changing the meeting to an afternoon meeting at one of their offices."

Ruth moved beside them. "I don't understand why Waldron wanted you to meet with Butler. I thought they were supposed to be on opposite sides of the issue." She sighed unhappily. "Cassie Waldron cut me dead not two days ago. Now you'd think we were bosom friends. I seem to have to learn over and over that things are never what they seem."

"He sounds almost too good to be true," Butler objected, slipping his spectacles into the case. He leaned back in his chair breathing deeply. His heart thumped in his chest and his body was covered with perspiration, though a heavy fall of snow had blanketed Washington, D.C., that morning.

"He's another Saint George Gore," Waldron insisted. "According to his business manager, he's got estates in the south of England, in Wales, and in Scotland. Income over a hundred thousand pounds yearly."

"*His* business manager," Butler scoffed. "But what about the British ambassador? What does he say?"

"He doesn't know him, but he knows of him. He looked him up in a book he had. Edgemont and

Canfield are both old names. Big estates. From his name this man is the descendant of both families. He's perfect. Perfect." Waldron was all but rubbing his hands in anticipation.

"But we don't know anyone who knows him," Butler objected.

"Ruth Westfall knows his wife."

"That makes me even more nervous. Ruth Westfall was from Chicago. Her parents—"

"Hugh, relax," Waldron insisted. "We're the ones who chased him down. He even refused to have lunch with us. He's got other fish to fry. You mark my words. Other people are trying to get him interested in their deals. We've got to sell Wyoming like it's never been sold before."

Butler sighed, his heart slowed, but then seemed to skip a beat occasionally. "Maybe you're right. I think we should have waited until we had him checked out—"

Waldron started to interrupt.

The old man heaved a profound sigh. "—but never mind. He's here. He's on his way. I just want this deal to go through." He closed his eyes.

The younger man stared at the huge body slumping in the oversized chair. Hugh Smith Butler looked like a corpse. And smelled like one, too. Waldron shook his head in disgust. The sooner he got this business concluded and went on to other deals the better. The senator was up for re-election in November. He didn't look as if he could stand the strain of another campaign.

"What we have to offer is a wild, untamed land." Butler finished his explanation with a clumsy flourish of his huge hand. "But it's a land literally filled with wild game."

373

He and Waldron looked at Shreve Cathervood, who sat straight in his chair, his eyes behind the dark glasses focused on Butler's face.

"How does that sound, Lord Edgemont?" Waldron nudged Catherwood in the side.

Catherwood turned in the direction of the voice. Waldron was an easy man to track. He touched people constantly, slapped their backs, shook their hands, patted their knees, nudged them in the ribs. "It sounds almost too good to be true. I understood that the only real land left was part of Indian reservations."

Butler cleared his throat noisily. Too much information from Ruth Westfall, he would wager.

Waldron shook his head vigorously. "Not at all. Not at all. Large quantities of Wyoming and Montana territories are virtually uninhabited. Except by wild game, of course."

"Magnificent hunting. The best in America," Butler declared. "The streams are full of trout, the sky filled with birds, the land—"

"Did I misunderstand your cousin, my dear? I thought she said that Wyoming was about to become a state." Shreve interrupted Butler's paean.

"I believe that is what she said," Miranda concurred. "Perhaps she was talking about Dakota. The names are very difficult to keep straight."

Butler sagged back in his chair, his fleshy lips compressed into a tight line. Lord Edgemont had appeared with not only his business manager, Mr. Windom, but his wife as well. The manager was bad enough, but Lady Edgemont's presence had not pleased him.

In his experience, women put a damper on a man's enthusiasm. Women wanted to know how much and what that amount purchased and exactly what the details were. And Ruth Westfall—he was sure—was destined to be his nemesis. She had created nothing but problems for him since she had returned.

Seeing Butler had fallen into a deep study, Waldron cleared his throat. "Wyoming will become a state. There's no doubt about that. But the timing has to be right. They can't become a state until they satisfy population requirements which you and your husband should be able to contribute to. Believe me, they'll welcome you with open arms."

"Where is this land?" Miranda looked at the maps spread out on the table beside them.

Frowning, Waldron nudged Butler. The old man opened his eyes looking around him dazedly. When he saw their expectant expressions, he sucked in his breath. With a smothered groan he heaved to his feet. "Er—if you'll step this way, I'll be happy to show you."

Shreve rose immediately and Miranda took his arm. George Windom closed up behind his other shoulder.

Butler shuffled to the other side of the table and began to point out the land he offered for sale. His pointer moved across the map of the northeast corner of Wyoming, where it touched South Dakota and Montana. Miranda recognized the lands of the Cheyenne and the Sioux.

She could feel the trembling beginning. These men condemned themselves with every word they spoke. Benjamin Westfall had been sent to drive the Indians to war so a slaughter could ensue and their lands could be taken. Since he was dead, they had decided to go ahead with the selling of the lands. Let the buyer beware. A real English lord would pour his pounds into their pockets and take off to the western frontier to hunt buffalo.

What he would find would be his death. The

army would be called in to avenge it and—she could feel the fever rising in her cheeks—Butler and Waldron would sell the land again.

Shreve could feel her body shaking against his side. Despite the impenetrable blackness, he glanced down at her. He tightened his clasp on her hand that had suddenly grown clammy. "If Mr. Windom could have these maps to examine," he began.

"But you're the one who needs to see—" Waldron began.

"Are you feeling all right, my dear?" Shreve asked Miranda

She started, tensed. He could feel the muscles jump. "I'm—"

"Why don't I send for Raymond to take the little lady into the outer office?" Butler made a poor job of concealing his irritation.

Shreve threw a black look in the old man's direction, then put his arm around her shoulder. "Do you want to go, my dear?"

Even in his alarm, he did not break character. The realization steadied her. "No." She touched her gloved hand to her forehead. "I just became dizzy for a moment."

"Raymond," Butler called from the door. "Bring something to drink for the lady."

"Yes, sir."

"No, really, I'm quite all right." She was in control again. "Please go on with your presentation."

Casting doubtful glances at each other, Butler and Waldron continued. Each extolled the virtues of the land, the wild, untamed qualities, the possibilities for ranching, and, above all, the hunting.

Shreve looked at each in turn as he spoke, pretended to study the map, and made appropriate comments in his clipped British speech. George

376

Windom made notes. Miranda watched them, feeling her emotions boiling inside her body at the same time she performed with calculated coolness.

When the senators pointed out and described the virtues of not only Indian lands but also lands of American settlers, she marveled that the atmosphere in the room did not burst into flame from her anger.

At last, the presentation was complete. Both men looked hopefully at Shreve.

Miranda smiled frostily. "I believe we should have a talk with Cousin Ruth and perhaps her friend, Mr. Lindhauer. He's from Wyoming. He should be able to give us an insight into what is the very best buy."

Shreve nodded enthusiastically. "Capital idea, my dear. Not that I don't believe you, Senator Butler and Senator Waldron, but talking to a native always gives a man a better feel for the place."

Miranda really wished Shreve could have seen their expressions. Chagrin, anger, disappointment swept across their faces. Then Waldron put on an affable smile. "Good idea," he managed. "But don't wait too long. These pieces will go very fast."

For his part Butler flung down the pointer with a clatter. Making no bones about his disgust, he stomped across the room and dropped into his desk chair. There he relighted the stub of an enormous cigar lying in a smelly ashtray.

His behavior was the height of rudeness in their presence. Waldron chuckled weakly as he escorted the trio out. "You'll just have to forgive Hugh, Lady Edgemont. He's just dying for a smoke."

"Something's got to be done about that Ruth Westfall." Butler's voice rumbled out of his chest.

Waldron looked doubtful. "I don't see—"

"No, you don't see. But I see. I see. You'd let an ignorant whining bitch be the one to decide whether our plans are a success. You'd let an English lord ask advice of a woman without an idea in her head except what's been put there by frontier rubes like Lindhauer and the rest of the Wyoming delegation."

"I suppose I could get Cassie—"

"Cassie! CASSIE! What does your wife have to do with this? See a problem, eliminate the problem. That's what a man does." Butler leaned forward in his chair, his hands spread out flat on the desktop. Their fishbelly skin was covered with brown liver spots.

"I don't see there's anything we can legally do," Waldron insisted stubbornly. "And I don't intend—"

Butler pointed his finger at Waldron. "Get out. I'll call you when I've handled the situation. Don't do anything. Don't 'get Cassie' to do a damned thing. Just get out."

"Now see here—"

"Get out!"

"What are you going to do?"

"You don't want to know," Butler stated flatly. His tone was accusatory. "So you don't need to know."

Raymond came in after Waldron left. "Can I get you anything, Senator?"

"Is Frank de la Barca still around?"

Raymond shrugged. "I don't know, sir. Shall I send for him?"

"Yes. If you can't find him, here's the name of a man I want you to find." He folded a piece of

378

paper and passed it to Raymond.

His secretary pocketed it. "Yes, sir. Anything else?"

"Send to the Pinkerton Detective Agency. Tell them to send around one of their best men."

"The delegations from all the western territories seeking statehood should be aware of what's going on," Miranda stormed. "You've got to tell them, Wolf."

"Calm down, Mirry."

She halted in her pacing. "Calm down! Didn't you hear me? Members of the United States Senate are selling land in the western territories to foreigners. They don't own any land out there to sell. They're crooks. They're thieves."

Victor looked at Adolf, who shrugged. Gently, patiently, her childhood friend took her hand and led her to the couch. "Mirry, it's something we're already aware of."

She gaped at him. "What?"

"We know all about it?"

"You know about it? And you don't do anything about it?"

Adolf looked decidedly uncomfortable. "Most of it's just speculation anyhow," he said offhandedly. "Men who make money want something to spend it on. They don't ever intend to come West and see what they've bought. They just turn around and sell it to someone else."

"But—" His words were like a punch in the belly. "Surely not all of the people are land speculators. Some people have got to buy the land and come West looking for it. Someone's going to be cheated eventually."

"Actually, they're pretty pathetic when they do,"

Victor explained contemptuously. "They come out expecting to find paved streets and farmhouses waiting for them. When they show up with their deeds of sale from some land development company in the East, we just direct them to the Badlands and let nature take its course."

"And that's it!" Miranda was astounded. "That's it!"

"That's it!" The future Wyoming legislator grinned a little sheepishly.

Suddenly, her childhood friend was a stranger to her. Her voice faltered. "But people are being cheated."

"Any man who's crazy enough to buy land without ever looking at it, particularly land in a place as far away as Wyoming, is just that. He's plumb crazy," Adolf rumbled. "Why Wyoming's like the back of the moon compared to this country around here!"

"He doesn't deserve to be cheated." Her voice trembled. She turned away from Victor.

Shreve heard her voice directed to him. "Miranda," he said softly. "Life is not like a play."

"No. I c-can't make this come together right in my mind. People are being cheated and everyone knows about it."

They stared at her pityingly.

A truly horrifying thought occurred to her. Her stomach burned with an all-encompassing fire. "The army wasn't sent out there to protect the poor people who had already been sold land, was it?" She looked at Adolf. "Was it?"

He shrugged. "That was part of the idea."

"But only a small part," she insisted, her voice breaking and turning shrill. "It was sent out to create the illusion that the land was well protected so the Senate could sell more and more of it."

Victor smiled sadly. He dropped down on his haunches in front of her. "Listen, Mirry, when we achieve statehood, most of these land swindles will stop. Maybe we'll even catch a few of the swindlers in the act, but for now, we really can't do anything. And we sure can't bring a U.S. senator like the Senior Senator from New York Hugh Butler up on charges. At least Waldron's playing like he's on our side."

"You don't understand anything, Miranda," Rachel informed her sister triumphantly. "Victor has explained so much of this to me."

Her fiancé shot her a warning look, but she refused to be silent. "This is all politics. That's why I'll be such a successful politician's wife. I understand it. No one is really doing anything that's so very wrong."

Miranda ignored her sister's snide remarks. She stared into the eyes of her childhood friend and found a terrible truth there. "You're cheating people, too. You don't care any more about them than the senators do."

A flush spread across the cheeks of the man she remembered as White Wolf's Brother. He dropped his eyes and rose abruptly. "It's not the same thing."

"I don't see the difference." Miranda's voice had a flat, dead tone. "Either way people get hurt."

Shreve rose and came to find Miranda's stiff shoulders with his big warm hands. "Let's go for a walk, sweetheart."

"Yes," Rachel agreed triumphantly. "Lead her away and explain things to her."

Miranda winced.

Adolf looked down at the floor.

"Rachel, shut your mouth," Victor ordered.

"But —"

"You want to be a politician's wife. Act like one. A politician's wife doesn't insult anyone. Nor does she burn bridges."

"Victor."

"Come on, Miranda."

Shreve was the one who opened the door and led her out into the hall. Though she looked where they went, he was the one who did the leading.

Twenty-one

Let gallows gape for dog; let man free.

"Mr. Henry Keller," Raymond announced.

Butler did not rise from his chair. Needles and pins tortured his extremities almost to the knees. He did not think his legs would bear his weight. He removed his glasses, straightened, and gave a pained smile. "Mr. Keller."

"Yes, sir."

"Please have a seat. You're from the Pinkerton Detective Agency?"

"Yes, sir."

"Good. Good." Butler stared at the rather nondescript fellow. In his plain brown suit with his brown hair, brown eyes, and even features, Henry Keller did not look like a detective. Certainly, he in no way resembled the saturnine Frank de la Barca. Butler's mouth tightened. "How long have you worked for them?"

"A little over ten years. In Chicago in the main office and now here since we've opened a branch." Keller seated himself in front of the huge desk. His trained eyes took note of the senator without appearing to. Besides the usual identification points, he took note of the advanced age and illness. The symptoms were evident everywhere. In the gray skin color and the palsied hands, in the facial tic pulling down the corner of the mouth and the shortness of breath.

The senator, too, studied the detective a minute more before he nodded. "Good, plenty of experience. I have a confidential assignment."

"All work that Pinkerton does is confidential, Senator Butler," Keller said mildly.

"Of course, of course, but this has to be more confidential than most. I want you to investigate a foreign couple who've appeared in town most recently. It has to be done quietly. No one's to get even a whiff of this. We can't take the chance of offending anyone."

"Pinkerton is noted for their discretion."

Butler cleared his throat in annoyance at the interruption. "I'm the only person you're to report to about this."

Henry Keller nodded, his expression unchanging.

Butler looked at him more sharply unable to see how his words might be setting with the man. Perhaps this investigator was more like de la Barca than he had first supposed. "It's strictly government business."

Keller nodded again. He did not inquire as to why a U.S. marshal might not have been called in to do the job.

Butler pulled out a huge pocket handkerchief and wiped his sweating palms. "I want their backgrounds checked thoroughly. Find out if they're really who they say they are."

Keller brought out his notebook. "Give me their names, sir, and then tell me why you think they are not what they should be?"

The senator let his breath escape in a long sigh as he slumped back in his chair. "It's just a feeling

384

I've got. Just a feeling."

Keller waited.

"They're a couple of Brits. Lord and Lady Edge-mont-Canfield." Butler said the name as if he detested it. He waited while Keller wrote it down. "She claims to be a cousin of Mrs. Benjamin Westfall."

Keller's pencil wavered, a slight frown creased his forehead.

"But Ruth Westfall's from Chicago. How would she come by a British cousin? Leastways anyone who'd want to claim her." Butler's head was bowed on his chest. The top of his pate was almost completely bald and very shiny.

"Anything else you'd like to tell me?" Keller prodded.

"The man claims he's a sportsman. He wears dark glasses to save his eyesight. He won't shake hands like a man. He's afraid he'll bruise his fingers or something crazy like that." Butler's head bobbed up. "Did you ever hear of anything like that?"

Keller shook his head. "No, sir. But I'm not a sportsman."

Butler shrugged his shoulders irritably. "I never heard of it. And my father was practically born with a rifle in his hand. Up in the Catskills he hunted—" He broke off. His eyes were red. "Get me their backgrounds. Every word from the moment they first saw the light of day."

Keller put the pencil inside and closed the notebook. "Yes, sir."

Miranda sat at the window staring out into the street.

George took a last snip with scissors at Shreve's

perfect mustache, then wiped the smooth-shaven jaw with a hot towel. "You're looking good." He complimented his friend. "Your color's good."

"Thank you, George." Shreve ran his hand over his jaw, then pressed experimentally at the underside. "Not saggy there?"

"Not a bit. Strong, tight."

"What do you think, Miranda?" Shreve called. He poked the underside of his face with his thumbs. "It feels a little soft."

When she did not answer, Shreve cocked his head in her direction. She must be brooding. She had sustained a terrific blow yesterday. "Thanks, George. It feels wonderful."

"My pleasure," the former actor declared. "When a man really gets old, he likes to work with a young face."

Shreve grinned at his friend. "Or a middle-aged one."

"Not you." George chuckled as he carried the basin and towels from the room.

"Miranda?"

"What?"

He came to her side and slid his fingers down over her shoulders, massaging gently. "Don't be upset."

"I've been a fool," she whispered angrily. "An idiot. I should have been locked up. I stopped growing the day my father was killed. I haven't made a practical decision since I was thirteen years old."

"Now you're talking like an idiot." Shreve kneaded the tense muscles of her shoulders and neck. "Sweetheart, don't punish yourself — "

She wrenched out of his grasp, rose, and caught his hands. Her voice betrayed her fury. "You've been right all along."

He grinned. "I seriously doubt that."

"Don't make jokes. Don't!"

"Miranda, sweetheart. I swear I'm not joking." He tried to soothe her with the sound of his voice. How he wished he could see her face!

Her hands were icy cold, her breath coming short, her voice raging. "I never really believed that what I was doing was wrong until today."

He frowned.

"Oh, I know, I was regretful, remorseful. I hated what happened to you. I hated what happened to George and Ada. I hated that man de la Barca and I hated Sergeant Trask and Benjamin Westfall. I hated him the most. And *I was never wrong.* I was on a holy crusade. I was Prince Hamlet with God and ghosts on my side to avenge the damnable sin of patricide." She began to laugh. Suddenly, she let go of Shreve's hands to wrap her arms around her body.

Her stomach burned like she had swallowed coals of fire. She moaned in pain.

"Miranda." He reached out for her, but she avoided the solace of his hands.

"No, let me say this." Her voice was heavy with sarcasm. "I never counted the cost too high. Because besides avenging my father's death and saving my mother and killing a man who needed killing, I was saving the whole of Wyoming for the settlers and the Sioux and Cheyenne."

"Miranda, don't be so hard on yourself."

"NO! Don't you dare excuse me. Don't you dare. Be honest with me just like you've always been. You've always said I couldn't play parts. I had to live them. No interpretation. Just emotion."

He heard her steps across the room. She was tottering, stumbling. "Are you ill?"

"Yes!" she all but screeched. "Yes, I'm sick! I'm sick to my stomach at what I've done."

"Sweetheart—"

"Just let me say it. I made my big speech to Adolf and my sister and to White Wolf's Brother— that honorable legislator, that noble savage, that honest, that true—" Her frustration expended itself in a vicious epithet.

Shreve made another sweep for her, but she avoided him.

"And they laughed at me. They didn't care that Butler and Waldron are a pair of crooks selling land that doesn't belong to them. It's been done before. And when the poor people who buy the land come West with deeds, the locals don't even tell them they've been cheated. They just direct them over to the Badlands, where they die of hunger and thirst and maybe get killed for their goods by thieves or scalped by Indians."

"If people are stupid enough—"

"The Indians!" she raged on. "Their chiefs have probably made land deals on the side all along and laughed at the whites."

He chuckled. "Could be. Didn't the Dutch or the English or some such group buy Manhattan Island for twenty-four dollars?"

She was silent for so long, he grew uneasy. "Miranda?"

"Has the whole world been making fun of me?"

"No."

"I know you've been laughing at me for years." She sank into a chair and bowed her head over her knees. "I can stand that. You've indulged me. You're indulging me now, just like you've always done. Trying to turn the whole thing into a joke.

388

I'll always be Juliet to you."

He came to her side. His fingertips found her back. He dropped down on his knee and touched her cheek. "Miranda," he said softly. "You'll always be Juliet, but not because you're immature. It's because as Juliet that I first came to love you."

She set her teeth until her jaw ached. "Oh, Shreve. I hurt so badly. I wanted to do the right thing. I wanted to make everything right. And now I find out"—she took a shuddering breath—"that nobody wants me to make anything right."

He put his hands around the back of her neck and pulled her forehead against his chest. *"Honour is a mere escutcheon."*

"What?"

"I said, *Honor is a mere escutcheon.*"

She jerked herself away from his chest. "Don't quote Shakespeare to me," she snarled. "I've lived by his words much too long. I've killed a man that, it seems, nobody particularly wanted killed except me."

"Benjamin Westfall wasn't a saint," Shreve reminded her. "Just from what he did to you personally, he deserved killing."

"But so many other people have died."

"I can forgive you for Sergeant Trask," Shreve told her dryly as he rose to his feet.

She allowed him to draw her up to lean against his chest. He put his arms around her and held her close. "I won't be stupid any longer," she promised, her voice hoarse with emotion and suppressed tears.

"I sincerely hope that's not true." He kissed the top of her head.

"I won't—What did you say?"

"Stupidity was what dragged me away from the

389

rail of the *Narragansett* in the middle of the Atlantic. A clever woman would have thought that I was doing the right thing."

She lifted her head and stared up into his face.

His eyes were closed, as if he were reviewing pictures in his mind's eye. "A practical woman would have taken George and Ada and walked right out of the hotel room in London and into a brilliant new career as a single actress. She wouldn't have tied her star to an old blind man who had given up."

"Shreve. I didn't — "

"You did, sweetheart. You didn't know anything but success. You believed that life is like a play, that dreams come true, that good triumphs over evil. You believed it so much that you made it happen."

His words were like balm to her wounds. "But you wouldn't have been blind in the first place if it hadn't been for me."

"I've thought a lot about that, too, and maybe it would have happened anyway," he said seriously. "Maybe the weakness was always there."

"You don't believe that."

He laughed. "No, but if it makes you feel better — "

She hugged him hard. "Whatever it takes to get you and Ada and George out of this, I'll do it. I don't care about anything anymore. Not the Indians, not Rachel and White Wolf's Brother, not Adolf — "

He stilled her roll call. "Come and lie beside me."

"Yes. All right."

He led her to the bed, laid her on it, and removed her shoes. He slipped his own off and

390

stretched out beside her to gather her in his arms. With a gentle hand he stroked her back, rubbing away the knots of tension in her spine, holding her while she dozed.

Her sleep was disturbed. Her muscles twitched, she murmured and fretted, stirring restlessly against him. Suddenly, she jerked awake. "Shreve!"

"I'm here."

She subsided against him. "I love you."

He held his breath. "Enough for me to make love to you?"

"Of course. Always. Forever. Whenever you want." She lifted her lips to his.

He kissed her long and thoroughly. His tongue caressed hers, his heart beat faster. When he lifted his head, it was to say, "I want to put my child inside you."

"Shreve!"

"I think we're both ready to be parents, and I want you very much."

She pushed both hands against his chest. "You really think everything will be all right?"

"I know it will." He cupped his hands around her shoulders. "Everything will be fine."

"Is the tragedy really over?"

He laughed aloud. "Marriage for everybody. Fertility rampant. Let the comedy begin."

Swept away by his exuberance, she arched her body against his and reached for the fastening on the back of her skirt.

When they were naked, her thighs spread wide to welcome him. Instead of plunging into her, he lifted her knees to his shoulders and pulled her hips up.

"Shreve," she groaned. "What are you doing?"

"Giving my all." His chuckle was little more than

391

a gasp for breath.

The feeling of fullness drove an ecstatic moan from between her clenched teeth. Never had he seemed so totally inside her. He was touching the very quick of her, pushing against the mouth of her womb.

"Rock with me," he whispered. "Rock with me, sweetheart."

Together they moved, the motion back and forth on her shoulders, providing the surges for his staff to slide in and out. The friction was building, her lips, her sheath swelled around the pressure, gripping him tighter.

"Shreve," she keened. "Shreve!"

His face was a study in passion, the cords of muscle beginning well below his collar bones. They strutted his neck and pulled at his jaw. His teeth, incredibly white beneath his black mustache were bared in an impassioned grin. His black eyes were fixed, staring into space as his body went beyond itself.

"Romeo," she whispered. "Oh, Romeo."

Whether he heard the name or not, she could not be sure, but his head dropped, his eyes stared directly into her own, creating the perfect illusion of sight. They seemed to look into her soul.

"Are you ready?" he gasped.

"Ready," she cried. "Oh, yes, ready!" she demanded.

He threw back his head and drove in deeper than before. One foot was braced against the foot of the bed. One knee left the mattress. Her body rocked up onto her shoulders with the force of his thrust.

Hot liquid flooded her, copious, life-giving.

Her womb contracted, then opened, then contracted again. She could feel it sucking at him, draining him of every precious drop of the life he had to give her.

For a wonderful minute, the feelings went on and on, a roaring in her ears and the blood hummed through her body, ecstasy of flashing stars and suns before her eyes.

His blackness, the terrible blackness, seemed riven for one shining instant with a shower of gold. But it was only memory. His own breath rasped from his heaving chest and sweat slicked his body.

She groaned.

He lifted himself off her, pulling out limp, exhausted, wetness dripping from him.

She relaxed on the bed, curled herself into a ball, and put her hand between her legs to hold the feeling and the life inside her.

He curled himself spoon fashion around her and pulled the covers over them both.

"Are you Billy?"

A deep voice called to him from the dimness of a carriage. He straightened away from the wall where he lounged, his cap pulled low on his head, his ankles crossed.

"Who wants to know?"

"Are you Billy?" The voice was more imperative this time.

"I might be."

"If you're him, then I've got a fifty for you."

"Fifty ain't much."

"There might be more if I could find Billy."

Billy bent low to the window to stare into the depths of the carriage. "I'm your man, but I don't do nothing for anybody I can't see."

Out of the shadows a hand moved bearing a

393

purse that clinked with the unmistakable sound of ten dollar gold pieces. Billy stared at it. "You can see all right," the voice said. "You can see what's in this purse. And that's what you're doing business with."

"What ya want me for?"

"A Mister de la Barca recommended you highly."

"Oh, he did, did he?" Billy scoffed. "News to me."

The figure in the shadows hesitated. "I need a job done."

"Yeah."

"There's a woman — "

Billy cursed virulently. "Another woman. Christ. Don't you guys ever pick on someone your own size?"

"Do you want this money?"

"Yeah, sure. But I want fifty to do it and fifty later, to keep it quiet."

"Fifty is enough."

"Not much," Billy sneered. "Last time me an' m' boys got beaten up twice for our trouble."

"You were stupid."

"Goodbye!" Billy started off down the street.

"Wait!"

The insolent face appeared again in the window of the carriage. "Yeah."

"She won't present the problem the other one did. She'll be alone."

Billy straightened up and looked in both directions. He shifted from one foot to the other on the icy street. Then he stooped to put his face close to the window. "I'm listening."

The man inside the carriage leaned closer. The lower half of his face was a white blur. "She'll be coming out of her hotel at nine o'clock in the morning two days from now. She will be wearing widow's weeds. She goes everywhere alone and heavily draped in black. Damn her."

The carriage horse stamped impatiently. It swung its head around and snorted twin puffs of white fog breath into the night. The carriage rocked forward half a revolution of the wheel.

Billy had to move along with it cursing. "Here. Hold that blasted horse."

The speaker went on without noticing. "Washington is very dangerous. There's heavy traffic in front of the hotels. She could have an accident. A wagon, a covered one, of course, like the one you used before, might come lumbering down the street."

Billy grinned malevolently. "Might run her right over and the bugger'd keep right on going. Never look back. There's that kind around."

"Exactly." The purse opened and five warm solid gold pieces clinked into Billy's outstretched hand.

"And then you'll come back here the same night and bring me fifty more?" he asked cheekily.

"Absolutely."

Billy straightened and stuffed the money down inside his pants. Then he set his hand on the window. "Don't think of leaving me short, Senator."

The silence in the carriage was profound.

The street tough gave a malevolent chuckle. "You don't know a thing about finding out stuff. You ought to be living by your wits on the street if you want to learn how to find stuff out."

"Here's the name of the woman and her hotel," the voice finally ground out. "Do the job and I or someone will bring you fifty dollars the night after."

"Better be sure it's you, Senator." Billy turned his

395

hand over palm up. "I won't take it from a hand that's got a shiv in it."

The note was thrust into his outstretched hand at the same time a cane rapped on the top of the carriage. The driver clicked his tongue to the horse and the vehicle rumbled off into the night.

Billy pocketed the money and the note with a laugh.

Twenty-two

I hope here be truths.

A chill slid down Miranda's spine. Her scalp prickled. Someone was watching her. She hunched her shoulder blades, but the feeling persisted. Turning suddenly from the hotel desk, she surveyed the room.

Only one man was visible, seated in a chair across the lobby. A newspaper had fallen from his slack hands and lay open across his lap. Their eyes met. His betrayed shocked recognition.

Too late, he tried to gather up the paper to shield his face. A couple of pages slid to the floor. His face reddened. Then as if seeking to deny that he had been watching her, his eyes broke contact with her own. Stooping, he gathered up the paper, folded it haphazardly, and laid it across his thighs. His gaze skittered across the lobby to study an older man drowsing in a sunlit corner.

Miranda frowned. His face was somehow familiar.

He slid his hand into his breast pocket and withdrew a cigar with studied nonchalance. Using a silver cutter to snip off the tip, he struck a match on the sole of his high-topped shoe, and puffed hard to get the smoke going.

The trained actress recognized the performance

for what it was. Perhaps he had merely been a gawker. She was used to people staring at her. In the part of the English milady, people pointed her out and whispered behind their hands.

However, something was different about this man. His performance was too good, too studied. Likewise, something about him became more familiar with each passing second. A cloud of blue smoke veiled his face.

"May I be of service to you, Lady Edgemont?" The desk clerk leaned toward her solicitously.

She turned back around. "My key please."

"Yes, ma'am." He handed it to her.

"Are there any messages or mail for either Lord Edgemont or myself?"

The desk clerk stuck his hand back into the key box. "No, ma'am."

Like a bolt a name flashed in her mind. "Henry Keller."

"What's that, ma'am?" The desk clerk turned back.

"Henry Keller." She spun around. The chair was empty.

Key in hand she dashed across the lobby. His cigar smoke laid a trail behind him. Out on the sidewalk, he had turned left. She followed her nose only until she caught sight of him striding briskly away.

"Henry Keller!"

The center of his back straightened as if a rifle round had gone into his spine. He took one more step.

"Henry Keller!" She caught up her skirts to run.

He turned to face her, a small smile lifting the corners of his mouth. "The Magnificent Miranda. I can't believe you remember me."

She halted less than a yard from him. Their eyes

398

met. He was pretending innocence. She could tell instantly and his very effort to pretend gave him away. Since he was acting, he must be doing so because he wanted to conceal something by his performance. She would bet her bottom dollar he had been hired to investigate her. "Are you enjoying my performance?"

His mouth dropped open as if he would protest. Then he shrugged. "I had only just sat down. I haven't really gotten to see it."

"It's every bit as exciting as Lady Macbeth, I assure you." She bit her lip. "You're still working for the Pinkertons, aren't you?"

"Yes."

"And someone hired you to investigate Lord and Lady Edgemont." It was not a question.

He nodded.

She shivered and shuffled her feet as the cold of the pavement slipped up through her boots. "Will you join me for coffee in my suite? I was just going to have some."

He hesitated. "I don't think it's the professional thing to do."

She took his arm as if they were old friends. Her smile was only a little strained. "But think how easy it will make your job."

He should have extracted his arm and walked quickly away, but her blue eyes compelled him along with the fact that he had never forgotten her beauty. He nodded stiffly. "There is that."

"Then come along."

She was still the most beautiful woman that he had ever seen, the most beautiful woman he had ever been close to, and certainly the most beautiful woman he had ever taken a cup of coffee from. He watched her graceful hands with their perfectly manicured nails hold the cup and saucer and pour from the silver teapot.

"Sugar?"

"Yes, ma'am."

"Cream?"

"No thank you."

She passed him the steaming drink and then poured one for herself. She drank it black and scalding.

He watched her and waited.

She set the cup down and looked at him with her magnificent blue eyes. "Did Senator Waldron or Senator Butler hire you?"

"I'm not at liberty to divulge my client."

She lifted one shoulder daintily. "Butler, I'd wager. He's a truly unscrupulous man. He believes everyone is as dishonest as he is, so he has everyone investigated."

He stared at the liquid in his cup, then raised his eyes. "In this case he was right."

Her smile was a little sad. "I remember you investigated Rachel Westfall for me."

"I did indeed." He half closed his eyes. "I remember that and more. Rachel Westfall had an older sister, a girl who disappeared. The girl's name was Miranda Drummond." He looked at his questioner. "You are Miranda Drummond."

"I'm Miranda Catherwood."

He took a sip of his coffee and found it excellent. The coffee in a posh hotel was much better than the stuff he made himself. "Miranda Drummond was the subject of an investigation by Benjamin Westfall," he remarked as if pulling items of information from his memory. "But you already knew that."

"Yes, I did."

400

He closed his eyes remembering the exact details of the case. "He found you with a troupe of actors. You were acting with them, when you were only sixteen years old. A detective named Parker Bledsoe did the investigation."

"And he was murdered."

"A terrible thing that happened to Bledsoe." He set his coffee down and put his hands on his thighs. He shook his head. "He was murdered, walking to his lodging from the office on the day after he found you. He wrote the report and then everything ended abruptly. Your stepfather paid the bill, even though there really wasn't a closure to the case. Or perhaps there was?"

"I'm sure there was," she said dryly.

"I seem to remember a home for wayward girls."

"I remember it too—quite vividly. And I seem to remember that Parker Bledsoe died in a particularly terrible way."

He frowned, remembering the description in the files. "It was never determined absolutely."

Her expression remained level. "I believe there was a suspicion of a saber."

"It was only a possibility. But Parker Bledsoe was—er—decapitated."

She looked at him pityingly. "And you Pinkerton people call yourselves detectives. I'm as sure as I am of the sunrise tomorrow that Benjamin Westfall did it. Since that time, I've experienced firsthand what the man was capable of."

Keller flushed. He pulled out his notebook. "Perhaps you'd better tell me."

"Why?" Her words raked him raw. "You can't do anything about it. Benjamin Westfall is dead."

"Yes, we heard that in Chicago. Assassinated by a disgruntled soldier. Another unsolved crime."

So that was the official story. Miranda bowed

her head. Perhaps—just perhaps—"That's right. I heard about that, too."

"But you say he was capable of anything?"

"He was certainly capable of putting me in that prison for wayward girls."

"But you survived."

"I was rescued within twenty-four hours by Shreve Catherwood and George Windom. Now they are my husband and business manager."

Keller did not make note of their names. Instead he observed, "The place has been closed down for years, but if I remember correctly a girl had to be referred to that place by the courts."

"Mrs. Mortimer would accept anyone if she could see a profit."

Henry Keller nodded. "Probably Bledsoe's next report would have stated that. He had to file a report with Pinkerton. Company policy requires that all detectives report any crimes they may uncover to the proper authorities."

"What if their clients commit them?"

"Especially if their clients commit them. All clients are informed of that before Pinkerton will take a case."

"So Parker Bledsoe objected and"—she paused for emphasis—"Benjamin Westfall cut him down."

"We don't have any proof."

"No. Nor will we ever have. Just like we'll never have any proof that Archie Doight was hired by Benjamin Westfall."

"Who's Archie Doight?" Henry Keller scribbled the name down.

"Archie Doight was a discharged soldier who set fire to a theater in Chicago."

Keller stared. "I didn't hear about that."

"It just happened to be the theater where Shreve and I were playing. It was started back stage at the end of a performance of *Macbeth*. Thanks to my husband's quick thinking, the fire was put out with only minor injuries and minimum damage. Archie Doight was a former soldier so stupid that he'd been seen by the theater manager. The police found him with coal oil on his boots. He had almost a hundred dollars in his pockets. He said he'd been hired to play a joke."

Keller looked appalled. "And you think Benjamin Westfall hired him? Do you have any proof?"

She shook her head, her lips curved in mocking smile. "Doight didn't know who hired him. He just knew it was an army officer."

"What did the police say?"

"They arrested him, and I suppose they sent him to jail for a few months. They might have let him go. Once everything was over with and the excitement had died down, he had only done it for a joke. And it was only a theater anyway."

"It was arson," Keller insisted.

"If hundreds of people had died—which they very well could have done—then he would have been tried and executed, but not before every Federal marshal in the country had moved heaven and earth to find out who hired him." She looked at the investigator bitterly. "But since no one was hurt, nobody really cares what happens to a theater or to actors. They're not important."

"That's not true."

She smiled. The warm light came back into her eyes. "So, Mr. Keller, did Senator Butler hire you?"

He closed the notebook. "I'm still not at liberty to tell you that, Mrs. Catherwood."

"Miranda—please. Did you know that Senator Hugh Smith Butler was responsible for Benjamin Westfall's going back to Wyoming? Westfall went with a grudge. He was going to rebuild Fort Gallatin and provoke the Indians until they revolted. Then he was going to exterminate them."

Keller stirred uncomfortably. "Well, the Indians have been—"

"The Indians have been persecuted by the U.S. Army for generations. Only a couple of times did they really hurt anyone—at Fort Gallatin and at Little Big Horn. They've paid for that at Wounded Knee and Sand Creek. They've signed treaties for their land. But Senator Butler and men like him want that land. So why not send a killer like Benjamin Westfall to drive them out?"

"You don't have any proof of that."

"No, I don't, but I'm trying to get it. Lord and Lady Edgemont-Canfield have been offered the opportunity to buy a great deal of land in Wyoming. We're to buy it from Butler of New York and Senator Chester Waldron of Virginia. Now where did those men gain access to land in Wyoming?"

"I can't imagine," Keller said dryly.

She smiled. "They hoped that Westfall would make it available for them. When he was killed, they decided to go ahead and sell it anyway to a gullible Englishman and his silly wife."

Keller sat back, his hands limp. "I guess this is why I'm hired. My client doesn't leave anything to chance."

"May I pour you some more coffee, Mr. Keller?"

"I'd appreciate it if you'd call me Henry just once."

She smiled. Her hand curved gracefully around the teapot's silver handle. "Please have another cup of coffee, Henry. You seemed to enjoy the first cup so much."

He hesitated, then he smiled himself, a little stiffly, as if he did not smile very often. "I'd like

404

that very much, Miranda."

They drank together in silence, then he set the cup down. "That was delicious. Thank you."

"You're most welcome. Will you have more?"

He shook his head regretfully as he rose. "I must leave, Lady Edgemont."

His use of the name froze her cup halfway to her saucer. She looked at him searchingly. "I wouldn't want you to do anything that you'd get in trouble for."

"I won't get in trouble. It'll just take me longer to check on your stories. Letters to and from England take six weeks to three months. Until that time's passed, I won't really know anything."

She followed him to the door and extended her hand. "Thank you, Henry."

"My pleasure, Miranda." He pressed it. "And may I say you have the most beautiful eyes?"

Ruth caught at the heavy black veiling as the freezing wind picked it up and blew the ends behind her. A glance upward revealed the heavy clouds that promised more snow.

When Hugh Butler's message had been delivered last night, she had felt a wild hope. Because she could not think what he might have to say to her, she had been in an agony of suspense all night long. Now she was early for the appointment.

Like a small black bird, she fluttered across the snow-covered street and carefully negotiated the high curbstone.

A delivery truck came out of an alleyway behind her, the horses trotting briskly. She did not turn her head as it rattled toward her. She heard the driver call to the team. His whip cracked. The horses picked up the pace.

The iron-shod hooves pounded faster. They were galloping now.

Still unconcerned, she did not turn until the very last minute. The horses thundered straight for her on either side of her. Fog breath whooshed like smoke from their flared nostrils. Yellow teeth champed the heavy bits. One plunged onto the sidewalk. The wagon bumped, tilting crazily. The whip cracked over the tossing heads.

Stunned, paralyzed, she stared in disbelief.

The wagon tongue struck her in the chest, knocking her flat. Her arms and legs flew wide. The back of her head hit the sidewalk. At least four hooves pounded her against the stone, but the wagon wheels passed on either side of her, missing her completely.

A messenger brought the news to Miranda before he went to Rachel. As Lady Edgemont, the cousin of the injured woman, she was considered the most consequential member of the immediate family.

The doctor, a short, balding man with a black beard, intercepted Shreve and Miranda in the hall outside her mother's room. In a hushed drawl he described her mother's condition. "A fractured skull, a fractured sternum, a crushed right hand—"

Miranda listened, her face white as a lily. Her mother. Her mother had been in an accident. Run down in the street.

"—multiple bruises, cuts, and possible internal injuries. A blow, probably a horse's hoof just over the spleen."

She listened to all he had to say, then, for the first time in her life, fainted in Shreve's arms.

* * *

Shreve's face swam into view hanging above her. The doctor, his expression concerned, held smelling salts beneath her nose. Coughing, she waved him away.

"I'm sorry," were her first words.

"Don't apologize." The doctor screwed the top down tight on his salts. "I'm the one who should be apologizing to you. You're a gentlewoman and I'm describing the injuries to you as if you were a colleague."

"I wanted to hear them," Miranda insisted. "I want to know the worst. My mother is going to live, isn't she?"

He raised his black eyebrows and shot a look at Shreve. "I was under the impression that you were a cousin of the injured lady."

Suddenly, Miranda no longer cared. The game was up. Henry Keller knew and would have to give the information to Butler once the proper amount of time had elapsed for inquiries to reach England and return. She and Shreve had found out what they had come to find out. Unfortunately, the information did no one any good. And worst of all, her mother had been injured. She choked. "I'm her daughter."

She fumbled for and found Shreve's hand. He squeezed hers with perfect understanding. She swung her legs over the edge of the bed and stood, leaning against his strength.

The doctor glanced from one to the other. The man's eyes through the dark glasses were fixed on him, but something about their unblinking intensity made him wonder. He shifted his weight.

"My husband is blind, Doctor," Miranda said angrily. Her expression was murderous.

The doctor cleared his throat. A flush mounted in his cheeks. "He hides it very well."

"Thank you," Shreve said.

"I'd like to see my mother."

"Of course. If you'll follow me. I can't of course make—" Discomfited by his remarks, he backed to the door, fumbled with the knob.

Miranda regarded his movements dispassionately. "I understand, Doctor."

"Of course." He took a deep breath and preceded them down the hall. "Now when you see her, she won't know you. She's asleep because I've given her laudanum for the pain. A nurse is with her, keeping snow packs on her body to keep the fever and swelling down."

"Won't she take a chill?"

"I don't think it's likely. Especially if the room is kept warm. Winter is a good time of year for healing bruises because there's a good supply of snow." The doctor obviously was supporting a favorite treatment. "We don't know how much people hear when they're unconscious. Particularly, when they're sedated. Talk to her as if you think she's going to be all right."

"She is going to be all right, isn't she, Doctor?" Fear and weakness set Miranda to trembling at his last remark.

He took a deep breath, his hand on the doorknob. "She's a very little woman, and those were very big horses."

They walked around the corner and almost collided with Rachel and Victor.

"Miranda!" Rachel's face was drained of all color. Victor had an arm around her waist to support her. "Miranda," she repeated piteously.

"Rachel." Miranda held out her arms and her baby sister staggered into them. Tears flowed down her own cheeks as she held Rachel and murmured soft words in her ear. The three men stood helplessly by as the two sisters grieved together.

Finally, Rachel was able to get herself under control. Shakily, she straightened and fumbled in her coat pocket for her handkerchief. "Have you seen her?"

"Not yet. We were just going in." Miranda kept her arm around her sister's shoulders. "Doctor — I'm sorry I don't know your name."

"Harl Thompson."

"Doctor Thompson had just finished explaining that Mother's unconscious."

"Oh!" Rachel gloved clapped her hands to her mouth. The tears started again.

"But it's because he's given her medicine to keep her from being in so much pain." Miranda hastened to reassure her.

"Rachel, it's the best thing." For the first time Victor spoke. His voice was deep and grave. "She's fragile. It's good she doesn't have to suffer needlessly."

Rachel looked from one to the other. "But I want to talk to her. I have to talk to her. She's got to be all right. She will be all right, won't she, Doctor Thompson?"

He looked steadily at Miranda. "I promise I'll do everything I can."

Rachel let out a wail. Victor pulled her face into his shoulder. "Ssh. You must be brave."

Miranda agreed. "Crying won't help, Rachel."

"Perhaps it would be better if you did not go in until she has regained consciousness," the doctor suggested to her mildly.

Instantly, Rachel raised her head and swiped at her eyes. "I have to see her."

"Then you must be very brave and not cry. She might hear you and think she was dying. We want her to know that she is going to live." The doctor opened the door.

A nurse was just laying a folded cloth across Ruth's forehead. She stepped away from the bed when she saw the doctor.

"Oh." Rachel let her breath escape in an agonized whimper.

The doctor frowned, but Miranda was scarcely able to conceal her own shock.

Her mother's head was wrapped in bandages. Her eyes were sunken and surrounded by deep reddish-purple bruises. Her right arm lay on a slanting board that elevated the hand which was also bandaged. Rubber bottles frosted with cold beads had been placed on either side of the hand. Another bandage bulked up around her waist beneath the sheet and blanket.

Miranda could feel the blood draining from her head. Sternly, she steadied herself. "Mother." Keeping her arm around Rachel she moved to the bedside. "Mother, we're here."

The body lay still.

Rachel looked from Ruth to Miranda and back again. Her skin was almost translucent. Miranda squeezed her shoulder. "Talk to her, Rachel."

"M-mother. We're—er—right beside you."

Miranda took up her mother's left hand. The fingernails were blue, the fingers cold. "Mother. I'll take care of everything. Get well soon, so we can all go back to Chicago together. Mother, I need you. Shreve and I are going to have a baby."

Rachel's color rose in her cheeks. "Are you really?"

Miranda shrugged. "Yes," she lied. "Shreve doesn't know yet, but I'm sure."

"How wonderful!" Rachel managed a weak smile. "I'll be an aunt."

"That's right. You have to get well quickly,

Mother," Miranda continued. "You're going to be a grandmother."

Perhaps she only imagined the tiny flicker of movement at the corner of the mouth.

"Why that is good, dear lady. You are going to be a grandmother." Dr. Thompson took their mother's hand and counted the pulse. "Very good," he announced. "You are definitely stronger. Now you must rest so the healing process will continue."

Miranda smiled weakly. "Mother." She bent over to kiss the drawn cheek. "We'll be back soon."

Rachel kissed her, too. "I love you, Mother."

Outside in the hall, Miranda went into Shreve's arms. He held her while she shivered. Her stomach and head were both burning. Horror piled upon horror. If her mother died, she would ultimately be to blame. Would this tale of revenge never end? Dear God! Was her mother Gertrude, Denmark's queen, an innocent victim in the blood duel between Hamlet and Claudius?

In her heart she began to pray.

"How is she?" Victor asked Rachel. The younger girl tottered blindly into his arms.

"Awful."

His voice came from far away, but it roused Miranda. "No one could have hit her accidentally. She was dressed in black on a snow-covered street. Was the road icy? Was it a runaway team? What was she doing out at that time in the morning anyway?"

Rachel sucked in her breath. "Senator Waldron sent for her."

"I wonder if he really did," Shreve speculated.

Victor's face was stern, the Cheyenne clearly visible in his expression. "You can't mean that someone tried to kill her. She's a woman. A lady. No one makes war on women."

Miranda shook herself away from Shreve. Her gaze raked her childhood playmate. "Don't be stupid, Victor. Indians and white men have been killing each other's women for years. And children, too."

"Not on the streets of Washington."

"Murderers are murderers, no matter where they live. I'm sure there were women and children in those wagons that you and your father directed out to the Badlands."

"Miranda!" Rachel cried.

Victor turned white. "I—I deserved that."

"Yes, you did."

"No," his fiancée moaned.

Shreve put his arm around Miranda's shoulders. "This is getting us nowhere."

Victor swiped a hand across his forehead. "I take it that you're pretty sure Senator Butler was responsible for this?"

Miranda tried to organize her whirling thoughts. "I can't prove it, but if she received a message, it came from him. Waldron probably didn't have anything to do with it. He's not vicious, just greedy. But Butler. He could put her out on a certain street, at a certain time. It would be easy to hire someone to run her down. If they use a delivery wagon, I'll bet it was the same one they used in the attempt to kidnap Rachel."

"But why?"

"He had just told my mother to leave town. He probably thought frightening Rachel would get her to do it. But he didn't know how determined my mother was." She smiled at her sister who clung to her lover's arm. "Nor that my sister would get herself engaged to her rescuer. When Mother didn't

412

go, maybe he decided to get her away permanently, before she persuaded her 'cousin' not to buy the land."

"You're making him out to be a monster."

"The death of one little woman is nothing for the breed of men who'll send a troop of soldiers out to die or set fire to a theater full of people or rob Indians of their ancient lands."

"Mrs. Catherwood!"

At the sound of her real name, they all turned to see a man striding down the hall toward them.

"Mr. Keller." Miranda stepped forward to meet him.

"Mrs. Catherwood, how is your mother?"

"She seems to be all right, Mr. Keller."

"Who is this?" Shreve asked, stepping up behind her and finding her right elbow.

"He's a Pinkerton detective I hired in Chicago. He's now living and working here in Washington, D.C. As it happens, he's working for Senator Butler investigating you and me."

Keller stared at the actor, his quick brown eyes taking in the momentary fumbling of the man's fingers in locating her arm and noting the fixed stare behind the dark glasses.

"A pleasure to meet you, Mister Catherwood." Henry Keller thrust his hand at Shreve's, testing his theory by delaying the handshake for the space of several seconds. Then he seized the actor's right hand and shook it vigorously. "I had the opportunity to see you on the stage in *Macbeth* in Chicago. Mrs. Catherwood kindly provided the tickets. It was a really memorable evening."

"Thank you." Shreve's mouth spread in a smile.

"I'm glad to see you here, Mr. Keller," Miranda said, "but how did you know about Mother?"

"I saw it happen."

413

"My God!" Victor started forward. "And you didn't stop it?"

Keller allowed himself a thin smile. "It happened too fast for me to stop it, but I caught the man who did it."

"I suppose he doesn't know who hired him?" Shreve's mouth twisted.

"I believe that he does," Keller replied. "He's been very closemouthed, saying nothing, denying nothing. I believe that he expects someone powerful to get him out of jail."

Twenty-three

The first thing we do, let's kill all the lawyers.

"You can't go in there!"

Senator Waldron looked up as the door to his inner office swung open and the secretary's loud protest heralded the entrance of quite an angry group of people. Foremost was Lady Edgemont-Canfield, followed closely by a young woman who strongly resembled her. Three men, one of whom was Lord Edgemont, filed in behind them.

Miranda planted herself in front of the wide desk. "Senator Waldron, did you send for my mother this morning?"

He rose from his chair alarmed by the tone in her voice. Still, he managed an affable smile. Lord and Lady Edgemont-Canfield were quite welcome, but the other three —

He studied the trio. Rachel Westfall, of course, was Lady Edgemont's cousin. The second man was nondescript. Medium height, dressed in brown, with brown hair and brown eyes. His face displayed no emotion, nothing at all. Waldron dismissed him. The white Indian Victor Wolf was another matter. Waldron regarded the Cheyenne with some distaste mixed with trepidation. The Indian looked to be on the warpath.

415

The senator turned his attention to the two ladies. A closer look made him think they both looked quite ill.

"Did you send a message for my mother to come to your office this morning?" Lady Edgemont repeated.

"Your—mother? Why no. I don't know your mother."

"Perhaps I should tell you that my name is not Edgemont. It *was* Miranda Drummond. Mrs. Ruth Drummond Westfall is my mother."

He raised his eyebrows, not comprehending the reason for the deception. "What are you telling me?"

Shreve took his wife's arm. His eyes behind the dark glasses focused on Waldron's face. "She's telling you that we never intended to buy land in Montana and Wyoming, Waldron. We were gathering information on fraudulent land schemes. We are not English nobility. I'm an actor, Shreve Catherwood."

Waldron turned white, then red. "The hell you say! By what right? By whose authority? I want to know who hired you."

"They were working for the Wyoming delegation," Victor put in rashly.

Waldron glared at him. "You want votes in the Senate, sir, you won't get them this way."

"Be quiet, Victor," Miranda rapped out. "Don't jeopardize a whole state's future with some quixotic gesture."

"Miranda!" Rachel exclaimed.

"The fact is, Senator Waldron, that Shreve and I were looking for a man who has plagued our lives. We stumbled onto the fraudulent land deals as part of the plot. We discovered it was the reason why we were being hunted."

416

Waldron came around the desk and tried to edge toward the door. "I don't pretend to understand all these wild statements. I want you out of here immediately."

Before his hand could touch the doorknob, Henry Keller was there to block his way. "I think you'd better listen, Senator."

"Who are you?"

"Henry Keller, Pinkerton Detective Agency."

His words stopped Waldron in his tracks. He moved back to his desk. These people must be serious if they had hired a Pinkerton man.

Shreve made the formal accusation in his rolling voice. "You and Senator Hugh Butler offered us large quantities of land along the Powder River in Montana and Wyoming. From Mister Wolf and his father Adolf Lindhauer I discovered that the land in question is either already homesteaded or part of the Indian territories."

Waldron tried to bluff. "I assure you that they are mistaken. My information cannot be wrong. It's correct based on the latest U.S. Army Corps cartographers. These men"—he jerked his head contemptuously toward Victor—"are undoubtedly mistaken. Perhaps even lying for some purpose of their own."

Victor growled low in his throat. Fists clenched he took a step toward the sidling man.

Waldron instantly retreated, swallowing hard, but he stuck to his guns. "My sources are reliable."

"Your sources are wrong." Victor stood five inches taller than the senator.

Suddenly, Waldron became aware that he was the shortest man in the room. His chubby body was at a distinct disadvantage placed beside the others. Even Henry Keller looked as though he possessed a fine pair of shoulders to fill out his coat. "Er—ac-

417

tually, all I know is information Senator Butler has provided me with."

Victor Wolf's lip curled. "Suddenly, you don't know anything, do you, Senator?"

"Senator Butler is one of the most highly respected men in Washington." Waldron began to bluster. "He would never—"

"Did you send a message to my mother?" Miranda interrupted.

Waldron stared at her suspiciously. "I want to know what this is all about."

"A delivery wagon ran my mother down on the sidewalk. On the sidewalk—" Miranda repeated.

The younger girl whimpered faintly. The Cheyenne put his arm around her shoulders.

"The driver whipped the horses up to a gallop and drove them over a foothigh curb to hit her." After the dramatic deliveries of Shreve and Miranda, Henry Keller's voice was soft and flat, but it carried its own peculiar emphasis.

"My God!"

"She was on her way to have breakfast with you," Miranda continued. "You had sent for her."

"I sent for her?" Waldron backed across the room. "Where did you get that idea? I never sent for her! No. I assure you I didn't. I surely didn't send for her. The driver—Did you mean to say he did it deliberately?" He pulled his handkerchief out and wiped his palms. "Are you sure? How could such a thing happen? To a lady? Is she hurt?"

"Very badly hurt." Rachel's voice quavered. "She's in the hospital unconscious."

"This is terrible." Waldron scanned the faces of the two women. "This is the worst thing that I've ever heard of. You poor young ladies." He looked at Miranda searchingly. "Your mother, you say?"

She nodded.

"Please sit down. Sit down." He pushed a chair forward and took Rachel's hand as she sat in it. "You're like ice." He hurried to the door. "Fetch hot coffee and whisky. Now."

Victor placed a chair for Miranda to sit close to her sister and take her hand.

Waldron turned back to the room. "Gentlemen, please be seated. Now. Tell me everything from the beginning. As you know I've been working with your mother." His eyes skittered to Victor. "I'm most sympathetic with the Indian problems."

The Cheyenne grunted.

Surprisingly, they had little trouble talking to the senator from Virginia. Scarcely mentioning the death of Benjamin Westfall at Fort Gallatin, Miranda and Victor told the story of the plight of the Cheyenne and Sioux, as well as the settlers in the Wyoming and Montana territories.

Waldron played with the letter opener on his desk when Victor Wolf admitted with great shame that men in that territory treated the greenhorns who bought such land as fools.

"We see them coming in with cheap wagons, made of unseasoned timbers. Young wives and little children sit on the seat beside them. They show their deeds and ask directions. We send them running around like crazy chickens." The glance he threw Rachel was anguished.

"We point off toward the horizon, describe bends and turns and watch their dust settle behind them. Some of them may find land and settle on it, but who knows? Nobody cares just so long as they don't bother us."

"Of course, mistakes are sometimes made in land plats—" Waldron began.

"Senator," Miranda interrupted his defense. "You

tried to sell Lord and Lady Edgemont land that didn't belong to you."

"But no money changed hands," Waldron countered quickly. "You two are impostors. By all rights I should turn you over to the U.S. marshals."

"By all means, call them in." Miranda's color rose in her cheeks. Cordelia to the life, she scoffed at him. "I'm not just Miranda Drummond and this is not just some two-bit actor. He's Shreve Catherwood, Romantic Star of Three Continents. And if you haven't heard of him, down in Virginia, let me assure you that New York and Chicago and London have, not to mention Mexico City and Madrid."

"Sweetheart, you'll have me blushing," Shreve said mildly.

"We'll call a press conference. Remember you sent us letters, offers, detailed descriptions of the land."

"No money ever changed hands," Waldron insisted doggedly.

"I think we could find a lawyer who could prove intent, especially one financed by your opponent," Shreve countered.

Waldron shot him a furious look.

"Senator," Miranda said persuasively. "A woman is lying mortally injured in the hospital. I swear to you if you don't call off this vendetta against us—"

"What vendetta!" Waldron burst out. "I didn't send for your mother. I don't know anything about any messages. You can ask my secretary."

"Our mother believed you were helping her. That's why she made the effort to come so early in the morning. She thought you were going to help her in pleading the cause of the Indians," Rachel accused him.

Waldron threw down the paper knife with startling violence. "All right. All right! I admit I was playing along with her. I had no intention of actually doing anything about the problems of the Indians." He pointed his finger at Miranda, as if it were a gun. "But that is all I will admit to."

"Then who did send for her?"

The senator shrugged his shoulders. "Perhaps it was all just an accident? A runaway team? Teams do run away."

Henry Keller had been leaning against the wall near the door. Now he pushed himself up straight. "This one didn't. As a matter of absolute fact, the man who whipped up the team is in jail right now. The name he gave me before I turned him over to the authorities was Billy Steuben. He claims, of course, that it was an accident. Other than that he's keeping very quiet."

"Maybe it was," Waldron muttered.

"No, sir. A couple of other men were out taking a morning constitutional. They saw him swing the horses and whip them up. They will swear he tried to commit murder."

At the ugly word Waldron flinched. "This still has nothing to do with me."

"If my mother dies"—Miranda choked but managed to continue—"Billy Steuben will tell who hired him."

"Right," Henry Keller said. "He's expecting to be freed momentarily. That's why he's keeping quiet. If no one gets him out, rest assured he won't face the hangman alone."

"I have nothing to do with anything like that. My God! I'm a decent, civilized man. You're talking about murder."

"Undoubtedly. Murder." Shreve allowed the word to roll off his tongue. *"Murder most foul."*

Miranda bowed her head and clasped her hands

421

together tightly. "If my mother dies, it will be murder in the first degree. Who do you think might have done it, Senator?"

"I don't know. I don't know anyone capable of such a heinous act."

"Not even Hugh Smith Butler?"

"Never. Never. He's a senior senator. He's been in politics for decades. He's one of the most respected men."

"Is he respected, or is he feared?"

"Respected. Respected."

"But he's involved in swindling deals."

Waldron used his handkerchief to wipe his sweaty forehead.

"Who told you about these deals?" Shreve prodded.

"Well, Butler approached me. A great many people in Virginia have wanted to relocate especially since Reconstruction."

"And who would they trust more than their own senator," Victor snarled.

"It was a good deal," Waldron whined.

"It was never a good deal," the Wyoming legislator contradicted. "You've never been West, have you? It's a harsh land, hot and dry summer, raging blizzards in the winter. Nothing like your mild Virginia."

"But people live out there," Waldron insisted weakly.

"Of course, they do. And the land belongs to them."

He hung his head sullenly. "Butler approached me."

"And he secured the appointment of Benjamin Westfall to the Mountain District," Shreve added.

"Yes. He knew Westfall could be depended upon to create trouble," he muttered.

"What did you say? Speak louder. We can't all hear you."

"I said, 'Westfall could be depended upon to create trouble.' "

Miranda shuddered. "He'd already been responsible for the deaths of more than eighty men."

Waldron raised his head. "Drummond? Your name is Drummond."

"My father died in the massacre at Fort Gallatin."

His face was red as fire. "It was before my time."

Miranda looked around the room. She felt dizzy with nervous exhaustion. Her sister Rachel was drooping where she sat. The men looked fagged out. Only Henry Keller retained his impassive expression. He was a good investigator, probably one of the best. "Do you want to send for the police, Senator?"

He rose and faced her. "What do you want me to do, Lady—er—Mrs. Catherwood?"

She felt something break inside her. The fire in her belly flickered and began to die. Like a flood, hopes she had tamped down so long rose to the surface. She could dare to believe that an end to all this was in sight. But so long. So long. Almost two decades had passed since her father had died in the rocks outside Fort Gallatin.

They were all looking at her. She took a deep breath. It drew coolness into her belly.

"I want your word that no one will ever bother my mother or myself or any of my family again."

Waldron wiped the last bit of perspiration from his upper lip. "You've got it, insofar as I'm able to grant it."

"In writing, Senator," Shreve insisted.

He shot the actor a virulent look, but they were

all staring at him including the Pinkerton detective. The man was damned imposing. All of them, even the woman, were damned imposing.

Miranda continued with a quick glance at Victor Wolf. "I want your word that the fraudulent land deals will stop."

"Oh, of course. No question about that. Agreed."

Victor hesitated. His face had reddened under Miranda's arch glance. "We want you to cast your vote for Wyoming statehood. Likewise, we'd like you to influence as many of your constituents as possible."

Waldron's face broke into a shaky smile. "That was a forgone conclusion. I've always stood for progress and for uniting this great nation from sea to shining sea."

Miranda gave him a quelling look. "I want a letter to Butler."

His smile disappeared as if by magic. "I can't—"

"This man is probably guilty of murder," she interrupted. "You'll be helping to catch a dangerous criminal."

"Why don't you sit down at the desk and let's draft what you're going to say?" Shreve had maneuvered himself until his fingers touched the desk.

"I can't—"

"Sit down!" he thundered in his best *Macbeth* voice.

The senator sat. Fumbling a sheet of paper from his drawer, he dipped his pen into the inkwell.

Henry Keller shook Shreve's hand again and then took Miranda's. "I'm not coming back to the hospital with you."

"Where are you going?"

"To see if our friend Billy Steuben has decided to remember the name of the man who hired him."

"Maybe he doesn't know."

Keller shook his head. "Men like Steuben usually know who's hired them, especially if the job is murder. If Butler did it, he had to go himself to make the contact. He wouldn't send a secretary or he'd incriminate himself. Steuben would have followed the messenger in the first place. If not, he would most certainly have followed Butler's carriage when he went back to his office."

"How could Butler be so stupid!"

"He's without Frank de la Barca," Shreve reminded her.

"Who's he?" Keller drew his brows together and repeated the name silently, imprinting it on his memory.

"A man who's chased us from Wyoming, to New Orleans, to Mexico City, to London," Miranda told him.

"And you're sure he's not around now?"

"He was captured in London. He tried to kill Shreve and kidnap me. Shreve knocked him down the circular staircase from the dressing rooms. He broke his leg."

"The last time we saw him," Shreve continued, "the doctor was taking him away to cut his foot off."

Keller whistled thinly. "Poor devil."

"He blinded Shreve," Miranda declared angrily. "I hope he loses both feet."

Keller squeezed her hand and smiled. "I'll let you know the minute Steuben cracks."

"Mother." Rachel pressed her wet cheek against Ruth's pale drawn one. "Oh, Mother, do you know me?"

"Yes." The word was barely a breath. Miranda could not even hear it, She could only see it as Ruth's eyelids fluttered briefly. She waited breathlessly, but her eyes did not open.

"This is an excellent sign," Dr. Thompson pronounced. "You've called her back to consciousness. That's why it's so important for someone whom she knows and loves to be with her. Talking to her. The spirit heals the broken body much faster than a doctor can."

"Oh, Mother." Rachel's tears trickled faster. She wiped at them with her hands. "Oh, Mother, I was so scared. But you're going to be all right." She looked up at Miranda. "She's going to be all right."

Miranda smiled down at her mother's still body. "She's tougher than you think. We all are."

Rachel kissed her mother's cheek and straightened. "We're all the same, aren't we?"

Miranda shrugged. "Same father, same mother."

"I've been a terrible person."

"You were acting according to what you believed. You remained loyal to Benjamin Westfall. He was the only father you'd ever known. He was good to you. You'd have been less of a person if you'd just abandoned him on the say-so of a sister who abandoned you." Miranda smiled sadly. "You don't have to apologize to me."

The girls stood on either side of their mother's bed, each of them touching her.

"I'm saying this now," Rachel insisted, "where Mother can hear me. I've been a fool." She pressed her mother's hand between both her own. "I was the one who set Frank de la Barca on you and Shreve in the first place."

Miranda blinked. "Really."

Rachel hung her head. "Victor knew about it. It was the reason we had such a big argument in Wyoming. I almost lost him forever because I betrayed you."

The silence stretched long between them. At last Miranda spoke. "That explains a lot. I always wondered how he found us. I didn't think we had left any tracks, and then he showed up in New Orleans."

"I'm sorry."

"I can't be angry with you. You had your own vengeance. Why should I deny you the same thing I had taken upon myself?" The corner of her mouth quirked up. "Did you enjoy it?"

"It was the hardest thing I ever did. It made me feel awful. I couldn't respect myself. And Victor was so unhappy. Looking back, I think he understood me the same way you do." She choked. Her voice quavered. "I behaved like a child, so you're forgiving me like a child."

Miranda felt her mother's fingers twitch, even though they rested on the slanting board. *All's Well That Ends Well.* She bent and placed a kiss on her mother's soft cheek. "Let's just forget it and go on. From now on we're sisters and this is our mother."

Ruth's eyelids flickered again. For an instant both girls could see the blue between the slits. The still mouth curved slightly.

Later while their mother was sleeping, they went down to the hospital dining room to have some coffee.

"Victor's ashamed about admitting that he didn't do anything about those land deals," Rachel volunteered as she spooned sugar into her cup.

"He should be," Miranda said firmly. "He could have stopped a lot of this. Maybe Mother never would have been hurt if he and Adolf had done what they knew to be right."

427

Both girls sipped the coffee reflectively.

"They probably sold a lot of goods to those settlers," Rachel said suddenly.

"I expect you're right."

"When the time comes for him to make the right decisions, he's going to think of money first."

Miranda mouth curved in a slow smile as she stared at her little sister.

Rachel set the cup down and studied a spot across the room. "I hate that."

"Just so you don't hate him."

Rachel flashed her a glance. "I would have thought you would be the one to tell me to give him up."

Miranda shook her head. She reached forward and put her hand over her sister's. "They're just men. They're not saints nor heroes. I don't think they save us so much because they're good men as because we belong to them and they keep what they have."

"That's probably true. Victor's very possessive." She hesitated. "Now that we've made love," she whispered. From under her eyelashes she gauged Miranda's reaction.

Her sister merely smiled. "Shreve is the same way. He seduced me so I'd fall in love with him and stay with the troupe. He needed an actress."

"Oh, Miranda."

"In my case I wasn't much of an actress, but he didn't have to pay me anything."

"That's terrible."

"Not according to the way he looked at it. The troupe was everything. I suspect with Victor it's going to be the store. Or maybe the Congress, if he gets elected. Or maybe the governorship."

"But he's corrupt."

"He's not corrupt. He's selfish. What you have

428

to do is get him to see that doing what's right is to his advantage. In that way you'll be the force for good in his life."

"What if he won't pay attention to me?"

"Does he love you?"

Rachel thought about that for a minute. "Yes," she said positively. "He loves me very much."

"Then he'll want to keep you happy and he'll want to do the thing that will earn him the greatest profits because he can be proud of the way he's supporting you. That's what you want him to do." She shrugged and grinned. "Within reason."

"It's not going to be easy, is it?" Rachel sighed.

"Easy! No." Miranda's answer was a bark of malicious laughter. "Never. Nothing that's worth while ever is. But I'll always remember that Shreve didn't want me to go to Wyoming. He tried every way he could think of to keep me from going. I found out later he even bought a marriage license." She made her eyes go wide for comic effect.

"But you went."

"I finally had to run away from him. But in the end he came after me and helped me stage that ride into Gallatin. He's suffered for me. He's saved my life a half-dozen times over, sometimes at the risk of his own."

"You really love him," Rachel said wonderingly.

"I really do. Even though I know he'll never change. Remember, Rachel, a woman marries a man and a man marries a job."

"And they're happy together?" The younger girl's mouth was drawn down at the corners. She looked ready to cry.

"Absolutely. With Shreve I always know exactly how he'll behave, because I know what he is."

"And that is?"

"An actor."

The door opened behind Miranda. Rachel put on a bright smile. "We're here." She waved.

"Glad we found you." Victor guided Shreve over to the table. "What are you two girls talking about so earnestly?"

"You." Miranda said with perfect truth. "We've discussed and weighed all your faults against your virtues."

Victor's face darkened, but Shreve chuckled. "Sounds devastating."

"It was," Rachel agreed, reaching for her fiancé's hand and pulling him down in a chair beside her. "But we decided that we'll keep you anyway."

Twenty-four

O bloody period!

"A message just came for you, Senator Butler. It's marked urgent." Raymond placed the envelope in the center of his employer's desk and stepped back, his expression concerned.

The figure in the chair did not stir.

"Senator Butler?" Raymond called softly.

A sigh. The chair creaked ominously as the senator's weight shifted. He laid down his glasses and put his elbows on the desk. The chair creaked again as he leaned his forehead against the heels of his hands. "I hear you, Raymond."

"Yes, sir. Can I get you anything, sir?"

Butler raised his head. His color was not good. The network of tiny capillaries in his jowls interlaced skin with a decidedly grayish cast. Likewise, his face had a bloated look.

He attempted to clear his throat, a massive but ineffectual rumbling. He winced as pain shot up into his shoulder and down into his arm. Perhaps the heavy, choking feeling in his chest was a touch of pleurisy. "Nothing, Raymond. Nothing."

The secretary nodded and withdrew.

"Unless you can find a few good years to tack

on," he said as the door closed. He doubled up his fist and thumped his chest. "I could use a few good years."

He stared at the letter with little interest. It was addressed simply to him with no return address, no indication as to its sender. He lifted it, weighed it, looked from it to the trash basket and back again. Then with a shrug, he reached for the paper knife.

The contents of the missive brought him to his feet. He stared at it, read it again, and cursed vitriolically. Crushing the paper into a wad, he lunged around the desk toward the coat tree.

Once he would have covered the distance in three wide strides. Now pain hit him hard, staggering him back until his thighs bumped into the massive piece of mahogany. His weight dislodged it fully an inch across the floor. Sweat pouring from his face, he caught at his chest and massaged the area over his heart.

After several long deep breaths, he straightened cautiously. Placing each foot tentatively, he moved to the rack, donned his coat and hat, and opened the door. "I'll be back later today, Raymond."

"Yes, sir."

"Set up a meeting with Lord and Lady Edgemont for this evening at the office."

"This evening?" The secretary looked up doubtfully.

"That's right."

Raymond could scarcely conceal a groan. "Shall I stay, sir?"

"Oh, no, m' boy. That's not necessary. I'll handle the details myself. You don't have to spoil your evening." He actually smiled at the young man. "In fact, why not take the afternoon off. Yes, that's right. Write the invitation to the Edgemonts and deliver it yourself. Then after that, you're on your own. The snow's starting. Go home to a warm fire. There's nothing of importance going on here. Nothing that can't wait till tomorrow."

"Yes, sir. Thank you, sir." The secretary began to scribble the invitation with all haste.

Miranda thanked Raymond in her best English accent. She tore open the envelope and read its contents. "Butler wants to see us."

Shreve grinned. "The summons we've been waiting for."

She hesitated. "I don't think we should go."

"What?" He rose and came to find her and take her in his arms. "Are you sure?"

"I'm afraid that somehow he knows who we are. Even though Henry hasn't told him, Waldron might have."

Shreve stroked the silky hair and caressed the back of her neck. "Then we won't, if you don't want to."

She shivered and rested against him. Her eyes drifted closed.

He kissed the top of her head.

"I have to do it," she said at last.

He sighed. "Just a momentary twinge."

She nodded. "Oh, but, Horatio, *thou wouldst not think how ill all's here about my heart.*"

He caught her by the shoulders and shook her gently. "Don't be the fool Hamlet was. For revenge he walked right into a poisoned sword. We really don't have to go at all."

"I think we do. It's no longer revenge. It's a matter of freedom. We'll rise out of the ashes of the blaze I started." She lifted her mouth to kiss him gently and sweetly.

He complied with a chuckle. "Watch it, Electra.

You're moving into Greek tragedy now."

Perhaps half of the senatorial offices had lights burning in their windows as Miranda and Shreve alighted from the cab. She took his arm and looked up. "I don't know why he wanted to see us so late."

Shreve patted her hand. "Probably to have as few witnesses as possible when he tries to murder us."

"Don't joke." She punched him in the bicep. "Don't even think about such a thing, must less suggest it."

"Sweetheart, he wouldn't bring us to his own office building to kill us. His style is to hire someone to run us down in the street or kidnap us and kill us at leisure."

She shivered into her fur collar. "I know you're right, but I still feel uneasy."

He put his arm around her waist. "It's cold out here, let's at least get into the building out of the wind."

She looked over her shoulder in time to catch a glimpse of a man stepping out into the lamplight on the curb. His hat was drawn down over his eyes and his coat collar was turned up against the biting wind.

At the door to the senator's office, Shreve knocked once, then turned the knob. It opened easily. The secretary's lamp was lit, but the secretary was nowhere to be seen.

"There doesn't seem to be anyone here," Miranda observed.

"Senator Butler!" Shreve called in his strongest voice, guaranteed to lift the audience out of their seats in the upper balconies.

"Lord Edgemont." The door to the senator's office swung open. Butler stood in it, dimly lit by a single light on his desk. "Ah, and the beautiful Lady Edgemont. Right on time for our appointment. Do come in."

Miranda hung back on his arm, but Shreve urged her forward across the floor. "Senator Butler, my wife is a little reluctant to come out this late especially after what happened to her cousin."

"I can understand that," Butler said. "I really can. Terrible thing." He stepped back into the office and moved around his desk.

As Miranda passed through the door, a terrific shove sent her flying across the room. Her knees banged into a small table between two chairs and she fell heavily. It went over with her, tangling her skirts in its spindly legs. "Shreve!"

"Miranda!" He made a grab for her, but she was gone.

"Now, you bastard! Let's see you play your games in the light."

"De la Barca!" Shreve whirled in the direction of the voice.

A fist whipped out and connected with his chin. The blow staggered him back against the door slamming it behind him. He righted himself and came up with fists doubled to face his opponent.

His opponent laughed shrilly. "What's the matter, pretty boy? Can't find me?"

Breathing hard, Shreve followed the shuffle-thud, shuffle-thud that marked the man's footsteps. Wildly, he threw a haymaker for the source of the sound. In doing so, he stepped into another punch. It rocked his head back on his shoulders.

With a triumphant laugh de la Barca kicked out. A wooden peg cut Shreve's legs from under him. He went down heavily on his hip but rolled over and came to his feet. "Did you feel that, you

435

pretty-boy, son of a bitch? That wooden peg is all I've got left. Remember how I begged you to save me. And you just stood there. Well, how d'y' like it?"

A flurry of footsteps signaled Miranda's charge across the floor.

"Ah, the charming Miss Drummond." De la Barca pivoted to meet her.

Shreve heard the sound of breaking glass as an object crashed to the floor. Next came a slap and a feminine shriek of pain.

He struggled to his feet. With a cry of fury, arms outspread, he flung himself toward the sounds of the scuffle. His head thudded into what must have been the madman's torso. His powerful legs destroyed de la Barca's precarious balance. The two crashed to the floor together, Shreve on top.

"Help!" Miranda screamed with all the power of her lungs. "Help! Help!" She tried to crawl to the door.

"Stop right there and close your mouth," Senator Butler commanded. "Another word from you and I'll shoot him."

She froze. The monstrous figure leaned over the desk, a revolver pointed at her, dwarfed but deadly in his huge hand.

De la Barca got his good leg into Shreve's gut at the same time he caught hold of the actor's tie. Frenziedly, he swung a punch to the side of the head, but the shortness of the stroke made it do little more than sting. The silk slipped. He raised his other leg and heaved.

Shreve catapulted off him. His temple struck the corner of the senator's mahogany desk. Pain rocketed through him. He flopped limply to the floor.

De la Barca laughed as he climbed to his feet.

436

Miranda rose, her back against the wall beside the door. "Senator Butler, this man tried to kill me."

"He shouldn't have done that, Miss Drummond. He was to do that only if you gave him trouble." The senator sat down at his desk. The gun wavered. Its weight dragged the arm down. Butler clutched his heart. "I paid him," he gasped, "to bring you to me. To give me . . . names. The cartel . . . organized against me."

"Cartel." She laughed incredulously. "There's no cartel."

The senator closed his eyes and tried to breathe deeply. He could not. Short panting breaths were all he could manage.

De la Barca came toward her. Shuffle-thud. Shuffle-thud. "She'll tell you whatever you want."

On the floor, Shreve groaned and opened his eyes. Pain of truly monumental proportions streaked through his head. Pain so terrible that it had color. Flashes of light—red, yellow, a red glowing ball. Moaning, he closed his eyes. The pain was too much to bear. He lost consciousness again.

Miranda's face twisted at the sound of Shreve's pain. "There's nothing to tell."

"She's lying." Clawlike hands reached for her.

"Who?" Butler thundered. Unfortunately, his voice which had once resounded off the walls of the Senate chamber came out in a low moan. "Who sent you? Who paid you to kill Benjamin Westfall?"

De la Barca caught her wrist and twisted it viciously. "Tell the senator what he wants to know."

The office door opened. "I believe we have enough information without putting Mrs. Catherwood through anything like that."

"Henry. Oh, thank God."

437

"Who the hell are you?" de la Barca snarled.

"Henry Keller," was the cool reply. "Here, none of that." He caught de la Barca's punch on his forearm, transferred his hold, and twisted the man's arm behind him. De la Barca howled in pain.

Butler's eyes flickered to the man he had hired. Then closed. He slumped back in his chair.

De la Barca kicked backward, but Keller was no blind man. Nor was he the woman who had been attacked and knocked over a table. In a matter of seconds he had the man in handcuffs.

"I'm a private investigator," de la Barca protested angrily.

"I'm with Pinkerton myself," came the cool reply.

For a minute de la Barca was silenced. His eyes darted to the senator sprawled behind the desk.

"Shreve." Miranda dove across the floor to her husband. "Shreve, sweetheart. Oh, my dear. You're bleeding."

"Hurts," he panted. "Don't touch the head. Hurts."

"Oh, sweetheart."

He slitted his eyes. Again the red and yellow this time joined by blue. Despite the pain a terrible hope welled in him. His breath caught in his throat. "Miranda."

"What, dearest?"

"Is there a light directly overhead to my right?"

For an instant she could not answer. Her heart pounded like a triphammer. "Yes." She held him by the shoulders.

"And the ceiling's sort of gray?"

She looked to heaven. *Oh, God, please, please, let it be true.* "Yes."

"And you. You're wearing a blue dress."

438

"Oh, yes. Oh, yes. Oh, yes. Oh, Shreve. Oh, dearest." She dared not touch him, but she could not keep from pressing her cheek against his forehead. "Oh, my love."

"Pain's awful," he murmured. "Can't get up."

She looked at Henry. "Please take that man out of here and bring an ambulance. Shreve mustn't move."

Henry put his hand on de la Barca's shoulder. The fight seemed to have gone out of the crippled man. He glanced at the man sprawled back in the desk chair. His eyes were closed. His hands clasped his chest. "I'll take care of it right away. Let's go."

"I'm a private investigator," de la Barca protested again. "I've got a license." He had no choice but to be collared out.

"Just lie still, sweetheart," Miranda cooed. "Don't move. Don't open your eyes until we get a doctor to tell you what would be best."

"I can see," he whispered. "I can see. I don't know how much. But I opened my eyes and I can see." Tears slipped from the corners of his eyes and slid into the graying hair at his temples.

"I know, dear. I know."

"Miss . . . Drummond." The hoarse voice came from above her.

She froze. How could she have forgotten the senator was in the room? Easily, considering her excitement, her hope.

Keeping her hand on Shreve's shoulder, she rose up on her knees. Her clenched fist braced on the corner of the desk. This evil old man would not come near her love.

Butler's eyes were barely open. His face was gray, his mouth hanging slackly. "Why?"

She tried to understand.

"Why what?"

439

"Why . . . Wes'fall?"

She set her jaw defiantly. "He killed my father. He sent Francis Drummond and eighty men out to die, so he could marry my mother."

The blood-shot eyes widened. "Only . . . reason?"

"Eighty-one men are good and sufficient reason, Senator. They died horribly. Their families grieved for them. How many widows and orphans did they leave behind? How many families ruined? My mother's life was practically destroyed. My life was changed forever."

"Revenge. Not . . . plot. Only . . . re . . . venge." Butler's breath left him on a sigh.

The eyelids did not close. The irises relaxed leaving black wells with no sight. The great mouth slacked open, drooling. The body seemed to settle in the chair, then gradually, it tilted forward. Thudding and thumping, the great ugly carcass slid into the wall behind the desk.

Miranda shivered. *"Whiles rank corruption, mining all within, infects unseen."*

From the floor, Shreve made a faint scolding sound. "I really must arrange for you to play *Hamlet*. You know the part better than I do."

She knelt at his side and slid her icy hands into his warm ones. "I know it because I've lived it."

Epilogue

Prosperity's the very bond of love.

"My wife wouldn't be the least bit happy about this. I literally had to sneak him out of the house." Shreve Catherwood shot a guilty look over his shoulder.

"So. You'll sneak him back in again and who'll be the wiser." Nehemiah Horowitz, the owner of the new Imperial Theater in Chicago, waved his hands expressively. "I've got a reporter in the house. The papers'll carry the story. We'll extend the run. We'll all be richer."

"We're already doing very well."

"With *Julius Caesar,*" Nehemiah scoffed. "Two women in the show for about five minutes. You tell Miranda—from me—this is her contribution to the show. Otherwise, we could all lose our shirts."

"She'll be mad when she reads it in the papers," Shreve objected.

"So. You'll hide the paper and say it never came. Do I have to tell you how to do everything?" Nehemiah gave a disgusted snort.

Shreve shook his head. Brutus's golden crown of laurel caught the lights from the stage.

From the bundle in his arms came a cooing sound. A tiny hand reached up and waved uncer-

441

tainly. It closed around a chain hanging against the polished corselet. The baby tugged.

On stage Marc Antony told the world that Brutus was *the noblest Roman of them all.*

Shreve grinned down into his son's face. "Can't wait to jerk my costume off, can you?"

The baby cooed and chuckled.

Shreve freed the chain before it found its way into the rosebud mouth.

"So call the field to rest, and let's away, to part the glories of this happy day," Octavius finished. The trumpets flourished. The cast waited for the curtain.

Instead Nehemiah Horowitz stepped on stage, waving the audience to silence. "My friends. Tonight, a first for the new Imperial Theater. My good friend Shreve Catherwood has the most blessed of announcements to make."

Shreve walked to center stage with the baby in his arms. His son had really been born in Ruth Westfall's house with doctor and nurse in attendance two weeks before, but as Nehemiah said, they could extend the run. And *Julius Caesar* was a hard show.

"Ladies and gentlemen, in his stage debut, may I present—my son." Shreve held the baby up to the lights. "Drummond Catherwood."

"Born in a trunk back stage!" Nehemiah yelled, as the applause rolled over them and the audience came to their feet cheering.

"Born in a trunk!"

To the Reader

You've finished the last act and the epilogue of *Acts of Love*. Just as with *Acts of Passion,* I have begun each chapter with a quotation from the plays of William Shakespeare. I hope the quotations have piqued your interest and that you have had the fun of testing yourself to see how well you remembered their sources. If you've again taken the test, then again here are the answers in the back of the book.

I.	"Well, well! there's one yonder arrested and carried to prison was worth five thousand of you all."	*Measure for Measure*
II.	"Receive what cheer you may The night is long that never finds the day."	*Macbeth*
III.	"I will not consent to die this day."	*Measure for Measure*
IV.	"All the world's a stage, And all the men and women merely players: They have their exits and their entrances."	*As You Like It*
V.	"The Lady doth protest too much."	*Hamlet*
VI.	"Double, double, Toil and trouble."	*Macbeth*

443

444